I0645540

AGE OF DRUIDS

BOOK NINE IN THE DRUID'S BROOCH SERIES

CHRISTY NICHOLAS

GREEN DRAGON PUBLISHING

Irish pronunciation is very different than English, despite using a similar alphabet. See the first pages for a pronunciation guide and glossary for Irish names and terms.

There is also a link in the back for a family tree of all the characters in this trilogy. Be warned, there may be spoilers!

Table of Contents

Dedication
Pronunciation Guide
Chapter One
Chapter Two
Chapter Three
Chapter Four
Chapter Five
Chapter Six
Chapter Seven
Chapter Eight
Chapter Nine
Chapter Ten
Chapter Eleven
Chapter Twelve
Chapter Thirteen
Chapter Fourteen
Chapter Fifteen
Chapter Sixteen
Chapter Seventeen
Chapter Eighteen
Chapter Nineteen
Chapter Twenty
Chapter Twenty-One
Chapter Twenty-Two
Thank You and Links (including a link to a Family Tree)
Other Books by This Author
Historical Note
About the Author

Dedication

Sometimes that which we pursue is not what we truly need or want. I dedicate this novel to those who realize their dreams are sometimes unwise and turn instead to nurture their own lives and loves.

I give thanks to my wonderful authors' group, who give fantastic feedback on my work, and my beta readers such as Ian, Julie, and Joe. Siobhan of Bitesize Irish is always helpful with the Irish pronunciations of the native words I use.

Thanks to Walker Metalsmiths of New York for the use of their wonderful brooch for inspiration for the cover art.

And with this final book in my Druid's Brooch series, I thank my husband, Jason, for all his patience and support.

Pronunciation Guide

People
Adhna — Eye-na
Aebh — Ayv
Aileran — AY-leh-ran
Áine — Awn-ye
Ammatán — Om-ah-tawn
Aoibheall — Ee-vul
Beacáin — bee-KAYan
Bodach — Bud-ukh
Brighid — Breed
Cailleach: The hag goddess — CAY-lukh
Ceatha — KAY-he
Cerul — che-RULE
Clíodhna — KLEE-uh-na
Éanna — EY-naa
Eógan — OH-wen
Fachtna — FAWKT-nah
Gabha — GAV-uh
Grian — GREE-ahn
Grimnaugh — GRIM-naw
Lugh — Loo
Macha — MAKH-ah
Manannán — Ma-na-NAWN
Maol Odhrán — MAY-ohl O-rawn
Micoll — MY-coal
Oisinne — oh-SHEEN
Tirechan — TEER-i-shan
Tuireann — TOO-reen
Wannaig — WAN-ig

Places
An tSionainn: The River Shannon — an TAN-een
Baile Átha Luain: Athlone — BAWL-yuh A-ha LOO-in
Tír na nÓg: Land of the Ever Young — Cheer nah Nohg

Other
Aos Sídhe: The Fair Folk — Ays shee

Bealteaine: Start of summer months — BYALL-tin-uh
Druí: A priest or priestess of the old gods — DROO-ee
Faoladh: a werewolf — FAY-lah
Fir Bolg: The people who lived in Éire before the Túatha Dé Danaan: People of the Bag — feer bol-ug
Géis: A curse or requirement — gesh
Grugach/Grugachann: A household Fae — GROO-gakh/GROO-gah-khan
Léine/Léinte: A long belted tunic (singular/plural) — Lay-na/Layn-tah
Túatha Dé Danaan: Fairies or people in Ireland before the Sons of Mil — TOO-a-ha day DAH-nan

Chapter One
Late winter, 442 CE, Loch Rí, Éire

Her baby Aileran's skull-piercing screech stabbed through Clíodhna's skull, making her want to abandon everyone and escape into blessed silence. Anything for a little peace and quiet, and several days of sleep.

She wished she could run somewhere in the forest, maybe up a hill, surrounded by buzzing bees and yellow flowers. Or flying over the rolling hills with a flock of starlings.

Her brief fantasy crashed to earth when another scream broke through. She picked up the babe, rocking him against her shoulder while stirring the iron pot. Clíodhna cast an eye for her middle child, Donn, who helped a lot, but tended to wander off and get into trouble. He wasn't inside, but she heard him yelling at the chickens, so he must be doing his chores.

Aileran cuddled into her shoulder, let out a wet burp, and promptly fell asleep, a warm weight against her neck. His hand curled around a hank of her black hair, pulling just enough to make her wince.

At the same time, his adorable smile invoked her own. Despite her frustration, she loved her baby boy. It had been a dozen winters since her womb had quickened, but she'd been glad of the new child after so long, especially after losing a daughter at birth.

Clíodhna glanced out the window of the large roundhouse. She glimpsed Donn unharnessing the plow with practiced hands. Though he had but fourteen winters, he'd stepped up as the man of the house ever since his father disappeared.

The baby fussed again, whimpering in his sleep. She rocked him while stirring the stew in the pot. They'd only a few meals of dried lamb left from autumn harvest, but had plenty of onions and turnips, as well as chives and garlic. At least Oisinne left them a workable farm before he disappeared. She used to sell small wooden carvings she'd made, but who had time for such frivolity now?

A sharp whiff of char caught her attention. "Curse the crows!" She swiveled the pot off the fire. She'd have to add more water before it scorched. Baby still in hand, she bent to the bucket, trying to lift it without waking the child.

His screams shot right through her skull, a physical pain that made her drop the bucket. The water splashed on the flagstone floor.

"Son of a diseased donkey!"

"Clíodhna! Such language!"

Ita, her friend from the village, stood in the doorway, a hand upon her heart.

"Sorry, Ita. Can you help me for a moment? I need about five extra hands."

"I can see that. Here, let me take the wee one." She reached out to take Aileran, who yanked on Clíodhna's black hair so hard, it brought tears to her eyes.

She tried to be patient with her son. "Let *go*, Aileran; there's a good babe."

A crash outside made her curse under her breath.

Ita smiled. "Go. Check on your lad out there. I've got Aileran well in hand. Don't I, wee thing? We're going to get on just grand." She touched the baby's nose, eliciting a giggle from the ungrateful wretch. Then the babe grabbed her blond hair and gave a hard yank.

Clíodhna gave them one last lingering glance before she rushed out to find out what trouble Donn had fallen into.

The boy lay half under a bale of hay, struggling to pull his leg out, his face screwed up in a comical grimace.

Trying to suppress a chuckle, Clíodhna lifted the edge so he could get free. "How did you get under there, Donn?"

He pouted, wiping straw from his *léine*. "When I brought Tinn into his stall, he reared. I staggered back and hit the pile. The top one fell on me. It didn't hurt, though!"

Clíodhna eyed the stack of hay, assessing the sturdiness of the remaining bales while trying to stifle a grin. "They look stout enough to me. You must have hit the bale hard."

He stared at his foot, shuffling it in the dirt. "Yeah, I hit it hard. Tinn reared pretty high."

Clíodhna gave him a pat on the shoulder. "I suppose a full-grown horse rearing up high can be rather scary, even to a sturdy lad of fourteen winters. I'm glad you were smart enough to back up. A frightened horse can be dangerous."

"I know, Ma. Uh, am I in trouble?"

"Of course not. But you still have chores left. Can you fetch me two more buckets of water?"

He squinted at her. "Didn't I just bring one in before I plowed?"

"Unfortunately, I dropped that one trying to put more water in the stew. Oh, my stew!"

She rushed back into the roundhouse but Ita had moved the stew well away from the hearth.

Clíodhna let out a sigh. "Thank you, Ita. I'm sorry to leave you with him for so long."

The older woman grinned, handing the baby back. "He's been a lovely lad. I miss my own babies. They're all grown and starting families of their own now. Hopefully, I'll have grandchildren soon to play with. Oh, that reminds me, I saw Etromma in the village. She said to tell you she might be later than she expected."

Clíodhna's eldest daughter spent far too much time with the blacksmith's boy, Tirechan, for her peace of mind. Etromma had sixteen winters, a marriageable age, and had made her choice clear. But the blacksmith would never pair his son, full of high status, to Etromma.

As the daughter of a single woman with a small farm, they held very little status. A blacksmith stood second only to a bard or *drui*, as he knew the magic of creating iron. His sons could choose any woman they wanted, but their father would pick the most advantageous mate.

In the meantime, Etromma would only make a fool of herself hanging around, trying to impress the lad, and possibly get herself with child. None of which would increase their status in the slightest.

She'd almost forgotten Ita was still standing in her house. Her guest stirred the pot idly while Clíodhna lost herself in musings.

After clearing her throat, Clíodhna asked, "Did you come over to ask something, Ita, before I so rudely recruited you into being an assistant?"

With a chuckle, Ita glanced up from the stew. "I was wondering if you would like to join me for the next meeting with the monks tomorrow morning?"

Clíodhna cocked her head. "The monks? You mean those strange men up in the glade? Why would I do that?"

Her friend gave laugh. "Well, for one, you can bring your children. It might give them something to do other than get in trouble. They teach classes, skills like beekeeping or baking."

Clíodhna waved her hand. "I already know how to bake."

"You do, yes. But does Donn? And being part of the community means you might have more help with the children when you need an extra hand." Ita raised her eyebrows and glanced at the baby.

Aileran was now sleeping in her arms as Donn came in with two buckets sloshing full of water. He grinned at Ita and carried them to the hearth. With a glance at Clíodhna, he poured some into the kettle and swung the iron arm back over the fire.

Ita glanced at him. "Good lad. You'll make some woman a grand husband someday."

Clíodhna resented the other woman saying it before she could. Donn was *her* child, not Ita's. Her friend had raised *her* brood already.

Then Clíodhna chided herself. Her friend just wanted to help. And the gods knew Clíodhna needed any help she could get. She hadn't enjoyed a good night's rest in moons. Five, to be exact. Ever since Oisinne left.

Clíodhna kept trying to convince herself his absence wasn't her fault. They'd had no argument, and she knew of no other woman, no long-lost relative came seeking help. He'd simply gone out hunting one day.

When he didn't come back the first night, she'd thought little of it. He often stayed out overnight, especially if he found no deer. By the second night, she'd grown concerned.

By the fourth night, she'd gathered several men from the village and together, they'd combed the nearby woods, searching for sign of either the hunter or his belongings. They found nothing.

The best trackers in the village found not one clue. Not even the trace of his footsteps in the mud. Clíodhna even lost her last horse to the search, when he got mired in a bog and broke his leg trying to escape. She'd loved riding that horse to escape life when she still could. That time was over now, with three children to care for.

Speculation as to Oisinne's fate ran rampant through the community. The most common theory was he'd been taken by the Faeries. Others guessed he'd just left to start a new life, or he'd fallen into a bog and suffocated, or he'd hidden himself and laughed at them all for their searching.

He'd always been fond of playing jokes, and the latter seemed plausible. But as the season marched with no sign of him, a joke appeared less likely.

Clíodhna muddled on as best she could, vacillating between resentment, freedom, loneliness, and despair.

At least he'd left her with a full pantry and dried lamb, beef, and fish from his hunting and fishing forays. He'd been a great hunter. His skill with the bow was unrivaled.

Before he left, he'd taught Etromma to shoot the bow, and she had a great deal of skill. She'd brought down two deer this winter, which helped tremendously.

Donn would never be a great hunter, but he adored fishing. Between the two of them, and her own weaving, they'd survived the winter. But she'd found it difficult to tend the house and raise the children at the same time. Perhaps being part of this monk community might help.

Clíodhna glanced at Ita, still stirring the kettle, waiting for her answer. What could it hurt to see what these monks had to say? "Very well, Ita. I'll come with you tomorrow. When?"

"Just after dawn."

Her eyes grew wide. "Dawn? That's when we milk the cows."

Ita waved her hand. "The cows can be milked earlier, can't they? Just give it a try. There is a Lovefeast afterward."

It turned out that the cows didn't mind being milked before dawn. If anything, they were more placid than usual. As darkness faded, Clíodhna gathered her three children and trudged to the outskirts of the village.

Etromma whined as she rubbed the sleep from her eyes. "Ma, where are we going?"

"I told you, dear one. Ita invited us to the monk's house. They're giving some sort of lesson. She thought we'd enjoy it."

"But it's so early! Why do we have to wake up extra early?"

"Because that's when they do the lesson. If we don't like it, we can leave."

Etromma answered with sullen silence and a few resentful glares.

Donn chucked her on the shoulder. "Mornings are the best time of the day, sister. Don't you love watching the sun rise? We always greet the dawn with Ma anyhow."

She rolled her eyes. "Yes, but that's dawn. This is *before* dawn. It's unnatural."

Clíodhna hid a smile and kept walking. Her roundhouse was some distance outside the main village, if village was the proper term. A collection of twenty families and a few single craftsmen clustered near a bend in the river.

About a dozen more farms like hers circled the village. Past that lay a low, flat hill where the monks built their community. The river running through town eventually fed into the sea, where Clíodhna had grown up.

She missed the salt water and storms across the ocean. Memories of swimming with dolphins and sharks sometimes tickled her dreams.

Seven monks had settled in this area the summer before last. They'd built apiaries, planted gardens, and helped the people in the village with tasks now and then.

Oisinne had attended their meetings once or twice but came back grumbling under his breath about dead gods, so he never went back. For Clíodhna to go without his blessing would be rude and unseemly. Besides, she'd never felt the need before.

Now, with Ita's urging, she pulled Etromma, Donn, and little Aileran in a sleepy string along the forest path toward the monks' place.

Others met them on the road. A smile, a nod, but not much conversation peppered the pre-dawn light. The sun shot rays up through pink clouds, but it was still chilly. Her toes grew numb from the mid-winter frost, and now wet besides from the dew. *This had better be worth the effort.*

About thirty people gathered at the wattle and daub square structure. It wore an odd little attachment on the chimney, like someone nailed two straight sticks together, crosswise.

The interior was dark, but at least the walls cut the winter wind. A small hearth burned near the front, and two braziers filled with glowing coals stood in back corners. Near the fire, a small table stood with another pair of crossed wooden sticks. A monk dressed in white robes and a colorful neck scarf stood next to it, his hands clasped in a patient pose.

Some of the villagers sat on the floor, so Clíodhna found a place along one wall and did the same, arranging her children in front of her.

As they waited, Donn poked Etromma in the shoulder, eliciting a yip of surprise and outrage. She shoved him back.

Clíodhna whispered, "Quiet! Both of you."

"But he—"

She held up a finger. "Shh!"

"Ma—"

"I said shh! Not another word."

Etromma fell back into her habitual pout. Clíodhna tried to think back to when she'd been that age. Had she been so petulant and whiny? She didn't think so. All *her* causes had been righteous and worthy, or so she believed at the time. Her parents probably would have disagreed.

Clíodhna remembered falling hopelessly in love at least a dozen times in those seasons. Perhaps being in love with just one boy at one time would work out better for Etromma.

It had taken a long time for Clíodhna to settle on a suitor, and she'd chosen poorly. Oh, Oisinne had been a fine storyteller and never failed to make her laugh. But, as much joy as he gave with his tales, he'd abandoned them all with no word.

Many times, Clíodhna imagined what might have happened to him. Many times, she came up with no answers. She'd even tried to ask the Good Folk, but they either refused to answer or didn't know. Or her offerings weren't enough. Their dissatisfaction was sometimes indistinguishable from their sheer contrary nature.

Back before she'd gotten married, Clíodhna had spent a lot more time with the nature spirits. Several *Aos Sídhe*, the people of the faerie hill, were her friends. She'd bring gifts and songs for them, and they'd reward her with dances and magic. Nothing powerful, but little magics, like a flower that blossomed with light, or a wind to caress her cheek.

Some seemed tiny enough to fit in her hand while others towered over her like mighty oak trees, but as insubstantial as mist.

Now that she had three children, she had nothing resembling free time. Caring for them consumed her entire day, attention, and energy. Tending the animals, the crops, and being a judge between Donn and Etromma took everything she had.

Still, she found joy in her children, as she had from her husband. When he left, he took some of that joy, some of that pleasure.

That reminded her of how many moons it had been since she'd lain with a man. Oisinne disappeared five moons past. She'd never gone that long since she'd discovered the pleasure a man could bring.

A monk in white robes raised his hands, his sleeves falling back. *Druí* knotwork tattoos, faded with age, entwined his forearms. A *druí* who became a monk? Clíodhna frowned, glancing around to see who else noticed. *What betrayal is this?*

He intoned several phrases full of harsh consonants and guttural sounds. Clíodhna couldn't understand a word of it. This new religion came from the lands beyond the sea, so they must have their own language. Did they expect everyone who came to these meetings to understand them?

The monk finished his speech and lowered his arms. His hair had been shaved across the top, bearing a large brow and forehead. The other monks bore similar hairstyles, and in Clíodhna's opinion, they looked silly. Still, she felt certain the *druí* required odd physical changes for their dedicants.

Some *druí* painted permanent marks on their skin with needles and dyes. Others spent several seasons in solitude, seeking wisdom from the gods. The gods only knew what other privations their dedications required.

Now speaking in their own language, the monk relaxed into a more conversational tone. He spoke of a god born hundreds of seasons ago, in a land near the desert, as per an ancient prophecy.

This god was born of a pure woman and a carpenter. Not only a god, but the son of a god, which confused Clíodhna, as hadn't they just said he was the son of a carpenter? He performed several acts of magic, including rising from the dead.

But then this demigod angered the local chieftains, and they executed him for his actions. His followers took up his cause and spread the word of his work.

Why would this southern desert god care for an island covered in trees and rain? Surely this land lay far away from his power. Still, the tale seemed intriguing, if a bit legendary and ponderous.

Like everyone else she grew up with, the druid in her village taught her to honor the gods with her heart and her mind. Legends of the gods were part of every song and story, lessons taught to each child.

Their druid recited histories at each fire festival, with smaller stories told around the hearth fire at home. Tales of the Dagda, Manannán, Brighid, Macha, and Lugh. These gods and goddesses went on quests, bore children, fell into tragic love, and fought heroic battles. From what she learned of this new god's life, he seemed relatively boring.

Clíodhna glanced at her daughter, who stared at the monk, entranced in his recitation. Donn also sat in rapt attention. At least they weren't bickering. Aileran had fallen asleep in her arms, lulled by the monk's calm voice. Clíodhna loved holding her son like this, the sweet smell of his hair tickling her nose and making her grin.

Maybe she could find a few moments of rest for herself as the monk spoke. His words became a slow rhythm, losing all meaning. Instead, she floated in the darkness, drifting along in wooly comfort.

A loud clap startled Clíodhna awake. Everyone was shuffling to their feet, so she hastily joined them. The monk sang a song with repeated phrases, encouraging those assembled to sing it back.

Again, these words were in that strange language. Clíodhna believed in the power of words and refused to chant something she didn't understand. A few people glared at her silence, so she mouthed them instead of voicing them.

The instant censure of her neighbors annoyed her. Why must she follow like a sheep? She was just a visitor.

As the song ended, people milled around, chatting and visiting in clumps. She turned to Etromma. "Are you ready to leave?"

"Not yet, Ma. I want to go and see what's on that table up there."

Donn pulled his shoulders close to his body. "I want to talk to the monk. I have a question about his god."

Several monks had set up trestle tables along one side of the building and brought platters of food. This must be the Lovefeast Ita spoke of. It looked delicious after several weeks of little but dried fish and last autumn's apples and Clíodhna's stomach rumbled.

Despite her hunger, the press of all those people pushed in on her. The crowd grew oppressive, and her mind spun.

Clíodhna found Ita and put a hand on her arm. "I'm a bit dizzy. Ita, I need to go outside. There's a garden, just the place to clear my head. Can you come fetch me when you're done?"

The blond woman gave a kind smile and nodded. "I'm glad you came today."

After hefting Aileran against her other shoulder, she exited the sturdy building. The walls had been well-constructed, at least. No uneven spots or crumbling bits showed.

The garden was laid out in a large grid, with medicinal herbs, food herbs, and vegetables in separate sections. The surrounding edge might have ornamental flowers once spring arrived, but for now, bare bracken guarded the perimeter.

Clíodhna thought this must be a lovely place in the summertime, with butterflies and bees flitting amongst the lush growth. Perhaps she'd come back then to enjoy it.

"Do you approve of our garden, then?"

Clíodhna whirled to find a monk with dark curly hair and a brown robe regarding her with a half-smile. A dimple in one cheek gave him a roguish air, and the corners of her own mouth turned up. "I'm not used to so many people inside. I needed to escape."

He let out a warm chuckle. "Perfectly understandable. We're already building a larger structure, but stone takes longer than wattle and daub. Did you enjoy the service?"

"Service?"

The monk gestured back to the building. "That's what we call this. Service is a daily dedication to God, a sermon, and then a final benediction of song."

She gave a tentative smile, as if she understood. Many of those words were new. Could they be from the new language?

Aileran chose this moment to wake. Instead of a gradual build up, though, he launched straight into an ear-splitting wail.

Clíodhna winced and bounced the child, turning to her companion. "I'm so sorry."

He grinned. "Not to worry. I've a wee boy of my own, just about that age. Alas, he's away with his mother in another land."

She cocked her head. "Another land? Did she not come with you?"

"No, my wife stayed with her family. She didn't wish to travel to this dangerous frontier, you see. She prefers the luxury of Rome. So, we divorced, though we remain friends. I miss them both very much."

Aileran settled down after his initial outrage and burbled as she held him close, murmuring to him in a low voice. "I'm Clíodhna, and this volatile child is Aileran."

The monk bowed deep, another half-smile on his face as he rose. His dimple reappeared, and his eyes were deep brown. "And I am Odhrán. I'm only recently called to God, and this is my first assignment from Palladius."

"Assignment?"

He closed his eyes briefly. "Yes. We each get assigned to a particular area, to speak to those who live there about our God. It's a mission of peace and information."

Clíodhna had never heard of a peaceful god. Kindly, yes. Good, of course. The Dagda was called The Good God, after all. But peaceful? Tales and legends of the gods dripped with war and betrayal, even worse than real life power struggles. She bit at her lower lip. Maybe war and betrayal were planned for later. "Does this mission of peace herald something else?"

Odhrán gave a shrug. "No, we're here to spread the word, nothing more. We have no mandate to force anyone to our beliefs."

Clíodhna rarely felt shame, but her cheeks grew warm. "I didn't mean to impugn your word, Odhrán. It's the concept of a peaceful god that I can't quite comprehend."

He let out a low chuckle, a gentle sound. "That's fair. God himself has performed plenty of violent acts. However, his son, our Lord Jesus, is a man of peace, and it's his message we're spreading."

"Is Odhrán a Roman name, then? It sounds local, and you speak our language well for a foreigner."

He gave a half-smile. "I was born with a different name but adopted one more familiar to the people here. Many of us do that. It helps us grow closer to the communities we serve. And I learned your language from another man of this land, several winters past."

She'd been about to ask him more about his demigod when Etromma cried out. "Let me go! Let me go!"

Clíodhna's eyes grew wide, and she ran to find out what her daughter got herself into. She rushed out of the garden toward the building.

Etromma stood before the entrance, an older monk gripping her upper arm.

Aileran sobbed again at being jounced. She jiggled him to quiet his fussing. "Etromma? What's this?"

The older monk, his straggly beard combed into two forks, scowled at her. "The impudent girl questioned our Lord's power!"

Clíodhna stood straight. "Is that all? For a healthy curiosity, you presume to hurt my daughter? How dare you lay hands upon her!"

Odhrán came up behind her, panting from his run. "Fachtna, what have you done?"

"It isn't me, Odhrán. This creature—"

"Fachtna! Watch your tongue. These are our hosts, and we must be respectful."

Fachtna curled his lip, still keeping a grip on Etromma's arm. "The girl did not respect me *or* our Lord God!"

Etromma let out a whimper, looking toward her mother with entreaty. Clíodhna wondered where Donn had gotten to. Probably off with that girl he was courting, rather than guarding his sister, as he ought.

Her blood began to boil, but just as she was about to launch into a tirade, her new monk friend spoke in a calm but firm tone. "Let her go, Fachtna. Your duty is not to discipline non-believers. In fact, if I recall, your specific mission is to help those in need. Am I misremembering?"

With a growl, Fachtna released Etromma, who ran to her mother. Clíodhna enclosed her in a hug with her free arm as Aileran began fussing again. She glared at the older monk. "I demand an apology. This man has assaulted my daughter with no provocation."

The monk spluttered. "No provocation!"

"Fachtna! You must offer an apology to the woman and her daughter."

By now, several other monks had gathered, drawn by the shouting. Clíodhna spied Ita far in the back, a frown on her face. Most of the monks stood behind Odhrán, but one or two stood behind the other man.

"*I* must apologize to *her*?"

Odhrán crossed his arms and planted his feet wide. "To both, yes."

Several monks murmured agreement, though they'd have no idea what started this fracas. Odhrán commanded respect and trust from his fellow monks put in him. A man to be watched.

Fachtna mumbled something under his breath.

Odhrán tapped his foot. "Louder. We cannot understand your words."

He gave another scowl. "I said, I apologize. I should not have touched the... young woman."

Odhrán stared at the older monk for a few more moments before nodding. He turned to Clíodhna, who'd finally managed to quiet Aileran again. "Will that suffice, Clíodhna? Or do you require further assurances of his good behavior?"

Clíodhna lifted her chin. "That will do. Thank you."

With dignity, Clíodhna took Etromma's hand and walked away, well aware that the entire community of monks, as well as many villagers, were staring at her back.

Chapter Two

Once out of view from prying eyes, Clíodhna let her tears come. They dripped down her cheeks unchecked, since Etromma still held her hand and Aileran was again asleep on her shoulder.

She sniffed twice and glanced back. "Etromma, where did Donn disappear to? Do we need to go get him?"

Her daughter also had tears on her cheeks. "No, he went to find Mugain, but she's visiting her aunt, so went back home. I stayed behind to ask more questions. That's when that man got angry. He started yelling at me, using strange words. He said I would go to a place called *Hell*. Do you know where that is?"

While swallowing back an angry sob, Clíodhna clenched her fists. "No, darling. Maybe it's where he came from. The monk I talked to said he came from Rome. I've heard of Rome, but not of Hell."

They fell into silence as they followed the forest path through bare trees and muddy ground, last autumn's fallen leaves forming a slippery carpet. When their roundhouse and farm came into view, Etromma released her mother's hand and ran inside.

Donn came out in an instant, holding the staff he always carried. "Ma? What happened? She was fine when I left!"

Clíodhna entered the house, put Aileran down in his straw bed, and moved her shoulder back and forth. "It's taken care of, Donn. Pay no mind." Her muscles would be aching for hours. "Did you enjoy the visit before that?"

He glanced at his sister's alcove. She'd drawn the curtain, but no sobs escaped. "Sure, but I didn't feel like asking questions yet. I might go again to learn more."

She hid her disappointment. If her son was intrigued by the monks' *message of peace,* it would do her no good to speak against it. "If you would like that, we can arrange some classes. I understand they will be teaching, like bards or *druí.* Does that sound interesting?"

Donn made a noncommittal grunt and gave a shrug, but Clíodhna recognized that as a sign her son was, in fact, interested.

What would the monks want in exchange for such lessons? They didn't have much. Perhaps she could offer some service. She had some skill with gardening, and they might not be familiar with local plants.

She hadn't been able to gauge the health of the plants in mid-winter, but come spring, her skills might be in demand. If only she could do so without having to interact with that odious Fachtna.

A sound outside made them both glance at the door, still standing open. She rose, massaging her shoulder again, but Donn waved her back down. "I'll go see what that was."

He grabbed his staff and went outside. Clíodhna sat next to Aileran's cot. What if that awful monk had followed them? He'd been a tall, solid man, despite his age. He could hurt any of them. There were warrior women, but she wasn't one and neither was Etromma, and Donn was barely fourteen winters old.

This helplessness infuriated Clíodhna. Why should she feel vulnerable in her own house? Why should men have all the power?

They often wielded emotional power, as well as power over others' lives. A true chieftain led by example, but more often, men led through fear or sheer might of arms.

Did these monks rule in the same way? Was their venture into her community merely to soften the village for a power grab? Despite the kind monk's assurances, she vowed to keep her eye on them.

Donn reappeared and laid his staff against the wall. "Just a squirrel. I'll go check on the cows and other animals. When I come back, do you want me to watch Aileran, so you can take a walk?"

Clíodhna narrowed her eyes. "Do I look like I need a walk?"

He grinned. "You look like you need to run away, screaming and tearing out your hair. A walk would be much easier. I don't know what happened in the village after I left, but something shook both of you. I'll get the details from Etromma when she's ready."

Wondering how she'd raised such a thoughtful son, Clíodhna glanced at the baby. He should sleep for a while, gods willing. She'd fed him recently enough, and her breasts didn't ache yet. When Donn returned, she kissed his forehead and left.

As Clíodhna walked outside, she breathed in the chilly air. The day was clear but crisp. She needed time to sift through the events of the day.

She climbed down the flagstone path to the riverside and followed the riverbank downstream. The village lay upstream, and she wanted to be away from people.

Clíodhna had never been comfortable with crowds. In her youth, she'd lived in a larger village near the mouth of *an tSionainn*, a huge river which emptied into the sea at a great estuary.

While she adored swimming in the ocean or imagining herself flying along the coast with a bird's wings, she hated the press of the surrounding people. She'd left that trading hub when she married, and never looked back.

Bracken along the river's edge tore at her *léine* but hid nothing. Squirrels and tiny birds huddled in cages of bare branches until her footsteps startled them. They scampered and flitted for safety as she drew near.

A huge stone perched at a bend in the river, hulking over the water. It had a smooth depression on top where she'd often sit cross-legged, contemplating life. A perfect place to think.

Clíodhna climbed to the spot, slipping once on the ice clinging to the stone. With a grimace at the ice, she looked forward to warmer days. Perhaps the true thaw would come soon.

For several minutes, she did nothing but listen to the water with her eyes closed. Clíodhna listened to the song of the current and breathed it into her soul. The magic of the natural world flowed through her like the river below, bringing her rest, strength, and confidence.

Every morning, she greeted the dawn with a similar rush of power. Every evening, she said farewell to the sun. Each magic held a different flavor, overlaid with its own characteristics.

Dawn burst forth, brilliant and energetic, full of life and hope. Each evening fell somnolent and quiet, full of depth and intrigue. The river, though, was eternal and immutable, promising endurance and strength.

A male voice behind her said, "If you continue to draw power without using it, you might falter."

Clíodhna whipped around, her heart pounding. She didn't recognize the man but judged him to be about her own age, perhaps just past thirty winters. He wore a full, dark beard with just a wisp of gray in the center. His ink-black, wavy hair wasn't pulled up in warrior braids, but some of his beard was.

Clíodhna rose to confront him, noting his tall, lean frame and his mischievous smile. She'd always been fond of men with a strong sense of humor.

She matched his smile. "Did you say something?"

"Indeed I did, Clíodhna. You're not using your power wisely."

Her whimsy disappeared in an instant. *How does he know my name? Does he live in the village? One of the new monks?*

He laughed. "I have no wish to confuse you, dear woman. True, I'm a stranger here, but I've known of you for some time. I sought you out."

Clíodhna backed up a step, wishing she wasn't standing on a precarious ledge over a raging river. She had nowhere to retreat to, as he blocked her only escape.

Her heart pounded as she surreptitiously put her hand on the hilt of her belt knife. "Why did you seek me out?"

He took a step forward and she tensed, her hand now gripping the knife handle. Her heart raced faster and her skin tingled with rushing power, but she didn't know how to direct it.

The stranger halted, frowned, and then took several steps back. "I didn't mean to frighten you, truly. I will sit over here on this log. If you like, you may leave, and I won't bother you again. Or you can come sit next to me and chat."

Clíodhna stood still frozen, though her heartbeat slowed. Sweat formed on her brow and threatened to drip into her eyes, but she didn't dare wipe it away.

The man sat on the log as he'd promised and waited. He didn't fidget but sat in silent anticipation.

Should she trust the stranger? He knew of her. Had he questioned her neighbors first? Or her children?

Her glance flickered in the direction of her house, concerned that something had happened to Etromma, Donn, and Aileran.

She was standing on the balls of her feet, ready to flee, when he spoke again.

"I assure you, your children are fine. You need not rush off to them. Your Donn is quite the young man and has everything in hand."

Clíodhna didn't like this, not one tiny bit. But she had to discover how he knew her and what he intended, both for her sake and that of her family.

With a decisive huff, she strode over to sit next to him. She faced him, though, so she could watch his reactions, and her hand remained on her knife. "Very well. Talk."

"Oh, dear. So prickly! Well, I suppose it's the best I could hope for, sneaking up on you in the middle of your ritual like that. I shall be certain to avoid such in the future."

In the future? He presumes much. She narrowed her gaze.

"You will want to know how I've heard of you. Well, I once knew your own parents, long ago."

Clíodhna clenched her jaw, old pain hammering on her heart. Her parents had died years ago, when she was a child. "You can't be much older than I am."

He laughed, a gentle sound that caressed her ears, trickling over the rocks like a babbling brook. "Oh, my, that's quite rich. No, Clíodhna. Do not take my appearance as proof of my age."

His cryptic comment made her head swirl. Little clues piled up, and a suspicion formed in her mind, one she'd need to test. "May I request something from you?"

"If I can grant it, you may."

Clíodhna yanked her knife from its sheath, pointing it straight at his heart, a good strong piece of worked iron. "Touch this."

He wrinkled his nose and pulled back. "You must be well aware I cannot."

I knew it. He's Fae.

Clíodhna stumbled to her feet, taking several steps back while still holding the knife out. But instead of holding it like a weapon, ready to stab, she held it in front of her like a talisman, a charm against the man still sitting on his log.

His shoulders slumped. "Danú, I've been making a right mess of this. Clíodhna, do please sit again. I vow to you upon my Queen's life that I mean you no harm. I am not here to hurt or entrap you or your children in a spell, contract, or *géis*."

Clíodhna had grown up playing with the small *Aos Sídhe*, those sprites of the woods and the land who were tied to their places by their nature. They might not be precisely Fae themselves but were protected by the Fae.

She'd seen them all her life, though most did not. Clíodhna didn't fear the spirits or the Fae, not categorically, but all the tales spoke of the dangers in dealing with a higher Fae, and this man—no, this Fae—must be a higher one.

Still, Faerie folk also held much magic. Perhaps he sought her out for something to her benefit. His vow seemed tight enough. She couldn't figure out how he'd wiggle out of it to do her harm, but she'd stay vigilant.

With a fluid motion, she sat on the log but kept the knife in hand. "Now, tell me first, who you are, second, why you are here, and third, why I should deal with you in any manner at all."

Eyeing Clíodhna's knife, he readjusted his seat on the log to face her. "I am Adhna and, as you have obviously surmised, I am Fae. I come from the Queen of my kingdom, Áine. She's noticed your power and sent me to assess you."

Spikes of fear coursed through her blood. A Faerie Queen knew of her and her magic. So much for his assurances of safety. This could only spell danger. "Assess me? Am I a farm to be valued for purchase?"

"You are not a farm. You are a human with magic. If you'd like, I can teach you how to harness that power and use it rather than simply raise it and let it dissipate."

Her fingers clasped around the knife hilt were beginning to ache. "Everyone does magic. What could you teach me?"

Adhna shook his head. "I don't speak of low magic, the sort of spells every woman performs in their kitchen. I speak of higher magic, that of the Fae and the nature spirits."

"And how would such teaching serve your Queen?"

Adhna shrugged. "It may serve her, or it may not. I am granted some latitude in my mission. I could make the argument that such lessons would make you a better tool should Queen Áine wish you to serve her. On the other hand, if she sees you as a threat, association with me might keep her from destroying you."

That cold statement made her heart drop. "You promised that you meant me no harm."

The side of his mouth rose in a charming half-smile. "And I meant it. You know Fae cannot outright lie. However, her will may override my intentions. I would rather you know this at the outset."

Clíodhna's ability to see the forest sprites aside, her independent nature had always been viewed as odd. Other than women warriors, she'd rarely encountered women of power, and while she could wield a knife or a bow readily enough, she'd never pass for a warrior.

But what sort of power might she gain with her magic? Especially if she actually learned how to use it?

When she'd been young, she'd craved to learn the *druí* craft, but her father wouldn't allow her to join their enclave. This might be the only chance she had to learn such mysteries.

Despite her pounding heart, she made her decision, re-sheathing her knife. "Very well. I will take one lesson. After that, I will decide on further actions."

Adhna rose, giving her a grin. The mischievous twinkle returned to his blue eyes. "Then I shall not yet ask you to take a formal vow. I will offer the first lesson free of any obligation or repayment."

"I accept these terms. One lesson with no payment necessary. When?"

His grin deepened. "This time, but tomorrow? We can meet here if you like. You're comfortable in this place, and the local power responds to you."

As much as she ached for time to herself, time to simply be alone, Adhna's offer intrigued her to her soul.

She took a deep breath. "Very well. The bargain is made."

Clíodhna needed someone to watch her children during these lessons. So, the next morning, she traveled to the village. Donn had been of great help the day before, but if she would be out for a lesson half the day, she needed someone more reliable. While Donn was mature for his age, he was still a young man, and she knew he had his eye on Mugain as a future wife. He might wander off when she returned from her aunt's.

That kind monk had offered to teach the older children. Perhaps she could also find someone to care for Aileran. Elsewise, she'd have to bring the baby along on her lessons with Adhna.

She'd dreamt of the Fae man all night. Her dreams shifted from dangerous flights across the countryside, pursued by some unknown danger, to sweet fantasies of making love under the full moon.

By all the gods, it had been *much* too long since she'd been with a man.

After greeting the dawn, Clíodhna fed and cleaned the cows, chickens, and pigs. She swept the house out but left any other cleaning to the evening.

Etromma, despite being awake since dawn, still rubbed at her eyes and yawned. Perhaps she'd had a bad night after her encounter with the angry monk.

They trundled down the forest path in silence. Halfway to the village, Donn asked a question which had obviously been niggling at him. "Why are you bustling us out today?"

Clíodhna had prepared an answer for this, but it flew away from her memory like a startled finch. Instead, she stalled. "Didn't you say you wanted to learn from the monks?"

He shrugged, his eyes on the muddy path. "It seems interesting. But I didn't think you were so keen on the idea yourself. Why the sudden change of heart?"

Clíodhna let out a deep breath. "I need some time to myself. I've got some decisions to make before the summer comes and thinking with the three of you in the house is nigh on impossible. Besides, learning skills will serve you better in life. I just hope they don't require anything too dear in payment."

Donn's eyes brightened. "I can offer to do some work around their place for payment. Their walkway is muddy. I could find some flat slate and pave it for them."

Clíodhna clapped her resourceful son on his shoulder. "An excellent notion."

That seemed to satisfy his curiosity and she breathed more easily.

As they approached the monks' houses, Clíodhna noticed several of them in the garden. She craned her neck, trying to recognize the kind monk who'd spoken to her. What had his name been? Odhrán.

Clíodhna spied his brown curls on the far side of the garden, stretching his back. He noticed her and waved.

After a brief discussion with another monk, he came toward them. "Greetings on this bright day. Clíodhna, is that right? I don't believe I caught the names of your children."

"This is Donn, and Etromma," she touched each one's shoulder in turn, "And the babe is Aileran."

"Well met, all of you. So lovely to see you again so soon! Have you come to take me up on my offer, then? To learn a few of the skills we can teach?"

"We have. Well, at least they have. I can't attend today, but I may wish to in the future." Aileran began fussing and she shifted him to the other shoulder.

"And the babe? We have a young monk who is excellent with the babies and younglings. He'd be delighted to have another charge."

Clíodhna swallowed back unexpected grateful tears. "That would be most kind."

He clapped, startling her. "Excellent! Let's get you settled in one of the rooms. Donn, you look like a sturdy lad. Would you like to learn some carpentry skills? Brother Cronan is building a long table for the guest hall, and he could do with an assistant."

Donn glanced at his mother, and she gave him a smile and a shrug.

Then the monk turned to Etromma. "And what would you like to learn, lass?"

Her daughter ducked her head, uncharacteristically shy. Perhaps she feared a reaction like yesterday's fiasco.

Clíodhna asked, "Would you have anyone cooking? I've taught her what I know, but my skills are basic."

Odhrán tapped his lip. "Let me think. Brother Éanna is skilled at making bread. Would that suit?"

Her daughter gave an enthusiastic nod.

"Now, if I can take this lad from you, I can place him in Brother Manchan's care. He tells stories to the young ones, tales of history and legend. Some are too young to understand the words, but his gentle voice puts many of them to sleep. He's been fed recently, has he?"

Clíodhna handed over the child, suddenly reluctant, but knowing she needed to. "Just before we arrived."

"That's grand, then. Now, run off and do what you need to do. Can you return just after midday? We normally run our services then, and the brothers need to attend."

Clíodhna glanced at the sun, judging how long she had. Spring mornings light didn't last long. Still, it should give her enough time for Adhna to prove his worth. "I can do that. But you haven't told me what you'd like in return for such lessons."

He chuckled, a pleasant, round sound. "Let's get the children off first, eh? Etromma, see that building back there, the one with the huge chimney? That's the baking hearth. Run in there and tell Brother Éanna I sent you. And Donn, your lessons will be in the yard past that. You can't miss the pile of wood and planks."

They both scampered off to their assigned places and Odhrán turned back to Clíodhna while hefting Aileran in his arms. "You owe me nothing at all. I hope you don't mind, but I asked a few people about you and your family after we spoke yesterday."

His words made her skin crawl. Clíodhna didn't like people asking about her.

"I heard about your husband's disappearance, and one of our missions is to help and support those in need, and you and your children, begging your pardon, seem in need. The labor of your family as they learn is payment enough for the skills we'll teach."

She didn't trust charity, especially in such genial form. But his expression seemed clear of guile. She gave a reluctant nod. "I thank you, Brother Odhrán."

"I'm not a brother yet, as I've not yet taken my vows. You may call me simply Odhrán."

Clíodhna grinned much too widely, echoing his own. "Then I thank you, Odhrán."

The skin around his eyes crinkled most becomingly, and her cheeks grew warm. She must leave this man's company before she did something silly. With a backward glance filled with guilt at leaving her children, she hurried home.

Her steps were unusually light and free as she walked away from the village. Ever since she'd married, duty had weighed down her life, made heavier with each new child. For the first time in many years, she had no responsibilities, at least for a few hours.

In a moment of sheer joy, she skipped along the path, grabbed a tree trunk and whirled around it, laughing with childlike abandon.

A rustle made Clíodhna halt but couldn't hear anything else. A bird flitted from one branch to another, chastising her for being too close to its nest. She grinned again. She hadn't been this giddy with delight since Oisinne courted her.

There had been several men before him, but none had made her laugh like he did. His stories enchanted her, and she wanted to keep him forever, to entertain her for hours.

She must admit, he did entertain her, even after they wed. However, he began staying out hunting longer and longer as the care of the children grew more and more time-consuming. Eventually, he just never came back.

On alternate nights, she blamed herself, blamed the children, blamed the Fae, blamed the weather, and of course, blamed Oisinne. But none of the blame had brought him home.

Torn between the desperate need for a nap without children and the burning desire to learn magic from the Fae, Clíodhna passed her roundhouse and climbed to her perch on the viewing rock. Her erstwhile teacher hadn't yet arrived, so she sat in contemplation of her river.

The calming rush of water lulled her into a much-needed nap, and she startled awake when Adhna spoke in her ear. "Are you ready, Clíodhna?"

She jumped up and whirled around, instinctively ready to fight, but the man chuckled. "Fear not, child. Remember my vow. I will not harm you."

Once her heart stopped racing, her temper flared. "Those may be the words of your vow but frightening me into falling off a rock wouldn't be directly harming me, would it? I'd be just as dead on the rocks below, though."

He cocked his head, still wearing that charming half-smile. "I wish to help you, Clíodhna. This will go much easier if you accept that basic truism. If not, this lesson might well be wasted."

Setting her jaw, Clíodhna forced herself to calm down. Being prickly had often caused her trouble. With deliberate calm, she sat cross-legged, folded her hands, and waited.

He blinked twice. "Wonderful. Now, the first lesson is to teach you about the power you've been pulling on. You may already be aware it's part of the land itself. You can draw upon the essence, the life-force of the land. It can be refreshed and even changed, depending on the will and strength of the person manipulating it. You've been pulling it in and then just letting it go away. While this isn't harmful to the land, it can fray your own soul if you do it too much without purpose."

Fray. What a wonderfully descriptive word.

"Now, this energy isn't limitless, but the purposes of any human, it may as well be. Only a god or goddess could drain even a portion of this energy from the land. Even a Faerie Queen could damage the land if she so chooses. Though I can't think of a reason they might, unless they went quite mad."

Faerie Queens featured in many of Oisinne's tales, and rarely did any human come out the better for encountering them. A traveler might gain some great ability, such as the gift of song or power over the waves, but they always lost something precious. A child, their voice, a leg, their sanity… or their life. She had no wish to make such a gamble.

But wasn't that what she was doing now? A shiver ran through her body.

Adhna raised one eyebrow. "When you pull power up through the land, how do you do that?"

She considered her answer for a few moments. "I see it, like a blue-white light, threading up through my contact with the ground. It's like delicate tendrils from a growing vine. It caresses my bones and my muscles, spreading warmth and energy. But it feels odd, like I'm pushing something through a barrier."

He clapped his hands. "Excellent description! The barrier is because it's earth magic. You're more tuned to air magic, I think. And then you just stop?"

"My mother taught me how to pull it up, but she never told me I should do anything with it. She said to always remember to honor the dawn and the dusk with my rituals. Earth and air magic?"

Adhna gave a solemn nod. "As well she should. They are worthy of honor, as is the land. Many humans, Fae, and gods cultivate that power to keep the land healthy, as the land's health reflects our own. If the land dies, so do we. I want to continue to teach you earth magic, and then we can move to air magic once you have a solid grounding in the earth."

The words felt right to her, and truer than the words of the monk yesterday.

"Now, let's do some exercises. I shall instruct you on how to both pull the power into your body, which you have already done. Then how to control it, which you have not done. First, I want you to draw power, but not as much as you can. Just a little. A small tendril, as you described, up your spine."

Clíodhna closed her eyes and imagined that thin, blue-white line branching up her back, through each of her bones until it reached the base of her skull.

"Good, good. Now, keep it there. Don't let it dissipate. Don't let it grow. Don't let it meld through your body. Just hold it in place."

The tendril quivered within her, aching to spread, to move, to disperse, but she clenched her jaw and kept it in place. After several moments, she trembled with effort, but refused to let the power win.

"Excellent! You're quite strong. Now, release it, a small portion at a time."

Clíodhna let the power escape, bit by bit, back into the earth. It tingled as it disappeared, almost like a wave goodbye. When she'd released all the power, she felt as if she'd run three leagues. Sweat dripped from her face, and her breathing came hard.

Adhna pursed his lips, his head cocked. "I think that's enough for a first lesson. Would you like to learn more tomorrow?"

Despite her exhaustion, she gave him a happy grin. She needed to learn this, more than anything in the world. This one lesson had left her both energized and exhausted at the same time but craving more. "Yes, please!"

"Then we must formalize our arrangement. Are you willing now to make a pact with me?"

Clíodhna stood to face him and he took both her hands, though hers trembled. Whether from tiredness or nervousness, she couldn't tell.

Adhna's tone turned formal. "I, Adhna of the Court of Queen Áine, do take Clíodhna to be my student, to teach her to wield her power with strength, wisdom, and heart. In return, Clíodhna, do you agree to abide by my teaching until our lessons are complete?"

Clíodhna hesitated, glancing back toward her home. "How long will that take? What if I can't make it here because of my children? I don't want them to suffer for my absence."

He gave her a kind grin. "It will take as long as it takes. If you decide you need to halt our progress to care for your family, such a delay is acceptable. However, completing the lessons is important. Half-trained is all dangerous."

After Oisinne had left, she'd been lonely and bereft of purpose, even with her family to raise. This may just be what her soul craved, something to strive for, and something to occupy her active mind. With a nervous swallow, she gave him a weak smile. "Then I do so vow."

A shimmer spread out from them in a wide circle, somehow both changing the land and leaving it the same. She shivered, wondering if she'd just made a horrible mistake.

Chapter Three

That afternoon, as Clíodhna returned to the monks' place to retrieve her children, she basked in the remnants of power tickling her muscles. Every time she moved, she left little fluttering sparks, almost like the intense pleasure lovemaking invoked.

Odhrán greeted her at the garden entrance and took her by the shoulders, wearing a wide grin. "You look radiant, Clíodhna. Your rest must have been recuperative."

"I'm much better, thank you. I don't think I've felt so good since I birthed Aileran."

"Well, he's been a positive delight. Etromma chafed at first, but now she's fascinated with the herb breads. Donn has learned well and may just have a knack for carving wood, though he likes the more decorative aspect rather than the constructive parts. Still, woodworking skill is valuable. Today has turned out well for your family."

Grateful for the positive news, Clíodhna asked, "Does that mean I can bring them again some time?"

"Absolutely. How about tomorrow? A regular course would be most beneficial. Unless you need them at home?"

Her children might not thank her for this decision, but it would be to their benefit as well as her own. Clíodhna waved her hand. "They can work the farm in the mornings and evenings. I think they're old enough to do both."

The monk's expression turned solemn as he clasped his hands. "Our order believes that hard work benefits a soul, and that idle hands breed mischief."

In her own childhood, Clíodhna had bred plenty of mischief despite all the work she did, but perhaps she had a special talent for it. The memory made her smile.

Odhrán let out a deep sigh. "Clíodhna, your smile brightens my day. Your children aren't quite finished with today's lesson. Will you sit and chat with me while you wait?"

Suddenly, her muscles ached from her work with Adhna, and sitting down would be welcome. "I'd be delighted to join you."

They settled on a wooden bench facing the ornamental portion of the garden. A few crocuses had poked up through the remnants of snow, and a daffodil bulb showed its head. Soon, the island would be in the full throes of spring, thrumming with life and growth.

Clíodhna felt the most alive in spring. Her body marched with the seasons, and with her husband gone, she must find someone to enjoy the fertile time with. Adhna might be a candidate, but should she be so intimate with a fae? A teacher and a student should also be careful with their relationships.

Odhrán might be a wiser option. So far, his conversation kept her interest, he enjoyed her company, and, despite the odd hairstyle, was pleasant to look upon.

Their thighs touched and the warmth of his skin radiated through several layers of cloth, despite the chilly wind gusting through the garden.

Odhrán cocked his head. "So, have you lived in this village all your life?"

"No, I only moved here when I married. My husband is… was from here. His family lived in this area for several generations, but they've all passed now. I grew up near the sea, to the east."

"Do you miss it? I lived near the sea not far from Rome. I used to love watching the waves come in during a storm."

Clíodhna shut her eyes and took a deep breath, placing her hands over her chest. "Oh, yes. Watching a storm over the ocean is my favorite thing. The sharp smell of lightning, churning whitecaps, violent wind. Frightening but fascinating. I never got enough of it, even when my mother made me come in out of the rain."

He gave a low chuckle. "I can see you loved it. Your face lit up when you spoke."

She opened her eyes to discover Odhrán had leaned toward her, and their faces were barely a hand-span apart. Startled, she asked the first thing which came into her head. "What was your home like in Rome? You said it was near the sea?"

The edge of his mouth quirked up. "On a cliff near the mouth of a river. The weather is much milder than here, let me tell you. Still, some lovely storms would surge across the water during the dark season. I thrilled at their power."

Clíodhna grinned and placed a hand on his. "I used to love wading in the surf every evening as the sun colored the waves red. Dolphins would come and play with me in the water, over-enthusiastic like dogs. Does your god have power over the ocean, like Manannán mac Lir does?"

Odhrán covered her hand with his other one. "He has power over all the world, ocean and land and heavens above."

Her eyes grew wide. "All of that? However does he manage?"

His expression turned solemn again, and he withdrew both his hands, so Clíodhna put hers on her knees. It had been many seasons since she'd flirted, and felt awkward. "Our Lord is omnipotent in all things. He can watch the fall of every sparrow and yet create powerful earthquakes."

Thinking back to her lesson with Adhna, Clíodhna said, "Such power in the hands of one being can be dangerous."

Odhrán waggled a finger at her. "God is incorruptible. He's not like the Greek or Roman old gods, with their petty jealousy and infidelities."

"But you said he had a son of a human woman. Is that not an infidelity?"

"No, God has no wife in heaven. He rules alone. Is it not the same in your beliefs? I've tried to find out more of the local religion, but your priests won't talk to me."

Clíodhna let out a rueful laugh. "Well, the *druí* guard their knowledge unless you're their student. But ruling everything alone... that sounds so utterly lonely."

They fell silent for a few awkward moments before she spoke again. "Danú is the mother goddess, but she has no consort. She has many children, however. Her children are our gods, such as The Dagda, The Morrigú, Brighid, and many others. Each one rules over different aspects of life. Brighid, for instance, is the goddess of the hearth, of creativity, and of healing. She is also sacred to blacksmiths and brings in the spring. This is her time, the time when the land wakes from winter slumber and bursts forth into teeming life."

"That's a delightful image. God has no such helpmate."

She gave a scowl. "How can a god rule without a goddess? There is no life without fertility."

Odhrán placed his hand on her hand this time. His skin felt warm and dry against hers. "He relies upon his children to be fertile."

Just as Clíodhna's blood began to grow as warm as her hand, a man's voice cried out. "Odhrán! Odhrán, are you out here?"

Startled apart, Clíodhna caught her breath. A thin, young monk came around the corner, Aileran in his arms. "This wee one is fussing strong. Is this his mother? I think he's hungry."

She held her hands out for her baby, suddenly needing to hold him. "Yes, I'll take him. Thank you so much. Brother Manchan? Is that your name?"

The man nodded, his spare frame full of eager energy. "Yes, indeed! He slept most of the day, but when he woke, he simply wouldn't stop fussing, so I came in search of you. I did feed him a bit of cow's milk, but he probably prefers yours. I must get back to my other charges." He left with a jaunty wave.

Odhrán cleared his throat. "I'll go fetch your other children. They should be finished now. Will I see you tomorrow?"

Clíodhna gave him a nod, unsure if she'd embarrassed him or not. But they'd done nothing to be embarrassed about. Her husband was gone, and he didn't seem to be attached. Perhaps she misread the situation. Regardless, she'd ask him tomorrow. That would be better than guessing wrong.

She rocked Aileran and hummed a nonsense song to him, his soft skin warm against her cheek. When Etromma and Donn joined her, Odhrán didn't reappear.

"How did you like the lessons? Do you want to return tomorrow?"

Etromma shrugged. "I really liked picking out the herbs and preparing them, but kneading the dough hurt my hands. Brother Éanna is good about explaining things, but he does it all in one long sentence."

Hiding a chuckle, she turned to Donn. "And what about your day?"

His face lit up. "I loved it! I can't wait to go back tomorrow. I helped Brother Cronan build a bench but then I got fascinated by the pattern in the wood grain. So then he showed me how to polish a finished piece, and I asked him if I could carve a decoration in it and he didn't want to do that, but he gave me a small burl to work with but I'm only halfway done."

Etromma gave her brother a sidelong glance. "Exactly like that."

Clíodhna lost the battle to suppress her laugh. After her joy of the morning, her intense lesson with Adhna, and her emotional chat with Odhrán, her need to laugh was far more powerful than her ability to hold it back.

The next morning, when Clíodhna dropped the children off at the monk's enclave, Odhrán met them, grinning from ear to ear.

After Etromma and Donn went off to their respective teachers, and she'd placed Aileran with Brother Manchan, Odhrán asked her to join him on the garden bench. She had some time before meeting with Adhna, so she agreed.

The monk wouldn't meet her gaze and held his hands clasped tight in his lap. "I wanted to speak with you about my actions yesterday, Clíodhna. I should not have been so forward to a married woman, and I want to apologize."

Stunned, she gaped. "But there's nothing to apologize for. My husband is long gone."

Odhrán's face turned several shades of red, and he glanced down, fiddling with his fingers. "Within the rules of my church, you are still vowed to him. Therefore, I am not free to make advances toward you. Such an action is counted a grievous sin."

She let out a genuine laugh. "I enjoyed the attention. In fact," she put her hand on his, halting his fiddling, "I enjoy your company very much. Do you not find me attractive?"

His blush deepened further, and he visibly swallowed. "Thank you. You are delightfully intelligent and alluring, and I *do* enjoy your company, very much. That, however, is not the issue." He took a deep breath. "While I'm not yet vowed to the church, I am still permitted to… have relationships with women. But the Church frowns on such… relationships outside of marriage. And when I take my vows in a few moons, I must renounce such relations."

Confused, Clíodhna cocked her head. "What sort of idiocy is that? Why would they cut you off from half of all people?"

He shrugged one shoulder. "Not completely, or at least, not for most monks. We can interact with both men and women within defined parameters. Some of us seek a hermitage and live away from all people, but most of us become a part of a community. No, the stricture is particularly on… *carnal* relations with women."

She pursed her lips. "So, are they all expected to take male lovers? Some men prefer that, but many do not."

Odhrán coughed and she helpfully patted his back, but he waved off her help. "No, no carnal relations at all."

"But how do you honor the fertility of your land? It's an insult to the goddess to abstain."

He bowed his head, drawing his hand from hers, and resumed playing with his fingers. "This is becoming a most distressing conversation, Clíodhna. I'm so sorry that I'm having trouble explaining it. Please understand, we're meant to hold ourselves pure, away from the temptations of the flesh."

"*Temptations of the flesh?* You make it sound so… sordid."

He clasped his hands over his stomach. "In the eyes of our Lord, it is, unless the relations are within the sanctified relationship of marriage."

"I don't understand your god. I don't think I want to, not with *that* bizarre belief."

After taking in a deep breath, Odhrán let it out again and turned to face her. "Nevertheless, it is *my* belief. I must abide by it and be true to my heart."

That fragment of peace she'd felt in his company seemed to be melting away, but she didn't want to lose it. "Does this mean we can't have discussions? Must you shun my company?"

His eyes grew wide. "Absolutely not! First, I'm not yet vowed. Second, I'm charged to work within this community, and you *are* part of this community. And third," he cleared his throat, "third, I truly enjoy our conversations. You make me consider things I'd never examined before. I appreciate learning, and maybe we can learn more about each other's beliefs through such conversations."

She didn't want to just talk to him. She wanted to kiss that worried expression from his lips and run her hands through his hair. But, despite the desire still tingling within her, Clíodhna took a deep breath and decided upon the more diplomatic route. "If that's all we can share, then I shall treasure our friendship."

Odhrán took her hand again, his skin warm against hers. "Thank you for your understanding. I prayed last night that my weakness in touching you hadn't been a horrible mistake. Your own wisdom and generosity are a balm to my spirit and conscience."

Her desire rose again, but she must honor his request. "May we talk each morning when I bring the children? I would very much like that."

Odhrán gave her a dimpled grin. "As would I. Some mornings, I might have other duties, but when I can, I shall meet you at the abbey entrance."

"Abbey?"

He gestured around them. "Our name for this enclave. Our leader is an Abbot, though we temporarily have none. They've sent one from Rome, and should be here in a few moons."

Suddenly worried that she'd tarried too long, Clíodhna rose, casting an eye toward the sun. "I should leave you to your duties, then. Thank you, Odhrán, for explaining this to me."

"Safe travel home, Clíodhna."

Her journey to her house was full of both frustration and chagrin. She'd been so sure he would make a delightful lover. This new religion seemed harsh, but some of the druidic rules might be just as severe, if not more so. At least he wasn't locked away in an oak grove for twenty winters, and she could still enjoy discussions with him.

Adhna was waiting for her at the viewing rock. He raised his eyebrows as she climbed the hill. "Should I have come later?"

"I apologize, Adhna. I got entangled in a fascinating conversation while dropping off the children. Have you met any believers from this new religion?"

His eyes clouded with anger. "I have not, and don't intend to. They label my kind to be some sort of daemon, inherently evil and only good for banishing."

Clíodhna narrowed her gaze. "Oh?"

"Most assuredly. They splattered another of our kind with some blessed water and told them to flee before the power of their god. Of course, the Fae just laughed at them, but then the man held up a piece of cold iron in the shape of a cross. The Fae escaped, but left some surprises for the priest."

"What sort of surprises?"

Adhna raised one eyebrow. "Would you like to hear tales or learn magic?"

Clíodhna bowed her head. "I'm sorry. Yes, I'd rather learn magic."

"Very well, let's begin."

Adhna took her through several exercises like the one yesterday. Afterwards, her body felt wrung out but vibrant, like she'd just run along a beach at full speed and her skin buzzed with the edges of power. She rubbed her eyes and scrubbed her fingers in her hair to relieve some of the itch.

The Fae clapped his hands once. "Now that you've gained a level of control, you will do something with that power. Draw your tendril back in. This time, pull it in through your arm to your right hand."

As Clíodhna did so, she could almost see the blue light with her physical eyes, rather than just her imagination. It sparked and twisted within her palm like lightning in a thunderstorm. The air grew dark. Rain clouds gathered above them.

He followed her gaze. "Danú's paps! Well, I know humans don't wish to stay out in the rain, so we should end our lesson there. I shall see you again tomorrow."

The first drops plopped on the stone beside her. As he rose and dusted off his hands, she did the same. "Would you like something to eat? I don't imagine it's any more pleasant for you to get soaking wet. I have bread at my house."

With a wry twist of his lips, he asked, "Would you happen to have any cheese?"

Clíodhna laughed as they ran to safety. "I have plenty of cheese!"

Shaking the water from their *léinte*, they crowded into the doorway and the now-dim interior of the roundhouse. The sullen glow of her banked peat fire gave off little light. After she coaxed it to life, she rummaged through her pantry and brought out flatbread, cheese, and some wizened autumn apples.

"I'm afraid I don't have much fruit left, but I've got some honey. Would you like that with the cheese?"

His face lit up and he looked even younger. "That is the most delightful offer I've had all season."

She fetched the honey and laid it on the table. As her guest ate, she studied him. He had pleasant humor and manners, and he wouldn't be constrained by any silly stricture of this new religion.

If she couldn't honor the spring with Odhrán, perhaps Adhna would be an interesting alternative. She owed it to her own beliefs to honor the life of the world. Such obligations were much more enjoyable with a well-chosen partner.

Adhna devoured the cheese with single-minded intensity. His hair and skin was clean, well-kempt, and almost shining in the low light. He was tall, with a lean strength to his muscles. His teeth looked even and white, and while he didn't have Odhrán's dimple, his eyes crinkled with true mirth when he laughed.

She appreciated genuine folk far more than physical beauty, but he had both. But, of course he was attractive. He was a magical being.

Still, Adhna was her teacher, her mentor, by bound contract. She shouldn't rush into any complication of that relationship. Clíodhna must consider her options and the dangers inherent in each. True spring was at least a moon away, perhaps more. She had some time yet to choose her partner.

Chapter Four

Clíodhna and her family fell into a routine. Each morning for six days, she brought her children to the abbey for their lessons. After a brief discussion with Odhrán, she returned for lessons with Adhna. Occasionally, she came back to the abbey in time to chat with the monk again before her children finished.

On the seventh day, the monks rested and worshipped their God. Odhrán invited her several times to attend with them, and she did attend a few times. However, she discovered several beliefs within their doctrine she just couldn't agree with, especially their censure of her daughter just for questioning one of their beliefs.

Still, for appearance's sake, Clíodhna continued to attend at least every other seventh day. Her children were happy to go each week and began discussing the finer details of their theology between themselves.

Would she lose her children to this religion? Clíodhna gently inserted other ideas into their conversations, closer to her own beliefs.

Sometimes Etromma agreed with her and other times she argued. Donn stayed quiet at such times, but he paid close attention to both sides. As long as her children kept open minds, she'd be content.

Clíodhna's favorite conversations with Odhrán were those comparing their beliefs. Each belief had a dedicated group of people, taught the deeper mysteries of the religion, to greater understand the message of their gods.

One bright day, Odhrán explained the iron cross affixed to the top of their worship building, which he called a church. "When the Christos had seen but thirty-three winters, political intrigue resulted in his execution by being hung on a cross with nails through each wrist and one through his ankles. He hung upon this cross, in desperate agony, and yet did not denounce his torturers, the Romans."

"That's the city you're from?"

Odhrán let out a low chuckle. "Yes, but he didn't live there. He lived in a different city called Jerusalem, far to the southeast and across a vast sea. But the city of Rome is home to the Roman Empire, which spans an enormous distance around this sea and beyond. Jerusalem is part of that Empire, and thus the government is Roman."

Clíodhna's head spun with all these names and places, trying to imagine this empire's scope, but she concentrated instead on the demigod. "So, he died on his cross?"

He gave a grim nod. "He did. They buried him in a cave. Three days later, he rose again, reborn as proof that he was God's son."

Clíodhna clapped her hands. "Oh, like The Dagda! He could bring people back to life with a blow of *lorg mór*! Or in his cauldron. But that was usually during battle."

Odhrán blinked and cocked his head. "*Lorg mór*? What's that?"

"A magical club. He could slay nine people with a single blow, but he could also bring them back to life with the other end."

He shook his head, frowning. "This wasn't from a mystical pagan artifact. This was a miracle, one of many based on His own divine heritage."

She furrowed her brow. "What is the difference between your God's miracle and my gods' magic?"

He gave her a sweet smile, his dimple showing. "A miracle is the grace of God in this world, while your magic is your own creation. Magic can be used for evil, while a miracle is always for good."

With raised eyebrows, she remembered Adhna's mention of daemons. "Do you see my gods' magic as evil, then?"

Odhrán hesitated and then shrugged. "Not inherently, no. The power itself is neither good nor evil. While some in my order might label any magic evil, I grew up with an aunt who was a witch. She used her spells and potions to help people, especially women wanting children, and life is sacred. She cautioned about ever working with lamia or daemons. Such workings were dangerous."

There were the daemons. "Dangerous to her? Or in general?"

He shook his head. "She never said. But if she had been caught, she'd be sentenced for six winters' penance."

"Six winters? For working with Fae?"

Odhrán set his lips in a line. "I don't think the Fae are the same as daemons. But I'm no expert on the matter. Perhaps the abbot could answer your questions more precisely."

Clasping her hands, she went back to another aspect of confusion. "You mentioned your God died. Why would you celebrate his death? How do you, in this far land, benefit from someone who died in a desert so many leagues away?"

"Our Lord returned from the dead and declared that He'd made a sacrifice so we wouldn't have to die for our own sins. He took the punishment for us. Because of that miracle, we worship the symbol of the cross to honor His sacrifice."

Clíodhna chewed upon that concept, still not understanding. Then she remembered the sacred kings.

In some ancient legends, if the harvest was poor for several seasons, the *tuath* elected a sacred king. This king ruled without bound during a full cycle of the seasons, given anything he desired. Women, food, riches, all things were his.

Then, at the end of this cycle, he'd be sacrificed with great ceremony and given back to the land, begging the gods to return the land's health and wealth to those remaining. Clíodhna could glimpse a similar idea within this demigod's death.

She glanced at the cross on the church, stark and black against the morning sun. Someone had also carved it on a vertical stone in the center of the garden. This one had a circle surrounding the top part.

Clíodhna frowned, concerned at such a dark and brutal sublimation of her beloved sun. "But why do you put the circle around it, like the Druid sun symbol?"

"That's only here in the northern lands. You already used the cross with the circle as a sacred symbol. We lengthened one arm of it to resemble ours, to make the transition between beliefs easier."

She found this explanation both ingenious and manipulative. His church had both intelligence and ruthlessness. A dangerous combination for any native belief.

Clíodhna glanced at the sun again, worried about how high it had risen. "I thank you for the information, Odhrán, but it's time for me to go."

He put a hand on her arm. "Wait, just for a moment. You aren't going to rest, are you?"

She flashed him an impish grin and shrugged.

"May I ask what you use this time for, then? I'd hoped to relieve you from work by taking some of the burden from you. But you do seem to have more energy. If you aren't resting..."

She sat again and let out a sigh. "And I appreciate and value your help, Odhrán. I truly do. But I'm taking lessons of my own, lessons I need to keep my mind and soul intact."

He narrowed his eyes and studied her expression. Whatever he saw there must have satisfied him. "Very well. Perhaps someday you can speak of these lessons to me. In the meantime, have a care. I don't wish for you to become more frazzled than you must."

Clíodhna gave him a happy grin and took his hands, squeezing them. "Speaking with you every day helps me to relax far more than an hour's nap would. You enrich my mind, Odhrán. I value that."

The monk smiled back, showing his dimple, and squeezed back. "I'm happy to be valued for such a thing. Now run, lest you be late for your lessons."

As spring grew closer, Clíodhna still hadn't made her decision about Adhna. She lay in bed in the pre-dawn darkness, considering her options.

Adhna acted, in equal measures, harsh and kind as a teacher. She worked hard to please him and master her lessons, but some didn't come easily, to her intense frustration.

Did she even want him as a lover? His body would please hers, she had faith in his experience. But his alternating flightiness and hardness confused her. Perhaps this stemmed from his Fae nature, but it might make an intimate relationship challenging.

But when had she ever backed down from a challenge? Was she getting old?

With that mindset, Clíodhna threw off her wool blanket and pulled on a clean *léine,* washed her face, and walked out into the early morning.

First, she stopped at the stables to milk the cows. Adhna had taught her how to increase their output, but she only worked magic on one cow each morning. She didn't know what sort of ill effect this Fae magic might have on her kine, but she didn't want to risk harming them as she practiced.

Clíodhna sat on the low stool and drew in the tingling bits of magic from the earth. It surged much too strongly, and she struggled to tamp it down, trying not to flood the poor beast with too much power.

She wasn't comfortable with this earth magic yet. It felt odd to her, as if it didn't belong in her blood.

The cow lowed and mooed, stamping her hoof as Clíodhna pulled back. The beast hadn't even produced a normal amount of milk.

With a frown, Clíodhna glared at her cow, but the creature couldn't be faulted for her own inability to control her magic.

She'd practiced Adhna's lessons every morning, before greeting the dawn and heading into the village for the new church lecture. Sometimes her efforts brought brilliant success, but other times were either no effect at all, or near-disastrous failure.

Clíodhna gritted her teeth and tried again.

As she drew in power and drew only a thin tendril into the cow's body, her milk erupted into the bucket, splashing up to cover both her and the cow with warm wetness. She spluttered before mopping the white liquid from her face.

At least her garden magic had been more successful. She glanced toward the herbs and decided she needed to do something that came more easily to calm her prickled pride. She rose, patted the cow on her flank, and stepped into the garden enclosure.

Clíodhna worked best when in direct contact with the earth itself. She sat in the dirt, her legs straight in front of her, her palms flat on the ground. After drawing in the gentle earth power, she took one faint tendril and touched it to the garlic plant. Just a feather-touch, nothing heavy or intense.

The plant stretched as if a child waking from a deep sleep and grew visibly. Moving to the next garlic blossom, she tapped each with a gossamer stroke, urging each to rise to greet the coming dawn with open love.

After the garlic, she enchanted the onions, the chervil, and each of the other herbs. When she finished, the entire enclosure seemed deeper, more lush, and most of all, more full of the joy of life.

Clíodhna rose and brushed dirt from the back of her *léine*. In the east, the sky was brightening, so dawn should arrive soon.

She still needed to make a decision about who she'd honor *Bealtaine* with. But if Odhrán couldn't be with her, then it must be Adhna by default.

While her older children ate, she took some time to play with the baby after he fed. Then they journeyed to the abbey in the pre-dawn light, the birds just waking from their slumber as the darkness faded. Clíodhna missed greeting the dawn, but she must make some sacrifices if she wanted to be to the church on time.

She still rolled that word around in her mind. It sounded strange to her, along with the other words Odhrán used. Church, liturgy, sermon… she'd never heard any of these before. Did the *druí* use them in their deeper mysteries? She had met with several *druí* before, and a few bards as well, but she'd never chatted with them as she had with Odhrán. Perhaps these words applied to all religions, and because she'd never studied druidic lore, they were new to her.

In truth, she appreciated that this new religion shared their teachings with their lowliest followers, and didn't keep all their mysteries for a small group.

The abbey yard looked as if someone had poked a stick in an ant nest. Monks scrambled around, rushing back and forth. Several villagers waited at the edge of the frenzy, gazing on the confusion with puzzled expressions.

Clíodhna found Ita and tapped her shoulder. "What's happening? Did someone get hurt?"

Her friend shrugged. "No, but someone important arrived in the night. They're rushing to get things presentable for him. He might be the new leader."

"The new abbot? Odhrán told me he'd be here soon."

Ita glared at her. "You talk with him a lot, don't you? Don't think we haven't noticed."

Surprised at the censure in her friend's voice, Clíodhna stared back. "Noticed what? We're just talking."

Ita waved her hand. "Yes, yes. But you've been taking all his time. He has other duties than entertaining you, you know."

Clíodhna's face grew warm thinking of the village women discussing her relationship with Odhrán. She wished she hadn't come to the abbey today. With all the confusion, no one would notice if she just left.

But that would mean the children wouldn't have their lessons, which meant she wouldn't have hers, either. The same day she'd decided about *Bealtaine*, too.

If she hadn't been certain Ita loved her own husband well, Clíodhna might suspect her of jealousy about Odhrán, but the woman doted on her man. Why should her friend be so concerned about the monk's time? He wasn't shirking his duties as a monk to be with her.

As dawn broke over the hills to the east, it bathed the valley with golden light and a bell rang. Clíodhna had never experienced such a deep and sonorous clang, echoing across the farmland. If anyone was still sleeping, they'd be awake now.

Ita clapped her hands. "Oh, I'd heard he brought a bell all the way from Rome! That must be it."

The sound was pleasant, but so loud. Clíodhna gave thanks to Brighid that her home lay far from the village. The sound might reach her, but they wouldn't rouse her from a sound sleep. Would they only ring the bell at dawn?

The yard emptied of rushing clerics. Ita and Clíodhna exchanged a confused glance.

When the bell stopped ringing and the last echoes faded, a procession of religious men wended out from their sleeping quarters. Each monk stepped in time, one by one, perfectly spaced.

Clíodhna had never seen them all together before and counted as they passed. Twelve, thirteen, fourteen… twenty-four in all. Behind them, a stranger in shining white and blue robes carried a standard with a strange symbol.

With measured steps, he marched stiff and formal. The symbol looked like a six-armed star, with a sideways loop on the top middle arm. Clíodhna made a mental note to ask Odhrán what it meant.

The new man looked just past middle-aged with long, dark hair shot with white and a gray beard. He was wiry and slim, despite his shapeless robes. He kept his eyes forward, not glancing side to side at any of the fascinated on-lookers.

After he entered the church, the bell gave a single peal. The villagers milled about in confusion until one monk poked his head out and gestured for them to enter.

With muddled reluctance, each villager complied, but Clíodhna held back. Aileran was sleeping soundly against her shoulder despite the bell. When Etromma reached for him, she allowed her daughter to take the baby. He didn't wake during the transfer but snuggled into the fresh shoulder with a sweetness which made Clíodhna's heart ache.

The interior was stuffed so full of people, Clíodhna felt crowded and wanted to immediately leave again. But her curiosity over this new abbot won out over her need for solitude. Clíodhna stood along the back wall, as here was no room for sitting during this sermon.

The new abbot stood at the altar and handed his standard to another monk, who then stood behind him.

The abbot then cleared his throat and held his arms up. Whispers and side conversations halted, all eyes to the front.

Once everyone silenced, he spoke in a full voice with deep tones and rich syllables which caressed her ears, though his accent spoke of foreign birth. "Welcome, people of Hibernia. Welcome to the one true church, the home of God, our Lord Almighty. Pray attend to the liturgy."

His next words must have been in the language of the new religion, Latin, but she still understood none of it. The words were harsh and guttural, not flowing and liquid like her own language.

The abbot's resonant voice, pleasant though it was, did not make the words softer. Instead, they prodded and poked into her mind, pushing against her. Clíodhna tried to think of other things, but they intruded upon her thoughts, crowding everything else away.

He switched to her own language, and she almost wished he hadn't. Now he praised his own God to the exclusion of all others, framing anyone not Christian as evil, full of nasty intentions to subvert their "flock."

His implication that all other beliefs were wrong bothered her, and she didn't want to stay to listen to more vitriol. Would she insult this new leader if she left during his sermon? It might be more polite to remain, and it might not be wise to upset a community leader. Still, she hated listening to this.

He switched back to Latin, more of a chant than a speech. Her head pounded in time to the foreign syllables.

When his liturgy ended, he spoke in their own language again. "Greetings be upon you. I am Abbot Pátraic, newly arrived from Rome, the eternal city, and the Holy See. Please welcome me into your community as you have welcomed my brethren before me."

He opened his arms wide. "I bring not only news from Rome, but also blessed tidings from our Emperor Valentinian the third, of the baptism into our blessed Lord's faith of your King Eógan mac Néill in the north, and of the latest pronouncements upon our faith by the newly inaugurated Pope Leo."

Clíodhna didn't know what a baptism was, and she'd never heard the Emperor's name, nor that of the northern king or this pope. Whatever a pope was.

"In the meantime, I shall work to strengthen the habits and rituals within this abbey and community, that it may better serve our Lord God. Now, please, we are offering our Lovefeast outside for your sustenance. Join us."

Thankful the speech had finished, Clíodhna bolted out the door. Monks had set up their trestle tables outside and already half laid the table, but her pounding head made her stomach roil too much to eat. She needed to be away from people. Now that the sermon had ended, she no longer feared insulting anyone by escaping, and her absence wouldn't be noticed amongst so many villagers.

Clíodhna escaped to the gardens, taking deep sniffs of the budding flowers and smiling at the few bees who'd braved the chilly morning. Several breaths later, she drew upon the power of the earth and growing things to strengthen her nerves.

As the sun played hiding games amongst the clouds, she wished it would shine upon her. A shiver ran through her body, and she'd welcome the sunlight.

The clouds, as if listening to her plea, parted to reveal the morning sun. She closed her eyes to bask in the warmth.

As the bright sunlight suffused her skin and body with life-giving heat and the earth surrendered its power to her muscles, she regained her strength, just as Adhna had been showing her. With a satisfied sigh, she rose and turned to leave the monk's garden.

The new Abbot was looming right in front of her. His chin held high in blatant disapproval and his scowl deepening. "What do you seek here, woman?"

Still suffused with the earth's power, she met his gaze with confidence. "I meant no harm. I come here often, to be at peace among the growing things."

He stared at her for a few moments, as if taking her measure. His eyes took in her stance, her clothing, and was probably assessing her status. "This is the abbey's garden, and if you should wish to visit, arrangements can be made. In the future, I prefer that you enter with an escort."

Clíodhna pursed her lips and bit back an angry retort. Instead, she sidestepped him to escape his piercing regard. Once out of sight, she let out a deep breath. She didn't dare mention that Odhrán often asked her into the garden. She didn't want to get her friend in trouble. The gossip Ita mentioned would be bad enough.

Then Clíodhna searched for her children. She spied Donn out in the carpentry yard and Aileran in the nursery. Etromma was likely at the bakehouse.

Freed from her duty, she scanned the abbey for Odhrán, but couldn't find him. He'd probably be busy with the new arrival and had plenty to do other than to spend time with her today. With a final glance around, she left the village.

She almost turned back to brave the village rather than go to her lessons with the Fae. Today would be the day she spoke to Adhna about *Bealtaine* rites.

Never in her life had Clíodhna felt so nervous. Not when her husband had asked her father to marry her, not even the first night of her wedding. But she'd made her decision and today, she needed to implement it. She meant to ask Adhna to be her lover today.

The entire walk back to her home, she rehearsed how she'd broach the subject. First, she'd mention the spring thaw or point out daffodils bursting through the thin layer of ice. Perhaps she'd speak of the budding trees and how sacred life once again pushed through to the world of men.

Then, she'd ask him if he wanted to be part of that process with her. Her imagination fed her responses ranging from excited delight to horrified rejection.

As she approached the viewing rock, Adhna sat cross-legged in her usual spot. He turned, his face grim. "I'm afraid I must leave you for a little while, my dear student. I've been called back to Faerie for now."

Clíodhna's heart dropped. The dismay must have shown in her expression. He stood and took both her hands, his skin soft against hers. "Worry not, my dear Clíodhna. I will return, hopefully soon. Perhaps even in a few days, but it might be as long as a moon. My Queen needs me, and I must obey."

Clíodhna hugged him goodbye, wishing with all her heart that he didn't have to leave. Clouds blocked the sun, and the wind picked up as they released each other. She stared into his bright blue eyes, wanting to kiss him before he left but not daring to.

She expected him to walk away. And she didn't expect him to dissolve in her arms. Her skin tingled where they'd touched. Clíodhna sat down on the viewing rock and cried in a mixture of grief and frustration.

Chapter Five

Her days no longer occupied with lessons, Clíodhna took some much-needed rest. As *Bealtaine* approached and the weather grew warmer, she did repairs on the roundhouse, prepared her garden for new growth, and kept her mind busy.

Clíodhna still needed someone to honor the spring season, but if Adhna might be back in time, she must wait for him. No one else in the village came close to being suitable or as attractive.

Odhrán, though she would have delighted in sharing his body, had made his position clear, and it would be unfair to pursue that avenue. Besides, she hadn't seen much of him since the abbot arrived. They stole a few moments of treasured discourse when she picked her children up, but the abbot had given him new duties which kept his days full.

She'd attended another sermon to discover more about Abbot Pátraic's intentions. His words sounded reasonable enough, if strident. He didn't seem to have any room in his philosophy for those who weren't part of his church.

Clíodhna didn't care for that exclusion. She'd never been good at obeying commands from authority figures. They made her want to do the opposite out of spite.

However, he had outlined several worthy projects, including regular teaching for all children, community workshops to spread knowledge, and charitable projects for those in need.

These reflected the ideals Odhrán had spoken of, and she appreciated that the new religion valued such ideas. *Druí* also held such beliefs, but only educated those dedicated to the path.

To fill her mornings, Clíodhna volunteered to help with the monk's garden, and using the techniques Adhna had taught her, encouraged the plants to grow quick and strong. Several monks remarked at how well the garden grew under her care. She found it amusing that the abbot had once told her she'd require permission to enter.

One day, as she helped make soup for the abbey, the new Abbot passed by. She braced herself for his habitual frown of disapproval, but he granted her a nod instead. She both hated herself for wanting the approval and glowed with the warmth of acceptance.

They were giving soup to poorer folks in the village, an activity which Clíodhna heartily approved of. When she stood at the table, handing out bread with the soup, she liked the changes this church brought.

Not that the village would ever let someone die of starvation, but many did scrape by to fill their bellies, especially in the spring when nothing yet grew in the gardens and the autumn slaughter had long since been eaten.

However, there was another change the abbot had brought, the acceptable behavior of unmarried women. He dictated that they should remain modest and protected by their fathers or brothers until they married.

Clíodhna did not like this change one bit.

Not only did it affect her directly, as a widow, but she seethed at the assumed authority. How dare he dictate women's behavior and abilities? Did they not equal men in wisdom and reason?

Under Brehon Law, women could hold property, divorce, and stand equal to her husband. The *druí* had no such disdain for females, and counted many women in their leadership. This new church had no women in places of power, from what she could discover. How dare he come into their land, their society, and begin making demands of change?

He'd given that sermon last week, but Clíodhna hadn't attended that day. It had set all the women talking, and Ita had passed on this news to her.

Clíodhna couldn't believe Ita had gotten the details right, so she sought Odhrán's counsel after dropping off the children the morning before *Bealtaine*.

The young monk wasn't near the stables, nor in the blacksmithy. She checked the leather workshop next, but the place was empty. Finally, she found him in the practice field. He was sparring with another monk, both using wooden quarterstaffs. The *clack clack* of the weapons made a gentle, regular rhythm. They were only sparring, barely touching the stout poles.

When he noticed her, Odhrán bowed to his opponent, replaced his staff on a rack, and mopped the sweat from his forehead. "Good day, Clíodhna! How are you on this fine morning?"

She pursed her lips, glaring at him. "What do you know about this new edict by your Abbot?"

His cheerful expression dissolved into a grim line. "Oh, yes. That. I expected to hear from you on this."

She waited with her hands on her hips. "Well?"

With a shrug, he wiped his face again. "It's a rule in Rome that Abbot Pátraic and other leaders are charged to spread throughout the Christian lands."

Clíodhna refused to grant him leniency, despite their friendship. "These are not Christian lands. These are Eirish lands, and not subject to rule by your empire. They don't even call it by the proper name. We are not Rome's to take. The abbot would do well to remember that fact."

Odhrán shut his eyes and breathed in deep. When he let the breath out, his eyes opened, full of entreaty. "Please understand, Clíodhna. I have no say in this decision, and no way of changing his mind. His superiors have ordered him to do this and I've been ordered to support him."

She clenched her jaw in frustration and lifted her chin. "Then who do I appeal to in Rome?"

He stared at his feet, his hands clasped. "They would not heed your appeal. You are a woman, and women do not have the right."

Clouds blocked out the morning sun, shrouding them in shadow. Wind began to whip through the practice yard, and the first fat drops of an impending downpour fell. Odhrán glanced up and gestured toward the armory to seek shelter. With poor grace, Clíodhna followed him as the storm grew in fury.

They shared the space with staves, leather armor, barding, horse tack in for repair, and a few old, pitted swords. The smells of rust, leather, and dust tickled her nose, warring with the musty odor of the rainstorm.

A crack of lightning struck the well-flattened dirt of the empty practice yard, making Odhrán jump.

He turned to her, placing his hands on her shoulders. "I am sorry, Clíodhna."

Clíodhna shrugged them off. "Don't patronize me, Odhrán. You know better than that."

"I do, and I didn't intend to patronize you. Will you calm your prickles for just a moment? I do have some news for you."

She pressed her lips together and gave him a sideways glance. "Oh?"

He bowed his head. "I'm to go away in six days."

Startled, she blinked. "Away? How long will you be gone?"

"Away for good. I've been reassigned to another community."

Suddenly realizing how much she'd miss her friend and their conversations, her anger cooled. "Where? How far away?"

He shrugged one shoulder. "I'm not sure. Someplace north, called *Ard Mhacha*. I'm to help establish a church for Abbot Pátraic. He's charged me with finding the best site to build and organize the construction."

Ard Mhacha. She'd heard of it in the *druí* tales, a place sacred to the goddess Macha. It was far to the north and east, at least six days' travel from here in *Loch Rí*.

She might never see Odhrán again.

Wanting to keep him close, she wrapped her arms around him and held him tightly. He hesitated at first, but then hugged her, his hands strong on her spine. She drew back, their faces but an inch apart, and they exchanged a soul-felt gaze, their eyes drinking in each other's essence.

With tender affection, she kissed him softly on the lips. The kiss lasted much longer than she'd intended, though she never wanted it to stop. *Bealtaine* was tomorrow, and she still needed a way to honor the gods.

Odhrán's hands caressed her back, her waist, and she deepened the kiss, opening her mouth. She pulled him against her body, feeling his need rise between them. He dug his fingers into her hair, and her own desire responded, tingling through her like the lightning crashing outside.

A whoosh of wind made the door slam shut. They stopped, startled from their passion, but then returned to their ardor with intense hunger.

Clíodhna loosed the urges she'd repressed for moons, eager to enfold him in her desire. A willing participant, he pulled her to the floor, amidst hay and dust.

Odhrán ran his hand down her waist to her thigh, pushing up her *léine*. The soft skin of his palm against her breasts made her shiver in delighted anticipation. She moaned when he kissed her neck and shoulder.

Clíodhna pushed up his léine and cupped her hands on his buttocks, caressing the downy hair and strong muscles.

His eyes widened as she pushed him to the ground with a grin. She yanked up his *léine* all the way up, pulled hers up around her waist, and straddled him. He groaned and closed his eyes as she rocked with gentle motion, rubbing against his manhood with a barely controlled craving to feel him inside her.

Clíodhna, unable to wait any longer, lifted and guided him in. He let out a deep groan and clasped her hips, digging his fingers into her flesh.

With measured rhythm, she moved up and down, guiding their lovemaking with practiced passion. He shuddered and wriggled beneath her, making her peak more quickly. She didn't want it to be over yet, so she stopped, squeezing deep within her.

His hands tightened on her waist, his nails scratching her tender skin. Clíodhna placed her hands on his chest, raking them across his breast and nipples, bending in for a savage kiss, biting his neck. He grabbed her head and stole a kiss from her lips, just as filled with need.

She moved again, stroking up and down with her hips as his cries rose in a crescendo, matching her own need and fervor. They both shrieked in time with a massive roll of thunder, the storm outside masking their passionate fury.

Her climax rippled through her body, still connected to his. He twitched and let out a whimper. Carefully, she dismounted and cleaned herself of his seed, rearranging their clothing with practiced hands.

Then, Clíodhna lay beside him, holding his hand to her chest as his breathing slowed from frantic to normal.

Odhrán glowed from exertion, but he then covered his face with his hands. "Clíodhna! Oh, my dear sweet God, what have you done to me?"

Confused, she turned to him. "Did I imagine your enjoyment, Odhrán?"

He turned, leaning his head on his hand. "Oh, I enjoyed it! You stole my very essence, and I loved every second. But I must leave in a week, and if I didn't want to leave you before, I certainly don't wish to now! At this moment, I don't think I could walk if I tried."

She giggled and stroked his cheek, her finger tracing a line of sweat. He grabbed her finger and kissed it.

Another boom of thunder shook the ground. He glanced at the door. "Perhaps we should get up. As much as I'd love to spend hours in your arms, someone will come looking for me when the storm eases."

"That would be wise."

The door slammed open, and the wind rushed in. Abbot Pátraic stood in the archway, his face filled with thunderous anger as he took in their positions. "How *dare* you? How dare you corrupt my faithful monk with your wanton, hedonistic ways!"

They both scrambled to their feet. Clíodhna brushed hay from her clothing and patted her hair into a semblance of order while Odhrán fell to his knees, his head bowed before his Abbot. "My Lord Abbot, I—"

"Silence! You will go to your cell, now. I shall deal with you forthwith."

Odhrán glanced at Clíodhna, fear patent in his eyes. She gripped his shoulder to reassure him, but the fear didn't fade. He rose and tried once again to plead with the abbot. "Please be merciful, my Lord Abbot. Clíodhna wasn't the transgressor. I am at fault. I—"

"I said *silence*! Go now, or you will make things worse for the wanton!" Odhrán slunk out the door and disappeared in the downpour.

Her spine straightening at this pejorative, Clíodhna said, "I request that you speak of me with more respect, Abbot Pátraic. I am a member of this community, and—"

Sharp pain exploded on her cheek as her head rocked to the side from his slap. Clenching her fists and her jaw, she glared at the abbot. "How dare you strike me! How dare you insult me! I will not allow such treatment from a stranger!"

He laughed, a nasty sound of someone used to power.

As the last echo of his mirth died, lightning struck the doorway behind him, making him jump away. Flames licked the wooden frame.

Clíodhna dove outside into the darkness and fled from the irrational Abbot and his abbey as fast as she could. She knew the path well, even without the benefit of sunlight. After slipping several times, she slowed her pace, confident that Pátraic wouldn't follow her.

Wrung out from the emotional adventures of the day, she dragged herself into her roundhouse, thankful to be safe home. Clíodhna had no idea how long she'd been in the abbey, nor when she had to fetch her children, but for now, she curled up in a knot and shook.

Her righteous anger, her inflamed passion, her abject misery, these all warred within her, threatening to burst forth with ferocious intensity. Her blood burned with swirling emotions, fighting to be free, echoed by the fierce storm outside.

Clíodhna bolted upright, a horrible thought occurring to her. What if Pátraic took his rage out on her children?

After grabbing her oiled leather cloak, along with Etromma and Donn's, she braved the fury of the storm again, the rain now blowing sideways.

Not three steps from her door, a hand on her shoulder made her whirl, knife in hand, ready to fight whoever interrupted her mission.

Adhna stood tall and untouched by the tempest surrounding him, his hair not even dancing in the wind. "You must come with me, Clíodhna."

Clíodhna glanced toward the abbey. "I need to get my children. They may be in danger."

He gripped her shoulder. "They are safe for now and will be so until you retrieve them. I've seen to that. You must come with me now."

She glanced to the abbey, itching to get to her children. "But why?"

"You must calm the storm."

The wind didn't blow his hair or beard. He stood like a statue against the maelstrom. Despite his assurances about her children, she wouldn't have followed him, if not for that patent sign of his powers.

Adhna led her along a path Clíodhna didn't recognize, and she'd lived here for many winters. How did she not know every path in this area? It rose with the hills, up and up into the blinding rain. Mud squelched beneath her boots, making her slip and slide until Adhna reached back for her hand, keeping her steady.

Hand in hand, they climbed higher, past the tree line, past rocky outcroppings looming on either side of the path. They passed through a strange mist, still despite the raging storm, and emerged onto a bare hilltop.

No, not bare. A single stone jutted from the grass, with smaller stones forming a circle. The little ones came barely to her knee, but the tallest monolith towered above her in sinister threat.

Adhna still clasped her hand, but she resisted when he drew her into the Faerie circle. She'd been so wary of a bargain with the Fae, why would she willingly enter such a place with Adhna? He had been true to her so far, but that held no meaning now.

"You must enter, Clíodhna. For your own safety."

Safety didn't exist. That Abbot would come after her now that she'd defied him. If she stood on this hilltop long enough, the storm might sweep her away into oblivion. Then she'd be safe from the abbot, at least. Safety in death hadn't been an option she'd thought of. But if her only other path lie in entering Faerie, perhaps death *would* be a better choice.

Despite her reluctance, he yanked her into the circle. Clíodhna cried out in pain and surprise. Adhna had never handled her with rough hands before. Didn't a human need to enter such a circle freely? All the tales said so. She stood within the stones, shaking from nerves and fear as the storm raged outside.

Adhna turned to her and took both her hands. "Now, calm the storm."

"Me? I have no such power, Adhna. How can I stop this?"

He raised his eyebrows, his expression sad. "You created this storm. It's a manifestation of your own rage, brought forth into the mortal realm. It's disturbed both your world and mine. My Queen has commanded me to show you how to halt the tempest."

She had caused this? How had she done that? Thinking back to the beginning, when she spoke to Odhrán, and how upset she'd become when he spoke of his moving away, a glimmer of understanding poked through her confusion. Then the passionate lovemaking and the fury at the abbot, well maybe she did have a hand in it.

With a painful swallow, she glanced at her mentor. "Very well. Show me how."

He led her to the center of the circle, facing the tall stone. "Sit. Draw in the earth's strength. Concentrate on the calming, gentle energy of the land. Be braced for pain."

Clíodhna did as he bid, the power flowing strong now. No gentle tendrils, but a rushing blue light tore through her spine, making her stiffen.

"Good. As the power channels up through you, hold your arms high and direct that power out into the clouds. Picture it unraveling the storm, like when you untie a tangled thread. Bit by bit, unknotting anger, pain, and rage from your emotional storm."

Lightning burst forth from her hands, burning through her blood, and she screamed in agony. She had little control on the surge coursing through her muscles and bones. It shot into the sky, blanketing the roiling, swirling clouds with pale blue crackles of light.

The pain became part of her as she regained control over her hands. Clíodhna physically pushed, as if the clouds were close enough to touch. Branches of light dug the clouds apart, breaking them into tiny wisps. They splintered into smaller dark puffs of her wrath. Angry thunderheads quieted into sullen darkness.

"Good. Now draw the energy back down, into the earth."

Another shot of pain arched through her spine and she cried out. Stars danced in the darkness behind her eyes as she pulled the anger and rage back into the ground, coolness embracing the red until it dimmed into a sullen heartbeat.

When the sky became calm and the now drained storm clouds drifted away, she slumped on the ground, drained from her efforts.

Adhna curled around her, his body warm against her back. He held her as her heartbeat slowed from its frantic pace, as her skin no longer burned with earth energy.

When she could breathe again, she croaked, "Is it done?"

"It's done. Now sleep, Clíodhna. You've done well, but it's taken everything you have. I will protect you. Sleep, and when you have rested, we can retrieve your children. They'll be safe. Rest. I'm here for you."

She didn't want to sleep. She had so much to do, but she had no energy to move her body, and so she drifted into a deep slumber.

Her dreams grew dark and amorphous, full of chasing danger, but try as she might, she couldn't glimpse what pursued her. Clíodhna pushed through boggy muck, but whatever pursued her came closer.

She turned to face her attacker but found only darkness. She flailed with the spear in her arm. Spear? Where had she found a spear? The iron tip burned her skin when she touched it. Gloom smothered her, and she couldn't draw in a breath. Panicked, she ripped at the night with her spear, rending great gaps in the void. Beyond it, she saw nothing, only more black despair.

With a gasp, she bolted upright, awake and terrified. Adhna wrapped her in his arms, still pressed against her back. "Shh. Calm, now. The darkness won't find you. I'm here. Your dreams are of the future, not of the now. A future far, far away. A future for a people, not a person."

Her breath came in short gasps, despite the brilliant sun above them. The mist and storm had all burned away, and the grass glistened in bright sunlight.

Clíodhna breathed in deep, taking in the sweet aromas of wet grass and clover. Her head cleared and she needed to move. She'd laid down for far too long. Etromma, Donn, and Aileran needed her.

She scrambled to her feet, but her knees buckled. Adhna supported her until she regained her balance, but her legs still wobbled. "What in Danú's name is wrong with me?"

Adhna laughed, the sound rippling around her. "My dear Clíodhna, you just worked a major magical conjuring and then pulled the energy from the very earth to quell it. You're still drained, despite the sleep. Let me help you home."

"I must get my children first!"

He placed a hand on her upper arm, his skin warm against hers. "I shall fetch the young ones. You need to rest. At dusk, I'll bring you back up here for *Bealtaine*, and we can complete your healing."

Dusk. The beginning of the fire feast, the time when the veil between the worlds grew thin. Clíodhna thought back to her lovemaking with Odhrán and wished she dared bring him to this hill. While she'd honored the goddess with their act, it hadn't been in quite the right place nor quite the right time. But now Adhna was back.

With Adhna's arm around her shoulders, she stumbled down the green hill, through the looming gate stones, and into the valley below.

Clíodhna still didn't recognize the path, but it brought her to her farm. She didn't quibble when Adhna made her lie on her bed, pulling a wool blanket to her chin. He placed a cool hand on her forehead and spoke a few words in an ancient language. Despite her determination to remain awake, and the brightness of the midday sun, she faded into slumber.

This time, she had no dreams.

Chapter Six

A spring breeze caressed her face, and Clíodhna touched her own right cheek, imagining it to be Odhrán's hand. Remembering the heat of him, she stretched and glanced around her home. Etromma was chopping turnips at the kitchen table, humming to herself while Aileran slept in his cot. Donn was nowhere to be seen.

Adhna sat by the hearth, stirring the pot with a wooden spoon. "Ah, just in time! Etromma, can you serve the stew? Your mother will need a hearty meal when we return."

Etromma flashed him a smile in agreement and grabbed the ladle to fill a bowl.

Clíodhna didn't think Adhna had even met her children before. Now her daughter was acting as if she'd known him all her life.

She narrowed her gaze at her daughter. "Etromma?"

Etromma brought her the bowl. "It's fine, Ma. Adhna told us everything."

Everything? Her stomach clenched at what the Fae might have shared with her children.

"Adhna collected us from the abbey. He explained he's been teaching you, just like the monks have been teaching us."

"That's all?"

"Was there more?" Etromma bent back over the table and began chopping onions.

Not everything, then. She breathed more easily and shook her head.

Adhna put out a hand to help her rise. "I wish I could allow you more rest. as your body still needs physical recovery. But today is *Bealtaine*, so I must take you back up to the hill. Dusk is coming, and tonight is too special to squander. Besides, I have some information for you."

She got to her feet and rubbed her face. "Information? About what?"

"Not until we're safe in the circle. Come."

Clíodhna relieved herself in the sand basket near the door before they left. "Etromma? Will you and Donn look after Aileran?"

Her daughter didn't look up from her task. "Of course, Ma. Do what you need to do. We'll be fine."

Only sixteen winters old and her daughter seemed ready to run her own household. She still pursued Tirechan, the blacksmith's boy, although his father wasn't pleased with the match. Soon, her daughter would leave home and start a family of her own. Clíodhna's throat caught with impending loss and glanced at Etromma with both pride and trepidation.

In silence, Clíodhna and Adhna trekked back up the mysterious path and through the stones. They didn't seem so sinister in the afternoon sun. The stone circle looked almost cheerful. Golden light bathed the inside surface of the large stone in the east. As she glanced toward the setting sun, she decided the stone glowed with more than just sunlight.

Adhna drew her around the circle one time, twice, thrice, all while chanting in some ancient language, words too slippery for her to grasp their meaning. His voice echoed across the space, swirling around her like playful mist.

With each march around the perimeter, the glowing stone grew brighter. The smaller stones pulsed with faint light. By the time they completed the third circuit, the main stone shone almost as strong as the sun, which was just touching the horizon.

Their world turned orange, red, and yellow. The light pulsed with the earth's heartbeat, slow and steady, strong and stolid. They entered the circle, hand in hand, with deliberate steps. Clíodhna's heart raced as power slammed against her.

This was no gentle earth energy, tendrils of blue-white light that she'd been using. This energy surged with seasonal strength, the power of the sun, far more forceful than the placid land. Clíodhna fell to her knees.

Adhna knelt next to her and pulled her into an embrace. He still spoke in that ancient chant, his voice encircling her with comfort. She clung to him as the power swirled around them.

He touched his lips to her in a passionate kiss.

Suddenly, Clíodhna wasn't ready, not so soon after Odhrán. She wiggled to escape his grasp, and he let her go. She pulled back and stared at him. Yes, she wanted him, and had wanted him for many moons now.

But her poor body balked at the effort. "I can't, Adhna. Not after all I've gone through today."

"I can lend you strength, if you wish. You can say no, and I won't be upset in the slightest, but another opportunity like this won't come for another six moons."

"Must it be right now?" She glanced at the sun, knowing the answer.

He followed her gaze and shrugged. "We might hold off for a little while, but not much. We must complete the ritual before the last sliver of sun disappears behind the hills. Would you like to wait? Or will you allow me to help? I can give you the energy now, and you can decide then. The ritual will be flawed if you participate under duress. I need your full willingness."

Clíodhna swallowed, staring toward the descending sun. She needed something. Someone to lean on, someone to lend her stability. This day had been far too chaotic for her to make sense of what she ought to do.

Then she gazed into Adhna's concerned eyes. She saw compassion there, and even affection. Maybe even love. Her spirit called out to his, eager to join.

She spread her arms and bowed her head. "Lend your energy. I'll try."

Adhna grasped her shoulders. "Are you certain? I don't wish to press you into this against your desires."

She straightened her spine, determined to be part of his ritual and to share the spark she saw in his eyes. "Yes. I want this. Please."

The Fae placed his hands on her forehead, his skin warm. Strength flowed into her head, through her torso, and into each limb, making her fingers tingle. Clíodhna quivered with the energy, unable to stop her arms and legs from twitching. The pleasure rushed through her blood so strong that it hurt, both worse and better than any pleasure in lovemaking. As the flow peaked, she arched her back with a soundless scream.

As the rush of energy dwindled, Clíodhna sprang to her feet and shook out her arms, rubbing the skin to remove the intense prickling sensation, like thousands of tiny ants biting her glowing skin.

"You took that well, Clíodhna. I'm proud of your ability. You've learned much since I first met you."

Flushing at the praise, she flashed him a nervous grin. Energy now coursed through her, too fast, too strong. She wanted to run up and down the hill at full speed, bare feet gripping the soft grass. Peering at the gate rocks, she wondered if she could climb to the top.

"I told you I have information for you. Now is the time to tell you."

Clíodhna halted, her hand pressed against her breast, feeling her heart thump like a drum. "What information?"

He interlaced his fingers. "I know something of your ancestry, something you must know now."

Forcing herself to sit, she fidgeted her fingers as she tried to pay attention to his words. Buzzing echoed in her ears and she kept looking for flies.

"I knew your family, seasons ago. Specifically, your mother's father. Do you remember him at all?"

She'd never met her grandfather, as he'd died long before she had been born. Clíodhna shook her head as she ran her fingers through her hair, suddenly aware of how straggly it felt. Swinging her head back and forth, she watched the clumped strands swish by, fascinated with their heft.

Adhna gripped her shoulders and gave her a tiny shake. "Clíodhna! Pay attention. Your grandfather wasn't human."

She halted and stared at Adhna. "He what?"

"He was a Lord of the Fae Court, under my Queen Áine. He traveled to the human lands, fell in love with your grandmother, begat a child, and then returned to Faerie."

She leapt to her feet, pacing back and forth, shaking out her hands. "No, that can't be right. He lived with my grandmother for many winters. My father remembered him when he courted Mother. They used to go hunting."

The Fae shook his head, wearing a frown. "That man married your grandmother later. Not your true grandfather."

She stomped her feet, reveling in the solid thumps they made. "That makes no sense. Who was this Fae? Wait. Does that mean I'm part Fae?"

A grin broke Adhna's serious demeanor. "Yes. That's what I'm trying to tell you, Clíodhna. You have Fae blood. It courses through your veins. This is why you have magic, why you can call the storms from the sky. This is why you called a maelstrom with your rage and passion, and why I could show you how to dismiss it."

Clíodhna touched her knife hilt, tracing the cool metal wire, delighting in its rough texture. "But why can I touch iron?"

"Your human blood protects you from cold iron."

She plopped down on the grass, suddenly weighted down by the knowledge.

"This is why I've chosen to teach you, and why I'd like you to be part of the *Bealtaine* ritual. Are you still willing? If so, we can delay no longer."

She glanced over her shoulder at the barest sliver of the sun still showing over the distant hills. Mists had risen, but a faint orange glow still pushed through the dusky fog.

With a deep breath and a brief wish that she could be with Odhrán instead, Clíodhna bit her lip. "I would be honored to take part in your ritual."

Adhna offered his hand, and she took it. He drew her into his arms, kissing her gently on the lips, and then they touched foreheads, gazing into each other's eyes.

Where her earlier tryst with Odhrán had been frantic and eager, Adhna moved slowly, gently, with more care than she might have believed. She'd had several lovers, but none as deliberate, considerate, and attentive as the Fae.

He broke off their gaze and again, they circled the stones three times. Again, he chanted in that slippery, ancient language. Again, he drew her to the center.

This time, he drew her down beside him and placed a finger on her lips. "Let me attend to you. You're the goddess tonight, the beloved of all men. You're the fertile ground within which seeds grow. You're the earth, full of life and fecund magic."

His hands caressed her shoulders, her waist, her hips, her legs, every inch of her skin, with feather softness. Energy coursed through her muscles. She sat up, wanting to touch him back, but he eased her back down.

Clíodhna squirmed, his touch both tickling and arousing her. She ached to pull him down on top of her, to satisfy her desire in delicious release, but he teased, slow and deliberate.

Finally, he bent to her cleft and tasted her dampness, making her writhe even more. His tongue flicked and then licked, and she rocked her hips to catch more.

When she cried out in passionate bliss, he mounted her, entering her with easy grace. She met his rhythm with her hips, her crescendo rising again. Together, they cried out as the darkness of *Bealtaine* evening enveloped them. Their burst of fertile satisfaction and joy honored the gods.

This time, Adhna let her sleep as long as her body demanded. Despite his infusion of energy before the ritual, magic could only do so much, and she'd been drained in the ritual, body and spirit. Both required time to heal and recover.

When she woke in her own bed, she realized he must have carried her all the way down the hill, tucked her in. She glanced quickly for Aileran, but he slept peacefully in his cot, so Adhna must have fed the babe with cow's milk.

While she'd been slowly weaning him these last two moons, her breasts were full to bursting. If she had slept too long, they'd be horribly painful. Adhna's magic might have helped with that. Her cheek ached, and touched it, trying to remember why. She had to cast her memory back to recall that Abbot Pátraic had slapped her. That seemed like a lifetime ago.

Clíodhna rubbed her face, then touched her hair. It was greasy and needed a proper wash after such an intense day.

Adhna wasn't in the roundhouse, but Etromma was curled up on her bed. With a glance outside, Clíodhna judged it to be midday. Had she slept through the night and half of the next day?

Her muscles ached, but not as much as they should. Adhna's magic must account for the difference. She stretched her legs and arms, reaching for the ceiling, stretching her back. When her spine cracked, she pulled back in, startled by the sound.

To think she'd imagined her life boring. The last few days had been much too full of excitement. Clíodhna needed some time to recover. Thankful that her children seemed to take everything in stride and care for themselves, except the baby, she crawled back under the warm blanket and curled up. She luxuriated in the unusual act of rest without sleep. A hint of Adhna's magical energy might still be crackling in her blood, because she almost felt as if she could fly.

Bees buzzed outside to the rhythm of birdsong as motes of dust danced in the slanting afternoon sunbeam shining through the open door. Donn's low voice answered a whinny from a horse, speaking in reassuring tones.

Satisfied that all seemed right in her world, she drifted back into a light slumber.

When Clíodhna roused again, the sunbeam slanted much more sharply, so it must be late afternoon. She stretched again, now eager to both relieve her full bladder and slake the thirst clawing at her throat.

Etromma no longer lay in her cot, and neither did the baby. As she wandered outside in search of her children, a cow mooed and Etromma laughed.

Her daughter was sitting next to the supply hut, playing with Aileran, while Adhna and Donn moved their three cows from one pasture to another.

Once they'd penned the animals, Donn waved to the Fae and strode toward the horses, while Adhna turned to her. "Are you well rested, Clíodhna?"

She gave him a tired smile. "I am, but my breasts are about to burst. I need to feed Aileran."

After taking the child from Etromma, she turned to the Fae. "I'm afraid letting me sleep all day means I have nothing planned for the evening meal."

Etromma piped up. "Don't worry, Ma. I have beans and dried fish soaking, all ready for stew."

She put her hands on her hips, surveying her children. "Well, it looks like you have everything in hand. I don't see why you even need me anymore."

Clíodhna could only hold her stern expression for a moment before all three burst out laughing. Donn hurried up, wanting to be let in on the joke.

As she sat to feed the baby, she stroked his downy head. How does one explain sheer silliness? She didn't have many moments like this in her life, though when the children had been younger, they had plenty such laughs.

Back when Oisinne was there, his stories often gave wonderful joy and good cheer. True, some brought dread and horror, and a sleepless night or two, for such was the nature of tales, but he balanced those with fun stories.

Clíodhna missed her husband. Not just for their physical relationship, but for the wonderful words they shared, like the conversations she'd had with Odhrán.

She hoped Odhrán hadn't suffered too much for their lustful games. He was already being sent away. With luck, nothing had changed his prospects for the worse. Still, his Abbot didn't seem the forgiving type.

Should she approach the abbot to offer an apology? She ought to take blame for the situation so Odhrán didn't get punished. They'd both given in to their passion, but she owed her friend support.

"Etromma, Donn, you both missed your classes today. Will you want to return tomorrow?"

Donn quirked his mouth up. "Today's rest day, Ma."

She rubbed her temples. "Oh, yes, well, my days have gotten mixed up."

Etromma raised one eyebrow and glanced at Adhna. "We both go back tomorrow. I can bring Aileran in the morning, if you don't want to come into town."

Determination and loyalty won over caution and she clenched her jaw. "I should go speak to the abbot, regardless."

She spent a restless night of tossing and turning, deciding what she should say to Abbot Pátraic. Nothing she could think of seemed right.

The next morning, she approached his quarters with great trepidation. She'd already dropped off all three children, but Odhrán was nowhere to be seen. Even if he'd already been sent away, she owed him a try.

Clíodhna steeled herself and, with spine straight and shoulders back, she knocked on the doorframe.

"Enter."

She stepped into the high-arched room, large windows letting in plenty of light. Pátraic sat at a tilted table, scratching a piece of vellum with ink. Odhrán had told her about *writing*, making pictures with sounds, and even showed Clíodhna a few examples, but it still seemed like magic to her.

Pátraic's scowled when he recognized her. "I banished you, wanton."

She swallowed the angry retort which rose to her lips and forced herself to speak her prepared words with a measured tone. "With respect, Abbot Pátraic, I am no wanton. I'm simply a local farmer and the mother of three children. You have my abject apologies for the situation yesterday," Had it only been yesterday? "I would like to speak on Brother Odhrán's behalf. He has been most kind to me and my family, and I would not wish him to come to harm for fulfilling your church's rule of helping the poor."

Abbot Pátraic stared at her wordlessly for several moments before his expression changed. Instead of a thunderous glare of anger, the lines of his face gentled into indifference. "It matters little. I've dealt with Odhrán. You will leave now. Do not return."

Taken aback, Clíodhna cocked her head. "But is he well? I would like to speak to him. And my children are taking lessons here."

His jaw clenched. "Your children are welcome to take classes. They did not sin. In fact, if you wish to repent your ways and join them, you are more than welcome. Odhrán, however, is beyond your wicked reach now, and will remain so. If you will not repent, you must leave. Begone. Now!"

Someone walked up behind Pátraic, the odious Brother Fachtna. He growled and she realized anything she said would fall upon deaf ears.

Abbot Pátraic stared at her so hard, it was almost a physical blow on her cheek, an echo of the slap he'd given her yesterday. Her cheek still ached from it. Clíodhna's face flushed with anger and embarrassment, and she left.

At least her children could still take classes. Clíodhna hadn't ruined their lives, as well. An older monk walked by, his eyes fastened on the ground before his feet. Could another monk bring word to Odhrán? No, she might get him in further trouble.

She'd failed her friend. Unsure of what else she could do, she trudged home, hoping Odhrán would survive her meddling.

Adhna was standing in the doorway and said nothing as he enfolded her in his arms. Relieved at not having to explain, she allowed his murmured words to calm her, his soft hands and lips. She trembled with the memory of her own mistakes and uncertainty for her future.

This Abbot had already become a community leader, and therefore a dangerous man to cross. How could she fix what she'd already done?

"Stop thinking of him, Clíodhna. I'm here to help you and your children."

Unexpected and unwanted tears pricked the back of her eyelids. "He hates me, Adhna. He'll find a way to hurt me. I know that sort of person. I could see it in his eyes."

He placed a finger under her chin, forcing her to look up at him. Their gazes met, and his spirit soothed hers. "Fear not. I will show you how to withstand his power."

She bit at her lower lip. What would she do, call down the lightning to smite him? The notion seemed ludicrous. And yet, she'd called that storm yesterday. Getting rid of it hadn't been effortless, but she'd done it once. With practice, she could do it again.

Clíodhna chastised her tears and straightened her back. "Very well, Adhna. Teach me."

Chapter Seven

Adhna covered his face with his hands. "No, Clíodhna, not like that! Just a slight touch. You need to tamp down the power and only draw the slightest amount of earth energy into the cow, like pulling a single thread from a rope. Otherwise, you might make her milk curdle in her udder. Now, watch again."

He drew a tiny tendril of energy, barely wider than a hair, emerged from the ground. Adhna coaxed it up the cow's leg and through to her udder, expanding into a gossamer net. The net pulsed with the earth's heartbeat, glowing and fading with gentle power.

When Adhna released the tendril, it faded back into the earth, and the cow's udder, previously empty, was almost bursting with readiness. Clíodhna grabbed a pail to relieve the poor cow.

"That, my dear, will be the sweetest milk you've ever tasted, I assure you. Now, try again."

As she finished milking, she said, "Let me use another cow. This one will be tired."

He gave a prim nod. "As you prefer."

Clíodhna moved the black and white animal into the main pen and pulled her sister into place. After several tries, she pulled the strand of energy up, but it wouldn't attach to the cow's leg. Instead, it whipped around like an eel, flailing as if searching for the ocean.

She pulled away, shielding her face, then tried to grab it with her hands, but it kept sliding out of her grasp.

"Put it back! Put it back. Now, relax, breathe in, and try again."

This time, the hair-strand of energy found the cow's leg, but it shot up her flank and crackled, making the cow cry in pain.

Adhna let out an exasperated sigh. "Stop, stop! Watch me again."

Three times he showed her the right balance of power and delicate touch. On the third attempt, she finally got the power into the right place and formed a mesh around the udder.

After harnessing her own heartbeat, she set the mesh to pulse with that rhythm, but now it contracted tightly, too tightly. The cow cried out, her rear legs buckling.

Horrified, Clíodhna let the power go. It snapped to her own heart and knocked her so hard, she fell on her backside.

The cow rose again, only limping a little, and Clíodhna let out a sigh of relief. At least she hadn't hurt the beast.

Adhna drummed his fingers on a rock. "That's enough for now. I'll leave you to practice, but not on a living creature. Use…" he scanned the yard, "use that rowan bush over there. Rowan offers a good amount of resistance to Fae magic. That should increase the challenge without risking one of your kine. I must take care of some errands, so I'll come back tomorrow."

Without waiting for her response, he left.

Clíodhna gritted her teeth, glaring at the cow. Not that the beast had done anything wrong. Her own inability to master the delicacy of this magic made her fume. She'd rarely had to work so hard at mastering a simple technique. Her fists clenched in frustration as she grabbed her stool and stomped over to the rowan bush.

Ten times, she practiced teasing the tendril of magic from the earth. Ten times, it fought her, writhing from her grasp and once, whipping her in the face. Clíodhna only had better control when the power came thicker and stronger. Tiny, fine control was elusive and recalcitrant, eager to fight her.

After grinding her teeth, she tried an eleventh time, but a rustle in the trees made her whirl. She scanned for any movement, her senses tense.

Nothing moved.

Self-consciously, Clíodhna returned her gaze to the rowan bush, but she didn't work more magic. Instead, she kept her senses attuned to the surrounding area. Certain that something was watching her, she did nothing abrupt or unusual. She sat on her stool, evidently observing the rowan bush.

Another sound made her leap to her feet, crouching with her knife in her hand, ready for whatever came. However, it was just Ita walking toward her house.

With a final glance over her shoulder, she put her knife away and went to greet her neighbor.

Her friend gave her a hug. "Clíodhna! I haven't seen you for a few days. Is all well?"

Grateful for the distraction, she said, "Well enough, and you? Come in for a drink of cool ale. The day's warm."

While pouring small ale for them both, she noticed Ita shoulders looked tight, and she didn't relax.

After they both sipped their drinks, Ita sighed. "I'm sorry to come so quickly to the point, but I must ask what happened the other day. Wild rumors are flying, and I want to find out the truth."

With a narrow gaze, Clíodhna asked, "What have you heard?"

Ita fluttered her hand. "Oh, so many bizarre stories! One had you flying into the storm and directing lightning to burn the church down. Another had you in a lustful orgy with all the monks, young and old. Another had you turning into a selkie and slapping the abbot with your tail. I know none of these could be true, so I came to find out the real story from you."

Lips pressed in a thin line, Clíodhna was grateful for Ita's direct approach. "You're a true friend, Ita. Thank you for that."

"Well? What really happened?"

How much should she tell? Nothing about Adhna, but Odhrán's reputation was at stake, and she mustn't make things worse for him. Still, Ita had come to her for the truth, rather than believe the gossip. Clíodhna owed her friend an explanation.

"Odhrán has been kind to me and my children. We've developed a close friendship over the last few moons."

Ita rolled her hand for Clíodhna to continue.

She cleared her throat. "On *Bealtaine* eve, he told me the abbot has reassigned him, and he's moving north, to *Ard Mhacha.*"

The memory of that conversation began to replay in her mind, both the intense sorrow of losing her close confidante and the highly charged sexual aftermath.

Clíodhna swallowed to regain control over her emotions. "We may have gotten out of hand saying goodbye to each other."

Her friend tried to stifle a giggle. "Gotten out of hand? You have a talent for understatement! From the gossip, the abbot found you on the floor, still joined at the hips!"

Clíodhna gritted her teeth. Who was spreading such details? Odhrán wouldn't have said anything. That Pátraic must have embellished.

They'd both already been getting to their feet when the abbot opened the door. "But that's not how he found us."

Ita narrowed her eyes, nodding once. "Fair enough. Odhrán left yesterday. With your permission, I can correct the worst of the rumors with the truth."

Her stomach dropped. "He's already gone?"

"Aye, he went off with three guards and two other monks yesterday at noon. I saw him myself."

Clíodhna clenched her hands, her nails digging into her skin. "I'll miss him."

"That may not be wise."

After looking up to Ita's concerned expression, Clíodhna lifted her eyebrows. "Oh?"

"The abbot isn't happy with either the circumstances, or the rumors flying about them. He's sent Odhrán away, but the gossip remains, as do you. He might make things difficult for you if he can."

Clíodhna's grief melted away, her heart now racing with anger. "If he can. What does he think he can do to me?"

Ita placed a gentle hand on her arm. "Don't try him, Clíodhna. The abbot is well-liked, and his church is becoming more powerful every season. He's converted one king already. The man is incredibly persuasive. He exudes charisma like no one I've ever seen. Most of the villagers are enthralled."

She scowled out the door, toward the village. "I don't find him persuasive in the slightest."

"*You* are biased. You already dislike him. And I'm worried that might make things more difficult for you. You're a woman without a husband, and you have three children to protect. That makes you vulnerable to any man, especially one with power in the community."

92

Ita's words sobered Clíodhna's determination, and she let out a deep sigh. "You do make a fair point. I'll be careful."

Over the next two moons, Clíodhna split her time between learning magic from Adhna, caring for her farm and her children, and avoiding Abbot Pátraic. That last proved to be the most difficult task.

He'd evidently embarked upon a campaign against the old beliefs, a systematic vilification of the old gods, goddesses, Fae, and magic.

While she couldn't care less what his personal beliefs were, he preached his bias every day to the community. Despite their own strong ties to the old gods, such daily vitriol made its mark.

Each rest day, after their liturgy, either Pátraic or another monk would urge the villagers to destroy any mushroom circles. They spoke of pulling down the Faerie stones and plugging any sacred caves or springs.

Some locations were preserved by re-dedicating them to the new religion's saints, the half-divine humans who did works for the new god. Clíodhna didn't understand quite what these saints were, exactly, but she equated them with the Fae lords. They had power, but not quite the power of the gods.

Etromma tried to teach her the difference between the saints, but she didn't really comprehend.

One morning, Donn explained how this new God was three Gods at once, but still just one.

She really did try to understand, for her son's sake. "Like the Morrigú? She has three aspects, depending on the need."

"Well, not quite. But we can use her as an example. For God, it's the Father, the Son, and the Holy Spirit."

Clíodhna had never heard that last phrase. "What, precisely, is a Holy Spirit?"

He screwed up his face. "Uh, I'm not sure. Let me ask Brother Cronan. He can explain it better than I can."

But she didn't need an explanation, not really, She didn't need to have faith that this new god existed. The old gods were still very real to her. She'd supped with Fae and worked their magic, which ran through her own blood. The blood of her children, as well, though they wouldn't acknowledge that part of their heritage.

Her children's dedication to the new religion just made her more determined to master Adhna's lessons.

When Adhna returned the next day, he stared at her, his gaze traveling from head to toe. "Clíodhna! When were you going to tell me?"

At a loss, she replied, "Tell you what?"

He gave her a scowl, as if she were being obtuse. "That you're with child! How long has it been since you've bled?"

Startled, Clíodhna counted back, trying to remember. In all the kerfuffle since Odhrán left, she'd barely kept track, which was unusual for her. "At least before *Bealtaine*, I'd say. Oh!"

Her hand drifted to her belly, though nothing would show yet. Another baby. Aileran was barely a full cycle of the seasons old. She clenched her hands, suddenly worried about her future.

Adhna gripped her shoulders. "Clíodhna! Don't be sad. This is delightful news. Wonderful! I'm joyful!"

"But how will I care for another child? Adhna, it's hard enough with three."

"I vow I will help, Clíodhna. Have I not helped already? We Fae so seldom have new babies. This new babe gives me hope."

Fear clutched her heart, despite his assurances. "But what if it's not yours? What if this is Odhrán's babe?"

He searched her eyes and put his hand on her belly. The energy flowed into her from his hand, warm and tingling. "No, it has strong Fae blood. You carry my son."

"A son?"

"Yes, my dear. A son of the Fae, strong and magical like his mother." Adhna pulled her into a tight embrace.

At first, she tried to wriggle free, unwilling to let happiness dampen her distress, but his bliss infected her. Clíodhna allowed a smile to creep across her face.

Then another thought occurred to her. "The village. They'll believe it to be Odhrán's, no matter what I say. You don't exist to them. Abbot Pátraic already detests me. He's gotten some villagers hate me, too. A few hissed at me when I pass."

He scratched his beard. "Hmm. That may be a problem. I shall work to alleviate that. Now, how did you complete on the assignment I gave you last week?"

Eager to leave the subject of her pregnancy behind, she launched into a recounting of her activities. "I replanted the Faerie ring in a more secluded part of the forest. The *Aos Sídhe* followed well enough, though they chittered and complained about the move. I had to do it at midnight, no moon at all to see, lest the villagers notice. They'll all believe someone stomped it."

"Good, good. And what about the *sídhe* in the village square?"

Clíodhna frowned. "I tried to get folks interested in preserving her home, but they kept threatening it with torches. They'd frightened her enough with the fire that she came willingly. I found an oak, even older and larger than her old home, right near a bend in the river. She clapped with elation when she saw that isolated place."

"Good, good. What have you got next on your plan?"

Clíodhna put a finger on her lip, considering the options. "The *Grugach* near the tannery are unhappy there. The waste the tanner dumps in the river hurts them. I could move them upstream, near the three hills."

"What else?"

Clíodhna thought of all the *Aos Sídhe* she'd met in her seasons there. The spirits of the water, land, and air, the trees and flowers. Magical creatures who existed just out of most humans' peripheral vision, who only showed themselves to a select few, or to the very young.

These creatures, both delicate and eternal, playful and capricious, needed her help. The village had changed, and they were no longer safe. "I'm not sure. I have to find out who else is unhappy."

"You're doing excellent work. This church man is on a mission, and his determination is strong."

After that, Clíodhna fell into a routine. She took her children to the abbey, but didn't enter, as per Abbot Pátraic's command. Etromma took Aileran to his minder on her way to the bakehouse. Donn had moved from carving wood to carving stone. He'd shown her several of his creations, some of which looked like dignified men in long robes, while others were grotesque creatures wearing ridiculous grimaces. His details were yet crude, but he was gaining skill with steady practice.

Clíodhna used to love carving when she'd been younger. Before she had children, she'd delight in taking a small boll of wood and revealing the hidden creature inside. She'd never reached the level of master, but she could create something lovely. She missed the texture of raw wood beneath her fingers, the slow removal of the extra bits to unearth the life beneath.

Occasionally, Clíodhna glimpsed Abbot Pátraic around the abbey grounds or in the village. He'd glare at her, and she'd glare back. He had no right to come to her village and drive her away. She wouldn't cede this to him, not now, not ever.

Working in the shadows, she corrected and redirected the evil rumors Abbot Patraic spread, to try to remove the taint he'd attached to her good name. This subtle campaign slowed the wave of negativity sweeping through the village.

She tried to get support to help the Fair Folk, but the sermons of these new Christians had long since delegated them into the role of evil creatures. They believed the Fair Folk to be of their Christian devil. An absurd notion. They were of the very land, so how could the land be evil?

Even before Odhrán had left, she'd asked his help with the matter. He'd listened with a sympathetic ear but wouldn't help. "It would be against our scriptures to traffic with such creatures, Clíodhna. I am so sorry."

Over the course of several weeks, she spoke to those that might still listen, urging folks to think of the Fair Folk. A few of the other women, including the tanner's wife, still left out offerings to the Fae every moon. A saucer of fresh cream to keep her cows full of milk, or a bit of honey to keep the bees happy. These practices had been part of the history of their people.

And when that didn't work, she simply spoke of the land, and how precious it was. However, as she visited several people, trying to drum up concern about her concerns for the wild places, she found mixed success. The blacksmith didn't even invite her in. Ita asked her in for a chat but didn't have much time to visit. The tanner kept glancing at the river when she spoke of the waste dumped there.

The blacksmith had been a hopeless case. He'd fallen well into the Christian dogma, even before Abbot Pátraic had arrived. Ita, while sympathetic to Clíodhna's plight, had similar views.

If she couldn't convince the villagers to help, then she'd have to do her duty alone, and save the Fair Folk herself.

When the night of the next full moon arrived, she approached the ash trees next to the abbey. She'd learned from Odhrán these trees were to be removed to make way for a new house for their writing. And so the sylph living in one of the trees needed a new home.

Holding a bowl of cream, she waited until the last monk went to bed. She approached the tree while humming a soothing tune under her breath. At the same time, she drew in a tendril of power from the earth, so the sylph would recognize her as magical.

She placed the bowl on the ash tree roots. "Sylph, I have a gift for you."

At first, nothing stirred within the rough bark. A flicker of pale, gray light shone out from behind the wrinkles. It winked in and out several times before seeping into the chilly night. It formed into the outline of a slim woman, impossibly tall and wispy. "Who calls to me?"

Bowing with respect, Clíodhna touched the bowl. "I am a friend of the Fae. I come with news and a gift."

The sylph glanced at the cream and licked her lips. Her gaze returned to Clíodhna. "What news do you bring?"

While clenching her jaw, Clíodhna let out a deep breath. "The sons of man who live here plan on hurting your tree. I come to show you a new place to live in peace, if you would follow me."

The sylph inched toward the cream. "Will you make me move?"

"I will not. However, I cannot stop the men from killing your tree. It will be safer for you to move before they attack."

The sylph swirled around the tree at the word "attack," lacing through the branches of the tree like fish through flowing seaweed. While the dance was beautiful, the sylph must be agitated.

When the creature finally settled at the roots, she took a long sip of the cream. "Very well. Show me your place."

As Clíodhna led the sylph into the hills, her companion winked in and out of every tree, as if visiting each one on their journey. Clíodhna didn't know if any had resident sylphs, but few trees did anymore. Many Fair Folk disappeared when men moved into an area.

They reached a tall hill with a grove of over twenty ash trees, tall and straight in the center. The sylph clapped her hands in delight and performed another dance around each one, as if testing for the best home. She finally decided on one near the center and flicked into the bark. The glow grew bright and then faded into nothing. Two more brief flashes were both a dismissal and thanks.

By the time she'd settled the nature spirit into her new home and stumbled into her own, dawn already glowed on the horizon. Grumbling about impossible nights, she walked back outside to greet the dawn, as she did every day. Clíodhna braided her hair and piled it on her head. She almost fell asleep while pulling the energy from the earth.

The sun topped the hill and she let out a deep sigh. More nature spirits came into danger every day. Adhna had charged her with helping as many as she could. He only visited every week now, to monitor her progress.

At each visit, they honored the gods with their lovemaking, and she looked forward to those days. Nothing compared to that first time on *Bealtaine,* but that had been a mystical coupling, sympathetic magic symbolizing the union of god and goddess on the cusp of the season. Acts between a mostly human woman and a Fae man created much less magic. And they enjoyed talking afterwards, intimate conversations while wrapped in each other's arms, a precious prize.

Clíodhna rose from her dawn ablutions, eager to catch some sleep before dropping the children at the abbey, but when she turned, she almost barreled into someone standing right behind her. She grunted and backed up three steps, stunned to see Abbot Pátraic.

She raised her eyebrows. "What are *you* doing here?"

He raised his chin and his gaze traveled up and down her body, a sneer on his face. "Performing pagan rites? That's not acceptable for one who comes to my church."

Clíodhna planted her feet and crossed her arms. "What I do here is my concern, not yours. We're not in your abbey now."

He clasped his hands. "Ah, but your children come to my abbey every day. A grace I have bestowed out of the kindness of my heart."

The statement required no answer, so she offered none. She narrowed her gaze, wondering what he would say next.

"It has come to my attention that you have no husband. Raising three children without help must be difficult. One purpose of our church is to help in such situations. I have therefore decided to relieve you of that burden."

She forgot how to breathe. "What? What do you mean?"

"We shall take Etromma, Donn, and Aileran into the abbey and raise them as good Christian children. Your wanton, pagan taint shall not sully them further. Their lives will be much purer." He turned and waved forward five burly monks who had emerged from the forest.

With a cry, she ran for the house, but Pátraic caught her around the waist. Clíodhna screamed and clawed for his eyes, twisting in his arms. He let out a screech and pulled back from her attack, his grip slipping.

Wriggling free, she made it to the threshold before the first monk could enter. She planted herself in his path. "You will not come inside my house! I do not give you permission to touch my children! Get away from my home, all of you!"

The wind whipped up and gusted so hard, two monks staggered back. The others searched the sky in panic as dark clouds roiled in, blackening the rising sun. Screaming ethereal creatures rode within the wind itself. The gossamer horrors, all mouths and sharp teeth, would be *Sluagh Sídhe* intent upon harassing the monks. Clíodhna hadn't called the creatures, so they must have joined in the fun once they noticed the storm.

Abbot Pátraic glanced to the heavens and moved his hand from shoulder to shoulder, then to his forehead and his chest. He turned toward the village and gestured to the monks to follow him. Before he left, he turned back to her. "This is not finished, wanton. Mend your ways and I might relent. But continue your pagan practices, and I will have no choice but to act in the children's best interest."

Once they were gone, Clíodhna's knees buckled under her, and she sat on the threshold. She gave in to the shakes and put her hands over her face. Tears leaked out between her fingers.

Donn poked his head out, his brow furrowed. He must have been up and listening to the argument. "Ma? Ma, what's wrong?"

Clíodhna sniffed to clear her head. "Nothing, Donn. But I can't take you to the abbey any longer for lessons."

"Why? What did I do?"

"Not you, Donn. Me. I've defied Abbot Pátraic, and now he wants to take you from me. You, Etromma, and Aileran."

Her son sat next to her on the threshold, wearing a deep scowl. "I don't understand. Why would they take us from you? Are you going away?"

She put her arm around him, hugging him tight against her right side. "No, Donn. They want to take you all away from me to teach you to be good Christians. I'm too pagan for them. Do you know what pagan is?"

He picked at his nails. "The monks say the word, but I don't really know what it means."

"Odhrán told me it used to just mean people who live in the country. But now it's what they call people who aren't Christian. Anyone who doesn't believe like they do. They use it as an insult to all of us who don't follow their ways."

Donn bowed his head and Etromma's sleepy voice drifted from the darkness. "Ma? What's wrong?"

Clíodhna rushed to her daughter's side. "Go back to sleep, love. You don't have to get up early today to do chores before lessons. Donn will tend to the animals."

Donn gave a nod and headed toward the stable while Clíodhna lifted her baby to feed him.

Would she have to run away? Take her children and flee in the night like criminals? She gripped Aileran so tightly he whimpered.

No. She wouldn't allow this. She'd been here for many winters, ever since she married Oisinne. Since before Etromma was born. Besides, her parents had died of a fever when she was young, so she had nowhere else to go.

Clíodhna would not permit Abbot Pátraic the satisfaction of running her off.

When Adhna returned the next week, Clíodhna let out a sigh of relief. Since Abbot Pátraic's visit, she'd been jumping at shadows, twitching at each sound, worried they'd returned to take her children. With Adhna here, he could help her keep watch and maybe teach her how to make her home safer.

When he arrived, he searched her face. "Clíodhna? You look distraught, child. Come, let me help you." He placed his hands on her forehead and that sweet, strong energy infused her body, rushing through every muscle and bone.

She let out a deep sigh and sat on the bench outside the roundhouse. "Thank you, Adhna. I've gotten little rest this week, and my work has suffered."

"Oh? It seems that there's a tale to tell. Let's sit and you can relate it. Might you have a bit of cheese to hand?"

Clíodhna chuckled and fetched the wedge she'd kept for him. His love of cheese had become a joke between them, but he had an obsession. Made from goat's, cow's, or sheep's milk, he didn't care.

He'd told her that Fae aren't very good at making things, unless they were a specific kind of Fae. Cheese, bread, milk, each required physical labor the Fae didn't care for. Despite Adhna's ability to create milk within a cow's udder, doing this regularly didn't appeal to him, even if it supplied him with endless cheese. Thus, such gifts from humankind had become well-loved by the Fae.

"What's happened this week to make you so frazzled, Clíodhna?"

She related the details of Abbot Pátraic's visit and his threats. Adhna clicked his tongue and tugged at his beard several times as she spoke, her anger seeping through her words despite her determination to speak in a calm tone.

When she finished, he let out a deep breath. "I'm afraid there is little we can do about his rise to power, at this point. Perhaps when he'd first arrived, we could have finessed some of the other villagers… but it's too late now."

"But I've tried talking to others! Even the few who aren't enthralled by him are reluctant to say anything against him."

"Just so. He's grabbed hold of the community, and he'll not let go of that power. This means we must work within his rules."

Clíodhna's blood went cold. This might get messy. At Adhna's advice, she packed several bags of essential items in case they needed to flee quickly. These stood next to the door, one for each of them.

Then, Adhna helped her work out the details of a plan to approach each villager, starting with those who still honored the magic of the land. Without aggressive tactics, they'd emphasize the benefits of keeping the Fae happy as integral to the health of the land, the kine, and their children.

Clíodhna pursed her lips. "But what about the Christian ideas that the Fae are something from their devil?"

"We'll just have to convince them the Christians are mistaken."

"The monks have drawn pictures, though! Little Fae creatures stabbing people and stealing their souls, all with a laughing horned creature looking on."

He let out a chuckle. "They can draw all the pictures they want. The truth must win out."

A voice came from behind. "Indeed, it must."

They both whirled to see Abbot Pátraic had returned, this time with more monks. Clíodhna counted ten, including several she recognized, like Brothers Fachtna and Cronan.

She scowled in the latter's direction, and he gave the briefest of shrugs with his lips pressed together in grim apology. Fachtna, however, grinned in horrific delight.

Clíodhna stood and stepped in front of the roundhouse door. Was Etromma still inside? Donn had been with the cows earlier, but she seemed to remember him returning. Aileran was inside sleeping since Clíodhna fed him. With a glance at Adhna, she braced herself on the doorframe.

Adhna spoke to her under his breath. "Get the children." Then he turned to the abbot. "I understand you are a leader in this community. Pátraic, is it?"

The abbot waved his hand in a dismissive gesture. "I don't know who you are, but you're not of this village, so I need not answer to you."

Clíodhna grabbed Aileran and several blankets. She shook Etromma from her nap. Donn was stoking the hearth. "Donn, gather those bags of food, the flint, the iron pot, and tools. Etromma, grab the clothing and blanket bundles we made. We must leave, quietly. Now."

Her children scrambled to their tasks as Adhna and Pátraic exchanged barbed words outside. She paid little attention to what they said, simply grateful that they'd been prepared. The abbot's tone conveyed all she needed to know. He'd come for her children, and she must not allow it.

Clíodhna emerged from the doorway, clad in dignity and carrying Aileran. Donn stood behind her, clutching a blanket wrapped around household tools, a wheel of cheese, three loaves of bread, and some apples. Etromma had a similar bundle over her shoulder.

Pátraic tensed as they emerged and snapped his fingers. His monks fanned out to block off her escape, almost surrounding the roundhouse.

Adhna glanced at Clíodhna, and then at the sky.

Clíodhna gave a solemn nod. The sky had been bright and clear, but now the dark clouds swirled overhead, turning into a whirlwind. The point of a miniature tornado touched the ground to the right, on the path leading away from the village. This same path led up toward the hills, where the hidden stone circle stood.

The monks in that spot scattered. A boom of thunder echoed across the valley. She glanced back at her two eldest children and gestured to the path. As one, the family marched toward the retreating, twisting windstorm.

Abbot Pátraic screamed to his monks. "Catch them!"

Adhna took the rear position, his hands held high, as Clíodhna pulled her children down the path. A monk tried to grab them but froze until they passed. Another, mumbling a prayer under his breath, pushed through almost to the point of touching Clíodhna, his fingers coming but a hand-span from her arm. She clung to Aileran, keeping the baby from the intruder and walked on.

Brother Cronan stood next to the path, his shoulders relaxed. He gave them a tiny nod as they passed, his hands out in a half-hearted attempt to grab her arm. She flashed him a grateful smile for his obvious reluctance. Donn whispered thanks to the monk who had been his mentor for the last several moons.

Pátraic rushed the small column of escapees and with his God's name on his lips, he shoved his way through the stickiness of Adhna's barrier. He laid his hands upon Etromma's shoulders, but she spun and kicked him squarely between the legs. He collapsed with a cry of pain, and Clíodhna shouted over the wailing wind, "Well done, daughter!"

Once away from the monks, they wended up the sacred hill, past the guardian stones, and to the circle itself. Clíodhna didn't want to bring her family to Faerie, but she must find a safe place. She turned to Adhna, a protest leaping to her lips.

He stalled her words with a raised finger. "You needn't enter the circle. There's a large, dry cave nearby. I'll make a place for you. It won't be ideal, but I'll do what I can."

A violent thunderstorm raged outside, but Clíodhna could no longer control its fury. The pouring rain and gale served an excellent purpose, making it more difficult for the monks to find them and obscuring any record of Clíodhna's passage through the forest.

Adhna must have anticipated this need, as baskets of food and supplies were piled in the back of the cave. Several blankets, a bronze pot, wooden bowls, and utensils filled one basket. A second one held turnips, onions, garlic, and herbs. Dried fish, a bag of rowan berries, a jar of honey, and oat flatbread filled a third, along with a small box of precious salt.

A small stream flowed along one edge of the cavern, though it might dry up when the storm faded. Etromma and Donn each grabbed a blanket and curled into an exhausted sleep.

She stared at the bronze pot Adhna had stowed and the iron one they brought. She could use the bronze to store water and the other to cook with.

Aileran began to fuss, so she pulled up her léine to feed the child. At first, he didn't want to suck, but after some coaxing, he took his fill. Her milk didn't flow freely and might be drying up. She'd need to prepare some soft food to wean him properly.

Clíodhna shuddered to think what an angry mob might do to her home, her cows, pigs, and chickens, and her beloved garden. Rage at the short-sighted bigotry of the abbot warred with disgust at the easily led minds of men. *How dare he?* Fury at the man's sheer gall to steal her family made her blood boil. *How dare he try to take her children?*

Thunder crashed, making them all jump. With a sympathetic glance at her children trying hard to sleep, Clíodhna did her best to damp her ire, lest those she loved suffered for her unbridled wrath.

Several hours later, the storm petered out to a mere drizzle. Clíodhna rose and stretched, then peered outside. Mists still obscured the hilltop with velvet gray. Nothing moved but the droning drip of water on leaves. The earthy scent of rain on soil mingled with the musty odor of the cave.

In a sleepy voice, Etromma asked, "Ma? I'm hungry."

With a chuckle for her daughter's priorities, Clíodhna handed her a flatbread. "I believe Adhna's magic hides the path to this place. I wasn't able to find it on my own and I doubt the monks will have any better success."

Etromma's eyes grew wide. "Are we prisoners?"

Clíodhna opened her mouth, but closed it again. Adhna had never been cruel or controlling. He'd been acting in his role as mentor, friend, and sometimes lover. And yet he was still Fae, and such folk were notoriously unpredictable. She swallowed and gazed into the mist. "That remains to be seen, my love."

Etromma nibbled on her bread in silence as water dripped in a steady tattoo. Aileran shifted in Clíodhna's arm, and she moved him to her other breast.

Donn roused and after washing his face, he started organizing their supplies. He created sleeping areas for each of them and, with Clíodhna's advice, arranged the food supplies and cooking implements.

When he rooted around the bottom of his sack, he leapt up. "I found it!"

Clíodhna chuckled. "Found what? The Dagda's Cauldron?"

Donn gave her a tired look. "No, Ma. I found my flint." He held it up with a smile, but his joy faded as he glanced outside at the sodden weather. "But we won't find any dry wood for a fire in this."

Clíodhna held up her hand. "No fire. Not until we know we're safe from discovery here."

He furrowed his brow. "How will we know?"

"When Adhna returns, he can tell us."

Etromma turned to her. "Ma, who is he? We met him at *Bealtaine,* and I've seen him a few times in the village. I know he cared for you when you were ill, but after you recovered, he disappeared again."

Taking a deep breath to gather her thoughts, Clíodhna let it out before answering. "He's been my friend and teacher for a few moons, Etromma. I trust him, for the most part."

Her daughter raised her eyebrows at the last phrase.

With a half-smile, Clíodhna answered the unspoken query. "He is Fae, and therefore not safe to trust completely. But he *has* protected us and taught me. I believe he has our survival and best interests at heart."

When she mentioned him being Fae, both children frowned, and exchanged a glance. In the silence, a distant rumble of retreating thunder rolled across the hill, a gentle growl in the darkening mist.

Aileran fussed, spilling milk down her breast. Clíodhna mopped it up and lifted him to her shoulder, patting his back with gentle thumps. He rewarded her with a deep burp and a dribble of spit.

Etromma put her arms out. "Here, Ma. I can take the baby for a while. Go relax while Donn finishes finding places for everything."

With weary steps, Clíodhna trudged to one of the blanket piles. She curled inside one, the itchy wool scratching her skin. The still-steady beat of dripping water lulled her to sleep more quickly than she imagined, and she descended into the darkness of sweet oblivion.

It seemed but a moment until the clattering of hooves on stone woke her. At least half the day had passed, judging by the darkness outside.

Dim shapes moved in the shadows, but the clip-clop rang clear, echoing through the cave. Adhna's voice trickled through the gloom. "Clíodhna? I've brought you a friend."

She rubbed the sleep from her eyes, trying to focus on the white mass moving toward her, much too large to be her Fae mentor. "Adhna?"

"She'll give you milk every day. I tried to find a chicken, but the monks have your home well-guarded. I borrowed this bonnie cow from an acquaintance of mine. She asks no payment for the loan, though a bit of cheese might not go amiss now and then."

Clíodhna's throat clogged with dryness. A gift from someone who liked cheese. He could only mean another Fae. She was wary of owing too many favors to the Fair Folk.

The cow stepped into the beam of moonlight near the cave's entrance. The white of her hide stood out, but her ears looked dark. Clíodhna struggled to her feet, brushing off her *léine*, and patted the cow's large head. The animal mooed, accepting the caress.

"Thank you, Adhna. And for the supplies you left here."

He blinked. "Supplies? I left no supplies."

She turned to glance at the contents of the baskets, now laid out in neat piles. "You didn't? But…"

The Fae chuckled. "Oh, those weren't from me. Those must be from the nature spirits, the ones you've been helping, I'd venture to guess. They'll have realized where I must bring you and expected your needs."

As if in answer, a tinkling laugh echoed from a dark corner of the cave. Clíodhna narrowed her eyes. "Can you come out, please? I'd like to thank you for the gifts."

Nothing stirred in the shadows.

With slow movements, she bent to test the cow's udder. The distended skin felt full, so she gestured to Donn to bring her a vessel. He grabbed the iron pot.

Clíodhna gave a sigh. "No, silly, never iron. Bring the bronze one."

Chagrined, he did as she bid. She knelt to grasp a teat and squeezed out a stream of raw milk. Still moving carefully, she brought the bowl to the shadowed corner. Clíodhna placed it on the ground and retreated.

The laugh tinkled once more, and the bowl disappeared.

Chapter Eight

Over the course of the next few days, Clíodhna made cautious friends with the local *Aos Sídhe*. A very young *nucklevee* named Ishc, who lived in the stream running through the cave, had gifted most of the dishes.

The creature hid in the shadows, but occasionally she caught a glimpse of a horse-like shape and a fish's tail. His skin looked raw, as if he had no skin. He'd likely stolen the dishes from the villagers over many winters, plucked from riverside meals.

An old, grizzled mine Fae lived in the cave with them, but didn't respond to gifts or words. They learned to leave him alone, though he probably gave the flint.

A sweet *sylph* lived in a copse of trees near the stone circle but seemed too shy to speak. Clíodhna accepted their gifts of acorns and berries with a solemn nod.

After a half moon had passed, they grew used to their new lives. No monk nor human came close. An ever-present mist clad the hilltop in chilly mystery and enveloped them in a blanket of safety.

After the first few days of inaction, both older children grew cranky and petty. Finally, she sent them both out to hunt and fish to keep their minds and bodies occupied and to give Clíodhna some rest from their complaints.

Each evening, they'd talk about their options. If they'd have to move to another village, what they'd do if someone found them, and if they would go to Faerie.

Every sound outside put them on alert. Etromma kept her bow to hand, while Donn practiced swinging the iron pot and chain. Clíodhna asked Etromma to show her the bow, but she didn't have Etromma's slender build, and her breasts kept getting in the way.

Clíodhna was thankful for the wee *nucklevee*, as he was the chatty sort and told outlandish tales. He glistened in the dim firelight, brown and green, mottled like a trout. In the liminal hours of dusk, he kept them entertained. During the full day and deep night, he slumbered beneath in his watery home. He wasn't as chatty or as playful as the dolphins of her youth, but she felt an odd nostalgia for the wee creature.

Still, she felt like a caged bird, unable to spread her wings.

One evening, as the mist darkened into dim twilight, Ishc froze mid-sentence. His head popped up and his eyes grew wide, staring at the entrance. Alarmed, Clíodhna turned, clutching Aileran to her chest.

But the cave mouth was empty against the mists swirling outside.

Forcing her heart to slow, she laid Aileran into his sleeping palette and picked up a stout wooden cudgel. Donn grabbed the heavy iron pot. He'd practiced enough to get surprising accuracy swinging it.

Etromma raised her bow and notched an arrow. They'd practiced this response every day, though this was the first time they'd had the need.

No sound came through the mist. She glanced back at Ishc, but the *nucklevee* had disappeared into his stream.

Clíodhna's skin turned clammy in the waiting darkness. Still nothing stirred, but she felt watched. Someone, some*thing*, was out there.

She wished Adhna was there. He visited every five or six days to bring news or supplies.

She felt woefully vulnerable with her two half-grown children and a baby to protect. Her fingers ached from clutching the wood too tightly. She hefted her cudgel again, settling it into a more comfortable grip.

Outside, wind rustled leaves. She strained her ears to hear footsteps, a snuffling animal, a bird wing's flutter, anything to tell her what lurked near her cave.

A twig snapped outside. She gripped her club harder, her nails biting into the rough bark.

Etromma stood stock still, with her arrow aimed at the cave mouth. Donn waited on the other side of the entrance, his iron pot swaying on its chain.

A brief, horrible image of Abbot Pátraic and his mob finding their cave and trapping them inside filled her mind. She pulled on earth magic to calm her fear and erase her terror. While it didn't completely work, she could breathe more easily.

A dark shape loomed in the mist, drifting slowly closer to the cave.

When it resolved into a man's shape, relief flooded through her blood, thinking Adhna had returned. Yet, as it came closer, she didn't recognize the creature. His bark-like skin made him obviously Fae, but no one she'd met.

Her hands ached but she kept a strong grasp of her weapon. "Who are you?"

The creature halted his steady approach. "You ask me a question, human?"

"Who are you?"

With a rough laugh, he threw his head back. "Do you not know me?"

Clíodhna placed her hands on her hips. "If I did, I wouldn't ask. Who are you?"

"Three times you ask, and therefore, I must answer. I am called Bodach, and I have come to help you."

Clíodhna narrowed her eyes and noted that both her children remained in battle stance. "Help me with what?"

The crackle of his skin echoed in the silence. "That is not hard to say. I'm here to help you to safety. Do you not realize humans search for you below?"

Panic seized her heart as she peered into the deepening gloom. "I hear nothing."

The creature chuckled again. He stood at least three hands taller than herself, even taller than Adhna. Where was her friend? He should be here protecting them, not leaving them alone with this strange Fae.

Aileran let out a plaintive wail. Etromma pulled her string back. With an unconscious gesture, Clíodhna put a hand over her belly, protecting her unborn baby.

"You need not fear me, mortal woman. Adhna spoke of you, and I came to help you escape. I can bring you to a place where the men who search for you can never find you, not in a thousand winters."

He did not specifically say Adhna sent him. Clíodhna clenched her teeth, not sure what to do.

Bodach took a step toward her, his arm outstretched. His fingers had half-formed buds on them, like flowers trying to break free of thick bark. She gulped and took a step back.

His mouth stretched into something resembling a smile, the bark creaking. "If you come with me, sweet Clíodhna, you may live in my home like a queen. I shall shower you with wealth and beauty. All the flowers of the spring shall be your hair, and all the rainbows of the rainstorm will be your cloak. You will dance until the Faerie Queen herself falls into slumber."

Visions of Faerie spun in her head, whirling bodies of beautiful dancing, gossamer fabrics, and bright laughter clothing her imagination. Clíodhna ran her fingers through her hair, trying to dispel the visions. Had Bodach planted them in her mind with Faerie magic? She'd never seen such things in her life.

And yet, his offer seemed so tempting. She'd grown so tired of straining, working hard to protect her family, life, and independence. Didn't she deserve some luxury?

His smile deepened, perhaps sensing her doubt. One finger stroked her forearm, tracing a delicate line along the muscle.

Clíodhna shivered. His touch had been feather-light, like Adhna's kisses that first night. A sweet burning traveled up her arm and into her bones in a sensual wave of release. Tingling crept down into her belly and cleft. Her breath shuddered at the sheer potency of his caress.

Without thinking, she placed her hand over his, covering his rough bark with her palm. Energy flowed through his skin to hers, crackling like lightning. She couldn't move, rooted to her spot with desire and terror.

His power, both destructive and sexual, coursed through her, fiercer than any river rapids. Stronger than any pleasure she'd ever felt, more intense than calling forth a thunderstorm. It rippled into her bones and out to her fingers. Her head pulsed with unbearable pressure, thrumming with both ecstasy and agony.

Clíodhna let out a soundless scream, her body frozen. Aileran cried out and suddenly, she could move. She finally dropped her hand and the power faded. Her vision went gray, and she collapsed.

Donn's voice filtered through her haze. "Ma? Ma! What did you do to her?"

The twang of Etromma's bow, a thunk, and Bodach's scratchy laugh drowned out her son. "Younglings, have no fear. Your birth-giver is unharmed. She will rise again. But you should all come with me, for your own survival."

Etromma's answer came firm and steady. "We will *not*! And we won't let you take Ma, either!"

After forcing her eyes open, Clíodhna watched as Bodach approached Etromma with an open hand. She must not allow the Fae to touch her daughter. Pushing to her feet, she stumbled forward until she fell into the intruder.

His bark-like skin seemed as solid as an oak trunk. No wonder he laughed when Etromma shot him. How could mere mortals harm such a creature? But for her childrens' sake, she must try.

Clíodhna gathered earth magic through the cave floor, pulling in strong tendrils and snaked vines of blue power, building it into her hands. She scrambled to position herself so that Bodach was between her and the cave's mouth. Both Donn and Etromma moved behind her, weapons still ready.

Once she steadied her feet, she lifted both hands and shot her blue, crackling earth power out like an arrow, at Bodach's woody chest.

His eyes grew wide, and he took several staggered steps back. She didn't wait for him to recover. After drawing in power once again, Clíodhna slammed it against the intruding Fae, pushing him further. He fell almost to the cave mouth.

His gaze narrowed as he pulled his own power around him, snapping orange lightning in his flower-fingers. "You will not be so lucky next time, mortal woman! I leave you to your misery. But take heed! You will regret rejecting me."

His form faded into nothing. Clíodhna couldn't tell if her own fatigue affected her vision, or if he actually disappeared. She didn't care at the moment. All her energy and power drained in the battle, she collapsed again.

Dimly aware of Donn pulling a blanket over her, and Etromma guarding the entrance with her drawn bow, a distressed chittering came from behind her. She turned her head to see Ishc, the *nucklevee*, peeking above the water line. "Is it safe? Is he gone?"

She mumbled some reassurance before falling into an exhausted sleep.

Clíodhna's dreams haunted her, filled with images of wealth, treasure, and inhuman delights but also exquisite torture and yearning hunger. She drifted in and out of consciousness, her recovery slow and painful.

Her stomach gripped with throbbing pain, keeping her from healing rest, and she feared for the wee babe growing inside. Tossing and turning, a few times she even rose without waking, stumbling into the cave walls.

Her eyes flew open and she couldn't move. She saw only darkness, and her limbs were tied down. Clíodhna struggled, her panic rising as her heart raced. Then she screamed.

Her scream echoed against the cavern walls, bouncing and increasing with each breath, making her screech even harder. The sound hurt her head and she clutched at her ears, rocking back and forth to ease the anguish.

Donn's voice came from beside her. "Ma? Ma, it's alright. I tied you down."

Etromma whispered in her ear. "Ma, it's fine! You're fine. You're awake. Nothing is wrong. We're safe."

Her mind was still muzzy from sleep. Was Bodach pretending to be her son? Was she trapped somewhere in his realm? "You what?"

"I tied you down, to keep you from wandering off as you slept. Wait a moment, and I'll get a torch and untie you."

The hearth glow flared up and he came near with a burning stick. Then he patiently untied the twine around her wrists and ankles.

Her panic receded into the distance, the sound of her scream still drumming against the inside of her skull and fading into a dull ache. Etromma brought Aileran to feed and Clíodhna fell once again into a restless slumber.

Days passed like this, and still she did not regain her full senses.

Donn and Etromma's voices drifted into her hearing, concern and uncertainty clear in their voices. Clíodhna concentrated on their words, trying to make sense of them. Reason and order seeped into her thoughts.

Etromma sobbed. "What if she never gets better? Should we take her to the healer in the village?"

"No, no, never that! The abbot would take us away."

"But what should we do?"

Donn clicked his tongue. "Maybe we can find Adhna? He had magic. He might be able to cure her."

"But how do we call him?"

"I'm not sure. Let me think about it."

Clíodhna wanted to tell them Adhna didn't come when called, like a hound. He arrived precisely when he wished, like the clouds. She might call the clouds now, with the rain, thunder, and lightning.

Clíodhna should have used her air magic against Bodach, but how do you pull wind into a cave? She'd drawn on the earth, the only thing she could touch in the cave, to protect herself and her family, rather than air magic.

She vowed to ask Adhna to teach her more elements when he finally returned.

Clíodhna licked her lips, dry and cracked. When she tried to ask for water, only a raspy croak emerged.

Etromma leapt to her side. "Ma? Ma, what do you need?"

"Wa-er."

Her daughter pressed the water skin to her mouth. "We got you to drink when you woke, but you always babbled. You sound better now."

Sweet, cool liquid dribbled down her cheek and into her throat. Clíodhna drank a sip, swished it around in her mouth, and took another. After her thirst had been slaked, she pushed herself up onto her elbows. "How long?"

Her children exchanged a glance. "A while. But you sound better now."

Frowning, she pressed. "How long did I sleep?"

Another nervous glance, and Donn answered, "Eight nights."

Bolting upright, Clíodhna swore. "Eight nights? Son of a diseased donkey. Eight nights!" She searched for Aileran, but he was sleeping soundly. Her breasts felt normal, so Etromma must have placed him there for feeding. *Eight nights!*

Flashes of memory seeped into her mind, wrestling with each other and fighting for attention. She couldn't tell if they were real, dream images, or something different. Clutching her head, Clíodhna scrunched her eyes shut, trying to block the visions and noises assaulting her.

When she emerged again from the chaos, both children were hugging her tightly.

Someone darkened the cave entrance, and she tensed, fearing Bodach's return. Instead, a stranger stood glowering in front of their only escape. Hairy and unkempt, he looked like a wild man.

120

Etromma snatched her bow from where it had dropped and aimed it at his face. "Who are you?"

Donn retrieved his iron pot on its chain. Clíodhna didn't attempt to rise, knowing her legs would fail her after so long asleep.

Instead, she scowled at the intruder, waiting for his answer. How had this stranger found them? Adhna had assured her the cave was hidden from anyone in the village. Humans shouldn't be able to find the path. Sure, that Bodach creature had found them, but he'd been Fae.

The rough stranger grunted, an animal sound, neither word nor response. His gaze swiveled from Etromma to Donn and finally rested on Clíodhna. He growled out, "I know you."

She exchanged glances with each of her children, searching for some knowledge of the man in their eyes. Etromma shook her head, while Donn visibly gulped.

But something in his voice touched a memory. If only hers hadn't been scrambled, she might be able to place where she remembered him from. If this wasn't just a shred of a dream.

He grunted again, then let out a gravelly cough, dribbling spittle into his tangled beard. A wave of noisome rot reached Clíodhna, and she coughed at the stench.

He lifted a gnarled, dirty finger and jabbed it in her direction. "You. You're my wife."

Horrified, Clíodhna grasped at the memories she held of her husband. Branches and leaves stuck in this man's tangled beard and hair, dressed in gray and brown rags, with dirt rubbed deep into the creases of his skin.

Oisinne hadn't even been gone a cycle of the seasons. How had he become this… this creature? He looked like a wild Fae, something from the depths of the undergrowth, a forest *sidhe*.

And yet, his eyes held a hint of a twinkle, of that humor she remembered. Those crystal blue eyes, surrounded by laugh-lines when he told a story. Images fell into place, and she recognized him for her long-lost lover, her husband, the father of her children. "Oisinne? Is that really you?"

At the sound of his name, his wandering eyes snapped to her. With hesitant steps, he approached her.

Etromma refused to relinquish her bow, but Donn put down the pot and helped Clíodhna to her feet. When Oisinne was close enough, they shared an awkward embrace before his pong made her gag.

She held him at arms-length, both out of concern and to keep nausea at bay. "Oisinne, where have you been? We thought you'd died!"

He cocked his head but didn't answer. His gaze darted from place to place within the cave, nervous and flighty like a hummingbird.

Clíodhna cleared her throat. "Well, the first thing we need to do is get you a bath. Come, there's a stream in the back of the cavern. Let's dunk you in."

Ishc the *nucklevee* fled upstream into the darkness.

Clíodhna got Oisinne washed and dressed him in clean clothes, but she couldn't coax any details of his disappearance from him. His eyes darted constantly to the dark corners of the cave.

Her husband might have been taken by the Faeries. All the old tales told of people disappearing and then coming home, confused about time and place. This described Oisinne precisely, and he might have been gone for many seasons to get this ragged.

He hummed and rocked at odd times or stared into space. Out in the forest, he'd startled into a violent spasm, as if something had hit him.

Regardless of where he'd been, Clíodhna was relieved he'd returned. While she cherished her freedom, she also treasured the safety of her family. With a man in the house, she'd be less subject to the prejudice of the abbot and the other villagers. They might even be able to return to their home now.

But not until Oisinne had healed some.

Adhna hadn't visited in a while with more supplies, and after her husband had been back a few days, they'd run out of meat and bread. Besides, it might be awkward to get help from her Fae lover, now that her husband had returned.

Rain drummed in a steady rhythm. Rivulets described artistic spirals and swirls in the trodden dirt outside, reminiscent of artwork on ancient stones, curvilinear and complex.

How her life had changed in the last few moons, like those curved lines. Doubling back, crossing, braiding, and twisting in a single line, yet full of complexity, beauty, and confusion. The pattern had balance and symmetry. While she'd lost much, she'd also gained much, with her newfound talent for magic, the knowledge of her Fae blood, and now the return of her husband.

Oisinne swung between violent madness and quiet peace. Occasional snippets of conversation with actual sense peeked through now and then, and Clíodhna treasured these few windows into her past marriage.

Perhaps they should go home now, regardless of Oisinne's condition. Maybe with a husband, Abbot Patraic might not feel so threatened by her independence. Clíodhna would have to broach the subject carefully to Oisinne as they ate their supper.

She leaned her back into him as they sat around the small fire. Oisinne shifted to put his arm around her, like when they courted. "Are you comfortable, husband?"

"I am."

Pressing her hand on her still-flat stomach, Clíodhna grasped at a bare memory of Adhna's love, but pushed it away. Oisinne squeezed her shoulder. Sure, his smile seemed tentative and confused, but that should change with time.

He rarely started conversations but might answer when spoken to. One-word answers were better than growls or grunts, she supposed. Someday, she might even get her laughing, storyteller husband back again.

A brief flash of Odhrán's infectious laugh intruded, but she shook that away, too. That part of her life had finished. He'd long since gone to his new post, and she'd never see him again. Her body tingled at the memory of that last night and their passionate lovemaking.

Oisinne rubbed her arms and squeezed her shoulders. The caress wandered up to her neck, where he traced a single finger along her cheek line. He hummed with no tune as he touched her. Clíodhna had forgotten how considerate a lover he'd been. Not as gentle as Adhna, but maybe he could erase her longing for Odhrán and Adhna both.

His voice rumbled as he turned to their daughter. "Etromma, we're short of meat. When the rain lets up, can you go hunting? It's been a long time since I shot the bow, but I hear you've kept practice."

Startled, their daughter nodded. Donn exchanged a glance with his sister and then looked at Aileran. "I could take Aileran down to the river. He likes to watch the fish when they jump."

Oisinne chuckled. "Good."

This conversation contained more words than he'd yet said since his return. Perhaps her husband would heal more quickly than she'd thought.

His hand traveled down her spine and to her waist, kneading the muscles of her back.

Clíodhna leaned forward. He took the invitation and rubbed all along the length of her spine, pressing hard into her muscles. She let out a small moan of pleasure.

Etromma stood, grabbing her cloak. "The rain's lightened. I'll go now."

Clíodhna sat up. "Etromma! You'll get your bowstring wet!"

Her daughter gave her a cocky grin. "I'll keep it dry while I'm tracking. My cloak is oiled."

Donn stood, glancing in the direction his sister went. "Maybe I should check the traps I laid yesterday."

He, too, disappeared into the now misty day.

Oisinne whispered. "It seems we've raised wise children."

She turned to face him, cross-legged on the cave floor. "They are at least observant."

He put a finger on her lips and leaned in. Clíodhna surrendered to his kiss, though his lips still felt rough and cracked. He pushed her back, kissing her neck until he lay on top of her.

With warm hands, he pushed her *léine* up to her hips and pulled his manhood out. It already stood stiff and thick, but she wasn't ready yet.

Clíodhna pushed him back. "Wait, we can go slowly."

His lip curled as he pushed her down on the floor and shoved inside her. She cried out in surprise and pain, but as he rocked in and out, she forced herself to relax to the inevitable.

As she bit back a second cry, she reminded herself that Oisinne was her husband. He had the right to take her. As his wife, she must accept his attention.

While she gritted her teeth, the sexual tingling in her own body finally responded. By the time he finished, she'd almost reached her own climax, their sweat intermingling with the mud on the cavern floor.

Oisinne lay upon her, his heavy weight pressing down. It reminded her of when she'd woken, tied to the ground, and she needed to be free. Clíodhna struggled to get out from under him.

He opened his eyes and laughed. "Oh, you want more?"

She didn't want more, but he stroked her below until his manhood was ready. At least he moved from on top of her while he readied her, giving her time to breathe. By the time he re-entered her, her body welcomed him, even as her mind denied him. Again, they rocked in passionate rhythm.

Once, making love to her husband had been a joy. Now it seemed a chore. He was a stranger, someone with high demands but little familiarity. At least this time, he brought her own pleasure to a peak before he spent his.

Snoring roused her from her post-coital drowsiness. Clíodhna pulled herself from her husband's flaccid embrace and went to clean herself. As she wiped, she glanced down at her belly, knowing she'd show soon, with Adhna's child.

Her husband's return and his reassertion of his rights might be exactly what she needed, for her own reputation.

After they ate their morning meal, Oisinne packed up the rest of the food. He stuffed dried fish in with rowan berries and a sliver of hard cheese. Next, Oisinne scooped the bowls into the iron pot.

He turned to glare at them. "Well? What are you waiting for? It's time to go home! Time to go! Time to go! Time to go!" He hopped around, then studied the edge of the table, the central hearth glowing with coals, and the doorframe with equal intent.

After shoving down her annoyance at his arbitrary decision, and rolling her eyes at his silliness, Clíodhna reminded herself that she did want to go home. She bundled the blankets to tie on her back. Etromma and Donn gathered their own packs as Clíodhna hefted Aileran. He was growing too big now to carry long.

Once they'd packed everything and she nestled Aileran into his sling around her neck and shoulder, she gave the cavern a quick glance. Ishc the *nucklevee* had never emerged after Oisinne arrived, but she said goodbye to him anyhow.

The trampled ground near the entrance and the charred ring of their fire were the only signs they left.

Oisinne danced around near the cave mouth like a manic pixie, the whites of his eyes glittering in the shadows. "Time to go! Time to go!"

Clíodhna let out a sigh and followed her husband outside. The day was as misty as ever, but Oisinne guided them. She'd never traveled the path without Adhna leading her in and out of the mystical place.

The path wended down the hill and into the forest below. The mists cleared as they got farther down, and eventually, their home came into view.

She'd half-expected a ring of monks to still be guarding the place, but after a moon, they must have given up. Still, relief flooded her when the clearing appeared empty. They trudged into the roundhouse, dusty and achingly bare, and dropped their heavy loads.

She put Aileran into his cot, though he fussed. Then she massaged the shoulder where he'd hung. Clíodhna still hadn't recovered all her strength from her magical battle with Bodach and her legs felt heavy after the downhill walk.

The roundhouse seemed smaller, somehow. Definitely not the warm homestead from last summer, before Oisinne had disappeared. Her life seemed so distended, unconnected, since then.

Memories of ringing laughter, tall tales, and ominous legends swam through her head. She'd been a part of Oisinne then. They'd worked together as one, enjoying a strong love and friendship. She'd lost that connection, and a part of her ached to have it back.

Clíodhna realized the flame of friendship she'd had with Odhrán sparked a similar vein within her heart. If he'd been free to stay, she might have forged a strong relationship with him. Her dalliance with Adhna couldn't reach that level as long as they were student and mentor. Would Oisinne be able to be that sort of partner again?

She silenced her musing with industry. Sweeping, clearing, organizing, all the things she needed done to get the farm back in working order. Someone had fed the animals and even milked the cows while they were gone. Clíodhna suspected Adhna had arranged that. She must ask him when he returned.

Would Adhna return? With her husband home, the Fae might stay away. Unexpected tears pushed behind her eyes at the prospect of losing her teacher and friend. She swallowed them away and wiped the sweat from her face as she mucked out soiled hay from the stable.

Etromma's querulous voice came from behind the roundhouse, but Donn's lower tone reassured her. Though Clíodhna strained to listen, she heard no one else. Oisinne might still be in the roundhouse.

A cry cut through her thoughts. She ran into the house, only to find her husband ripping his wool blanket into shreds.

Clíodhna gripped the doorframe as her glance flickered to Aileran's cot, but the child was safe. "Oisinne! What are you doing?"

His eyes had grown wide and wild, madness sparking inside. He clutched at the scraps of the fabric like they held his life's blood. "It's evil! Evil, I tell you. It tried to eat me!"

She yanked the remnants of cloth from him, wondering if he'd found faerie mushrooms. "Don't be ridiculous! It's wool. How could it possibly eat you?"

Like a cat, he batted at the dangling scraps, trying to grasp the ends. Clíodhna held them out of his reach. What had happened to her laughing husband? He acted like a crazed fiend.

Clíodhna backed away, still holding the wool strips, and tucked them from sight, and Oisinne calmed instantly. He sat on the floor, cross-legged, and rocked, humming to himself without a tune.

After swallowing hard, she fetched some food. A bit of cheese, dried fish, and flatbread. Placing it before him, she watched him notice the food. Then his rocking eased and stopped. His hand shot out to snatch the dried fish, nibbling on it like a squirrel. He swayed as he ate, humming in that same monotone.

Steps outside made her spin to confront a new problem. She caught her breath, recognizing Abbot Pátraic.

He pursed his lips as he peered inside. "It seems the rumors are truth. I was told your husband had returned. It's a miracle! I came to welcome him to our church."

Clíodhna didn't dare move. She hadn't forgotten that the abbot had tried to take her children. Were Etromma and Donn safe? Donn's chuckle filtered through the wattle and daub walls of the roundhouse and she breathed again.

Oisinne rose shakily, and extended his hands, palms up in welcome. All signs of madness disappeared as he became the consummate host. "Welcome to our home. I offer you bread and ale. Will you stay and sup with us?"

The abbot stared for a few moments before placing his hands over Oisinne's and shaking his head. "As much as I would like to, good man, I must refuse this time. I'd be honored if you came to our service on the morrow, just at sunrise. Please, bring your family, and join our community."

The words were more a command than a suggestion.

Oisinne grinned in a feral show of teeth. "That sounds grand! We shall be there as the sun rises." He turned to Clíodhna. "Do you know where we must go?"

Numbly, Clíodhna nodded, not taking her eyes off the abbot.

Pátraic beamed at her husband and opened his arms wide. "Excellent! We shall see you then." He shot an inscrutable glance at Clíodhna, the only time he'd acknowledged her presence, and left.

She turned to Oisinne, placing a hand on his shoulder. "Husband? Are you interested in his services? I've attended a few times, and much of it is in some strange language. Then he tells stories from his homeland and offers prudish advice."

Oisinne's grin deepened. "Stories! I love stories."

He strolled out of the roundhouse, whistling out of tune. Clíodhna had no idea how to react to this new person. Once he'd disappeared down the path to the river, she rushed outside to ensure her children were safe. Etromma and Donn were still working next to the stable, feeding the pigs. She let out her breath in relief.

Donn raised his eyebrows. "Did you see the abbot?"

Clíodhna set her lips in a grim line. "Yes. Did he speak to you?"

Etromma glanced over her shoulder. "We saw him coming and hid in the hayloft. He poked his head inside, but we covered up well."

"How did I raise such smart children?"

Donn cast a glance toward the river. "Speaking of children, is Da well? He's been acting strange. Well, stranger than normal. He looked at me this morning as if he didn't recognize me."

Clíodhna looked in the same direction, frowning. "I'm not sure, Donn."

The next morning, the family traveled to the village together. Clíodhna clutched Aileran tight to her breast, though he whimpered. He wasn't quite old enough to let him toddle beside her, not if they wanted to walk at a normal pace.

Donn and Etromma held hands and walked close to her. Oisinne wandered back and forth across the forest path, exclaiming with wonder at each new flower or bush, as if he'd discovered a tree with leaves of sunlight.

His childlike delight would have been wonderful in a boy of six winters. For a grown man, the head of a household, it chilled her spine.

When they arrived at the abbey, she stared at the complex. They'd added a new building since she'd last visited, high on the central hill. The thatch was still green, forming a long hall with a cross section on the end, the same shape as the crossed sticks over their smaller building. Work continued on the walls, but it looked like it might be ready before the winter.

Villagers trickled toward them and entered the smaller church. With so many people now attending, no one had room to sit, so they all stood and waited for the services to begin.

Abbot Pátraic processed to the table at the front of the church, dressed in a white, shining robe. He wore a mantle around his shoulders in heavy, brightly colored embroidery. Glints of gold shone with every gesture. Clíodhna had never seen clothing so decadent. He chanted a song in Latin, and several villagers answered him on alternate lines.

Within a few minutes, Oisinne began humming. Neither her own elbow in his ribs nor the abbot's annoyed glares did anything to silence him. He played with his fingers, moving them in complex patterns.

When another priest began the sermon, Oisinne swung his arms back and forth, like a child just discovering how heavy his hands felt. He hiccupped.

Glares came from the villagers and the abbot. Clíodhna put her arm around her husband. "Oisinne, be still. We are guests here and should listen quietly."

He hopped a few times from one foot to another, but at least he stopped humming. Etromma and Donn wore horrified expressions.

When the service finally finished, Clíodhna tried to rush her family out and away, but the abbot came straight for them. He held out his hands. "I'm so glad you took me at my word, Oisinne. I trust you enjoyed the service?"

Her husband cocked his head, as if listening to some new birdsong. His mouth twisted up at the corners with a feral twinkle in his eye.

Abbot Pátraic must have taken this as assent. "Good, good. I am so glad you came back to your family. They sorely needed some firm guidance. With you in charge, I'm certain they'll fall back into moral habits."

At that moment, Clíodhna had an incredible urge to punch that smarmy smile off the abbot's face, shove Oisinne down a dark hole, take her children, and leave this judgmental village once and for all. *As if I need a man—any man!—to tell me what to do!*

Instead, she gritted her teeth, gave the abbot a polite smile, and turned away. Clíodhna didn't trust herself to speak, but at least she could appear polite, for now. One day, she'd make that man pay for his insults.

As they made their way back to their home, Oisinne stopped dead in his tracks and stared at a gnarled oak tree. He stopped humming as Clíodhna almost barreled into him.

"Husband? What are you doing?"

He cocked his head as he had earlier. "This tree wants to tell me something, but I can't understand the words. They must be in some other language. Do you think that lad back there could translate for me? He speaks another language."

She pressed her lips together while Etromma and Donn exchanged a knowing glance. "Abbot Pátraic was speaking Latin, from where he lived in Rome, far to the south. I doubt the tree speaks the same language, Oisinne."

Clíodhna pulled his arm to move him along toward home, but he resisted. "The tree wants to sing to me, Clíodhna! Can't you hear him? He's whistling in the wind!" Her husband collapsed on the ground, laughing so hard he could barely breathe. His eyes teared up, and his face turned red.

With her children's help, she yanked him to his feet. "The joke is over! Come home, now."

Oisinne leapt up and swung at her face. Clíodhna ducked, but he aimed his next punch at Donn's stomach. Her son wasn't as fast and let out a pained grunt.

While Donn doubled over, Etromma grabbed her father's arm and Clíodhna reached for the other. This time, he hit her straight in the eye, and pain flashed as she let out a curse.

Etromma ducked low and kicked his legs from under him. He fell backwards, a startled look on his face. Then he giggled, a mad, freakish sound that left him in tears.

No one else was laughing.

As his family dragged him along the path to the roundhouse, Oisinne chuckled in random spurts.

They got him inside and tucked into his bed. He still giggled wildly at nothing as Clíodhna poured ale and made him drink it. Perhaps he'd fall asleep and give them all a rest. Though it was barely midday, she was weary.

He finished the ale and wiped his mouth with the back of his hand. Then he threw the mug against the far wall. She hummed a sweet tune and finally, he closed his eyes and slept, though he mumbled and tossed in his slumber.

Her entire body ached as she sat outside with Etromma and Donn. With a worried glance at the door, her daughter asked, "What will we do with him? He's lost whatever senses he had left. Do you think the abbot can cure him?"

Clíodhna let out a sharp bark of laughter. "That man couldn't cure a cowhide with a vat of tannin. I don't know what we can do, though. Remember, the village healer went north last moon, to her sister's."

Donn bit at his lower lip. "I want to ask one of the brothers. He cares for the herb garden and he fought in some war before he became a monk. He told me that he'd dressed a lot of wounds."

Etromma picked at her nails. "Dressing wounds isn't the same as healing madness."

He threw his hands up. "I know that! I know. But what else we can do?"

Clíodhna chewed on the possibilities. A well, sacred to Brighid, the goddess of healing, lay many leagues to the east. But getting Oisinne there might not be possible. What if they made the perilous journey and couldn't find the well? Or it didn't work?

Or Adhna's magic might cure Oisinne's madness.

She clung onto that thin thread of hope as Oisinne cried out in his sleep, a screech that cut across her nerves like a knife.

Clíodhna sat in the stone circle, despite freezing rain. *Why is it so cold in the middle of the summer?* The wind whipped her hair into painful snakes, so she tied it into a knot at the base of her neck. She clenched her jaw and faced the sky. She opened her arms and called out, "Adhna! I have need of you. Please come to me."

After the tenth repeat of this plea, someone cleared their throat behind her. She whirled, suddenly worried Bodach had answered her call instead. But there stood her lover, his black hair shining in the rain.

Clíodhna ran into his arms, pressing up against his chest, surprised at much the sight of him filled her with happiness. The rain died as they embraced, and the sun chased the storm clouds to the horizon.

It had been six days since she'd resolved to ask him for help, and every day was a further trial of her patience. Storms grew worse as her nerves got frayed. Even raising two strong children didn't prepare her for controlling an insane husband.

Three times now, she'd had to resort to tying Oisinne to his palette to keep him from punching her. He flailed his arms at the slightest provocation, not recognizing his own family, insisting they must be strangers, come to steal his stories.

Adhna's embrace was warm and comforting. Clíodhna didn't want to leave that haven.

Eventually, he held her at arms-length and studied her eyes. "You've not had an easy reunion with your husband."

She laughed, a slight tinge of hysteria coloring the mirth. "That's a bit of an understatement, lover."

He frowned. "You mustn't call me that, Clíodhna."

Her eyes grew wide. "And why would I not? We are lovers. It's a fact. And you're my teacher, my mentor, and at the moment, my only hope."

Adhna glanced around them. "No place is safe from unwanted listeners, Clíodhna, even this place. I believe you had an encounter with one such, a Fae called Bodach? He has spread tales of his meeting with you all through the Queen's court."

She shivered at the memory of the bark-skinned Fae. "He's a nasty one. Will he come back? What does he want with us?"

After giving a shrug, Adhna caressed her hair. "I'm not certain. He seldom interferes with mortals, but you have magic. He's drawn to power and must have felt your pull upon the earth."

All the fears and frustrations of the last days came bubbling to the surface. She shoved his chest away. "Then why in the name of all the gods did you teach me earth power first? He could have hurt my children! I fought him off, but fell ill for days with the aftermath! We might have all died!"

He placed both hands over his heart, entreaty in his eyes. "Clíodhna, I couldn't know he'd sense those lessons! You must believe me."

Clíodhna paced back and forth, the clouds once again gathering above her. She wanted to believe, but after days of keeping her temper in check around Oisinne, her rage spewed forth, and she didn't want to rein it in yet. "You left us open for attack and just vanished! Where were you when we needed protection?"

He clasped his hands. "I had duties at the court of my Queen Áine."

Her wrath morphed into an ugly jealousy. *"Duties,* is it? You lounged around in her arms while that Fae attacked us, is that it? Well, it's obvious you don't really care for me, otherwise you'd have set up some protections."

She stomped out of the stone circle, but he grabbed her arm and spun her around. "Clíodhna! You truly don't understand. I can no more disobey an order from my Queen than you can flap your arms and fly into the sun. It's not even a matter of will. I'm physically unable to defy her. She needed me, and as much as I wanted to return to help you, I couldn't."

Clíodhna's fury still bubbled within her, and he was her only available target. "Then you might have warned me!"

With sad eyes, his shoulders slumped. "Should I warn you to steer clear of the winter winds? Or the stormy sea? I can't prepare you for every danger, as much as I'd wish to. Just like any mentor, I must trust in you, my student, to learn how to survive. You've done well so far, and I'm proud of you."

She spat at his feet. "That for your pride, and that for your trust."

He ignored her vitriol and put his hands out, palms up, a gesture of welcome. Clíodhna glared at him a few moments more, still wanting to vent her wrath on someone, but his logic cooled her ire. She let out a long sigh.

Adhna wrapped her in his arms. Clíodhna sobbed against his shoulder as he hugged her tight.

All the frustration, anger, and helplessness she'd been feeling came crashing through her body. She let all the emotion flow into him until she was a wasted husk, devoid of all humanity.

When she'd calmed down to mere whimpers and sniffles, he stroked her hair. "What can I do to help now, Clíodhna?"

She rubbed at the snot on her face, wishing the rain would come back to clean it. With a mighty sniff, she let out a shuddering breath. "You might take Oisinne's madness away."

He didn't need to reply. The answer was clear in his face, his eyes even sadder than they'd been before. "I might calm his rantings for a while, in Faerie. But here in the mortal world? I don't have that power."

"Then who does?"

He shrugged. "Other than my Queen, I only know of one Fae who possesses power over madness. And you don't want to ask any favors of Bodach. You've already run afoul of his greed and temper once. I don't recommend a second encounter."

Bodach. That slimy, terrifying Fae who'd tried to trick her. After clenching her fists, she screamed toward the sky in her frustration. Clíodhna beat her palms against the slick, wet standing stones until they ached.

When she quieted, Adhna drew her into his arms again. "Let me come down to the house with you. Maybe I can at least calm him. It won't be a permanent healing, but it can you a few days of peace."

Numb, she rested her head against his chest for a moment of comfort. They descended the treacherous muddy path back down the hill, slick with the rainstorm of her own sorrow. She slipped a few times, but Adhna caught her.

As they entered the clearing, Adhna still held her hand in the crook of his arm. Oisinne was watching from the doorway.

His eyes glimmered with anger. "So, this is what you leave me for? To couple with a stranger?"

She held her hands up, glancing around for her children, but they must be in the barn, safe from his anger. "Husband, this is Adhna. He's a friend, nothing more. He's been teaching me—"

Her husband stalked toward them, jealousy in every line of his body. He clenched his fists so hard, the knuckles showed white. Thunder played across his face. "How dare you call yourself my wife!"

Adhna dropped his grip on Clíodhna's arm and opened his arms. "Oisinne, pray tend to me. You will not hurt this woman."

Oisinne swiveled to face the Fae. Without warning, he rushed Adhna, his shoulder dropped low to attack his midriff. Adhna stepped aside, unflustered by the assault.

Her husband slowed when he encountered nothing, turned, cocked his head, and staggered a few times, as if drunk. He glowered and lowered his shoulder to strike again.

Adhna chanted in an ancient tongue and raised his hands, the sleeves of his *léine* dropping back to reveal inked serpents wrapped along his arms. Oisinne shook his head and ran toward his opponent.

By the time he reached the Fae, though, his pace slowed and his head bowed low. After a few more stumbling steps, he crumpled into a heap at Adhna's feet.

With a cry, Clíodhna knelt next to her husband. "What did you do? Did you kill him?"

Adhna placed his hands on Oisinne's head. "He is well enough, Clíodhna. At least, as much as he can be. I made him rest. He should sleep for a few days, perhaps rousing now and then for food or drink. Even then, he'll be calm, as if in a dream."

Her fear when he fell made her realize she still had feelings for Oisinne, despite his madness. Donn had peeked around the house, and she beckoned him close so they could help her husband into his bed.

After they covered him with several wool blankets and tied netting, she returned to Adhna's side. "What happens when he wakes? Will he remember what you did to him?"

"He will remember nothing of this day. That's the best gift I can give you for now."

She glanced at her husband's sleeping form. "Can you show me how to do that?"

He bit his lip. "I can show you how to muddle the memory, but it's a dangerous tool. You must be careful not to do it too often. Sometimes the effects can become permanent, and it may backlash."

After steeling her spine, she said, "Show me."

The chant was simple enough, and she almost understood the words. They danced on the edge of comprehension, alien and familiar at the same time. But this magic drew from air and water, to wash the ephemeral memory away like a summer storm.

After she practiced drawing the power, Adhna explained how to wield it, but once again cautioned her against using it frivolously. "When I return, I'll teach you more."

"Must you truly leave?"

He gestured toward the house. "If I stay, your husband will only get worse. For your own safety, I must go back to Faerie now. I'll visit, but I can't stay and teach you any longer."

Her throat grew dry, and she threw her arms around him. Her lover clung tightly to her, his fingers digging into the muscles of her back. Clíodhna didn't want to let him go, and her blood chilled with both misery and despair.

Once they broke their embrace, he faded into the trees.

Chapter Nine

When her husband woke a few days later, he didn't mention Adhna or his attack. For this, Clíodhna thanked the gods.

Despite this reprieve, her days were chaos. Each night, Donn helped her tie Oisinne's ropes tight. Each morning, she had to wake before her husband to untie them.

But once, she was roused from her own restless sleep by his growls. The growls quickly turned to grunts and then shouts. "Let me go! Let me go!"

Should she untie him? He would just get angrier if she didn't. In the dark, she fumbled with the knot holding his right wrist.

Once that was free, she went to the other side, but before she could untie that, his fist knocked her aside. With a cry, she stumbled back, her entire face throbbed with pain.

"Don't touch me! They're coming! They'll get me!"

Donn whispered in her ear. "Come away, and I'll calm him."

She couldn't let Donn get hurt, though, so she shrugged her son off and untied the other knot. This time, his fist hit the side of her head, and her ears rang.

Untied, though, he calmed back into a deep sleep, and Clíodhna let out a ragged sigh.

Donn gave her a hug. "Ma? We don't have to stay here."

Clíodhna shook her head. "He's my husband. I must care for him. Besides, we have nowhere else to go."

She tried to get back to sleep, but the dawn crept into the sky before she could even calm her whirling thoughts.

At least so far, though, she'd been able to deflect his anger from the children. Once or twice, Oisinne pushed Donn or slapped Etromma, but they'd learned how to escape the house before his fury rose to physical violence. Etromma usually grabbed Aileran on her way out. The baby crawled fast but got little chance to explore when his father rampaged.

Clíodhna would stay to calm her husband, and to keep him from chasing them down. He paid her in a currency of bruises and lacerations. So far, he'd broken no bones, but she'd collected a twisted ankle, bruised ribs, and two black eyes.

Despite a painful limp, her only escape was long daily walks in the forest. Oisinne would rather stew at home. He didn't even go out hunting now.

Instead, Donn would fish or trap small game while Etromma hunted for larger prey. Clíodhna tended her garden but sometimes joined Etromma as her daughter tracked her prey, for a glimmer of freedom.

Each day, when they returned, Clíodhna would receive more blows, but at least she'd found a few hours of peace.

And each dawn, Oisinne insisted on going into the village to listen to the monks.

One day, he acted almost human. He greeted other villagers with pleasantries and small talk. Oisinne complimented the abbot on his sermon, and the progress of the new building. He even linked his arm in Clíodhna's, the very picture of a happy couple.

The next morning, Clíodhna opened her eyes to the cool pre-dawn darkness, hoping the day before heralded a phase of healing. Oisinne snored evenly beside her, still asleep, and she breathed a sigh of relief.

Rising, she removed the knots, Donn helping when she'd gotten half of them done. Just as she untied the last one, Oisinne leapt to his feet, his eyes darting around with wild suspicion.

Without warning, he kicked her left knee. Pain shot through her leg and she dropped to the floor, trying hard not to cry out.

Donn took Oisinne's arm and led him to the table, throwing a concerned glance over his shoulder. Clíodhna waved her hand while gripping her knee. The pain was already receding, so it must not be a break. But the quickness of the blow had been unnerving.

She hobbled to the table, pulling out the cheese and bread for their morning meal. At least he'd gotten the same leg she'd already twisted.

Etromma went out to milk the cows, Aileran on her hip.

Oisinne stared at the flatbread in front of him. "Clíodhna! What's this you're feeding me?"

"Rye bread, Oisinne. And here's soft garlic cheese to spread on it."

He flung the bread on the floor and stomped on it. Then he scooped his fingers in the cheese and smeared it on his face. He laughed with maniacal glee and smeared more on her face.

Exasperated, she wondered if she should use Adhna's spell to calm him, but remembered his cautions. She should only use it in need, not for convenience. After clenching her jaw, she wiped off the wasted cheese.

He hopped around and spoke in a sing-song voice. "Time to go to church!"

With a glance at the rising sun and a promise to honor it another day, Clíodhna hustled her husband out the door. With luck, Etromma and Donn could escape today's service and have some quiet time to themselves. They'd get a lot more work done without their father trying to help.

The sun had barely shot out rays of peach-gold light from behind the hills when they arrived at the church. Only a few people were inside, but she cast a smile at Ita, who stood with two of her children.

Her neighbor frowned, glancing first at her face and then at Oisinne. She answered Ita's frown with a sad shrug. Her friend steered her pregnant daughter to the other side of the church.

Abbot Pátraic processed to his dais. After his Latin chanting, he didn't launch into his normal lecture. Instead, he stared at several of the villagers, his gaze lingering long on Clíodhna. "It has come to my attention that several people have been consorting with evil."

Each attendee exchanged glances, as if wondering who. Clíodhna knew, somehow, that the abbot was speaking about her.

"Spirits and creatures of evil inhabit the woods and streams of our village, and trafficking with them is against the good words of our Lord God. He forbids such interactions, upon pain of being unworthy of God."

Now he glared straight at Clíodhna. She steeled her spine and glared right back.

Oisinne let out a high-pitched giggle and jumped toward Abbot Pátraic. Startled, the abbot drew back, but his attacker didn't strike him. Instead, he stood upon the altar, shoving the candlestick to the floor. Abbot Pátraic cried out and dove to rescue his precious silver candlestick. This gave Oisinne time to dance on the table and pull his *léine* off over his head.

Now naked except for his leather boots, her mad husband raised his arms as if offering a supplication to the gods. He let out a deep peal of laughter, something ominous and dark. His laugh bounced from the walls and several people milled around with nervous anticipation. A few escaped while others watched with gleeful expectation of what Oisinne might do next.

Clíodhna wanted to pull him down and drag him home, but she couldn't move, both horrified and fascinated.

Her husband spun around three times, the small altar rocking under his weight. He leapt down and ran outside, still with no clothing on. Clíodhna, finally able to move, hurried to catch him. Someone gave a nasty cackle as she ran outside.

Mist had risen with the sun. Golden beams of light made her naked husband almost glow as he sprinted through the village, pointing at each roundhouse he passed, shouting out nonsense words and imprecations.

Heads poked out of each house at his passing. Some returned to their homes, while others emerged and chased after Oisinne.

How can I catch him? He's much stronger than me and I can't run as fast with my ankle. Besides the harm that might come to my baby. Her hand strayed to her stomach.

As she considered her options, a hand gripped her arm. Clíodhna swung around to confront this new threat and came face to face with Abbot Pátraic.

"*You* are the reason for his madness, Clíodhna. Your infidelities caused this, and consorting with the evil that lies beneath the hills. God has spoken, and you are being punished for your crimes against him!"

Several villagers had gathered around them. A couple murmured agreement, though a few frowned at his harsh words.

Clíodhna drew in a deep breath. "You know nothing about me and my family, Abbot Pátraic. I suggest you pay more attention to your own affairs."

Thunder gathered in his expression. "Every person in this village is my affair, woman! I will not have your wastrel ways infecting honest, God-fearing people."

She laughed in his face, throwing her head back in genuine mirth. "Wastrel ways? What does that even mean?"

A crash from the blacksmith's roundhouse drew made them all look. Oisinne had fallen into the water trough and splashed about like a toddler in a pond.

With a final glare at Abbot Pátraic, she limped to Oisinne and drew him free of the trough.

The blacksmith approached, and she tensed, knowing how he felt about her. But he gave her a reassuring pat on her shoulder and whispered in her ear. "My grandda acted like this for a while. He regained his senses after a few moons. Take heart."

His son, Tirechan, the boy whom Etromma had been moon-eyed over, came with a large blanket. "This should keep him covered until you can get him home."

She gave thanks to both and pulled her husband from the judging eyes of the onlooking villagers. Even the monks frowned as she went by, but Clíodhna couldn't tell if they disapproved of Oisinne's actions or her own. In the more cynical corners of her mind, she felt their censure like a physical slap.

Once she got him home, Oisinne slept most of that day. His bouts with madness exhausted him, giving her some break after dealing with his rampages. At least this time, he hadn't hurt anyone.

After she'd cleaned and dressed him, and gotten him to sleep, Clíodhna fed Aileran. But after just a few minutes, a shadow in the doorway made her glance up, Ita glanced in, her manner nervous and tentative.

Her gaze flicked to Oisinne mumbling in his alcove, turning under the ropes, before she cleared her throat. "Clíodhna… have you been unwell?"

Rolling her eyes, Clíodhna flicked her hand. "Not me. Oisinne, definitely. I'm tired, that's all."

Her friend visibly swallowed. "We're all worried about you."

Clíodhna pursed her lips and regarded Ita with a steely expression. "About me? Or of me?"

Casting her gaze to the ground, Ita fidgeted with her fingers. "Both? You've been acting so odd lately. And Oisinne… he used to be… calmer." Her friend reached a hand toward Clíodhna's face, where the latest bruises ached. "His hand has grown heavy, as well."

Clíodhna batted Ita's hand away. "Oisinne is out of his mind. No sane man runs naked through the village. I'm handling it the best I can, but any changes in my behavior must pale against his, don't you think?"

Her friend stepped into the roundhouse and sat cross-legged in front of the central hearth. Ita blinked a few times in the gloomy interior and peered at Oisinne. "Is he like this all the time?"

Pressing her lips together, Clíodhna shook her head. She poured two mugs of ale and joined her friend, handing her one. "No, sometimes he acts almost sane, but still a shadow of his former self. It's safer and easier to keep him away from people, but he insists on going to your church each morning."

"The abbot has been making complaints of you."

"Of me? Not of Oisinne?"

"Yes, of you. You and your, well, he calls them a *legion of fornicators,* but he means lovers."

Clíodhna burst out laughing. "A legion of fornicators? He cannot be serious."

Ita sipped her ale, and her expression grew solemn. "He is, and he's convinced several of the village elders that they should deal with you."

With a scowl, Clíodhna stopped laughing. "Deal with me how?"

After glancing out the empty doorway and once again toward Oisinne, Ita whispered, "He's planning an attack on the forest spirits."

She furrowed her brow. "He's planning what?"

"You heard me! Don't make me raise my voice. He's gathering some villagers, armed with farm tools, and he's intent on clearing out the Fae and spirits from the woods near the river bend. Tomorrow morning."

Clíodhna rose to her feet so quickly, she knocked over her ale. With a grumble, she bent to mop the mess up. "Tomorrow morning, huh? We'll see about that."

"No! You mustn't interfere! That's why I came, to warn you. It's a trap. He knows you'll come to help, and he wants to catch you in the act. That way, he can accuse you as a sorceress."

"A sorceress? I don't know that word."

Ita fidgeted again. "According to him, a sorceress is a woman who consorts with daemons. A person filled with evil. Someone who will corrupt others into evil."

How dare this man come to her village and accuse her of such things? Clíodhna shut her eyes, drawing peace from the earth. "Ita, how many winters have you known me?"

With a shrug and another sip of ale, Ita said, "Fifteen, sixteen? Ever since you married and moved here."

Clíodhna leaned against the table, her back to Ita. "In all that time, have I ever done anything evil?"

She shrugged again. "I don't know. For a while, some people thought you'd killed your husband. He disappeared so suddenly and, well, you know how rumors work."

Throwing her hands in the air, she whirled around. "It's obvious that was a lie, isn't it? There he is, right over there. Mad as a hare, but very much alive! I swear, Ita, while I admire your honesty, sometimes too much isn't a good thing."

Her friend shrank away from Clíodhna's anger, bowing her head to stare her mug and the splash of ale left inside. "I didn't say I *believed* the rumors. Just that they existed. I really am trying to help."

Clíodhna let out a deep sigh and threw her head back. Once again, she drew magic from the earth, trying to calm her heart and temper. Ita always just wanted to help. She should be kinder to her friend.

"I'm sorry, Ita. I know you're trying to help, and you don't deserve my anger."

"Don't apologize. This can't be easy to hear."

Clíodhna spoke a few polite pleasantries to her friend and bustled her off, thanking her for the news. However, now she must plan on how to rescue the Fae without getting caught in Abbot Pátraic's trap herself.

Confronting the angry mob would be the most dangerous and least likely to succeed. One lone woman against maybe twenty grown men and an angry abbot seemed very poor odds.

She might sneak in before they arrived and bring each Fae to safety, but even if she had a week's notice, that wouldn't be enough time. That little bend in the river was a delightful sanctuary and she'd moved several Fae there from the more peopled parts of the village already. At least a dozen Fae lived there now, and they didn't move easily. Change required much argument, bribery, and cajoling for each of them.

She might gather help herself, but who else talked easily to the Fae? Etromma had some ability, but she didn't use it much since she began attending church. Donn never noticed the creatures, as far as she could tell. Ita would be too meek to try such a bold action.

If Odhrán still lived in the abbey, she might ask for his help, but he was gone. She daren't call Adhna back, not after the last time.

No, she'd have to deal with this mess herself. If she convinced one Fae to move, maybe the others would follow suit. Clíodhna had to at least try.

After asking Etromma and Donn to watch their father and Aileran, she dressed warm for the chilly night and stalked toward the river. The moon shone bright in the deep of the night, which helped her find the right path. Birds slumbered under the velvet sky, but crickets sang as she marched along.

As she entered the glade, the first Fae she encountered skittered away. Starlight flickered above as the wee creature hid behind a giant oak. "Please, come out! I won't harm you. I'm here to warn you of danger."

Only a tinkling of the wind answered. "You know me. We've met before. I helped move you here, remember?"

Another tinkling, this time stronger. "Angry humans are coming with the dawn, They want to hurt you, but I can bring you to safety. Will you come?"

Silence answered her urging, but behind her, something snapped.

Clíodhna whirled, expecting Abbot Pátraic. Instead, another Fae stood in the moonlight, a gossamer wisp of a woman. "You must come! He is in danger!"

Confused, Clíodhna furrowed her brow. "He who?"

"The dark-haired one who serves the Queen! He's trapped, and we can't free him! Come! Come!"

The pale Fae faded from view, leaving only the whisper of light and the sound of tiny bells.

"Stones and crows! Where did you go?"

The bells jingled to her right, so Clíodhna turned in that direction, taking several tentative steps. She glanced back at the oak tree, but that Fae must have fled during her distraction. Another few steps took her out of the glade and onto a path she'd not seen before.

As she stepped on the trail, she peered around for any sign of the Fae woman. A faint glow guided her forward. Abbot Pátraic couldn't lay a trap like this. It must be a true call for help.

Clíodhna crept forward, testing each step before putting her full weight down. She progressed down the glinting path until she reached a new clearing.

This was a dark place, darker than the dead of night, darker than a pit in the well of the earth. As used to magic as Clíodhna had become, she'd never seen a place so devoid of earth power.

A dead spot, with no energy from earth, air, water, or fire. No spirit lived within the dirt. Dead trees surrounded a deep hole, their rattling branches entwined in a wicked tangle. This tangle covered the top of the pit like a cruel cage.

Clíodhna shivered, unnerved by the ravaged land. The devastation curled into her bones, making her skin crawl. Nothing lived within this wasteland. Black tendrils of rot and desecration called to her with dissonant song.

If Abbot Pátraic sought something evil, this horrible place would be perfect. Maybe he *had* set this trap for her. One who seeks evil is much more likely to find it wherever he looks.

Clíodhna rubbed the goosebumps from her arms and peered into the murky pit. Despite the barren earth, something stirred inside the gloom. Someone moaned, a thready voice murmuring with pain and despair.

Her own voice quavered with fear. "Who… Who's down there?"

An eternity later, a faint voice echoed in the back of her mind. "Flee, Clíodhna!"

She spun, searching out the source, but the only person near lay in the bottom of that pit. "Who's there?"

"Flee! Save yourself!"

She recognized Adhna's voice, burdened with pain and fear. She'd never known him to show fear. What could frighten such a powerful Fae? What had the power to trap him in such a place?

Her skin turned to ice as a hand fell upon her shoulder. Clíodhna spun, only to find the Fae who'd lured her here. "Who are you? Did you set this trap?"

The pale woman smiled, her long tresses glittering with their own light. "I merely came to find you. Adhna needs your help."

"Why me?"

"You are of him, as I am."

Her confusion must have shown on her face, for the Fae continued. "He is my sire, and you carry his child within you."

Clíodhna placed a hand over her own belly, glancing between the Fae and the looming maw of the evil pit. With grim resolve, she steeled herself for the pain of pulling energy through dead earth.

Deep, deep into the soil she quested, pulling a bare tendril from the living land beyond the dead zone. The energy resisted her call, snapping back before she could draw it further than a hands' span, making her head reel.

A second time, she drew that bare thread of power, and it screamed with each movement, then snapped back.

Again and again, she pulled at the energy, each time gaining a little length. After her tenth attempt, she stopped to wipe sweat from her brow. Despite the chilly night, her efforts left her panting.

Another pull, another snap back to the living earth. Frustration warred with determination and failure. Each snap whipped at her soul, making her whimper with pain.

After she'd long lost count of her attempts, Clíodhna finally got the tendril long enough to touch it to Adhna's hand, deep in the earth. He cried out, but not in pain. An exultation of joy and strength which turned to a sobbing grumble when this, too, snapped back to the living earth.

However, her success now bolstered her fortitude. Clíodhna pulled the power again and Adhna held onto the tendril this time. He pulled, yanking her from her own feet. She fell onto the dead earth, but she kept hold of the energy. As Adhna drew it into himself, he created a lattice of energy to shield him from the evil blackness.

The Fae climbed this lattice, step by step, out of the grim pit. Once he reached the cage of dead branches, he raised his arms with a triumphant cry and shattered the surrounding desiccated limbs into a thousand pieces. Shards rained over them as she hugged Adhna with gentle glee.

His bones jutted through his thin body. He must have been starved of more than magic in his prison. Clíodhna worried she might snap him if she gripped too tight.

He held her at arms-length, searching her eyes. "Clíodhna, why didn't you flee when I bade you to?"

"Did you truly expect me to leave my teacher to such a place?"

His eyes darted into the gloom surrounding them. "I suppose not. But we must leave. He could return."

"Who did this to you?"

"Bodach."

She shivered at the bark-skinned Fae's name. They hurried down the glinting path to the mortal forest glade at the river bend.

Dawn threatened in the east, and Clíodhna halted with a gasp. "The Fae! The abbot is coming here to destroy them!"

Adhna's eyes glittered in the twilight. "How dare he do such a thing?"

She swallowed and turned to her lover. "He's trying to trap me by hurting them."

With a slow nod, he clenched his jaw. "Very well. We'll just have to take care of this quickly."

He cut the air with his hand, a line of fire burning vertically where he drew his finger. Chittering behind her made Clíodhna turn, only to find five Fae watching Adhna.

She addressed the watchers. "Who else is here? We must run to safety, before the sun rises. Will you gather the others?"

They backed away several steps, but Adhna turned. "Listen to the human woman. I'm making a passage into Faerie. You must escape."

The closest, a *sidhe* with knobbly green skin, bowed her head, fidgeting with her fingers. "But we live here. We are of *this* place. We can no easier move than our tree can."

Adhna cut another line, perpendicular to the first, at the level of his head. Without turning from his task, he said, "My magic can move you safely, though it may sting. However, waiting for what the other humans might do to you would be much more painful. You might even perish."

She turned to another *sidhe* with red oak skin. "Go fetch our kin."

A third line, parallel to the first, and then a fourth line as a threshold, formed a doorway. Clíodhna peered through the opening, but only a dim light shone through, more subtle than the dawning sun behind it, as if a hundred candles had been scattered across the green, rolling hills.

The light flickered with life and magic, making her heart leap as the memory of the dead place crept around her mind.

The oak *sídhe* arrived, with a line of Fae behind her. A tall, willowy water nymph, several rock gnomes, and a sprite stood in miserable caution, eyeing Clíodhna with suspicion and silence.

Adhna turned, his doorway complete. "Follow me. I will keep you safe and find you a home on the other side. You might not return to this world for some time, but you will be alive. Come, now."

Clíodhna grasped his arm. "Wait, Adhna! What about you? Will you be back?"

His smile faded. "Wait for me by the stones."

One by one, the Fae winked out of view into the fiery entrance. As each one disappeared, a bit of the magic in her world died. She felt each like a chink in armor, hailstones upon her skin. When the last one had gone, her heart felt smaller, as it had within that dead zone.

A clamor on the other side of the glade made her jump. Abbot Pátraic had arrived with his helpers. He swung a metal object with sweet-smelling smoke drifting from tiny holes, chanting in his harsh language.

Another monk flung water from a small mallet, back and forth on either side of the path. Clíodhna snuck into the still misty trees, seeking the shelter and solace of the living things, to escape the evil of men.

As she trudged toward the circle of stones in the mid-morning fog, Oisinne's cries echoed through the woods. He screeched at the top of his lungs, the sound reverberating in the mist. Etromma yelled back at him, telling him to shut his mouth and no one had hurt him.

Clíodhna glanced up the hidden path to the stone circle. Adhna had told her to wait for him there, and she wanted to spend her day in quiet solitude. She ached from the night's magic and every muscle in her body felt like Oisinne had spent all night punching her. But it wasn't fair to leave her own daughter to mind her husband. Clíodhna forced herself to go to her chaotic home.

Her husband had broken free of most of his ropes, but one still tangled around his leg. It tethered him in a precise radius from the central roof pillar.

Though he struggled against it, trying to pull it off by sheer strength, the knot held tight. The more he struggled, the tighter the tangle became. Etromma and Donn hovered just beyond his reach.

Donn held out a bowl of stew. More stew stained his face and clothing, so this must be his second attempt to offer food. Etromma held a fussing Aileran, bouncing him on her shoulder as she tried to calm their father down.

As Clíodhna entered, her daughter spun and glared at her. "We needed you an hour ago! Where have you been?"

Clíodhna closed her eyes, and then held out her arms for the bowl. "Battle of another sort. I'm sorry to have left you to this. Go get some rest."

With understandable anger, Etromma stomped out, taking the baby with her. Donn handed her the bowl. "Maybe you'll have more luck."

Clíodhna took the stew bowl and gestured out the door. "Go get some rest yourself. I'll take care of him."

Despite every limb feeling like soaked logs, this crisis warranted that magic Adhna had showed her. With that resolution in mind, once her children left, she drew upon magic.

But despite her call, it resisted her, unwilling to come. Had she injured her ability in the night, in that dead place? Maybe the power was a living, breathing thing with a memory of pain.

Instead of drawing on the earth, she tried to draw on the air and water around her, pulling the peace of a still lake into her mind. She couldn't calm her husband if she couldn't settle herself. At least Adhna had taught her this much.

Rather than pulling on the tempestuous power of the ocean, she drew on the still lake, placid in the pre-dawn world. She breathed in and out, once, twice, three times. Measured heartbeats and closed eyes helped her concentrate, despite Oisinne's mad ramblings. Clíodhna shut out external noise and concentrated on her own body. *In and out, once, twice, three times. In and out.*

Serenity suffused her, a sweet, beautiful tranquility. A calm pond in the dawn. The countryside when covered with fresh snow. The pure quiet of a moonless night.

When Clíodhna opened her eyes, she spread this pacific power through her hands and into her husband's anarchic soul. She unruffled his muddled mind, pouring honey on his angry mental wounds. His frenzied rage ebbed into a deep slumber.

As his snores filled the room, Clíodhna collapsed in a pile of exhausted bones. But her rest didn't come with peace.

The dead place haunted her dreams. She ran through the lifeless woods, terrified of the skeletal limbs reaching for her, ripping her clothing and tangling her hair. Once, she stumbled, grabbing handfuls of dirt, but nothing lived within. No bugs, no beetles, no roots. Nothing but sterile soil, unable to sustain life.

Trees loomed over her, laughing in glee at her helplessness. Clíodhna scrabbled away from their reach, but the dirt just slipped between her fingers. She cried out, sobbing in frustration and panic.

Pale light glowed on the horizon. The light became a man, arms outstretched in supplication. She didn't know this man, didn't recognize his face, but his presence exuded peace and love.

His face shone and his hair glowed white. He drew her back into her beloved ocean, to swim amongst the fish and sea creatures. The figure calmed her with her childhood memories, an innocent time before stress and danger took over her life. He reassured her by his very existence, and she fell into a calmer slumber.

She woke to the sound of Aileran screeching. The sound shot through her skull, and she shot straight up, worried about Oisinne. He lay on his side, curled up like a baby, snoring with vigor.

After letting out a breath of relief, Clíodhna gathered the real child in her arm and bounced him, getting her breast out to feed him.

Two moons past, Clíodhna had tried feeding him mashed turnips instead of her milk, but he resisted the change. But her breasts ached and her milk was fading, so Aileran had better wean soon.

The sun laid low in the west, so the afternoon had almost disappeared. She must rush if she meant to meet Adhna at the stone circle at dusk. Clíodhna braided her hair and twisted it into a tight bun.

Once she fed and burped Aileran, with his swaddling changed, Clíodhna rocked him to sleep. Aileran had just started crawling around, despite being a full cycle of seasons old. Etromma had already been crawling around like an awkward puppy at six moons, but Donn hadn't started exploring until almost eleven moons. Aileran looked like he'd follow in his brother's footsteps.

In search of her older children, Clíodhna walked to the stable. They'd fed the cows and pigs and cleaned their stalls, but now they'd disappeared. Had they gone to the village? Perhaps they needed an escape from Oisinne's care, just like she did.

If neither child returned before dusk, she'd have to take Aileran with her and trust that Oisinne would be safe. He *should* sleep under her spell. Despite Adhna's warning, she didn't seem to have suffered any ill effects, but she'd withhold her judgment until he woke.

What if she'd done something damaging to him with her magic? Would she be able to tell? Sanity and sense were already strangers to him.

Donn came in, carrying three hares from his traps.

She gave him a nod of approval for his hunting success. "Is Etromma with you?"

"No, she went into the village. Tirechan asked her to have a meal with his family."

Her eyes flew open with surprise. "After all that's just happened? I would have thought they'd shun our family."

He gave her a lopsided smile. "She said something about Tirechan's great-grandsire being mad, so they had sympathy. I guess having a father who's away with the fairies is less scandalous than having no father at all."

A sad commentary on their society. Clíodhna had been much happier without Oisinne around, and she'd bet good wool that both Etromma and Donn had enjoyed better lives.

Still, she had a duty to care for her family, no matter how mad they were. Clíodhna had made her vows, and family was the most important part of society. Someone who turned out their own kin because they became inconvenient would be shunned from any right-thinking village.

That didn't mean she didn't dream of running away, never to return.

With that thought in mind, Clíodhna gathered the baby for their trip to the stones. Donn, dressing the hares, glanced up. "Would you like me to mind him, Ma? I'm just going to make a stew, so I don't mind. Da's been sleeping well enough, right?"

But Oisinne was only sleeping well because she'd ensorcelled him. Her own husband, under a sleeping magic by her hand. Maybe she *had* fostered evil, as the abbot accused. Clíodhna swallowed down an unexpected sob.

After giving her son a thankful nod, she handed Aileran over. The baby giggled and yanked on Donn's brown curls, making nonsense sounds of delight. With a glance at the skinned hares, Clíodhna's gut roiled, nausea sweeping over her. She clutched her stomach under her *léine,* hoping Donn hadn't noticed. Her husband had only just returned, and any baby he begat wouldn't be causing sickness yet.

After her encounter with the dead land, her journey up the glittering path to the standing stones felt more ominous. Every shift in the wind, fluttering late summer leaves, made her cringe, and her eyes darted to every shadow. And the journey seemed to take all day rather than a few hours.

Bodach had entrapped Adhna. Had it been to catch her, like Abbot Pátraic's trap? Or had it been for some other reason?

Bodach didn't seem the type to craft a methodical plan for revenge. His personality seemed much more chaotic and random. Still, she knew little of Fae temperament. She'd only met Adhna and the local nature spirits.

When Clíodhna had asked about life in Faerie, he'd shaken his head. "That is not a lesson I wish to give, Clíodhna. Someday, I might bring you to visit. Until then, be content in your life here. It is, in some ways, much safer and more beautiful than Faerie."

All the tales told of the beauty of Faerie. Even those humans who'd escaped entrapment in Faerie spoke of the breath-taking loveliness of that realm. Perhaps Adhna spoke of something other than physical beauty.

Clíodhna passed the guardian stones just as the sun's edge dipped below the hills. The landscape, awash in deep orange, shifted into a cool violet. She shivered and drew her cloak tight as the day's warmth disappeared with the sun.

Black stones glittered in the dying light. There was no moon yet, and besides, it would be only a sliver this night. Another shiver traveled up her spine as she stared at the tallest stone in the north.

Spiral symbols had been carved on the inside face of this stone, though they'd worn with time. Barely visible in this twilight, she traced the pattern with her fingers, turning around once, twice, three times and then again and again. Three spirals connected in the center. A trinity of eternal movement.

Adhna's voice behind her startled her. "You look better rested, Clíodhna. You must have slept well today."

Clíodhna turned, a smile on her face. Her lover stood in the center of the circle, midnight robes covering his body in fetching mystery. "I did, though the exhaustion helped."

He narrowed his eyes, staring into hers. "You performed the calming charm on your husband, didn't you?"

Clíodhna swallowed, unprepared for the guilt attacking her conscience. She forced herself to stand straight and take responsibility for her decision. "I did. He might have hurt himself or my children."

He paused a moment before nodding. "It's as well. You'd have been tempted eventually, and I did show you how. There's no changing that now."

He reached into his robe and pulled out a small object wrapped in white fabric. It glinted in the darkness, almost glowing with its own light. "I have something for you. This is payment not only for freeing me, but also for helping the local Fae to safety."

Mesmerized by the glittering white, she asked, "What is it?"

"A gift from me and my Queen, mind you, but there is no price or payment asked in return. Will you accept this gift with a free heart and mind?"

Caution warred with curiosity. "But I don't know what it is!"

"I'll show you. But first, I must have your assent."

Breaking the spell, she glared at him. "How can I know if I want to accept if I don't know what it is? You might be handing me death, for all I know! It might be a gift like a humpback, or a tongue that can never lie!"

Her lover's eyes turned sad. "Do you believe I would treat you so, Clíodhna?"

Ashamed at her distrust, she bowed her head. "I don't think that of you, Adhna." Raising her head, she set her lips in a firm line. "However, I don't know your Queen, and have no way to judge her goodwill toward me. She might have commanded you to dispose of me, and you wouldn't be able to give me warning. Isn't that true?"

His mouth drooped into a frown and the hand holding the glittering white package fell.

She swallowed back her fear and decided that she still trusted him, despite everything she said. "That being said, I agree to accept your gift."

Adhna frowned with solemn finality. Then he gestured for her to sit in the center of the circle before unveiling his prize. "When you freed me from that pit, I lost something precious. I lost my ability to live fully in either Faerie or the mortal realm. Now, I must spend a certain amount of time in Faerie and a certain time here. Not an onerous curse, but one that will affect my future. Because of that, there may be times I cannot come to you when you need me."

He looked intensely uncomfortable, and Clíodhna wondered if he had a glimpse into a dangerous future.

"Because of this, I requested a boon of my Queen Áine. I asked her to enchant a piece of jewelry so that I may gift it to you and your descendants. This jewelry will give you a power or, if you already possess a power, enhance it."

He unfolded one side of the white fabric, and then another. A third revealed a brooch fashioned with exquisite detail, anamorphic shapes entwined in gold and silver. Four green gems glittered in the setting, glowing with a subtle gleam in the now near-total darkness.

She reached to touch it, but he moved it out of her reach. "Not yet. We must prime this magic to you and your family. Later, you can pass this on to one of your own, and they to another, as long as they are of your blood."

"Will they also possess my magic?"

Adhna shook his head. "They will find their own magic through the brooch. Be careful who you choose, though. They must be stout of heart and mind, able to wrestle with the power they accrue. Some people are not meant to wield such strength."

With a thought to Abbot Pátraic, and then to Oisinne, Clíodhna nodded. Power was dangerous in the hands of those with no respect for it. Those without conscience can use it to manipulate people to their own purposes, and those without self-control can use it to hurt people. "I promise to be cautious with my use of the power."

"It isn't enough to promise to be cautious. I must build a deterrent into the brooch. If you misuse or overuse your power, you'll feel ill."

Clíodhna wrinkled her nose. "Misuse by whose judgment?"

He gave her a half-smile. "The brooch itself. It may be in your family long after I have passed, or even Queen Áine. Any mortal judge would be of little use. The brooch itself, while it has no conscience, can nevertheless be immortal, if cared for."

"But how can a brooch make judgments of conscience?"

"It can look within the soul of whoever wields it, and judge whether they are doing something for selfish gain or the good of others."

She didn't care for that explanation. While the brooch drew her, intrigued her, it also frightened her. Such an artifact in the mortal world might be a dangerous weapon in the wrong hands.

"But how can I control my descendants? They may be rotten people."

Adhna stroked the metalwork of the brooch. "The brooch will not accept someone unworthy. Each holder must be primed into ownership, via a ritual I shall show you. If the brooch accepts the stout heart of the new bearer, it will make a clear choice. Either way."

The green stones of the brooch flickered, resembling luminous eyes of some underwater monster, ominous and dangerous.

Clíodhna clenched her teeth as she worked to recall the kinder denizens of the deep. The wise salmon, the playful dolphin, the curious flounder. Not some dangerous monster from the darkest depths. "Then let's perform your ritual. I want to see if the brooch accepts me."

Adhna rose without effort and reached his hand to help Clíodhna. She took his hand and rose, her arm brushing the white fabric. A shock of energy sparked and she pulled back from the sharp pain.

"Don't touch it yet! Not until the ceremony is complete. Now, walk around the circle with me, three times."

He led her in a stately march around the circle, sunwise. Then he led her to the center and held his hands up, cupping the brooch to the sky. Green light shone from the stones, bathing the entire hilltop in a menacing light, a portentous warning of dangers to come.

Small motes of brighter light danced in the darker green light, swirling like the carvings on the stones in a merry dance. The threatening mood lightened into cheery laughter as the lights skipped from the top of each stone, around and around.

These motes gathered around her, forming an almost solid blanket of shining green. Clíodhna grinned, delighted at the joyful atmosphere and their uplifting ambiance. Her spirit soared across the sky, on the wings of a starling in the bright sun of early dawn.

Now the sparkles dove straight into her heart. Pain shot through her and she crumpled to the ground. Still, the lights entered her breastbone, swimming within her blood, humming with impossible temper inside her bones.

Clíodhna stretched out her arm and cried out, "Help me! Adhna!"

He simply backed away three steps. "You are part of it, Clíodhna. I cannot stop the ritual now."

Lights streamed out of her fingertips, her mouth, her nose, even her eyes. Each one left with painful stings as if she'd been poked by a thousand sewing needles. Into her heart and out of her fingers, into her blood and out of her eyes. The pain just kept burning in her blood until blackness surrounded her. Her final thought was relief that she hadn't brought Aileran.

Chapter Ten

Clíodhna's entire body ached. She tried to open her eyes, but they refused to obey her command.

Instead, she groaned, which got a response from Adhna. "Well, I had no idea it would be so intense, my dear Clíodhna. I apologize for that. However, at least you survived the process."

She didn't see much to be joyful for. She couldn't move her arms. Clíodhna couldn't even talk.

"I suspect you're a wee bit sore. I'll do what I can for that, but I must admit I have little power at the moment. It took most of my reserves just to create the brooch before my Queen blessed it, and I'll be low for some time, especially after Bodach's attack and your rescue."

Clíodhna wanted to ask him to stop rambling and just cast whatever spell he had to take away the ache.

"Now, hold still…"

What else did he think she might do? Dance a jig?

He placed his hands over her belly. Warmth spread through her body, a sweet, fuzzy warmth, like being curled up in front of a peat fire covered in wool blankets and the arms of a lover. A delicious warmth like hot lamb stew trickling down her throat. A savory warmth, like the hug of a sleeping baby.

Heat traveled down her limbs and up around her scalp, making her hair stand on end. When it reached her lips, she tried talking again. "Did… did the brooch accept me?"

He chuckled, removing his hands. "If it hadn't, you wouldn't be asking about it, let me assure you."

She propped herself up on her elbows, her aches fading to dullness. Adhna held out the brooch, wrapped in its white cloth. "This is now yours, my dear Clíodhna. Guard it well, use it wisely, and be ever aware of its power."

Nodding, she touched it tentatively, recalling the pain from the transition. It tingled, but not painfully so. She then grasped it and held the brooch tight.

Adhna helped her once again to her feet. "As much as it pains me, I must leave you now, and I shan't be back for some time. I have to deal with Bodach's betrayal, and that will take time. Will you be safe enough here without me?"

Thinking of Oisinne, slumbering under her spell in the roundhouse, she nodded. "I think so. I hope so."

"Very well. If you have need of me, you know how to call me, but I may not be able to come right away."

She gripped him in a fierce hug, loath to let him go. "I wish I could come with you."

Startled, he returned the hug. "But you don't, Clíodhna. You truly don't. Faerie is not a place to escape to—it's a place to escape *from*."

She dug her fingers into his back, desperate for a solution. "I don't care. You're there, and you're the only one who truly understands me. I want to learn from you, talk to you, make love to you. You're everything in one, a friend, a lover, a teacher."

With a rueful chuckle, he kissed her with deep passion, and then gave a chaste peck on her forehead. "And you are all things to me, sweet Clíodhna. A stronger woman I have rarely met. I will come back for you when I can. That, I can promise."

Then, Adhna faded into the darkness.

With only faint stars to guide her, Clíodhna trudged back to her roundhouse with her mad husband and children. Clíodhna gripped the magical brooch until the edges bit into her skin, but she welcomed the pain. It didn't come close to matching the pain in her heart.

Much to her relief, Oisinne was still sleeping. Donn sat outside, tending a cheery fire in the clearing. Aileran sat next to him, playing with colored rocks, glowing in the flickering firelight. Etromma was nowhere to be seen.

Glancing up at the star-filled sky, Clíodhna clamped down on the panic rising in her belly. "Etromma hasn't returned yet?"

Her son grinned. "Oh, she came home, then left again in a huff. Evidently, Tirechan never learned how to track game, so she's showing him how."

Clíodhna frowned. Tracking game at night? She narrowed her eyes at Donn, surprised that he'd been fooled by such a flimsy excuse, but her eldest son just tickled Aileran to elicit a giggle.

Etromma had enough winters to wed, and she'd chosen who she wanted. His family's surprising reversal on her acceptance made Clíodhna suspicious, but if Etromma had found a good match, she'd be content.

Clíodhna just hoped that Tirechan didn't toy with her affections. If that young man hurt her daughter, he'd have to answer for it.

Clíodhna remembered young love. Back when she'd first wed Oisinne, he entertained her every evening with outlandish tales. Back when he'd made her body sing under the blankets, and they'd made love under the stars on summer nights.

But the giddiness of young love faded into content and comfortable. Magic died into routine. That was a long time ago, and now her husband lay in a spelled sleep, so mad he'd become a danger to his family.

Some tales spoke of madness when a human was tricked into visiting Faerie. And when he returned, he'd lost all sense. Adhna said this hadn't happened to Oisinne, but what if Adhna didn't know?

Clíodhna didn't want to blame the Fae for something that wasn't their fault, but still, her mind and conscience wanted a reason for Oisinne's madness. She wanted something to blame, some reason behind the change. Life didn't always give reasons, but she still sought one.

With another rueful glance toward the roundhouse, Clíodhna sat cross-legged next to her younger son and moved the rocks around in a pattern. He giggled and touched one, so she moved that one in a circle. They played that game for a while and Clíodhna realized that, even if she couldn't find joy every hour of the day, she could grasp moments of joy with her children. Perhaps that was enough.

After Etromma returned, somewhat mussed from her evening adventures, Clíodhna gave her a stern look and pulled her aside while Donn took Aileran inside and put him to sleep.

Etromma stood with her feet planted wide and crossed her arms. "Well? I hope you won't lecture me on my behavior."

Clíodhna raised her eyebrows. "Did you do something which deserves a lecture?"

Her daughter's haughty confidence slipped. "N-no."

With a half-smile, she put a finger under Etromma's chin. "My darling daughter, not so many winters ago, I was your age. Men can be lovely companions in the dark. Just be certain he will also claim your love after the sun rises."

Even in the dying firelight, Etromma's blush rose strong. "He does! Well, he *says* he does. His mother hugged me and made me eat three helpings of fruit tart."

Clíodhna chuckled. "And will you be spending more time with them, then?"

She gave a vigorous nod. "He's invited me to come on a trade journey with him to *Baile Átha Luain* in three days. His father needs more ore and tools, so he's sending Tirechan. His older sister is going, too, so we won't be alone."

Clíodhna narrowed her gaze. "How long will the trip take?"

She shrugged. "I'm not sure, but it's a two-day trip each way, so perhaps six days in total?" Her eyes held a tender appeal.

With pursed lips, Clíodhna gave a curt nod. "Just be cautious. Travel can be dangerous, and Tirechan is strong, but young. One man can only fight off so many others. The Fianna are still out and about this summer, and some aren't picky about the law."

Her eyes glittering in gratitude, Etromma nodded her head with such enthusiasm, her lightly tied hair fell loose. With a grin, Clíodhna picked an oak leaf from her tresses. "And be cautious with your young man. You should be vowed to each other *before* a baby is born. Does he make you happy, Etromma?"

Playing with the end of her plait, Etromma grinned. "He does, Ma. And he asks me all sorts of questions and listens to my answers."

"Questions about what?"

She shrugged. "Oh, my favorite weather, or if I like any songs, or if I like fish, that sort of thing."

"It seems he does want to learn more about you. That's good. It means he's interested in more than bedding you. I'll pack you some provisions before you leave."

Etromma bounced away into the roundhouse. Clíodhna chuckled, doubting that her daughter would get any sleep.

Sleep, despite her earlier exhaustion, seemed the farthest from her own mind now. Her imagination whirled with too many ideas. Adhna, the brooch, Oisinne, Etromma and Tirechan, Abbot Pátraic, everything swam in her memory, jostling for attention. She couldn't untangle any of these problems now, but none of them cared.

While nestling on her side next to the outside hearth, Clíodhna tried to relax her mind by thinking of something new, something fantastic. She imagined what the world of Faerie might look like. Despite Adhna's censure, it seemed a magical place of wonder and beauty.

As a child, she'd always wanted to visit the land of the Fae, colored by so many legends and tales, despite the dangers. What would it be like to stand before the Queen of Faerie? Would there be dancing and singing? Would she have magnificent courtiers?

Bodach's bark-covered face shoved into her imagination, and she clamped down hard on that vision. Clíodhna didn't want the evil Fae lord sullying her fantasy. He might be a true-life courtier of the Faerie Queen, but he had no business in her own image of the place. With a flick of her hand, she pushed him away.

He returned almost as quickly as he disappeared.

As she had so many times in the real world, Clíodhna pulled on storm clouds in her vision world, but they wouldn't come to her call. Frowning, she glared at the sky, but no clouds appeared. No sun, no wind, no rain. How would she use her power in a place with no weather?

She glared at Bodach in the flickering firelight, and he just grinned with maniac glee at her fruitless efforts. With a grim set to her jaw, she pulled instead on the magic of the earth beneath Faerie. This, she could do, thanks to Adhna's instructions.

Faerie held far stronger magic than in the mortal world, and instead of thin tendrils of blue-white light, enormous ropes of white power twisted and writhed in her bones. Pain impaled her as they engulfed her body, but she wrestled with these monstrous ropes, trying to control the sheer power pushing through her.

Clíodhna cried out as she grabbed a line of power. It slinked out of her grasp like a slippery eel, whipping back and forth with angry strength. A second time, she grasped it, but it slithered away again.

When she seized it a third time, the white-hot energy burned her skin. She grunted in pain but kept her grip tight. The force of the earth power slammed her into the ground. She gasped from the impact and then remembered they were in her dream.

Letting out a war cry that would have made her father proud, she jerked the power into place, in the center of her being. Clíodhna became a font, a vessel for this monstrous font of power. Now in control, she glanced around for her foe.

But Bodach had disappeared.

Disgusted by losing her quarry, she sent the earth power back into the land of Faerie.

It wouldn't go.

It still flowing through her, burning her blood with intense and exquisite agony. Again, she wrestled her will against it, pushing it back down, through her torso, her hips, her legs, through her feet and into the ground.

Finally released from the earth's power, a cry behind her made her turn to face this new threat. Had she let the power go too soon?

Now, Oisinne stood before her. Not broken and mad like in the human world, but tall and strong, his eyes twinkling with humor and intelligence. *This* was the man she'd married. The man she'd defied her own father for, the man she'd fallen hopelessly in love for. The man she'd laid with under the summer sky, making love for hours in sweaty abandon.

Oisinne reached for her, and for a moment, she longed to fall into his arms. She ached for that forgotten magic of young love, that giddiness and glee of discovering each other's bodies. She stretched her hand out, their fingertips brushing with a spark of power.

A flicker of movement on his hand caught her eye, and she spied something beneath the skin. Clíodhna squinted and the hand became a feral claw, cruel and sharp. She jerked away from his grasp and danced back. "Who are you?"

In a cloying, rasping voice, he said, "I'm your husband, Clíodhna. Do you not know me?"

Eying the claw, she said, "My husband is sleeping in my house. You are not Oisinne."

"But I am. Do you not remember how we met? You looked so tempting, with your black hair loose and long, wet from the river."

The memory swept through her mind. She'd been bathing, certain of her privacy, when Oisinne came upon her and stole her clothing. She'd gone on a merry chase through the woods but she'd caught him.

A smile crept upon her face, but she wiped it away. "You're not Oisinne."

He took a step closer. "I have his body and his memories. Who else would I be?"

Such an odd phrasing. Clíodhna didn't trust it, not here in Faerie. Though she wasn't actually in Faerie, was she? She was just in a dream of Faerie, an imagination of her own construction. This imagined Oisinne possessed her memory as well.

She took another step back and considered drawing again on the earth. Whoever this creature might be, she didn't trust him.

He laughed. Something in the tone triggered recognition and her blood chilled. She knew who she faced. "Bodach, go away, I don't want you in my dream. Begone!"

He took a step closer, his smile deepening into a leer. "But I want to make love to you like you have with your dear husband. It's his body, nothing new or unusual. I would taste your sweet nectar, my flower, and enjoy your charms as Oisinne has. As Adhna has. As your pet monk has. You have plenty to sate us all."

The earth hammered at her feet, eager to enter her body once again. Her skin, however, tingled with anticipation and desire, begging her to say yes. To feel hot hands run across her curves, hot lips on hers.

Bodach reached out to stroke her hair. "If you won't allow me to taste of your body, Clíodhna, let me swim in your memories. Tell me how Adhna escaped my trap, and I shall let you go free."

She took two more steps back, out of reach. "Ha! As if I'd believed any offer you gave me, Bodach. Go."

"But it's true, my honeysuckle. Sweet, sweet, Clíodhna. Adhna can't give you a fraction of the pleasure I can. He's bound to being kind and gentle. Sometimes gentle is too easy. I can give you intense bliss with just a little pain. All I need is a bit of information, and the ultimate delight is yours."

The tingling she'd felt when he touched her before returned, deep within her pelvis, but she ignored it. Instead, she called the earth's power. This time, she knew to control her draw, only pulling what she needed. Even so, it flooded her.

In the mortal realm, it had taken all her will to call up even a tendril, but in Faerie, that trickle was a rushing river. Blasted by the torrent, she shoved most of it back as she reeled.

Bodach let out a nasty laugh. "Do you believe your paltry powers can stop me, human? It's silly of you to try. It would be so much easier to just give me what I want. I promise you won't regret it. I vow to give you a fair exchange. Your body craves it. I can smell your sweet, salty desire. It calls to me."

With a horrid realization, Clíodhna realized he wasn't lying. Her body ached to embrace him and experience everything he promised. In her dream state, her body took two steps forward, despite her revulsion. Her skin itched for his touch, hot and desperate. Sweat shone on her arms, glistening in the light.

"Ah, yes, just like that. Come to me, my flower. Let me lick your petals and plunge my stinger inside your—"

She slammed him with earth power in the middle of his chest.

He stumbled back with a cry of rage. "Treacherous human! For that, your children will pay!"

This thread made Clíodhna's rage burn white-hot, and she stopped tamping down on the earth's energy. She pulled on the full torrent and blasted him.

With wave after wave of power, she pushed the earth magic into his chest like a raging rockfall until he stumbled back. Further and further, step by step, she pushed Bodach away from her dream-body. "You will not harm my children, do you hear me! Stay away from me, stay away from my family. Stay away from everything I love!"

Oisinne's skin melted away, leaving the bark-skinned Bodach. This form, too, splintered away, sparkling into tiny motes and those motes danced into the darkness.

Another voice echoed in her mind, a kinder, gentler voice. "Clíodhna, you must leave." Adhna's voice.

"Leave where? Here? I'm trying to!"

"You need to leave your home."

"What? I can't do that! I have to care for Oisinne. Where would I go? Will you get out of my head? I don't want to talk to nothing."

As shining motes danced back from the night, they formed into her lover's body. His mouth curved into a welcoming smile, his arms out. "You look well in dream-form, Clíodhna."

She stepped back. "Are you really Adhna?"

He dropped his arms. "I am, but I will not make you touch me to verify. However, I can't stay long. I only came to urge you to leave."

Clíodhna bit her lip. "I can't leave, Adhna. I have my children and Oisinne. And the new one on the way." She patted her stomach, just beginning to bulge.

They both shared a smile. "I know it will be dangerous, but the man of the new religion has been gaining power, and he's making a plan. He'll hurt you if you stay. He'll hurt your children."

She clenched her jaw. "I've had just about enough of people threatening my children! Adhna, if you have a solution, I'd like to hear it. Otherwise, you're throwing water into the wind."

"Come to Faerie."

She glanced around and laughed. "Here? Where Bodach can attack me? I think not."

He clasped his hands in front of him and placed his two index fingers on his lips. "I have a place where I can keep you safe, you and your children. I might even be able to help Oisinne's mind."

Clíodhna raised her eyebrows, still wary. "What sort of place? In the Queen's Court?"

His eyes grew wide. "Nothing so grand. A small cottage near a pond. It will be quiet and lonely, but safer."

"Safer. Not safe, but safer. I don't like that, Adhna."

He gave a sad shrug. "Safer is the best I can offer, Clíodhna. Even that will take all my power and influence. If you come, however, you will only be able to return once to the mortal world. That visit can be as long as you wish, but only one journey back."

Clíodhna lowered her gaze. "I'll think about it. If I agree, I'll come to the stone circle."

He bowed his head, and the motes flew away again, swirling up to form stars in the ink-black sky.

Chapter Eleven

Clíodhna stumbled out of her dream and back into the mortal realm. She shot up, woken by the crackle of the fire. Glowing coals had burst into a raging hearth fire, the flames reaching for her body. She scrambled back from the hungry, flickering flames and tried to regain her balance, both physical and mental.

Donn came out, rubbing his eyes. "Ma? Are you still out here? It's almost dawn."

After dusting off her clothing, she stood to face him. "Sorry to wake you, dear. I slept out here but had a bad dream." Clíodhna stared at her eldest son for a moment. "Donn, if we left the village, would you be horribly upset?"

He blinked a few times, still not awake. "Leave? To where?"

"A friend said he had a safe place for us all. A cottage near a pond."

"That Fae friend of yours?"

Asleep or awake, her son wasn't stupid. "The same."

He bit his lip, watching the fire. "I don't know. I love my classes at the abbey. But I haven't been going lately, because of your fight with the abbot."

She felt as if Donn had punched her in the gut. "*My* fight? He tried to take you away from me! How is this my fault?"

He picked at his fingers. "I don't blame you, Ma! But if you just acted more like the other mothers, maybe he wouldn't be so angry with you all the time."

Etromma stumbled out, her hair a tangled mess. "What's all the shouting about?"

"Ma wants us to move away with her lover."

Clíodhna rolled her eyes. "That's not what I meant, Donn, and you know it! I'm just trying to find a place that's safe for all of us."

Etromma stared at Clíodhna, her mouth agape. "Move away? But Ma, that would mean I'd have to leave Tirechan! You can't do this to me!"

After covering her face with her hands, Clíodhna rubbed it, trying to dispel the mounting fight before it escalated. "I'm just trying to keep everyone safe."

Etromma rubbed her arms and scowled at the fire. "I'll be plenty safe as Tirechan's wife."

Donn glanced at his sister, nodding. "And I'd be safe in the abbey, as Brother Cronan's apprentice. I should have a trade other than just fishing, anyhow, don't you think?"

Clíodhna glared at her elder children, not wanting to admit they'd grown into independent people, with their own thoughts and dreams. She'd have to let them go, and she didn't want to admit that, even to herself.

Aileran wailed, his voice piercing the pre-dawn silence. Clíodhna heaved a sigh, wishing for a way to start the conversation all over again. A bird darted across the clearing, almost straight at her. She ducked and cursed, then stalked into the roundhouse to comfort her baby. She sat beside the baby's cot, cradling him close and humming him back into sleep.

Warmth on her face woke her again. Clíodhna stared at the daylight and still clutching Aileran, she rushed out to greet the dawn. She'd neglected such devotions and felt strong guilt for her omission.

Almost as if in reaction, the dawn rose deep red, an angry, sullen color. A heavy blanket of dark gray clouds swallowed the sun mere moments after it rose. The air cooled considerably as it disappeared, and she shivered.

Setting the still-sleeping child next to her, she honored the dawn, silently begging the gods to forgive her neglect of her duties.

Clíodhna spoke no more of moving to Faerie, but her children whispered about it when they thought she couldn't hear. They made plans to escape, either to the blacksmith's home or to the abbey.

Why had she fought so hard to keep her children if they would only leave her at the first sign of trouble? No, she had to be realistic. They were fourteen and sixteen winters now, old enough to be on their own soon. They'd marry and move in with their spouses soon, regardless of her feud with the abbot.

With a sigh, she hugged Aileran to her bosom. At least she still had one son left, one who would love her a few more seasons yet. And another child on the way, a child of Adhna's blood. A Fae child.

Escaping to Faerie seemed a much better prospect now. How would Aileran and her coming baby fare in that strange land? At least they'd be with her.

A sound from inside the roundhouse made her guilt surge forth again. Oisinne moaned and coughed. With a sigh, she hefted Aileran into her arms and went to see if Oisinne had woken from her spell yet.

Her husband was still asleep, but he tossed and groaned when she knelt beside him. Aileran reached a pudgy hand out, but she kept the baby away from his father. "No, dear. Da can't hold you just now."

Clíodhna wondered if she'd ever again trust Oisinne to hold Aileran. His ropes looked loose, but day had dawned, so she ought to free him.

Just as she untied the last knot, her vision grew dizzy, and weakness swept over her body. She fell to her knees, grunting from the pain. As she fell, Oisinne sat straight up in bed, looking around with feral eyes, wide and unrecognizable.

They didn't have the same knowing evil as when Bodach possessed him in her dream. No, this was something different, a bestial, barren expression filled with vile hatred which chilled her to her core.

Scrambling away, she held Aileran close, but her crazed husband stalked her. She couldn't get up without dropping the baby, so she kicked at him. Oisinne clawed at her legs, ripping welts in her skin. Clíodhna screamed and pulled on the earth's power to shove him back, but she'd had no time to prepare.

Still weakened from whatever had made her woozy, the earth only gave her a trickle of energy. That bit of power shoved Oisinne back a few hand-spans, but no further.

"Donn! Etromma!" But they must have left after their heated discussion. Curse her for driving her own children away.

Oisinne dove for her again, his hands reaching for her face. Her heart racing, she planted one foot in his chest. He was too heavy for her to push away easily, but it kept his fingers from her eyes. He scrabbled at her, unable to get past her leg. She tried to push him further but had no leverage while holding the baby.

Panic rose in her chest. Oisinne yanked the edge of her *léine* and ripped, exposing her torso, but Clíodhna might as well have been a tree stump for all the effect it had on Oisinne.

Most men, when confronted with a naked woman, changed their expression. Their gaze held some level of leer, even if it also held love. Oisinne looked upon her only as prey.

If the earth would not obey her command, could she call the weather into the roundhouse?

Clíodhna drew a gale of wind inside the house. At first, only a light breeze answered her command, but as Oisinne's clawed hands edged closer to her face, her desperation increased her power.

A huge gust pushed him back. Not enough to let her escape, but enough for her to struggle to her feet. He lunged for her legs, wrapping his arms around them, but she scrambled away.

If only she'd learned to call the *Sluagh Sídhe* to help. The wild Fae liked her, but those had only appeared when Abbot Pátraic attacked her.

Clíodhna grabbed the brooch Adhna had gifted her. Nothing else but her baby mattered at the moment.

She sprinted for the door, clutching Aileran so tight he bawled in pain and confusion.

The mid-morning sun made her blink at the glare. A howl behind her made her turn, anger rising in her blood. She'd had enough of running for her life.

Now that she had access to the spirits of the air, she drew down power from the sky. Clouds roiled in inky blackness, a maelstrom of rage from her mind manifest in the heavens.

Just as Oisinne's crazed face appeared in the door, running straight toward her, a thick bolt of lightning cracked at his feet. He paused, wrinkled his nose, and came for her again.

After swallowing against her guilt, Clíodhna drew down lightning a second time. She'd given enough warnings. This one was aimed for Oisinne directly.

The energy crackled in her hands as her husband came closer and the clouds readied for her final strike. Her arm hairs rose as the energy escalated. A massive slam of power struck Oisinne, lighting his body with an eerie glow. He danced in place and then collapsed.

Unwilling to wait and see if she'd killed the crazed creature who had once been her loving husband of seventeen winters, Clíodhna ran up the path, toward the standing stones.

The rain didn't stop as she left the clearing, but Clíodhna didn't care. Somber weather matched her mood. Her guilt over attacking Oisinne with deadly magic had been barely balanced by his obvious insanity. He'd come for her and her babe. She couldn't have mercy upon such murderous intent.

Clíodhna wanted desperately to go back for her other children, but they'd grown into adulthood now, and were safer without her. She only hoped Etromma and Donn would find solace in their lives.

She didn't even dare return to make sure they settled. Would they mourn her? Would they mourn their father? She might never see her children again. Tears fell unnoticed with the raindrops.

Yet, Adhna had said she might return once again to the mortal world, should she escape to Faerie now. Perhaps, in a few winters, she might come back and see her children grown into fine adults, with families of their own.

Clíodhna hugged Aileran to her chest, anxious to keep her remaining child safe in her arms.

The guardian stones loomed black and slick wet, emerging from the mists like silent sentries. When the circle came into view, fog clung the tops of the stones, shrouding them in mystery. The day turned dim with her summoned storm.

Now thoroughly soaked, she sat in the center of the circle and gave in to her sobs. She heaved with misery, cradling Aileran and shielding him from the cold rain. He fussed and whimpered as he nuzzled against her chest, searching for milk but she couldn't even respond to this primal need.

I murdered my husband. No matter if it had been in defense, I killed him. And I drove off Etromma and Donn to their own fates, without a word of goodbye, a blessing, or a kiss. I'm a horrible mother. Aileran would be better off anywhere but in my arms, shivering and hungry on a Faerie hill.

The rain pelted them now and the ground began to rumble.

This last pulled her from her misery. She gave in to Aileran's quest and pulled out a breast for him to feed upon. The earth's rumbling continued, like a herd of horses galloping past, but no outside noise pierced the pouring rain and her own hiccups.

She had to call Adhna, but he said he might not come right away. What if she had to wait for days? She'd grabbed no supplies for a long wait.

Aileran had milk, but she had no bread, cheese, or meat. She'd never been a good hunter and besides, she had no weapons. She held only her brooch, her magic, and her determination.

After breathing the damp air deep into her lungs, Clíodhna stood, still cradling Aileran close. Raising her face to the sky, she called to Adhna, begging him to come to her and take her to Faerie. Three times, she called. The power of her request resonated through her blood, but no answer came.

With a sigh, she sat back down in the mud. Now, she'd have to wait. With an annoyed glance at the sky, she shoved the clouds away. She was done with the storm and was tired of being cold and wet. If only she had the power to dry herself.

That rumble returned, stronger than before. Her legs tingled where they touched the earth. She stood back up and placed her back to the largest standing stone, wishing she had a knife.

As Aileran fussed, she also wished she'd found somewhere safe for him, somewhere other than on this mystical Faerie hill with only a tired woman for protection.

A third rumble came. This time, hoofbeats accompanied the rumbling. Many hoofbeats, not just one horse. Rustling to the north made her turn to meet this new threat.

The first figure to burst forth from the tree line was resplendent upon a magnificent black horse. He had bedecked his bark-skinned body with ivy and vines, which trailed after him like pennants in the wind. Clíodhna recognized Bodach and her heart raced. She cowered against the nearest stone.

Behind the Fae Lord trailed at least ten lesser Fae, each one carrying a bronze, leaf-shaped sword, brandished for battle. They circled the stones with practiced precision, their swords pointed inward at her.

Bodach held back as they took their positions. Once they halted, frozen in posture, he dismounted and sauntered toward her.

"So, it seems you need some help, my lovely. I can taste your desperation, and it's delectable." He took in a deep sniff, as if savoring the aroma of roasting meat. After letting his breath out with a satisfied sigh, he smiled at her.

Bodach didn't have a cheerful smile, or even one of glee. His smile assured her he knew full well the terror he inspired within her heart, and he relished that knowledge.

Still standing with her back pressed against the stone, she drew upon the air, calling her power to her defense.

"No! None of that! Not this time!" He snapped his fingers, and his entourage raised their sword tips. Her swirling clouds had formed into a tight circle, ready to obey her, but the lesser Fae raised a circle of their own, made of wind. This wind twisted and dissipated her clouds with a snap of energy.

The backlash slammed against her, pushing all air from her lungs. She gasped for breath as Aileran croaked out a cry of protest. *Adhna, where are you?*

Rocked by the counter-magic, Clíodhna tried again. This time, she drew the tendrils of earth energy into her body, disappointed that she found no raging river of power to wrestle under control like in her dream.

Blue-white light traveled up her legs and body and shot out of her arm. She didn't direct it at Bodach, but at the sword hand of one of his guards. As the magic knocked his sword twirling toward the ground, he let out a cry of surprise.

Bodach reacted with a shout of rage. She disarmed three more guards before he attacked.

The Fae reached for her arm, his bark skin digging into her flesh. Clíodhna let out a scream but still threw power at each guard. Five disarmed now, and the others milled about, unsure what to do.

The first had dismounted and bent to retrieve his bronze sword, but it sparked when he touched it. He jumped back, cautious at the remaining energy held by the metal.

Pain shot through her arm as Bodach bent it behind her. She screeched in frustration and pain. But Clíodhna couldn't physically attack him, not with Aileran wailing in her other arm.

She directed her next blast at the Fae Lord, but he just cackled at her attempt. "Not so fast, my flower. You took me by surprise before, but now I've bolstered my own protections against your sort of power. You won't overcome me so easily this time."

He bent her arm further up her back. Gritting her teeth, Clíodhna refused to scream again and give him satisfaction.

"Come now, just another lovely whimper. I relish your pain so." He placed his other hand on her belly, pressing the small lump. "Oh, I see you're with child. Now that's an interesting development."

"Get away from me!" Clíodhna shoved her body against him, but he held her fast, almost embracing her with one arm behind her.

His breath, hot against her cheek, smelled of woodsmoke and the sickly sweet of rotting fruit. He placed his mouth on hers, though she drew back. She hit her head on the stone behind her, unable to escape further.

Bodach's cruel, passionate kiss made her body thrum with desire, despite her revulsion. Her flesh desired his with every fiber, pushing up against his body. Her nether region tingled with need, urging her to open her legs and welcome him.

The Fae's free hand roamed over her belly and around her hip. Then he stroked her buttocks, pressing her against him. She squirmed with both horror and pleasure.

"Ah, yes, exactly like that."

Aileran grabbed Bodach's lip and pulled hard.

The bark-skinned Fae snapped to one of his guards, "Tominn! Take the brat. It's time to complete this one's initiation."

"No!" All sensual compulsion fled as Clíodhna clutched her child tight, resisting Tommin's attempt to take him.

"Fool! I'll do it." Bodach released her arm and grabbed the child. Clíodhna swung her arm around and, with all the panic and fright of the day, punched him in the eye.

He jumped back with a shout. "Daughter of a pig! For that, your spawn will pay!"

Clíodhna sprinted from the circle, past the startled Tominn, past the guardian stones, and down the sparkling path. She didn't dare look back despite the hoofbeats chasing her.

She couldn't concentrate enough while running to call on her full air power or to aim, but she threw a few lightning bolts behind her, felling trees to impede their progress. She made it all the way to her roundhouse before her pursuers caught up with her.

Nothing lay in the clearing before the house, not even the smoking corpse of her husband.

Confused, she scanned the clearing, searching for some trace of Oisinne, but nothing remained. Had she imagined the attack?

But Clíodhna couldn't bother with it now. She must escape Bodach. *Adhna, where are you?*

She kept running to the village. While it had never been a sanctuary in the past, with a host of Fae warriors running her down, it was the only option left.

They wouldn't dare ride into a village full of mortals, would they? Abbot Pátraic would sooner banish her than hide her. She might be running straight into her own doom.

Maybe she could get to the river. Running water might stop the Faeries. But the river wasn't anywhere near the path, and would involve tramping through the forest, which would slow her down.

A voice hissed from the trees on her right. "Clíodhna! This way!"

Relief washed over her as she recognized her lover's voice. "Adhna? Is that you?"

"Of course, it is. You called, didn't you? Come, quickly now!"

Adhna pulled her through a rhododendron bramble, the thorns scratching both her and Aileran. When the boy cried out, she tried to shush him. In desperation, she stuck a breast in his mouth. He whimpered, but much more quietly.

Frowning at the baby, Adhna said, "We may have to leave him here, Clíodhna."

She halted, aghast. "What? What do you mean, leave him? He's my son! I can't abandon him!"

190

"Not so loud! Bodach and his lackeys are still searching for you. I left a false trail, but that won't fool him long. And I don't mean you must abandon him. You have a friend, Ita, right? We might have to leave him to her care."

"I can't leave my son, Adhna."

He tugged on her arm, urging her forward. "The passage to Faerie is dangerous for a mortal child. He'd be safer there, and we can escape more easily."

Clíodhna hugged Aileran to her chest as he dribbled milk. She mopped it up awkwardly as she followed Adhna.

He led her through bracken and down a deer trail toward the village, in a roundabout way. When they emerged from the woods, Ita's farm perched on the next hill.

Clíodhna panicked and backed up, clutching her baby tight and shaking her head. "No, no, I won't leave my last child!"

Adhna placed a gentle hand on her belly. "You have another coming. Our child. He'll be much better suited for life in Faerie, being of the blood."

"I thought you said I had Fae blood already? That means Aileran has some."

He placed a kind hand on her cheek. "Not enough, love. Not enough to shield him from the temptations and dangers of the land itself."

Clíodhna had no tears left, not after the trials of the day. With numb acceptance, she followed Adhna as he pulled her toward Ita's house.

Chapter Twelve

Adhna's cottage, on the edge of the Faerie marshlands

Adhna hadn't lied about the peace of his home. Clíodhna lounged next to the pond, watching insects who looked almost like butterflies dance on the surface, wheeling and diving in all the colors of the rainbow.

His cozy cottage had room for both of them and a delightfully carved wooden lintel. Images of wolfhounds entwined with hares along the edge and over the door.

Bees buzzed around them, but Adhna said he couldn't hive them here in Faerie like he did in the mortal world. She missed honey, as well as bread and cheese. Nevertheless, they ate well enough on fruit and meat.

Clíodhna missed her children with intense pain every day. Each morning as she woke, she sent a mental message to each child, wishing them success, health, and wealth.

They'd never hear such messages, but it made her feel better to say them. Her heart ached for Aileran. Such a wee baby, and he'd never know his mother.

Ita had been confused but welcoming when they showed up on her doorstep, child in hand. Adhna offered to bring gifts of food for his upkeep, but she refused, promising to care for him along with her own. After a tearful parting, Clíodhna left with Adhna, her heart broken.

Now, the growing babe within her womb helped fill a small part of that void. This child, much more active than the others had been, kicked and prodded at all hours of the day.

Not that there was any real day here. No dawn to greet. No night to rouse the insects. But she slept when she grew tired and when the child let her.

It felt so odd to have no real duties or struggle. They had no animals to care for, nor a garden to tend. She asked that Adhna at least allow her to prune the flowers growing around the pond and pick some to brighten the interior of the roundhouse.

Within a few sleeps, she'd grown heartily bored with this idle life. She didn't know what to do with herself. But when she asked about visiting other areas of Faerie, his expression grew grim. "Not yet, love. Bodach still searches for you, though he searches in the mortal world."

Clíodhna pursed her lips. "What about Donn and Etromma? Can he hurt them?"

He shook his head and placed a reassuring hand on her arm. "No, I've placed protections on each of your children, so he can't harm them directly. And he can't find you here, as I've built strong wards over the winters. This isn't the first time I've had to deal with predatory Fae Lords, and I doubt it will be the last. However, if you go wandering in the marshes, for instance, those protections would no longer keep you from his minions."

Clíodhna chewed her lip and let out a long breath. Her hands itched to do something. Perhaps she'd make some baskets. She'd never been crafty except for her carving, but she must find something to fill her waking time.

The baby kicked again, drawing her attention to her growing stomach. It distended now, as her time grew nearer. She didn't know how many moons she'd spent in Faerie, but her belly and her body told her what she needed to know.

This would be her fifth birth, though she only had three living children. A stillborn daughter still tugged at her memory. Her name would have been Samthann.

Sadness threatened to overwhelm her as Clíodhna grew nostalgic and morose. She felt more prone to such melancholy here, though it may be due to her pregnancy.

Still, she must fill her time. So, after asking Adhna for some cutting tools she'd taken up carving again. All the tools were made of bone or bronze, as nothing iron would be tolerated in Faerie. Adhna brought her several branches of soft wood to practice on.

Faerie wood reacted differently than wood in the mortal world. It had an odd suppleness that pleased her. It bent and molded to pressure, so she could almost shape it with her hands at times.

Her initial attempts came out clumsy and horrible, but with enough time, she might get as good as she'd once been. She might even become as good as Donn. That thought brought on the melancholy again.

After picking up her latest project, a length of soft wood she'd been carving into ivy around a pillar, a pang in her lower back made her groan. Clíodhna pressed her hand on that spot to ease the pain.

The pressure helped, and she bent to pick a carving tool. Choosing a curved bone pick, she stippled along the edge of an ivy leaf, pushing the soft wood down to raise the edge of the leaf.

One of the non-butterflies lit upon the end of her wood. Its wings shimmered with rainbow iridescence, making her grin with delight.

Faerie had an intense beauty, like nothing she'd ever before beheld. When she left again for the mortal world, a part of her would stay here, mourning the loss of that beauty to her dying day.

For now, she was content to enjoy the lovely things all around her. The insects, the trees, the dawnless light, and the still pond.

That still pond grew ripples, startling her out of her reverie. The disturbance became a head, something small and knobby, rising and coming toward the shore.

Clíodhna's heart raced as she grabbed a stout branch next to her, a future carving project. It would work as a cudgel, though she was in no condition for a physical brawl.

The creature emerged from the pond, dripping and pitiful. Wet hair matted along its back, and it shook like a dog, flinging droplets in all directions. Clíodhna covered her face from the onslaught and asked with caution, "Greetings. Who are you?"

Barely half her height but at least twice her mass, the creature looked like a boulder. His skin, except for the stripe of yellow hair down its back and on its head, was like polished granite, sparkling in the light when he moved. He crunched when he walked, as if stone scraped against stone. "I am Crunn. I have a message."

Adhna had just left to answer a summons from the Queen. Who else would know where to send a message?

He grinned, white pebble teeth showing bright. "From Fae you helped in the mortal world. They send word of your children. Adhna bid them keep an eye on your younglings, and to report anything unusual."

Clíodhna let out a ragged breath of relief. How considerate of Adhna to arrange for news. Her instincts for hospitality kicked in. "May I offer you food or drink? How are my children doing?"

Crunn sat on the shore, which allowed her to sit. "I require no sustenance, but if you would perhaps sing something for me before I leave, I should be most grateful."

"Sing? You enjoy songs?"

His mouth stretched even wider and creaked. "They're my greatest weakness, especially those of mortal women. I have thus found much trouble in my life."

Wondering idly what might trouble a magical creature made of stone, Clíodhna clasped her hands. "What news do you bring me? And I'd be glad to sing a song in payment."

"I have three pieces of news, one for each child. Would you gift me a song for each?"

She let out a chuckle. "Very well, three songs for three pieces of information."

"Your daughter, the one with the death iron man? She has made her vows to him and is with child, as you are."

The death iron man? Oh, he must mean the blacksmith. I understand why he would refer to a man who works with iron, deadly to the Fae.

Then the meaning of his words struck her. *Etromma married and pregnant! Our babies will be similar in age. But she is so young!*

"Crunn, how much time has passed in the mortal world since I've been here?"

The stone crunched as his smile slipped. "I am not sure how mortals measure time, nor when you arrived."

"We count the winters as one cycle of the seasons. So, it starts when the mortal world grows cold. When it becomes spring, then summer, then autumn, and winter again, that's one."

He considered this for some time, touching each of his fingers several times, shaking his head, and trying again. "I do not know." He hung his head, ashamed of his failure.

She placed a gentle hand on his head, and his skin felt like cold stone. "Don't worry. I'll ask Adhna. He's got a good grasp of mortal timer. What's your second piece of news?"

"Your older male child has also vowed, but with the men of the new god. He is a skilled craftsman, and was sent away to work on a new stone structure in the north."

In the north. Perhaps the same place Odhrán went, to start the new church? Would he remember Odhrán and speak of her? Nostalgia swept over her again and she took in a deep breath. "And your third news?"

"The baby male child has grown. He seems happy, as he laughs often. He is skilled with handling horses, and rides fast and long each day."

Aileran riding horses spoke more of the passage of time than any of the others. If her toddler was racing horses now, at least ten winters had passed.

Tears burned behind her eyes, but she swallowed them down for her guest's sake. How rude to cry in front of her messenger.

"I might even have a fourth bit of news."

Fourth? Did he speak of Oisinne? Or maybe Odhrán had returned? "Will you take a fourth song for it?"

With a slow nod, he agreed. "Yes, but it must be a special song. This information was difficult to discover."

Intrigued, Clíodhna agreed. "Four songs, with one being extra special."

"There is a female in your home. She moved in when you disappeared, and the children moved away. She did not live there before."

Not Oisinne, then. "Can you describe the woman?"

"She has great power. Red hair, strong arms, pale skin, spots on her face."

"Freckles, do you mean?" Clíodhna pointed to the ones on her own arm.

Crunn nodded with such vigor, his chin crackled. "Freckles, yes. She picks herbs and has a cow with red ears."

What an odd description. She searched her memory, but didn't recall having met someone like that. With a shake of her head, Clíodhna decided she must have taken over their roundhouse when they'd abandoned it. As peeved as she might be about the theft, she could do little about it, from Faerie.

Her back ached again, and she groaned when the pain gripped her spine. Crunn jumped up, his gaze darting around to find the threat.

She waved him back down. "No, nothing attacked me, Crunn. My back hurts, that's all."

"No, no, no! Your child is coming! Your child is coming! I must fetch her! Adhna made me promise I'd fetch her!"

Before Clíodhna had the chance to ask who in the name of the gods he meant, Crunn ran into the water and disappeared beneath the surface. The ripples died as the pain traveled up her spine and down her legs.

She stumbled toward the roundhouse, her carving project abandoned. With a great deal of grunting and cursing, she crawled to her pallet and lay flat, hoping to relieve some painful pressure on her back.

Would Crunn return? He must, in order to get his songs. Somehow, that realization comforted her as a wave of agony swept through her torso and down her legs, making her feet tingle as if she'd crossed them too long. Her arms burned and sweat dripped from her face.

I can't do this alone! Where's Adhna? He promised to find me a midwife.

Clíodhna didn't know how long she drifted in and out between bouts of aching and panting. Time lost all meaning when each breath came with agonizing pain, a burning throb through her body.

No sun meant the afternoon didn't wane. No birds heralded the dawn. No night clothed the hills in darkness. No relief came to her, despite all her curses, prayers, and pleading.

When someone darkened the roundhouse door, she stared at the form, trying to discern if it was help or threat. Not that she could give battle in her state.

A woman stood in silhouette, glaring at her. "You shouldn't have started yet, child! Well, done is done. Let me fetch some supplies." She disappeared again.

When the woman reappeared, she carried two bronze cauldrons of water. After depositing them along the wall, she then rifled through Adhna's things to find several cloths, a strip of old leather, and a meadskin.

She handed the last to Clíodhna. "Take a good swig of that, Clíodhna. It will help with the pain."

Clíodhna drank deep of the sweet, potent alcohol. The suffusing warmth through her limbs made her sigh as the pain dimmed. It would come back, but for now, she felt amazing.

"Now, let me just get you better situated. Did you just lie down on the bare floor? Tsk, tsk. You've had children before. You should know better. Now, a few cushions here, for under your knees, and one under your back. That should help. Doesn't it help?"

Clíodhna couldn't even form words as another wave hit her.

"Oh, I didn't introduce myself, did I? I'm Brighid, and as you may have gathered, I'm well-versed in midwifery. You might even say I'm an expert." Brighid let out a deep, loud laugh at her own quip.

Brighid. As in the goddess of healing? Clíodhna narrowed her eyes at the woman.

"Yes, the very same. You needn't glare at me, young lady. I know who you are and what you've done and who you're to be. At the moment, though, none of that matters. What matters now is that child you're about to bear. We shall bring him into this world as quickly and cleanly as we might. It's not every day a Fae has a child!"

Brighid examined her by peering between her legs, probing with her fingers, pressing against her belly, and mumbling under her breath. "No, that's not right. Danú take it, I'll need to turn the stubborn child before he hurts himself."

A sprite flew in, flicked to each dark corner, and flitted out again. Another followed, then three more. The small roundhouse buzzed with Fae creatures, their sharp little beetle wings clicking and rattling so loud, Clíodhna covered her ears.

Brighid waved her arms. "Out! Out, the lot of you! I have work to do. Now, Clíodhna, sip this tea. It will help relax your muscles."

She struggled to sit up, but Brighid held her down. "No, don't rise. I'll pour it in your mouth. Don't worry, it's not scalding hot."

The warm liquid dribbled in her mouth, and she coughed, choking on it before she mastered the trick of swallowing as the goddess poured. She jerked, causing more to spill from the cup and almost drowning her.

"Not so much, child! This is potent magic! Ah well, done is done."

Within a few moments, her muscles eased and melted within her body. Clíodhna's vision grayed to a pleasant fuzziness. She drifted on the cloud of whimsy, musing she might sleep for eternity.

"Now, with what little will you have left, I want you to push. The babe is ready to crown soon and needs a bit of help to finish his journey."

Familiar with the routine, Clíodhna tried to strain, but her muscles refused to cooperate.

Brighid *tsked* under her breath. "Oh, I must have given you too much. Never mind, it'll wear off soon enough. Try again."

Strain as she might, her body ignored her attempts.

"Danú take it, that baby is ready to come. I suppose I must do this myself. Be still." Brighid placed her hands over Clíodhna's taut belly, a warm magic suffusing the skin and sinking into her body.

Clíodhna moaned from pleasure and delight, rather than pain. Inside, the warmth felt delicious, like a summer swim in the hot sun.

The baby turned and twisted inside her. Her pain dulled, flying away on the chittering wings of a Fae sprite. She let out a long, low sigh at the release.

"Ah yes, much better. Now, the babe is ready to come out. Can you push yet?"

She tried, but her muscles remained in languid repose, refusing to obey her commands.

"Very well. Let's try something else."

Once again, Brighid laid her hands on Clíodhna's belly, but lower this time. The babe moved, pulsing like a heartbeat closer to her cleft. Once, twice, thrice, his head stretched her wide. Once, twice, thrice, the pain of the taut skin made her screech. Once, twice, thrice, her scream died into a whimper. Again and again, Brighid coaxed the child out of her womb, but the baby refused to get past a certain point.

Adhna rushed in, frantic and desperate eyes darting everywhere. "What can I do? How can I help?"

"You can help by getting out. Wait, have you any seaweed?"

"Seaweed? Why would I have seaweed?"

Brighid waved her hand. "Never mind. Get more water."

He scowled, eyeing the cauldrons. "You have plenty of water."

"Go get more! I need you out of my hair. I'm busy enough without babysitting a panicked father. Shoo!"

With a longing glance at Clíodhna and a blown kiss, Adhna ran out of the roundhouse. Clíodhna still floated on her relaxing cloud and didn't care. All that mattered now was the sweet relief from pain.

Once, twice, thrice, Brighid pulled the baby closer to birth. This time, his head crowned and the rest of the body slipped out, slithering in a mess.

"Another few pushes for the afterbirth, my dear. There we go. Much better, no? A wee, fine lad you've borne. Have you decided on a name?"

Her son's thin squalls filled the room, tugging her back from her cloud-dream. "Rumann. Adhna and I decided on Rumann."

"Rumann it is. A good, strong name for the youngling. He may not become a hero, but he will father a few, I'll tell you that. You've begun a strong legacy here, Clíodhna."

Eager to hold her baby, she stretched out her arms. Brighid cleaned and swaddled the babe after cutting his cord and placed him in his mother's eager embrace.

He nuzzled her, searching for his first meal. She wouldn't have milk yet, but the clear stuff should come. He sucked for a few moments before falling asleep against her sweaty skin.

Her own consciousness slipped away as the goddess' last words swam in her mind.

After endless darkness, something nuzzled her elbow. Clíodhna shifted to her side, and the seeker latched onto her breast, hard. She yelped and her eyes flew wide.

Memory of the difficult birth, Brighid's help, and her Rumann returned, and her expression softening to pure love. While cradling the soft skull with downy fuzz with her hand, she took a deep breath, smelling the sweet scent of baby.

Such a simple pleasure, forgotten as the child grew from milky fragrance to the odors of an active child.

A sprite flitted into the roundhouse and out again. It must be keeping watch, because Adhna appeared in a moment. "Are you rested, Clíodhna? What can I get you?"

"You can help me stand, Adhna. My bladder's about to burst!"

With a chuckle, he took Rumann from her arms and helped her to the basket of sand, steadying her when her knees wobbled.

Thus relieved, she hobbled back to the bed, but didn't want to lie down again. Yes, she was still exhausted, but she must regain her strength. She'd done so after each child, and she meant to repeat the habit.

Rumann grunted, searching Adhna's *léine* for milk. Clíodhna laughed as Adhna's expression turned to alarm and confusion. "Here, let me take him back. You can hold him after he's fed."

With great reluctance, he surrendered his son. His smile was so sweet that her heart ached for him. This must be his first child, to be so entranced.

But then she remembered her dream, the Fae who'd claimed to be Adhna's daughter. "Have you never had a child, Adhna?"

He let out a deep sigh. "Most Fae have a very difficult time with conceiving, though we live very long lives compared to mortals. Maybe once in five hundred of your winters, we'll sire a child."

Her eyes grew wide. "Five hundred winters! Adhna, how old *are* you?"

He laughed, stroking her hair, which only made her realize how badly she needed a bath. "Not so long, love. Merely a hundred so far. I'm but a child by Fae standards."

A hundred winters. Clíodhna only had a few over thirty, and she felt wise in the ways of the world. Her world, perhaps. But Faerie worked in strange ways. If she wanted to thrive here, she'd have to learn those ways. More so, she must master them.

She glanced at her baby. "As my son grows, we'll both have to teach him. Can we teach him the Fae magic, do you think?"

"It depends on his talent, but the odds are great. He's more than half-blood. Even if he shows no affinity for wild magic, his children might."

Clíodhna remembered Brighid's words about Rumann not being a hero and pressed her lips together. She'd prove the goddess wrong and teach her son everything he needed to be a great man. But to do that, she'd need to learn first. "You can begin by teaching me, then."

He gave her a half-smile, melting her heart. "What would you like to know?"

"I want to meet the different sorts of Fae. Talk to them. Work with them. You've taught me earth magic. I want to learn the others. Air, fire, water, and spirit. I want to be in command of my powers, not subject to their whims."

He chuckled and held out his hands. "Slow down, Clíodhna. That's a tall order. Why haven't you asked for this before?"

She patted her still distended belly. "I had other priorities. Now that the babe is born and healthy, I must move forward. For his sake *and* my own."

Adhna hugged her around the shoulders, planting a kiss on Rumann's forehead. The boy gurgled but didn't stop feeding. "Very well. I shall invite some marsh Fae here and we'll learn what we can of their ways. There are many types of wild Fae that might be friendly to you, and many others you should approach with extreme caution. Their loyalties may not always rely on the type of Fae, but the influence of a particular Fae Lord."

Clíodhna's blood grew icy. "Like Bodach?"

"Exactly like Bodach. He exerts a great deal of influence throughout the Fae communities and with the Queen's court."

Curiosity tickled her imagination. "What's Queen Áine like? What's her court like?"

Adhna shook his head with a half-smile. "Not yet. We don't dare approach the Queen until Rumann is older. We must ensure his safety before all else, wouldn't you agree?"

The idea of meeting the Faerie Queen both terrified and excited her. "But how can I protect myself from Bodach if I don't have the Queen's help?"

His expression turned grim. "There's no true protection from Bodach, Clíodhna."

She gave a reluctant nod. Rumann must be safe. But how could meeting the Queen be so dangerous? Would Adhna even be able to arrange a meeting?

True to his word, whenever Rumann fell asleep, Adhna summoned another Fae to meet Clíodhna. A series of sprites, *pukaí, grugachainn,* spirits of the pond, the grasses, the rolling hills, and the roundhouse itself. Each one told her their story, their hopes and dreams. She shared with them her own tale and made many friends.

Some frightened her with their grotesque appearances. Others took her breath away with sheer splendor. Each one possessed unique powers, personalities, and loyalties.

Clíodhna enjoyed having more friends than she'd ever had in her life. Now she had visitors every day, singing to her and playing with her hair, amusing Rumann with their antics.

Between visits, and when he didn't have duties for the Queen, she enjoyed Adhna's companionship.

He still taught her magic, but they no longer shared a student and teacher relationship. Having a child together cemented their partnership far better than any earthly vows. They lived and loved and laughed together as time passed and Rumann grew.

Crunn returned to collect his payment, so she sang him the first song. He insisted on only one at a time, so that he might savor each one.

With that first song, however, other Fae gathered. The assembled audience listened with rapt attention to her human voice. She could in no way compete with the perfection of Fae voices, but her human mistakes somehow made the songs more interesting to the lesser Fae. Her imperfections flavored it with intrigue.

One day, she was playing with Rumann while Adhna was on an errand for the Queen. She lifted her son up high to his delighted giggle and swung him low in a slow arc. He grabbed at the sprite who flitted out of his reach, but the sprite flew too fast.

A pond naiad, covered in green and blue scales, approached her, wringing her hands. Worry lines in her face spoke of obvious distress. "My mistress, I need help! My baby is caught in the reeds, and they won't let her go!"

With Rumann in her arms, Clíodhna tramped to the other edge of the pond where thorny reeds had caught a young naiad's gossamer fins.

With careful fingers, she untangled the young thing. When it came free, with only a small tear on one fin, she bobbed three times in thanks and dove under the surface. Her mother offered more substantial gratitude, a hug and a tear, before she followed her daughter.

After she helped the naiad, other Fae came to her for help. Caught wings, lost objects, spoiled food, each one required assistance of some type. Sometimes, she could help the Fae, but not always. At least trying made her feel useful.

Rumann delighted in the creatures and learned what he could get away with for each Fae. A few sharp raps with beetle wings or a lash with a whipping tail taught him to be gentle with each of them, and how much teasing was permitted.

Her son seemed to be learning how to survive in Faerie.

Chapter Twelve

With practiced fingers, Clíodhna pulled the thorn out of a *grugach*'s fleshy foot. The creature's eyes grew wide with abject fear and he fled into the tall grasses. The three sprites who'd been playing with Rumann followed suit, leaving the two humans alone in the clearing.

The ever-present light grew dim, so Clíodhna gathered her son into the safety of her arms and ran for the relative shelter of the roundhouse. She crawled under the table, well aware that it offered little real protection.

While weather didn't exist in Faerie, and she had no worries about heat, cold, or rain, that meant she had no way to call upon her best source of power. Therefore, any threat put her at a disadvantage.

The earth listened to her call, but she had yet to learn how to control the much stronger magic of the land of Faerie. She'd been working with Faerie earth, under Adhna's cautious tutelage, but she didn't yet have the skill she needed to defend herself.

The light dimmed more, and her heart raced. Rumann fussed against her chest, gripping her hair and pulling hard as he reacted to her fear. "Ow! Hush, Rumann. Shh."

"You need not silence your spawn, human."

She whirled to confront the voice, fearing Bodach had found them, but the voice booming through the valley sounded female. Powerful, confident, and strident. *Adhna, where are you?*

"Calling for your protector will do little good. He is powerless next to me."

Clíodhna cowered under the table, wrapping herself around her son. Something in this voice made her bones shiver.

The door darkened and a cold wind whipped into the roundhouse, making everything fly in a confusing mess. *Wind? Where had wind come from? Faerie had no wind.*

"Faerie has what I say it has. Show yourself."

Her body moved of its own accord, her knees straightening, but she maintained her death grip on Rumann. As she got to her feet, Clíodhna lifted her chin despite fear shooting through her heart.

The woman before her, if such a mundane term might apply to her, stood taller than any woman Clíodhna had ever seen. She wasn't slender or dainty, but had muscles and solid thighs, rounded curves.

Her clothing shifted from brilliant greens to soft blues, icy whites, and vivid yellows. Clíodhna had to blink from the radiance, despite the dimness.

Long, white curls framed an imperious, snow-white face with piercing black cat eyes. Her hands were planted on her hips as several tiny-winged Fae peered around at Clíodhna and Rumann, curiosity clear in their faces.

Three tall male Fae stood outside, their stiff postures and bronze spears making their position as guards obvious.

"Give me the child." Her voice split through Clíodhna's head and commanded obedience.

She stretched her arms out to hand over her child, but fought against the compulsion and pulled back. "No! You may not take my baby."

The tall woman laughed, the low rumble of a thunderstorm across the sea. "I will not take him from you, mortal creature. I wish to examine him. A child born of Fae is unusual enough that it requires my attention, especially when it's born in my very realm."

With great reluctance, Clíodhna complied with the woman, who could only be the Faerie Queen, and placed Rumann into her arms.

With lightning speed, Queen Áine shifted from commanding ruler to adoring mother. She beamed at the child, tickled his feet, and chuckled at his giggle. "The babe seems healthy. You may keep him."

Queen Áine handed Rumann back, and Clíodhna clutched him tightly. She tried to swallow away her nerves, but something blocked her throat. *Where was Adhna?* Rumann, startled by all the movement, fussed and chewed on her shoulder.

The Queen stared at Clíodhna, as if gazing into her very soul. Clíodhna tried to stare back into those black cat eyes, but she fell into their depths, as if hurtling down an endless pit. Her mind screamed as she fell, unable to look away or save herself. Pure terror took over her mind as she stood, frozen and staring.

Her strength against the Faerie Queen broke after only a few moments. She didn't dare look away, but she could blur her vision. Once blurred, she cast her gaze to the Queen's feet, a safer target than those eternal, dangerous eyes.

"You are a curious human. Not many can defy me. And you have gained much influence here. Did you think I wouldn't notice such a shift in my power base?"

The Queen's words chilled Clíodhna even further, and she bowed low in respect. "I had no intention of taking your power, my Queen. This place is isolated, and I am only trying to make friends in my new home."

210

Her voice turned even colder. "I do not like you, mortal woman. I do not want you living in my kingdom. However, the marsh Fae and some wild Fae have spoken for you, and Adhna is your loyal champion. You have borne a child of Fae blood. For those reasons, I shall allow you to remain, but only under certain conditions."

Clíodhna hadn't been of such political machinations while she fiddled with carving and telling stories. How many favors had Adhna pulled to be her champion? What had it cost him?

"You will raise the child by Fae standards and tutelage for as long as he dwells here. You will attend to me as a handmaiden as he grows. As my handmaiden, you will sing me your human songs each night. You owe them to Crunn, but the obligation has been passed to me."

Clíodhna's throat grew dry. "You've heard of my songs?"

The Queen's gentler manner disappeared. "I hear of everything that happens in my realm!"

Falling to her knees from the force of the Queen's disapproval, Clíodhna bowed her head. "I accept these conditions. What will my duties be as handmaiden, other than singing?"

"You will swear your loyalty to me, in word and in deed. Should you break this vow, your punishment will be swift and permanent. Come to my court when Adhna returns from his current mission."

By the time Clíodhna dared to look up, the Queen and her entourage had disappeared. The sky lightened to its former brightness, and the oppression of power lifted.

Clíodhna let out a long, shuddering breath. What had she just done? She'd barely considered her answer when she accepted a contract from not just any Faerie, but the Queen.

She cursed herself for being a prime fool and hugged her son.

Today, she must vow herself to the Queen.

When Adhna returned, she told him of all that had transpired. Then he wanted to take Rumann, but it broke her heart to give her last child up. She kept telling herself it was for his own safety, but she didn't believe it, not in her heart.

"I've found a safe place for him in the human world."

She let out a humorless laugh. "Safe? What's safe anymore?"

He gave her a kind smile. "A stolid fisherman and his grieving wife. Their own son died just days ago, and they'll welcome the new child."

Adhna placed a hand on the child's head. "They've agreed to keep his name Rumann. They wanted to change it to their dead son's name, but I convinced them it would cause them too much pain."

Clíodhna was grateful for the small favor. In the future, when she returned to that world, she might still be able to find her children.

He reached for the child, but pain struck her through her heart, and she pulled Rumann back. "No! No, I can't let him go yet. Please, just a little longer?"

Adhna let out a sigh. "For a few days. But I can't wait much longer than that, my love."

After that, she cuddled her son close, almost smothering him with her anticipated grief. Then, she steeled herself for her current task. Adhna sent her to court, as he was off on yet another mission for the Queen.

Clíodhna followed a glowing sprite down the path toward the court, fear rising with each step. As she reached the building, she stared up in wonder.

Soaring arches of delicate white branches met overhead, with autumn leaves forming a roof. A russet leaf, colored shining gold, fluttered down to the floor. Once it reached the ground, however, it disappeared.

Birds sang in the upper branches, but none came into view. As she gazed out through the tree trunks, the gently rolling hills of Faerie undulated like waves on the sea.

Clíodhna took in a deep breath and entered the graceful arched doorway.

Every courtier stared at the lone human as she walked through the massive chamber. Impossible shades of red and yellow, blue, and purple rioted in a rainbow of gossamer fabrics. Few of the Fae court resembled humans. Some had feathers or scales, or skin so vibrant, their clothing faded in comparison.

A short, squat toad-like Fae, had given her a solemn nod as she passed, the only sign of encouragement she received.

Once she reached the center dais, Clíodhna knelt in the grand hall, trembling and terrified, but unable to move a muscle.

Queen Áine sat on her throne made of living branches, woven into complex knotwork designs. Beside her, a smaller throne of curved stone sat empty. She had no consort to help her rule.

The Queen, resplendent in white and silver, rose with infinite elegance. Her pale skin glowed with its own light as she towered over Clíodhna, even when she descended the dais to stand next to her. She placed both hands upon Clíodhna's head and chanted unfamiliar words. The language seemed ancient, liquid, and alien.

Adhna had used this language for his spells, but he'd refused to teach Clíodhna. "It's the language of the gods. No mortal can learn it. The

Fae are permitted to use it only under strict conditions, and we cannot pass it on."

The Queen's words made Clíodhna's skin crawl. Power gathered as the chant came to a crescendo. Pressure rose, pushing against her lungs and making her hair crackle with energy.

The Queen stopped chanting, a question in her tone. Clíodhna's head moved of its own accord to look into the Queen's eyes. Those black, endless cat eyes.

She shivered and wanted to flee, but the Queen's gaze locked into hers. "Do you vow your honor and loyalty to me above all others, Clíodhna?"

Swallowing against the knot in her throat, Cliodhna glanced around at the courtiers, eager for entertainment if the human dared refuse. Her life would be forfeit in seconds. With a last thought of desperate pain for the children she might never see again, she gulped. "I do, my Queen."

A ripple of power spread out, an iridescent ring coloring everything in its path, along with a gust of cold wind. Clíodhna shivered and rubbed her arms, once she had bodily control again.

Something had latched onto her mind, something limiting and heavy. She suspected her vow had created a burden she must now carry everywhere.

A disappointed sigh rippled through the watching Fae, but the Queen's mouth twitched in the ghost of a smile. "Very well. Rise, handmaiden, and take your place at my side as part of my court."

Clíodhna rose on shaky knees. She turned to face the attending Fae, all wearing disapproving frowns, except the toad-like Fae, who gave her a slight smile and a wink. She took a deep breath and stepped back, hoping to shift focus away from her.

The Queen took her seat upon the throne again, the very essence of regality. She clapped once, and two Fae guards dragged someone down the long, mirror-smooth floor.

The prisoner was a brown Fae, with gashes in his dark skin, dripping something white like tree sap rather than blood. His clothing hung in rags and he wore a resigned expression.

The Queen's voice shot through the hall, filling the space with command. "What is his crime?"

A third guard stepped up, rapped his spear against the floor, and reported, his gaze locked forward. "This Fae attempted to steal fruit from the Queen's Garden. He claimed he did it as a favor for his pet mortal, in the human realm. She asked him for an apple of immortality."

The Queen threw her head back and laughed. "Did he believe such things of my humble garden? Oh, fool that he is. The usual punishment." She flicked her hand in a careless gesture. The guards dragged him away. Clíodhna burned to ask what his sentence would be, but realized she may not like the answer.

Several cases came before the Queen, each one judged with little deliberation, from what Clíodhna could tell. The one point of mercy the Queen granted was for a young Fae, small as a child. He'd wandered into a forbidden area, something described as the Dead Marsh.

For his crime, the Queen spoke to him in stern tones, reminding him that the marsh was dangerous, and that he should mind the rules better. The glimmer of human kindness gave Clíodhna a shred of hope that her new position wouldn't be as horrible as she'd feared.

Hours must have passed before the Queen clapped her hands three times. Two guards had been leading a supplicant in, but they hastily turned around, shuffling the black Fae outside.

The courtier crowds had grown during the Queen's judgements, doubling and then tripling in size. Now more than forty Fae milled around, waiting for their Queen's command. They watched her with eager anticipation.

Queen Áine rose, surveying them all with pleased confidence. Then she gestured to a cluster of three Fae in the back corner. They fumbled into the shadows and came out with several objects, but Clíodhna couldn't tell what they were until the music started.

Then the ethereal strains of strings and wind soared through the vaulted trees and caressed her ears. Entranced by the delightful melody, she began to dance, without a thought for propriety.

A hand gripped her arm and she grunted in surprise. The stout, toad-like Fae held her back, staring up at her with alarm. "You mustn't! No one dances without the Queen's permission."

"I didn't realize. I'm sorry."

He bowed and gave a wide grin filled with sharp teeth. "I'm here to help. I'm called Grimnaugh."

"Thank you, Grimnaugh. I'm Clíodhna."

"Oh, we're all well aware of who you are, human! The court has been abuzz about you ever since you came to Faerie. The Queen, in particular, is intrigued by you, a full human! She wanted to make you a handmaiden right away."

She glanced around at the other Fae in worry. "I thought I was safe. Adhna said he'd hide me."

"He hid you well enough. We weren't sure where Adhna hid his cottage. Only the Queen had that knowledge. But the court has been gossiping about you incessantly, and we learned you'd been helping the other Fae, both in the human realm and here. It's unusual for a human to be so useful, so you were the subject of much speculation."

He pointed out each Fae and told her the name they went by, and their relative rank in the court. "You, as the Queen's handmaiden, are ranked above them all, until the Queen chooses a consort. However, as a human, you have no real power. You're a… a curiosity, at most. She's been without a consort since the last one died, and they're all pushing for the position. Well, most of them. Adhna doesn't seem to be interested, though she favors him."

Mixed emotions swam inside her as Grimnaugh rambled on. She didn't want to lose Adhna, but if he had a chance at such power, why wouldn't he have taken it? "Adhna could have been consort?"

Grimnaugh's grin almost reached from ear to ear. "Many times past. But his heart, it seems, is promised elsewhere. He's wise to turn the Queen down. She wouldn't have tolerated such a split loyalty. Rejecting the Queen is dangerous, but she'd never play second best."

So Adhna had turned the Queen down because of his feelings for herself. Clíodhna felt both relief and guilt. She stared at her hands, clasped in front of her, terrified to move lest she violate some other court custom.

"Don't be so worried, Clíodhna. Adhna asked me if I would look out for you when he couldn't. We've worked together in the past, and I owe him a few favors. I'll help you learn what you must to survive."

"Thank you, Grimnaugh." She glanced up as several Fae moved to the center of the floor, forming a double line. "Is the dancing to begin?"

"I recommend you wait and study the steps before you enter the dance. Mistakes do not reflect well upon our Queen."

Clíodhna studied the elegant Fae as they glided across the floor. Each dance seemed to be full of precise turns of phrase, meaningful glances, and other subtle power plays within the Queen's Court.

Clíodhna's prior education in social customs meant nothing here. Every gesture and nuance carried tremendous meaning. Until she became familiar with the possibilities, she must keep silent and still. But she wasn't very good at either.

As she learned her duties as handmaiden, Grimnaugh was her shadow, whispering information in her ear. She adored the short, squat Fae and his help saved her life countless times. The Queen only acknowledged his presence at Clíodhna's side once, with a bare nod. Grimnaugh told her this qualified as high praise for any lesser Fae from his Queen.

When Adhna returned from his latest mission, he entered the great hall, looking ruffled and tired. After he gave his report to the Queen, she allowed them a few precious hours of time alone. He wouldn't speak of his errands, as they were the Queen's business, but they didn't talk much, anyhow.

Afterwards, Adhna thanked Grimnaugh for watching out for her with a precious wheel cheese and a jar of honey, and then he had to leave again.

Grimnaugh let out a cheerful giggle and a small dance at the gifts. "Adhna knows me so well! I grow weary of fruit and vegetables. He's so lucky, getting to travel into the mortal world."

Clíodhna cocked her head at the Fae. "You cannot?"

His shoulders drooped. "I'm not powerful enough. Only the courtiers and their ilk can go back and forth at will. The Queen has assigned some, like the nature spirits or the *bean sídhe*. But our place is here, at the pleasure of our Queen."

In the distance, rolling hills glowed with ambient light. "I wish I could show you a sunrise. It's a glorious sight and I miss them."

Grimnaugh looked in the same direction, but then shrugged. "Adhna said you may return someday. Will you do so, given the chance?"

"I must see my children again. They're all living in the mortal world, and I've trusted others to take care of them. Each one has left a hole in my heart."

Later, Grimnaugh introduced her to some lesser Fae who worked for the Queen. Those who prepared food, repaired garments, and decorated for her balls.

These Fae seemed more human-like, though too tall or short to be real humans. Some had wings or fins or feathers. Their voices sounded like tinkling bells or roaring winds.

A few times, when the Queen was busy with another matter, a courtier approached her during court. Grimnaugh whispered in her ear, giving her the Fae's rank, name, and purpose. Eventually, she got used to these supplicants, and the Queen said nothing against her helping them.

The Queen said she knew everything that happened in her realm, after all.

One such young Fae walked toward her during a ball. He looked very young, tall and thin, with snow-white skin like the Queen's and a young raven perched on his shoulder. His ink-black hair curled around his face and down his back, almost alive and writhing.

He bowed to her as Grimnaugh whispered, "This is Ammatán. He's recently admitted to the Queen's court, as his sire once served her. He's been living in another Queen's court for many winters."

The white-skinned Fae flushed when she beamed at him. "Greetings to you, Ammatán."

"I wanted to meet you as I've never seen a full human before. Oh, I hope I haven't offered insult?" His hand flew to his mouth in a very human-like gesture.

The sweet, anxious expression in his eyes made her soften. "I'm honored to meet you, Ammatán. What is your talent?"

He swallowed, bowed, and scampered off without answering her question. She turned to Grimnaugh. "He seems sweet."

With a nod, Grimnaugh frowned. "Sweet enough. He has yet to find a protector in court. That choice often colors a young Fae's future."

"A protector?"

"Someone to guide the youth, teach him the ways of the court, how to avoid the pitfalls. Adhna and I are your protectors, though he's by far the more powerful." As soon as the young Fae fled, another took his place.

This Fae towered over Clíodhna, stick thin and wispy, like a mare's tail cloud in the sky. Grimnaugh gave her name. "She is Cerul. Her position gives her power over the light in Faerie."

Clíodhna's eyes grew wide. "That sounds like a great deal of power!"

The tall Fae bowed once, her pale blue eyes shining. "I have little to do but maintain levels. The Queen prefers consistency. However, the work is important."

While cocking her head, Clíodhna asked, "Have you ever traveled to the mortal world?"

Cerul gave a slight smile but said nothing.

Clíodhna let out a sigh. "I miss the serene beauty and power of the sunrise. Can we do nothing of that sort here in Faerie?"

Cerul considered the question with more solemnity than Clíodhna expected. "I shall research." She left quickly before Clíodhna could thank her.

Grimnaugh introduced several other Fae. *Beacdin* raised mushrooms along the Great Swamp's edge, while *Gabha* worked bronze, creating the spears and daggers used in Fae warfare.

A third, *Ceatha Mil*, a rainbow-striped female, was the only beekeeper in Faerie. She told Clíodhna that no one else could coax the creatures to thrive here, but she'd never divulge her secret.

A disturbance at the entrance made them both glance toward the arched doorway. Clíodhna sucked in her breath when she recognized Bodach striding in with four guards, all marching in step. He approached the dais with brash confidence and gave a deep bow. "My Queen, I have returned from a successful mission."

Queen Áine smiled, but it didn't reach her eyes. When Bodach rose, he cast his gaze across the gathered courtiers until it fell upon her and Grimnaugh. He glowered and turned back to the Queen. "Your Grace, why have you accepted this human to your court?"

Her response came in a whisper, falling upon a sudden silence, like mist on a still pond. "Do you dare to question my judgment, Bodach?"

The bark-skinned Fae bowed again. "I should never dare to do so, my Queen." He retreated, not turning his back to her. Once he exited, the assembled court breathed again.

Grimnaugh curled his lip. "That one has incredible nerve. One day, it'll land him in a great deal of trouble."

"Has he always been so bold?"

"A few times. Most recently, when the Queen took a mortal lover. He has no love for humans, and believes their blood dilutes the pure Faerie blood. Which is ridiculous, because all of us are some mixture."

The hall grew quiet again as another petitioner approached the Queen. And then another courtier approached Clíodhna.

She'd expected Bodach's obvious disapproval to result in other courtiers to shun her, but several now queued up for introductions. That alone gave her more information about both Bodach's relation to the other courtiers and the strength of Queen Áine's approval.

Before she left the court, the Queen pulled her aside. "Be wary of Bodach, as he means you ill."

Clíodhna bowed her head. "I'm aware, my Queen. I shall be cautious. He attempted to destroy me in the mortal world."

Her gaze narrowed. "If he attempts anything in Faerie, he will feel my wrath."

Before Clíodhna could thank her, the Queen swept from the hall in a flurry of sparkling silver and white, like a soft snowdrift blown by a strong wind.

Chapter Thirteen

Clíodhna paced back and forth each day, weighing her options, what she should have said, what she might do now, what her decision would mean for her son, every imaginable aspect.

Try as she might, she couldn't find a way out of her vow. Unless she convinced the Queen to release her, she may now be bound forever, subject to the Queen's whim. The Queen even had power over Clíodhna's body and might compel her to say things even when she wished to stay silent.

Had she even vowed loyalty freely? Or had that been the Queen's compulsion? She shook her head for the thousandth time. She shouldn't dither like this, but she had nothing to take her mind off it.

Inside her head, the possibilities of what might have happened whirled like a waterspout, around and around, making no headway and solving no problems. Rumann whimpered for attention, but Clíodhna ignored her babe and thought of yet another impossible solution.

Flashes of memory sparked in her mind. The intense blue of the Queen's outfit, the endless depths of her black eyes, the flutter of wings from her Fae attendants. A glint of sparkling light on the bronze spear heads of the guards. These images swam in with Clíodhna's plans, constructs, and wild imagination.

When Adhna returned, three sleeps later, Rumann's cries had grown desperate and hoarse. He'd curled up around his mother's leg, tired of tugging at her for attention. She sat cross-legged on the floor, staring into space, ignoring her son. Old milk stains crusted under her *léine*. Her hair sprouted in unkempt tendrils, her face was slack-jawed, and her expression blank.

Adhna grasped her shoulders and shook. "Clíodhna, my love, what happened? Wake up!"

She didn't move.

He picked up Rumann and patted the boy's back, quieting his cries. The baby whimpered and nuzzled his chest, looking for milk. "I'm sorry, Rumann. I can't feed you. But I can put you in the right place."

Adhna lifted Clíodhna's *léine*, his nose wrinkling at the odor of sour milk. With a wave of his hand, he sent one of the Fae to fetch a washcloth and water. Then he tugged the soiled *léine* over her head and cleaned Clíodhna's caked breasts. "Clíodhna, wake up. Rumann needs you. Open your eyes. Open them, please. It's Adhna. I'm here to help. Wake up!"

Deep within her throat, Clíodhna let out a visceral groan. One hand drifted up to cup Rumann's head at her breast. Adhna fetched a comb and untangled her hair with gentle hands, brushing it into smooth waves that fell down her back. He cleaned the first washcloth and wet it again, wiping her face and shoulders, hoping the cool water would help to rouse her.

Through much coaxing and placing Rumann at both breasts, another moan escaped her trance. Clíodhna's eyes fluttered, half-blinking several times. Despite the mind-fog, her gaze became more focused, and she stared at him, confusion clear on her face. She gave a whispered croak. "Adhna? You're back?"

"I am, and I worried you had left."

She pursed her lips. "But I'm right here!"

After stroking her head, he said, "You weren't a moment ago, love."

"I don't understand. Is Rumann hurt? He looks like he's been crying." She reached for her son, nuzzling him for comfort.

"Rumann survived well enough. He's fed and happier now. Tell me what happened."

She told him of the Queen's visit, her own inability to resist, and her obsessive examination of her actions.

He shrugged with a sad smile. "A common reaction to meeting the Queen. She inspires uncertainty in some, robbing them of all confidence and poise. Either by magic or by words, she has the effect of stealing your belief in yourself. She doesn't do it on purpose, mind you, but many mortals are thus affected."

Her skin pebbled and she rubbed her arms, being careful not to dislodge her babe. "Will this happen every time I see her? I'm to be her handmaiden! How can I tell stories or sing when I'm worried about every word?"

His smile grew kinder. "No, usually just the first encounter. It may hit you from time to time later, but as you grow used to the effect, you learn how to push it away. I can teach you some tricks. Now, let's get you a clean *léine* and a dip in the pond. You, my love, have a powerful odor."

Clíodhna wrinkled her nose. "Ugh. Yes, please. You might have to help me stand, though. I must have been here for days to be so stiff!"

Adhna helped her stagger to the pond. "Queen Áine holds court, though sometimes she conducts business and other times entertainment. Often, one morphs into the other. There are great balls and tiny gatherings, all on her whim. She'll expect you to react to her desires. As her handmaiden, she'll also expect you to listen for gossip and report anything of concern."

Clíodhna scrubbed the grime from her arms and legs, reveling in the cool pond. "What sort of things would concern her?" Several tiny Fae fluttered around, playing in the splashes. A non-butterfly landed on Rumann's nose. His eyes crossed trying to look at it and he waved his pudgy hands.

With a bronze ewer, Adhna poured water over Clíodhna's hair, the clean water sluicing out several days' worth of neglect. Then, he brushed it out again. "Anything against her law or influence. Anyone complaining of how she rules her realm. Any complaints at all. In time, you'll learn to sift out the petty whines from the serious ones."

She rubbed the water from her eyes and blinked at him. "Will she grant me that time?"

He shrugged. "There's little telling what she'll do regarding you. She rarely takes on a human handmaiden." He stared at Rumann. "However, there is one thing I am dead certain of."

With a nervous glance at her baby, Clíodhna shivered. "What?"

"Rumann won't be safe in Faerie if you're the Queen's handmaiden. She's pleased there is a babe of the Fae, but won't tolerate a crying child around her."

Fear seizing her, Clíodhna backed up several steps. "No! No, you can't take my last child from me! I've lost all of them, and you can't do that!" She clung tight to Rumann.

"The danger is real. Not only will you have little time for his care, but he'll be a target for those who wish to influence the Queen. I can't be with him at all times to protect him. If you have him at the palace, his screams will anger the Queen."

Clíodhna scowled at him. "Then what am I to do? I can't shove him back whence he came!"

Adhna put out both hands to placate her. "His greatest chance is with a human family. Both the Queen and Bodach have less power in the human realm, and it'll be easier to hide him there. I'll find a kind couple who've lost their own child. I'll try to find someone near your own village."

Clíodhna had no tears left. First, her stillborn baby girl, then Etromma and Donn left in the human realm, and Aileran as well. Frustration and rage bubbled inside her at the injustice as she held Rumann tight. "If he can be so easily hidden, why can't I hide him with me?"

Adhna bowed his head. "Bodach has a bond with you now. His power and yours have intertwined, so he can find you anywhere."

"No, it's just not fair!"

Adhna hugged her and Rumann both. "I don't like this either, Clíodhna. But the life of our son is paramount. We *must* keep him safe. Don't you agree?"

Exasperated, she rolled her eyes. "Of course, I agree. I'm just not convinced we have to abandon him!"

He let out a deep sigh. "What would Bodach do if he found Rumann here alone?"

Clíodhna had no answer to that, not one she liked, so she sat in sullen silence. With a sudden thought, she asked, "What would Bodach do if he found Rumann with a human family?"

"He won't. I can hide him with glamor in the mortal world."

She gritted her teeth. "Very well. I grant leaving him here would be unwise, even in someone's care. But I still don't see why I can't bring him to court."

"The Queen doesn't tolerate such chaos in her court and has made her position on this clear many times in the past."

"Chaos? He's just a child. How much chaos can he create?"

Even as she said the words, she realized how silly they sounded. One child's cry could pierce the ears as well as the Faerie Queen on a good day. With a rueful smile, she admitted to herself that Adhna was right.

"May I at least know with whom you will gift my son?"

"Of course. I will find a nice, young couple with a good trade and a sturdy house. I'll send frequent emissaries to ensure his good health and maintenance, and they'll bring back news. In the human world, I can create a *géis* against Bodach's interference. It won't work in Faerie, but the rules are different there."

He took both her hands in his and kissed her fingertips. "I want you to have joy, my love. This will make you much less anxious, knowing someone is caring for our child."

She leaned into his chest, and he hugged her tight. "I hope you're right, Adhna."

Adhna left the next hour, along with her son. Clíodhna fretted at every sound, every snap, every rustle of the leaves. Finally, Grimnaugh came to sit with her, and distracted her with tales from the court. The Queen did not yet summon her to court, so he stayed for several meals and sleeps.

After what seemed like days, her erstwhile host, lover, and mentor returned, tired and bedraggled. She helped him wash in the pond and massaged his back, rubbing the weariness from his body. He sighed with delight and closed his eyes.

She sluiced water over his head and scrubbed his tangled hair. With an exclamation, she fetched a comb and attacked the tangles. Between his grunts when she pulled his hair, she asked, "Will you have to go away again soon? I thank you for thinking of Grimnaugh to help me while you're away, but I miss you."

He hummed in pleasure at her attention. "I've pleased the Queen with my last mission, or so she says, so I might not have to leave again soon. Several other courtiers have requested duties, and she's promised to spread the work around."

She pulled out a particularly stubborn tangle. "Can you share any of your mission details?"

"Not much. I can tell you I've been going to the courts of the other Queens. I suppose you could label them as diplomatic missions. This Queen hasn't had very amicable relations with the other realms in the past. It's been my duty to remedy that."

"What are the names of the other Queens? Where do they rule?"

He chuckled, shaking his head. "Faerie isn't a staid and physical realm like your mortal world. The locations can shift and meld like mist, and many lesser Queens are dotted in the hidden corners of Faerie. However, I can name the more powerful ones. Queen *Aoibheall* is my most recent visited. Some other Queens are *Grian, Una, Micoll,* and *Nic Nemhain,* though her realm lies far away."

The names swam in Clíodhna's head, but she had no tales to attach them to. "Tell me about each of them."

"Let's see. Queen *Aoibheall* is a Queen of fire, and she favors the creative arts. Poetry, art, and dance are her focus. She is rough on her favorites, though. If they don't produce works to delight her, she might rain fire down upon them. *Grian* is our own Queen's sister and has a penchant for transforming those who displease her into badgers."

Clíodhna covered her mouth to keep a giggle from escaping. "Badgers?"

Adhna grinned back, his eyes twinkling with amusement. "Yes, badgers. Sometimes she even turns them back when they repent. Sometimes."

He stared up at the sky. "*Nic Nemhain*, now, she's a dark one. She loves bones and is rumored to have a palace made of them, though I've never seen it myself. *Micoll*, she's the Queen of the smaller Fae, those wild Fae and sprites of the marsh you're so fond of."

"And *Oonagh*?"

"I've never met *Oonagh*. She lives to the north and west, along the shore. She's called the Silver Queen and loves music so much she will take musical mortals as pets."

Clíodhna shivered at the notion of being a slave to a Faerie Queen. Then again, how was that different from being a vowed handmaiden?

"You said you haven't met *Oonagh*. Have you met the others?"

He clenched his jaw. "I have. Some I hope never to meet again."

Something in his manner forbade Clíodhna from pressing for further details. Instead, she caressed his shoulders and wished he wouldn't be in danger again.

Adhna turned and clutched her hands, staring into her eyes. "Promise me, Clíodhna. Promise me that if you ever gain power within the court, to hold tight upon your good nature. Keep it safe inside you, and never let something from the outside eat into it. Don't give your kindness up for anything or anyone. Promise me!"

Startled, she blinked twice. "Of course, I will, Adhna! But, I'm a mortal in the Faerie court. What sort of power could I ever gain?"

He released her and looked away. "It happens from time to time. Pray it doesn't happen to you. Such power is a burden, and not for the weak of the soul."

As an answer, she said, "I promise. I will keep my goodness close and fast within my heart. If you promise to always be by my side when I need you."

He swallowed and gave a rueful grin. "I don't know if I can promise that, Clíodhna. I can promise to try my best, but if my Queen calls, I must go. You understand that."

Her heart, at first bolstered from his heartfelt warning, now sank. To fill the hole it left, she drew him in for a kiss, their lips both hot with the blood of passion and temper.

He ran his hands up her arms, slick from the water, and down her breasts. She wrapped her legs around his hips in invitation and he gave her that beguiling half-smile.

They made love in the warm water of the pond as the dim ever-present light shined upon them, sparkling in the ripples.

Chapter Fourteen

Clíodhna threw the wooden bowl to the ground in a temper. "But you said she'd send someone else!"

Adhna's shoulders slumped. "I'm aware of what I said, love. But Bodach is meddling again, and she has to send me now. I'm the only one she trusts to undo the tangle he's created."

She began angry pacing. "I don't understand why she doesn't just banish him."

"She can't. He holds too much power within the court, and he's been fostering some grumblings."

Clíodhna cast her mind back to something the marsh Fae had complained about. "He offered the marsh Fae and the wild Fae favors for future support."

Adhna scratched at his beard. "I suspect you're right. He may want to wrest control from her and take the throne himself. But she can do little against him, as per the rules of Faerie magic. He can't do anything directly to her, either. They must both work through proxies."

She arched one eyebrow. "And you're her proxy?"

"Exactly. As are you, so keep that in mind."

Her anger fled into solemn resignation. "I will. Stay cautious, my love."

Her lover clutched her tight as he kissed her. When they parted, her lips ached with bruising, but she didn't mind.

When Grimnaugh brought her to court that day, she considered the diminutive Fae before asking her question. "Does the Queen realize how much Bodach is trying to undermine her power?"

He gasped and glanced around, searching for anyone who might have overheard her question. "Don't say such things! Not here, it isn't safe."

The frog-like Fae grabbed her hand and dragged her back into the roundhouse. "Now, we're behind Adhna's strongest wards. What are you saying?"

"From some grumblings of the marsh Fae, I suspect that Bodach is working to undermine the queen. Adhna says it's a possibility."

Grimnaugh scowled as his grip on her hand grew tighter. "A possibility had better be a certainty before you bring it before the Queen. Have you any idea what Bodach will do to you if you accuse him of treason without proof?"

She swallowed, her imagination running rampant with horrible ideas. "How do I make certain?"

His eyes grew wide. "You could never be certain! If you find out anything for certain about Bodach, you can be assured he meant you to know it. Anything truly damaging, he'd never let you tell the Queen. His very life depends on it, and he values his life and power above all else."

Frustrated, she ground her teeth. There must be some way to bring Bodach's disloyal actions to the Queen's attention. Despite Grimnaugh's cautions, Clíodhna was determined to bring her information to the Queen.

When they arrived at court, several courtiers mumbled as she passed. She noted the censure on a few faces who had treated her with kindness. "Grimnaugh? Has something happened?"

He gave one young Fae a sideways look and let out a growl. "I'll find out. Bide for a while."

Clíodhna took her place, standing beside the throne and a few steps behind. The Queen made three decisions for petitioners before Grimnaugh returned.

They had to wait for a break in the proceedings before he could share what he'd discovered. Abruptly, the Queen called for a pause in court by striding out of the hall.

Once she left, Grimnaugh hurried to Clíodhna's side and spoke in a whisper. "There's something odd about Adhna's latest mission. I can't get a straight answer from anyone. That's nothing unusual, as the Fae aren't as direct in their speech as humans can be. However, be even more cautious than ever."

Her blood turned chilly, and she glanced around. None of the other Fae would meet her gaze. "I wish Adhna were here."

Grimnaugh cast his somber glance across the forty-odd courtiers. "So do I."

"Who's doing the most grumbling? What groups of Fae are they closest to?"

He stared off into the middle distance. "Cerul is in a foul mood, as is Terbhan. They both work with the wild Fae of the air and the marshes."

"Terbhan? I don't think I've met them."

He nodded toward one corner. "That's Terbhan, over near the twisted pillar. See? Pale blue skin and wicked sharp claws?"

"I see them."

"Coming to court at all is unusual for Terbhan. They prefer to be swimming in the land's power. Something must be very wrong for them to give that up."

Clíodhna bit her lip and stopped staring at the blue Fae. "Are they petitioning the Queen today?"

"Not that I'm aware of, but Cerul is on the list. But the Queen has more petitioners on the list than she normally has patience to deal with."

Then Queen Áine returned, forestalling further speculation between them. She glanced at her seneschal to call up the next petitioner. However, instead of calling a name, he said, "Cerul would ask you a favor, your Grace."

The tall wispy Fae stepped forward and the watching courtiers fell silent. However, the Queen rewarded her with an icy stare. "No. I will not hear Cerul today. Who is next?"

Murmurs flew across those assembled. Queen Áine stood and held up one hand. "I will have silence in my court. No more petitioners now."

She turned and exited once again, leaving in her wake even more mumbled conjecture.

Grimnaugh wrung his hands. "This doesn't look good. This doesn't look good in the slightest."

Clíodhna barely heard the frog-like Fae. She slipped away from him and the grumbling courtiers to follow Queen Áine. For the first time since she'd met the Faerie Queen, she seemed upset, and Clíodhna needed to find out why.

The back passageway into the hall, the one that led to the Queen's antechambers, was dark and chilly. Clíodhna rubbed the pebbled skin on her arms, hoping the Queen wouldn't blast her into cinders the moment she appeared.

When she reached the first open room, she squinted in the bright light shining from the walls themselves. Rich, shining fabrics in blue and white draped across every surface, their reflection making the glow even stronger.

The Queen pulled open a cabinet drawer and drew out a stone, then closed the drawer again. Without turning, she said, "What do you want, handmaiden?"

At first, her voice didn't work. Clíodhna cleared her throat and tried again. "I… I have some news for you, my Queen."

The Queen spun, a bare hand-span from Clíodhna's face. Her voice dripped with disdain and cold anger. "Do you know something you believe I am ignorant of?"

"I… I think so, your Grace."

Rage flared in the Queen's icy eyes. "You think so. But you are not certain. Why are you wasting my time? How dare you intrude upon my private quarters?"

Clíodhna's skin turned clammy as the Queen drew closer, their noses almost touching. She couldn't move her legs, not even to run away. After steeling her nerve, she forced words out. "Bodach. He's trying to…"

The Queen turned away from her and flung an arm out in a dismissive gesture. An invisible force hurled Clíodhna against the wall, and pain burst in her shoulder. "Do not speak to me of Bodach. I will not have Adhna's pet trying to manipulate me regarding my consort. Begone."

Clíodhna crawled from the antechamber with a frustrated sob, every muscle in her body screaming in protest.

By the time she struggled to her feet and made it to the main hall, everyone had disappeared. Only Grimnaugh remained, pacing back and forth, awaiting her return. When she poked her head through the entrance, he rounded on her. "I told you not to say anything! Didn't I warn you?

Adhna will have my hide for not protecting you. Why would you put us both in such danger?"

Chastened, she bowed her head. "I thought direct action would be better than this skulking around, but I was wrong. Faerie and human worlds work in different ways."

He shot her a frustrated glare. "You are speaking the truth. Keep it in mind, aye?"

As Clíodhna seethed with her foiled attempt at direct action, Grimnaugh led her back to Adhna's roundhouse. Bodach knew she lived here now, but Grimnaugh assured her that as long as she remained in the house, behind Adhna's wards, or in the Queen's company, the bark-skinned Fae couldn't hurt her.

There were some days the Queen didn't summon her. So, while Adhna still traveled, Clíodhna held her own miniature court with the marsh Fae and the wild Fae.

Some asked her for help or favors, but more often, they asked for her songs. Some of them also sang for her or related tales of their past endeavors, either real or legendary.

Clíodhna looked forward to the times she spent with the lesser Fae. While she spent a great deal of personal energy attending the Queen, her socialization with these Fae renewed her soul and kept her laughing.

Still, she also needed sleep, so when a yawn threatened to break her jaw, she had to dismiss her miniature court. They always protested, but she'd learned to insist.

As time went on, her court increased. Not only the marsh Fae and wild Fae, but some higher-ranked lesser Fae visited.

Each one asked her for a favor, and she couldn't bear to turn them away if she could help them. Most had minor enough requests, asking for a funny story or a sweet song.

Once she even saw that young Fae, Ammatán. When she noticed him, she beckoned him closer, but he fled. He must be a shy one.

Cerul came a few times and sat next to her, silent but supportive. She met the mysterious Terbhan, who had a lovely singing voice, and Clíodhna begged them to sing whenever they visited.

One day, when the Queen's court was packed with petitioners, she only heard a third of them. Even then, she chose from the list, ignoring others. The Queen had once again ignored both Cerul and Terbhan.

Once Clíodhna returned to Adhna's home, as much as she wanted to hold her usual court, the day had already drained all of her energy.

When she asked Grimnaugh to pass on her regrets to the others, he frowned. "I don't believe that's wise, my lady."

She gaped at the Fae. "My lady? When did you start that nonsense?"

He stared at his toes and murmured, "Some time ago, my lady."

With a sigh, Clíodhna placed a gentle hand on his shoulder, his skin rough and dry under her hand. "Please don't. I'm no lady, and I'm certain Queen Áine would be displeased at the presumption."

He mumbled something and glanced away.

Clíodhna took both his shoulders. "Grimnaugh, this is not a jest. I have no wish to take any of the Queen's power, nor do I wish her to believe it of me, even in error. She terrifies me."

"You have power already, my lady. You have the support of many of the lesser Fae. Even a few courtiers espouse you now."

Her eyes flew open with alarm. "I don't want courtiers! I don't want a court. Perhaps it was a bad idea to have anyone visit here to begin with."

Grimnaugh grumbled again, but wouldn't speak further, no matter how much she badgered him. Frustrated, Clíodhna stomped into the roundhouse and curled into bed, drawing her blanket up.

Despite her resolution, sleep did not come. She tossed and turned, thinking what might happen if the Queen suspected her of a power play. Her own imagination paled beside the Queen's ability to punish such a bold mortal.

After hours of futile attempts at sleep, with bleary eyes, Clíodhna rose again. The glade was quiet and peaceful, a gentle light glowing from all things, and yet, she felt deliciously alone.

Stepping into the pond, she immersed herself in the warm water, hoping to clear her head. What else should she do? She'd tried to warn the Queen of Bodach's machinations, and now she might be in peril of being accused of the same. Clíodhna must alleviate the Queen's suspicions before they fell on her.

She really wished Adhna would come back, but he'd been gone much longer than his previous missions. Clíodhna suspected Bodach had a hand in that, too.

A water Fae swam to her. This one had no voice, and it paddled around, playing with her black hair as it floated on the water's surface. Her fins tickled, and for a moment, Clíodhna forgot her concerns and played for the pleasure of playing.

Many winters ago, Clíodhna remembered playing. She'd had plenty of chores on the farm, helping her parents care for animals and clean the house. But she'd also spent summer hours playing in the water.

They'd lived on the western shore. Salty sea would tickle her nose when she dove under the waves. She'd play with the dolphins, riding them out into the deeps, almost out of sight of land, and back in before the storms came.

Once in a great while, a water nymph might be bold enough to let her approach. When she watched a wind sprite take flight and soar into the sky, she'd promised herself someday she would fly in the air like a bird.

Once, she had mentioned the sprites to her father, and received a lecture on fancies and tall tales, a lesson she'd remembered for many winters. A lesson that kept her from feeling playful too many times in her life.

What would her father think of her now? Playing with Fae within the very land of Faerie, and even attending the Faerie Queen.

Clíodhna let out a snort of derision. He'd probably dismiss it as the height of fanciful daydreams and tell her to get back to work.

With a sigh, Clíodhna rose from the pond and crawled back into bed, letting sleep claim her. Then she rose, attended court, and returned to bed. She had no energy for anything else.

Clíodhna counted at least twelve more long sleeps before Adhna returned. She'd just pulled her covers up when he stumbled in, tripped over something and let out a heartfelt curse.

After springing to her feet, Clíodhna peeled the soiled clothing from his body and made him lie down. He looked well-worn and rough. "You need rest, love. I'll prepare a meal, but you sleep."

He mumbled something about leaving again soon, but she shushed him. "Sleep! Not talk. Sleep."

Once his snores filled the roundhouse, she assembled bread and fruit for him, placing them on the table in plain sight. Then she picked his *léine* up with two fingers and, holding it out as far as she could, carried it to the pond. It reeked of stale sweat.

She dunked the stinking garment in, wrung it, and dunked again, until the stink went away. She hung the *léine* to dry and examined it, noting several places that required mending.

Clíodhna pulled out her sewing kit with a bone needle and repaired several rips. One had parallel cuts like an animal's claw had ripped it. She glanced at her lover, trying to remember if she'd seen any wounds on his skin when she readied him for bed. He must have already healed, for she recalled no cuts. Fae flesh healed quickly, but clothing didn't.

Someone cleared their throat. She spun to check on Adhna, but his snores still rattled the roofbeams. Instead, a group of five Fae stood in a line. The largest one, a mountain Fae, his skin gray and mottled, stepped forward, wringing his hands. "Please, my lady…"

She held up a hand, much like the Queen often did. "I'm not my lady. I made that clear to Grimnaugh. My name is Clíodhna."

He cleared his throat again, a noise like stone scraping together. "Yes, my lady Clíodhna."

She rolled her eyes and sighed, gesturing for him to continue.

"My lady Clíodhna, we've come to beg a favor from you. Will you listen to us?"

"Your name is *Cionnan*, right? How can I help, Cionnan?"

Another Fae twittered and giggled, hopping a few times in excitement. The mountain Fae cast her a withering glance and she calmed down, her wings still fluttering. "We ask you to rid our land of a blight."

Clíodhna narrowed her eyes. "What sort of blight?"

He stared at his feet and mumbled something, but so low she couldn't make out the words.

"Well? I can't help you if I don't know what to prepare for."

The stone Fae mumbled louder this time. "It's my lord Bodach."

"Bodach? Bodach is your blight?" As much as she feared the bark-skinned Fae, she also wanted to fight him, to once and for all banish his evil influence over those she cared for. Prudence overcame her urge for justice. "I'm not powerful enough to battle Bodach, Cionnan."

He grumbled again, stone grating against stone. Adhna emerged from the roundhouse, rubbing sleep from his eyes, wearing nothing at all. He blinked at the Fae delegation. "What's this, then?"

She gestured to her visitors. "These Fae would like my help in ridding their land of an evil blight. Bodach."

His eyes grew wide, showing the redness from lack of rest. "That cannot be done! Not by this human. Cionnan, what possessed you to come to Clíodhna? Even I would be a better candidate for such a mission, and yet I'm not powerful enough to beat him in a fair fight."

The mountain Fae stared at his feet again.

Adhna marched to the Fae and grabbed his shoulders. "Why? You should have gone to Queen Áine with this petition. Why didn't you do that?"

The stone Fae glanced at Clíodhna and back at Adhna, entreaty in his sad eyes. "We have tried. She won't hear our pleas."

With a curse, Adhna turned away and started pacing. "Bah. This is not good, not good at all. Clíodhna, stay here. I must speak to the Queen. You lot, head back home. Clíodhna cannot help you with your problem. The Queen is the only one able to do such a thing."

With that, Adhna stalked back to the roundhouse and donned a new, clean *léine*. He continued to grumble headed toward the Queen's court.

As soon as he left, Cionnan grabbed Clíodhna's hand, his skin cool and hard. "Please, please, my lady, at least come with us to see what he's done?"

Each Fae turned sad eyes upon her. She could no sooner stay now than she could take flight. With one last glance in the direction Adhna had gone, fear warring with the need for justice, she followed the Fae to their home.

Calling it a mountain might have been over-generous. The hill rose to a rocky outcropping, but the sides were grassy and gentle. A thin, lazy river curled around the base, wending through bracken and willow trees.

One of the Fae delegation, a *sídhe*, hopped with glee to be back near her tree and dove into the trunk, her smile brightening. Cionnan frowned and pointed to an area upstream. "See there? Where the water spreads out into a marsh?"

Clíodhna saw a wide marsh with several bedraggled weeds poking out of hummocks and some skeletal branches without leaves along the edge. "It looks rather gloomy."

He gave an excited nod. "Exactly. It used to be a cheerful place, with marsh Fae thriving amongst the reeds. It's become a dead zone. Bodach comes and plucks the magic from the land, and the dead area grows each time.

"Plucks the magic? What do you mean?"

"When one draws upon land magic, the way we do naturally, and the way some humans do, we always take what we need and return the rest to the land. That allows the magic to replenish, grow, and thrive. Bodach does not return it. He's found a way of hoarding the magic so he can use it later."

Something sounded in the distance, like a hunting horn. Clíodhna turned, but saw nothing except mist on the horizon. "Did you hear that?"

Cionnan tapped his fingers together, his gaze darting back and forth between the marsh and her. "What? I'm not sure what you mean, my lady."

"Stop calling me my lady. Can't you hear the horn?"

"A horn?" The Fae stared into the mist, his eyes growing wide. "It may be someone coming to take more of our land magic, my lady. We need your help to defend it."

She pursed her lips. "I told you, I don't have the power to protect you against Bodach. You've asked the wrong person. Even Adhna told you that."

The horn sounded again, closer.

Clíodhna looked around for the path they came in on, but the mist rolled in so fast, it obscured everything around them. The coolness made her skin pebble, and fear suddenly gripped her heart. "I shouldn't be here. Please, take me back to my roundhouse. Now."

He shook his stone head, his expression obstinate. "No, my lady, you need to defend us! You're the only one we trust!"

More Fae surrounded them now, melting out of the mist. They milled around with anxious frowns and pushed in around her. A third blast from the horn sounded much closer. "Son of a diseased donkey! You'll get me killed, Cionnan! Which way is home?"

Hoof beats rang out on the stone path. Mist parted to reveal Queen Áine, dressed in curvilinear-decorated bronze armor. Bodach rode by her side, wearing a smug smile. The magnificent white horse she rode wore elaborate barding in brilliant white and blue.

Now, the Queen pulled her mount up next to Clíodhna. The surrounding Fae pushed back but didn't make way for their Queen. "What is occurring here?"

Clíodhna raised her chin. "I apologize, my Queen. Cionnan asked me to come see his home, but I think I'm I've intruded on some ceremony. I shall leave." She bowed and backed away.

"Halt! Do not move. Cionnan, come forth."

The stone Fae crawled forward on his knees, his head bowed.

"Why have you lured my handmaiden into the wilds of Faerie? What game are you playing?"

His stone-crunching voice whispered, "Nothing, my Queen. We meant no harm, I swear it!"

Adhna came running up behind the host, out of breath and streaming sweat. "My Queen! My Queen, I tried to catch you at the palace. Clíodhna? What are you doing here? I told you to leave Cionnan alone!"

The Queen glared at Adhna, then Cionnan, and Clíodhna. Her face twisted into an angry frown and cast a sidelong glance at Bodach. "The wild Fae and the marsh Fae have formed a revolt, and I don't have time to discover what mischief they've created here. The time for battle is nigh. Adhna, I have another mission for you. Clíodhna, you're to return to Adhna's home and remain there with no exception, until I send for you. Cionnan, report to the palace immediately."

She wheeled her horse around and galloped back the way she came, enveloped by the mist. Bodach shot a knowing grin toward Clíodhna, raised his eyebrows, and followed the Queen.

When both had disappeared, Adhna let out his breath. "You heard the Queen, all of you. Especially you, Clíodhna. Did I not tell you to stay home? I'm not sure what this will mean when she returns. Go home, rest well, and stay safe. I can't be here to protect you from her wrath, but Grimnaugh will stay with you."

He rode off in a different direction and the mist swallowed his form. Clíodhna let out her own breath. What had she gotten herself into now?

She allowed one of the other Fae to lead her home, but her mind was numb. All her worst fears had come to pass, and she couldn't even fathom what the Queen would do. The only thing she could do was wait.

Clíodhna had never been very good at waiting.

Chapter Fifteen

Clíodhna paced with increasing worry in front of the roundhouse, then shifted to walking around the pond. Marsh claimed the far end, so she couldn't even do a full circle. Instead, she had to either detour around or turn back and do most of a circle in each direction.

Why had she been so stupid? While haring off to help the Fae seemed innocent enough, she realized how it might seem like she was trying to usurp the Queen's power over her own folk. A thousand times, she practiced her explanation to the Queen. A thousand times, she rejected the practiced words and started over.

"My Queen, I merely wanted to help a friend…"

"My Queen, how could I say no? He asked so nicely."

"My Queen, I wanted to save you the burden of such annoyance."

That last sounded so ridiculous, Clíodhna broke a branch off a bush and flung it into the pond, glowering as ripples fanned out.

She wished Grimnaugh would come. She needed to ask someone for advice, and he had good wisdom.

Gripping a stone in her hand, she tossed it into the pond. The ripples soothed her frustration, so she repeated the gesture several times before noticing how denuded the bush now looked.

Chagrined, she let out a sigh. While sitting cross-legged next to the bush, she pulled energy up from the ground. She'd forgotten how strong the magic flowed in Faerie, and for a moment, wrestled with the power. However, she'd only pulled a small tendril and she directed it to heal the torn branches. As she did so, the bush sang to her in thanks, its melody entwining with her power.

Once Clíodhna healed the raw, broken branches, she rose and returned to the roundhouse. If she couldn't trust herself not to hurt the living things of Faerie, she had no business tramping around in angry frustration. Instead, she should do as she was bid for once, and wait for the Queen to return.

Clíodhna detested waiting.

She ate and slept several times, but no one came. They must all be cowering in their homes, terrified of the Queen's wrath. Clíodhna couldn't blame them, as the Queen commanded more power than any of them combined, with the notable exception of her top courtiers.

Grimnaugh finally came by, but he didn't stay long. He whispered his explanation. "I have been assigned other duties, I'm afraid."

"So, I'm to be left all alone? Adhna is still gone."

He gave her a sad smile. "I'll visit when I can. It just won't be as often."

Clíodhna treasured his visits as welcome interludes. While she waited, she carved to pass the time. Soon, she'd amassed a growing pile of carved wooden figures: fish, birds, Fae, even a complex interwoven knot along a curved branch.

That last took the longest, but she felt great pride in the creation. She still didn't have Donn's innate talent, but she had some skill.

The reminder of her missing children—Donn, Etromma, Aileran, and wee Rumann—stabbed to her heart.

What might each of them be doing this very moment, in the mortal world? Etromma must have borne her child. Did she have a boy or a girl? Was Donn still working for the monks, carving beautiful stone sculptures for their buildings? She ached to see him and his work. Did Aileran still love riding horses? Had Rumann learned how to fish like his adopted father?

What sort of people had they grown into, without their mother or father to guide them? Would she never see them again?

Adhna told her she might visit the mortal realm once more, and she wouldn't waste that opportunity. When the time came, she'd travel back and see each of her children. She had no idea if she could return to Faerie after that visit, though.

When would the time be right? What if the Queen judged Clíodhna a traitor and executed her? If she returned to the mortal world, she might escape the Queen's uncertain judgment.

The notion of spending the rest of her life amongst her children, away from the machinations of this back-stabbing Faerie court, appealed to her. She rose, meaning to pack some supplies and do just that.

Then Clíodhna sat again, dropping her face into her hands with a new sob. She didn't know *how* to return to her own world, not without guidance from Adhna or Grimnaugh. She was trapped in her own misery.

At this moment, Clíodhna felt utterly alone, and the weight of that loneliness pressed hard upon her soul.

Tears burst forth from her in a flood, and she didn't even bother to wipe them from her face. Her breath came in ragged gasps as she sobbed, her arms curled around her shoulders as she rocked back and forth.

Clíodhna cried for what seemed like hours after that, soaking the half-carved dolphin in her hands so badly, the wood swelled out of proportion of the figurine.

Wiping her cheeks, she tossed the carving aside. She didn't have the heart to finish it now.

Just as she threw it into the pond, crunching footsteps made her turn. Grimnaugh trudged along the path, his head bowed and his feet dragging as if the weight of two worlds rested upon his shoulders. Every line of his body spoke of weary dread.

"Grimnaugh? What's happened? Has the Queen returned?"

He lifted his head, but his eyes were red and swollen. "She's returned. Yes, our Queen has returned. Forever."

Clíodhna stood in a snow-white *léine,* in a line of other courtiers. Each one dressed in simple garb, solemn and respectful, as the Queen's funeral bower approached.

Eight white horses, perfectly matched, drew the silver sledge. Lesser Fae marched behind, strewing snowy petals like flurries. The petals glowed and swirled in a slow dance, caressing her body in a curvilinear pattern. They drifted up into the sky, like the stars in the mortal realm, into the dim ambient light.

Cerul marched beside the sledge with Bodach and several other higher courtiers.

Behind them marched a line of mourning Fae, each with faces as still as stone. Fae from the upper echelons of power down to the lowest of the lesser sprites. Fae from the realms of man, Fae from water, earth, sky, and land. The Fae of modern thatched houses and ancient stone circles. Fae so beautiful that her heart ached just to glimpse them, and Fae so horrific, nightmares screamed in the back of her mind.

Other than the sound of horse hooves, dead silence accompanied the procession. No singing, no music, no whispers marred this silent spectacle.

Clíodhna only heard that she'd fallen in battle. Queen Áine had ridden out with a host to punish the wild and marsh Fae. Clíodhna's guilt over her involvement in that rebellion clambered against her conscience.

Both marsh and wild Fae walked amongst the mourners, so that particular question must be settled. Had they hated their own queen so much?

Some of her recent decisions were unpopular, but to commit regicide was treason. Even in the human world, to betray one's chief must be punished with death. A Faerie betrayal must be so much worse.

Her heart ached for those wild Fae that she'd befriended and hoped her actions hadn't convinced them to rebel.

As the sledge passed her, Clíodhna searched for something within the Queen's still face, though she wasn't sure what. As her gaze moved from the Queen, she met Bodach's eyes. Though his face remained solemn, his eyes danced with anticipatory glee.

Clíodhna's blood seethed at that brief glimpse into his eyes. He knew something. He may have even made this happen. She wanted to ask Grimnaugh, but she must remain silent until after the Queen's funeral.

Through the gardens behind the palace and up the hill, the procession marched. A stone bower, surrounded by beautiful flowers and graceful willow trees, lay waiting to receive its occupant.

When the courtiers laid the Queen within and sealed the top with the heavy stone slab, every Fae let out a sigh. Upon the strength of that sigh, a rare wind blew within the land of Faerie, a gale which fluttered everyone's clothing and made the leaves rustle in an odd farewell song.

A wall of pressure pushed out from the stone grave, invisible yet unmistakable. It shoved against each attendee, tingling power through their bodies. Clíodhna gasped as it flushed through her, invigorating her with energy and pain.

Her hands throbbed and her head pounded. She pushed her palms against her forehead, but nothing eased the ache. With a sob, she ran down the hill, disregarding all protocol and etiquette. Grimnaugh called after her in a fierce whisper, but she couldn't stay there. She had to escape.

Down the hill she hurried, dodging lesser Fae who were still walking at the tail end of the procession. She ran until her legs ached, her feet throbbed, and her lungs burned. She ran blindly, without direction or purpose, away from whatever exploded from the Queen's bower.

When she reached a meandering creek encircling the palace, Clíodhna collapsed on the shore. With cupped hands, she slurped several handfuls of sweet water, salving her parched throat. Liquid dribbled down her throat, bringing her voice back to life. She closed her eyes in sheer pleasure.

Clíodhna's head still ached, but at least now her mind worked. What had come from the tomb? Some death spell, perhaps? A final curse from the Queen? Some shifting in the magic of Faerie? She didn't know and didn't wish to know the answer.

Someone was behind her. Clíodhna didn't want to turn around. She didn't want to face anyone, not right now. Not until she'd gained more control over her thoughts. When would Adhna return?

Clíodhna glanced up to find Bodach leering at her with wry amusement. Bumps pebbled her skin and she swallowed down a surge of fear.

"You seem out of sorts, sweet Clíodhna. Let me help you to the palace."

He reached for her hand, but she snatched it out of his grasp. "I have no business there now. With the Queen's death, I am no longer a handmaiden. I shall wait for Grimnaugh to take me back to Adhna's roundhouse."

He gave a single nod. "That's correct. You are no longer the Queen's handmaiden. Instead, you are so much more."

She tried to gather her scattered thoughts. "You aren't making sense. Go away. I don't want you near me."

His smile widened into exultant joy. "But I must be near you, my Queen. My place is to be forever by your side from this day on. I'm now *your* Consort."

Stunned by Bodach's declaration, Clíodhna allowed him to help her to her feet. Cerul ran up, out of breath. The tall Fae glared at Bodach but didn't interfere.

A few other courtiers arrived, exchanging concerned glances. Bodach clutched Clíodhna's hand and drew her toward the palace. She resisted, but she had no strength to fight him.

Step by step, the palace grew closer, looming taller above her. Clíodhna's mind whirled as she tried to make sense of it all. The previously light, soaring towers and arches now loomed sinister, dark and foreboding despite glittering white stone with specks of blue.

Courtiers fell into step behind them, creating an informal procession toward the palace. The new Faerie Queen and her court.

Clíodhna didn't understand how this was happening. She was human, not Fae. Sure, Adhna said she had Fae blood, but a Queen must need to be full-blooded Fae, not part human, mustn't she?

Thoughts and contradictions clashed in her mind and the Queen's magic on the hill kept her from being able to make sense out of them. Shreds of ideas danced and swirled, not allowing her to settle on one spot and untangle the mess.

Clíodhna no longer had control over her own body. As soon as Bodach took her hand, he forced his will over her. She'd had no time to build up any defenses, as Adhna had taught her. Bodach's will made her feet take each step forward.

Step by step toward the palace.

As they entered the main archway, Fae rushed in to line the halls, bowing as she walked by. Bodach kept a firm grip on her hand, pulling her along as if they walked as equals.

Step by step toward the throne.

The glowing walls dimmed as she passed, light focusing on her. Did Cerul have control over that or did some ambient, low-key magic work as part of the palace itself? The throne looked wicked as they approached, its bare branches entwined in a hopeless knot, eager to reach out and catch her clothing, her tender skin, to pull her into its clutches.

Inside, she screamed, though her mouth would not move. Her face was frozen and yet her mind gibbered in fear. *I shouldn't be here! This isn't my place!*

Clíodhna glimpsed green skin to her left. Grimnaugh caught up to them. He seemed both panicked and hopeful. She grasped a modicum of peace in that assessment.

They climbed the dais and when she turned to sit on the throne, Bodach clutched her hand to his chest. "Wait, my Queen. The proprieties must be observed at all times."

Clíodhna froze, casting around for any sign of what came next. She still had no control over her body. Could she speak? She cleared her throat, testing her ability.

After darting her eyes to the right to see if Bodach was paying attention, she tried a whisper. "Adhna, where are you?"

Bodach squeezed her hand, her bones crunching under the painful pressure. He hissed under his breath. "You are not to speak, my Queen. Do you understand?"

She hissed back, infusing her anger into her words. "If I am Queen, I may do as I please."

He spoke in a fierce whisper. "You are only Queen by my power and support. I am the most powerful Fae remaining, even including your beloved Adhna. My place will be by your side as consort, and you will do what I say. If you take one step out of line of my commands, your children will suffer for it. And yes, I now know where all four reside in the mortal world. Pay heed, my Queen, and do nothing, and I mean *nothing*, but obey me in thought, word, and deed."

All the venom and power of his words sunk into her bones.

Her entire body went numb. Grimnaugh stood by her, but did nothing except give her an encouraging nod.

A slow, martial beat thrummed through the hall. Ponderous, inevitable, demanding. The sound grew louder, as if the drummers walked the endless halls of the palace. A parade of battle-wearied Fae tramped in with the slow tattoo, all in perfect formation.

Ranks of bronze spears, swords, a myriad of Fae mounts and soldiers of every description filled the hall. Clíodhna didn't think the space would hold so many, but it seemed to expand to accommodate the additional Fae.

As they all stopped in position, courtiers ranged next to the dais. The soldiers and other Fae stood before her, arrayed for her approval.

A bell tolled, reverberating across the room and the hills beyond. The bell rang again, and once more. Echoes of its ring died out and the silence fell heavy upon the gathered host.

The ever-present ambient glow dimmed, almost as dark as a mortal night. Clíodhna glanced at Cerul, who lifted her arms in a demonstration of power. The tall Fae twisted her hands in an elegant gesture and the stars came out.

In all her time in Faerie, Clíodhna had never seen stars. With no day and no night, only the ambient glow of the land itself, she missed staring at the twinkling lights in the sky.

A splash of white, the path of starlight, shone above her in sparkling glory. Gasps went up, as many of the Fae had never traveled to the mortal world.

Soon, glittering points of light traveled across the sky, sped by Cerul's magic. A glow on the horizon hinted with feather touches of teal and blue, turning to purple and peach.

When the sun rose in brilliant splendor, Clíodhna wept in nostalgic triumph. If she'd regained control over her body, she would have fallen to her knees to greet her old friend, the dawn she'd lost for so long.

This grandeur once colored her every morning for her entire life until she came to Faerie. Now, she beheld the wonder once again in exaltation.

This couldn't be the real sun. But Cerul's illusion imitated the mortal world so well, try as she might, Clíodhna didn't see a difference. What a wondrous achievement.

While trembling from the power of the gift Cerul granted her, Clíodhna took in a deep breath, trying to regain sway over her emotions. With Bodach controlling her physical reactions, at least she kept her mind in line.

The drumming came again, but instead of a slow, martial march, it rapped out a precise tattoo, as if announcing some great event.

When it finished, Bodach held her hand up in his, as if signaling a victory. "Our beloved Queen has perished. She fought bravely against those who rebelled against her, but her time has fallen.

"Now, we have a new Queen, a Queen who will take up the Faerie Mantle and lead us to victory. All hail Queen Clíodhna the Fair One!"

The sheer wall of noise of Fae cheers smashed upon Clíodhna like a physical assault. She closed her eyes against the onslaught, wishing she could cup her hands to her ears.

They cheered three times, a grand huzzah to welcome her. She opened her eyes to study the faces of each of her new courtiers.

Cerul's pleasure seemed genuine and after her coronation gift, Clíodhna understood. Cerul had been a supporter of hers for some time, without her realizing it.

Grimnaugh looked ambivalent. He must know she hadn't accepted this responsibility willingly. Other courtiers looked either thrilled, pensive, worried, or outright angry. She made a note of each reaction, to store them away and examine them later. For now, she must get through this day.

Something rumbled in the distance, like a team of galloping horses. She glanced up at the arches, but nothing dire seemed to be happening. The hallway filled with Fae, so no enemy could rush in without warning. Clíodhna shoved her unease away and turned to Bodach.

He grinned at her, a grin full of lascivious delight, kissed her hand, and gestured for her to take a seat on the throne, at long last.

Clíodhna glanced behind her to make certain the throne hadn't moved, took a deep breath, did her best to look regal and assured, and sat.

The rumble grew. Now, the walls shook and the ground buzzed. She gripped the throne's arms until her knuckles turned white, glancing at Grimnaugh for an explanation. He gave a shrug, his expression bleak. The other courtiers glanced around in patent confusion.

Bodach looked unconcerned, and still held her hand. She tried to extract it, but he gripped tight, crushing her bones.

"Bodach! What is that? Let me go."

"Not yet, my Queen. You have one more thing to do."

"What? What is that?"

"That, my Queen, is the power of the land of Faerie. You must survive its attack. Somehow."

Rumbling bounced the throne until her teeth rattled and her spine ached. Clíodhna clung onto the arms of the chair for dear life, begging it to stop. Bodach's laugh echoed in her ears as the noise drowned out everything else.

A wave of sparking power reached up from the ground and engulfed her like a giant hand, slamming her against the throne. She struggled to fight against it, but she had no defenses against such strength.

Just like in her dream, this power from the earth surged like a behemoth, a huge and unstoppable force. Its amorphous potency surrounded her, drowning her in its depths.

Clíodhna tried to pull in a gasp of air, but failed. Panicked, she drew energy from this attacking earth, pulling it into her body to wrest some control from it. A trickle seeped into her bones, but the vast majority of it ignored her command.

Ignore me, will you? I'll teach you better.

Angry now at its recalcitrance, she doubled her efforts, calling upon every trick Adhna had taught her. She yanked that rope of power, swollen with brute strength, and shoved it into her own body, under her governance.

It fought, bucking like a dolphin on the waves of an ocean storm, but she wouldn't give up. Clíodhna clung upon it without mercy, tightening her grip with each heartbeat, until it sighed within her clasp and suffused her muscle and bone, a surge of sweetness taking over every bit of her body.

With intense relief, she took a deep breath. Power buzzed through her, energy crackling along her skin.

Clíodhna turned to Bodach, whose lascivious grin fell a few notches. Several courtiers fell to their knees and bowed their heads to the floor when she rose.

Clíodhna became the Faerie Queen in name and power, and in command of this land.

Bodach took a step back, his eyes growing wide. She'd done as he'd wanted and survived the onslaught of power, and now he'd pay.

But then, his grin returned, and he trailed a finger along her arm. She narrowed her gaze, but he turned away, unconcerned.

Bodach clapped twice, and the Faerie host parted in precise formation. A column in the center opened, and a squad of Fae ran in, carrying tables and benches. After placing one table on the dais, they placed long ones in a center line. Then another squad hurried in with platters.

The platters gleamed in Cerul's fake sunlight, glinting with bright sparks as they traveled through the beams. Several Fae squinted either at the beams themselves or the shine from the plates. As servants laid the food upon the table, aromas wafted toward her, and Clíodhna remembered that it had been a very long time since she'd eaten.

How could she think of food? When her most dangerous enemy propped her up as a puppet leader, she couldn't do anything to stop it, and her body craved meat? How banal she had become, a slave to her base desires?

Still, she couldn't deny her body's craving.

The savory scent of roasted food made her mouth water. Glass goblets of exquisite grace and elegant design held potent mead. Had the Fae made these? Or were they artifacts from the human world?

With a feeling of ceremony, she rose, holding one glass up to the gathered Fae, and took a sip. They all cheered and drank from their own vessels.

The warmth of the mead rushing through her blood didn't feel like it had before. Now, it bristled and tingled in her blood, like tiny explosions throughout her body. Clíodhna sat with care, unwilling to appear unsteady.

Had the power shift morphed her, somehow? Changed her to a true Fae? Had it transformed her human parts? A chill traveled down her spine.

Some ancient tales told of mortals demanding someone prove they bled to determine they weren't Fae. As a test, she pinched her skin, not knowing how that would prove anything. She bled, but Adhna bled. She'd seen it and dressed his wounds.

Clíodhna nibbled at the food, not as ravenous as she'd been. The courtiers ate with cautious enthusiasm, each one sneaking a glance toward the dais. Bodach ate with fastidious manners. Clíodhna had imagined him with horrible manners, shoving food into his mouth like an animal. Instead, he cut each slice of meat with his bronze leaf-shaped knife and placed it daintily in his mouth. He chewed and swallowed each morsel before cutting another off.

Noticing her regard, he turned. "Do you not find the offering to your taste, my dearest? I can call for something else, if you prefer." He clapped twice. A young servant appeared at his shoulder, all eager eyes and nervous anticipation.

"What would be your pleasure, my Queen? A delicacy from the mortal world, perhaps? Or something sweet and unusual? Ah, I know!" He whispered into the servant's upswept ear and the youngster darted off.

Clíodhna watched the courtiers and noted each Fae's reaction to Bodach and to herself. She listened to the snippets of conversation that drifted through the hall.

When the servant returned, they staggered under a huge platter. On top was a miniature palace, almost like this one. It even had soaring archways of glittering white and blue, with living ivy entwined around the towers.

With an exclamation, Clíodhna realized the castle consisted of sweet cake. Even the ivy was edible. Her eyes grew wide, but she didn't want to ruin the incredible creation by eating it.

Bodach laughed at her hesitation and sliced into one hallway with his bronze knife, offering her a slice. "Eat of the sweets, my dearest. You are the Queen and should have all that is wonderful."

For just a moment, her heart melted against his perfidy. But then she remembered his cruelty and it hardened again. She bit into the confection and relished the intense sweetness. How many bees had toiled for this much honey?

She turned to her captor and Consort. "Tell me, Bodach, why did you wish me to sit on this throne? For you have obviously arranged everything."

He blinked with feigned innocence. "I have? That's curious. I didn't realize I could be so crafty."

The court grew quiet as her hissed response cut across the entire hall. "As your Queen, I forbid you to lie to me."

Still with a cheerful grin on his face, Bodach blinked. "As you are my Queen, I have no ability to lie to you, anyhow. Please, enjoy your coronation feast. Soon, there will be dancing!"

Bodach caught the eyes of a courtier hovering on the sidelines, and that Fae ran out of the hall. Clíodhna gritted her teeth. She'd confront him afterward, not before the entire court. She might not be familiar with being a Queen, but she'd learned some etiquette from her time as a handmaiden.

The courtier returned with a group of Fae, each carrying an odd object. They stood to one side of the hall, lifted the objects, and played.

Clíodhna had attended the Queen's court a hundred times already, and seldom had she heard instrumental music. They'd held balls and dances, but usually with a Fae singer or a group of singers. Perhaps the old Queen hadn't cared for such tools.

But how could anyone not be delighted with such an exquisite melody? The music soared up and down in graceful descants, at once describing the flight of a butterfly and a powerful rainstorm.

Clíodhna shut her eyes and lost herself in the music's magic, quite forgetting where she sat and who sat next to her.

When the music ceased, she gasped, as if someone had punched her in the stomach. The removal of such a glorious sound was a horrible loss. The room spun with music and mead, and perhaps with the sweet palace confection.

Her stomach roiled and her breath grew to shallow gasps. Clíodhna clutched at the edge of the table, unable to stand or leave without danger of stumbling. Queens didn't stumble. Nor could she appear ill in front of her people, especially not during coronation. She needed no one else to tell her what a bad omen that would be.

In and out. One breath. Two breaths. In and out. Her nausea subsided and she merely felt uncomfortable. Eventually, her head cleared somewhat, allowing her to pay attention to her surroundings.

The courtiers finished their meal during the first song, then servants cleared tables and dishes from the center of the hall. Fae formed clumps for a formal dance. Bodach stood and offered his hand, but she glared at it with repugnance. "I prefer to watch."

A flicker of rebellious disappointment colored his expression, but he sat back on his lesser throne. The musicians began their tune and the courtiers danced.

She'd never watched the balls from this vantage point. Up on the dais, she commanded a full view of the formations, a measured orchestration of perfect movement, both elegant and ordered.

Not one Fae stepped out of place, nor hesitated on the beat. Swirling clothing and glittering hair accompanied the dancers, as did the occasional wing or feathers. Clíodhna was entranced with the artistry of both the dance and the dancers.

Swirls and twirls of delicate tracery across the glittering dance floor. The sky above, with Cerul's artificial sun still high, now dimmed with colorful clouds dancing in a similar rhythm. Clíodhna watched the mirrored dance above until her neck ached.

Cerul had outshone herself with the sky today. She must remember to thank the Fae personally. That chance remark when she'd first arrived must have been the impetus to create this illusion, and she appreciated that personal touch.

Clíodhna glanced at the remaining palace confection and the other scraps of food. They hadn't been removed with the rest of the tables, as she still ate and drank, so she grabbed another morsel.

This was some sort of mushroom marinated in garlic sauce. She popped it in her mouth and nearly gagged at the strong taste. She took a long swig of mead to clear her throat, and her head spun again.

As the dance ended, Clíodhna stood and clapped her hand once in approval, as she'd seen Queen Áine do so many times.

The courtiers, out of breath from their exertions, fell apart from their rigid lines into knots of friendship and gossip. This freed her from her role as rigid hostess, and allowed her to dismount the dais.

Bodach placed a hand on her arm, halting her step down from the throne. "My lady, you still have a duty."

Clíodhna forced a smile on her face. "Oh? Do remind me, Bodach."

"You must punish those who rebelled against Queen Áine, of course. You cannot let them go free for their insolence."

She scowled. "But the marsh and wild Fae rebelled. Most of them are already dead."

His lip curled into a nasty smile. "Nevertheless, you must discipline the rest. Or else others will believe they can try to throw over the Queen with impunity."

The marsh and wild Fae loved her best, the ones who first came to her in their time of need. The ones who kept her company on lonely nights in Adhna's roundhouse. How could she punish them for trying to make their lives better? "I can't do that, Bodach."

He raised his eyebrows. "If you do not, the other Queens will take you to task, else risk similar resurgence in their queendoms. This is not merely a matter of your own realm, Queen Clíodhna. It's a matter for all of Faerie."

She ground her teeth with stubborn intransigence. She didn't want to do this, but his words made a horrid sense. "Very well. What do you advise?"

His grin stretched from ear to ear, the bark crackling at his glee. "I suggest a token punishment for their leaders."

Clíodhna drew in a deep breath and sat back on her throne. "Bring them to me."

Chapter Sixteen

It took some time to gather the leaders of the revolt, but after a few sleeps, they assembled before Clíodhna's throne. Every courtier she'd ever met came to watch her mete out punishment.

She'd consulted with Grimnaugh to gauge his opinion on Bodach's idea.

"I'm afraid he's right, my Queen. You must punish them. However, your punishment needn't be too dire. Perhaps banishing them to the mortal world for a time would be sufficient, at least for the leaders. Most of them survive well enough there, and enjoy their time, so it isn't a harsh punishment."

"Is that why I've met so many there? Did they all get banished from Faerie?"

He shook his head. "Oh, no! We go when we want if we're allowed. I've never been, but many travel there. The mortal realm works differently, and some enjoy those differences." Grimnaugh shivered, displaying his own opinion of the mortal realm.

Clíodhna had so many questions about that statement, she couldn't choose one. A flood of nostalgia washed over her, and an aching need to hold her children tight. Grateful that only Grimnaugh was here to witness her sadness, she gave in to her sobs and fell to her knees, her face in her hands. She cried silent tears, her shoulders shaking with the love of her children, away from her in the mortal world.

Grimnaugh patted her shoulder with awkward comfort and cleared his throat. When she dragged her sorrow back inside, she looked up, tears staining her cheeks. "Grimnaugh, have you ever missed someone so much it felt like something stabbed you?"

He cleared his throat again. His voice grew to a mere whisper. "Once, your Grace. Once, long, long ago, my dear lover. A piece of my heart died with him on the battlefield."

Still on her knees, she hugged him tight. At first, he resisted with a stiff back, but soon he melted into her hug. They drew comfort from each other.

Clíodhna drew back and sniffed. "If I must punish the rebellious Fae, let me do so in the kindest way I can. For the sake of those we miss. For they surely lost loved ones in the battle, and we might divide families with this edict."

Grimnaugh's brow furrowed in puzzlement. "But if you do that, other Queens may see you as weak."

"Then we must disabuse them of that notice. How often do the Queens visit each other?"

"Visit? The Queens? They don't, your Grace."

Her eyes grew wide. "What? Queen Áine never visited other Queens? They never came to this court? She sent Adhna as an emissary in the past."

"Never, ever! Not that any Fae in living memory can recall."

She tapped her lip, gazing out the window of her chambers. "Perhaps we should change that."

Grimnaugh swallowed. "But any Queen visiting would be at a horrible disadvantage, and in terrible danger! Your power base would surround her, leaving her vulnerable to attack! None would take such a chance."

She gave him a half-smile. "Even if I did so first?"

Grimnaugh wrung his hands. "I beg you not to do this!"

"If Bodach thinks he can control my actions when I'm the Queen, he's made a dire mistake. I will not sit idle and let him manipulate me because he holds power over my people and my children. If I can make allies with other Queens, the power structure will shift. I must try."

Grimnaugh's face had turned pale green and his spots had faded almost to invisibility. He spoke in a bare whisper. "What do you mean to ask the Queens for?"

She stared out the window again. Cerul's fake sun had faded after the coronation, so she only saw the ever-present glowing landscape. "Safe passage for me and my blood family through any of their lands. And I shall grant the same to them."

"But how can you guarantee Bodach and his loyal Fae won't attack them?"

Giving a shrug, Clíodhna said, "If he does, then I will no longer be Queen. I'm the only one he can control in that position, otherwise he wouldn't have placed me here. Therefore, it's in his best interest to keep me in place."

Grimnaugh's gaze darted around. "I don't like it, my Queen. I don't like it. Too much can go wrong. I don't like it one bit!"

"Grimnaugh, you've been my dear friend and invaluable help. But I never asked you to like it. Do you think it will work?"

He stared off into the distance, blinking a few times. A purple insect not quite like a butterfly flew across the window. "Your logic is sound, my Queen. It fits into how things work in Faerie."

Clíodhna stood, dusting her hands together in a gesture of final decision. "Excellent. Now, let's make some plans."

Still nervous, Grimnaugh asked, "What plans?"

"Since Adhna hasn't returned from his last mission, we must find another emissary to set things in place. Someone I trust above all pettiness." She lifted one eyebrow and frowned at Grimnaugh. "And as much as I value you by my side, only one choice remains."

He glanced around behind him three times before placing a hand on his chest. "Your Grace, you can't mean me! I'm no diplomat. Indeed, I possess no rank to be an emissary. I wouldn't even know what to say!"

Clíodhna let out a chuckle. "I have faith you'll know exactly what to say. You've been acting as Seneschal for me since I got here. You understand court etiquette inside and out. And above all else, you are unthreatening and humble. What more could I need in an emissary? Except two of you, so I could keep you by my side." She grinned with her last words, hoping to break the tension.

Grimnaugh let out a deep sigh. "Very well, your Grace. I cannot say no, though I will ask Cerul to take my place by your side. Will you agree to that? Wait, you could send Cerul! She's much more regal and acceptable as an emissary!"

"Which is why she cannot go. I need someone who will be unnoticed by Bodach and his agents. You will be perfect."

His last suggestion rejected, Grimnaugh hung his head. "Yes, your Grace. I will leave after your next court, when you discipline the rebels. I should be by your side in case you have questions on that decision."

Clíodhna placed a hand on his shoulder and squeezed. "As always, I will welcome your help, my friend."

Clíodhna tried to hide her trembling hands by clasping them in her lap. She'd never sat in judgment on someone before, other than her own misbehaving children.

How did she think she possessed authority and power to punish thousands of Fae? Powerful beings in their own right, a people who had lived in the marshes and wild places of Faerie and the mortal world far longer than she'd been alive?

And yet here she sat, as the perpetrators were being brought in under guard to answer for their ill deeds.

Their ill deeds. They rebelled against a Queen who had made unreasonable decisions. That Queen had died in the battle, which had made Clíodhna herself Queen.

In reality, she should thank these rebels, these insurgents whose refusal to accept oppression had vaulted her to power. Of course, that presumed she'd craved that responsibility, and she didn't.

Yet, if she thanked them, she'd send the message to the entire realm of Faerie that they'd acted under her direction, under her orders, despite the untruth of that assumption.

Clíodhna's head ached with political machinations, and wished she was sitting anywhere else but her throne at this moment.

As they waited for the prisoners, Bodach arrived. He'd been absent while they searched for the rebels. Clíodhna had relished his absence so much, she'd never inquired where he'd disappeared to.

When he sat on the throne, he took her hand. Clíodhna tried to pull it away, but he held it fast. She kept her face neutral as she hissed, "Let go of my hand, Bodach."

He replied with a sweet tone, almost sing-song. "We must appear to be in accord for this decision, my Queen. Any hint that we aren't a united front would damage your strength and reputation."

She glanced at him out of the corner of her eyes, and he grinned back, as if they were lovers sharing a joke. He patted their clasped hands with his other one. "When we finish with this duty, I will show you the rest of the Queen's duties to her Consort."

Clíodhna put as much strength into her voice as she could muster. "You will do no such thing."

His voice remained sweet. "Do you forget, my Queen, I know where your children live in the mortal realm? I can go to them and do what I like. They hold no magical protections, and you are trapped in this realm as the Queen."

Clíodhna must remember to ask Adhna about that. She had the previous *géis* about only returning once. Would that still hold true with her new role? Or were there new rules she must adhere to?

Bodach trailed a finger up her arm in a casual caress. Her skin tingled, the sensation moving down her body, warming her desire. She clamped her jaw to quench her reaction to his sexual magic, but it still thrummed through her.

The first Fae stood taller than any she'd seen. He stood higher than a mature oak tree, and he resembled one. He walked with long, lumbering strides, his bark creaking as he drew closer. Clíodhna wondered how much power those branch-like arms held, and if he bore any relation to Bodach with his bark-like skin.

When the Fae halted, his guard had to hurry to catch up. They glared up at their prisoner, but he paid them no mind. His huge, yellow eyes blinked twice and then bowed to her, almost touching the ground with his uppermost branches.

When he straightened, he spoke in a rasping voice. "Greetings to you, Queen Clíodhna. I am pleased to vow my loyalty to you, with that of my people. We are of the Wannaig of the Bog-Oak People. I command some wild Fae."

"Greetings to you, Wannaig of the Bog-Oak People."

Further conversation halted while the guards led the other leader in. She came less willingly.

Her screeches resounded through the hall, echoing off the walls in painful staccato. Clíodhna clenched her teeth, wanting to cover her ears but not daring. The prisoner's keening ululated, up and down along the discordant scale.

Bodach turned to her with a whisper. "She proved a formidable foe. You must punish her with harsh determination, or she will fight against you, as she did with your predecessor."

Two guards struggled with a dark mass, dragging her forward with great effort. The prisoner raked at their eyes with sharp claws, but they pulled back out of reach. They both wore thick leather armor that covered their arms and legs, with leather helmets. They must have dealt with this prisoner before to have taken such precautions.

A stench preceded her, the stink of rotten vegetation and swamp gas. Her skin oozed black and green, leaving a trail of slime behind her. She cackled once and then screamed again, the sound cutting to Clíodhna's mind.

A third guard stood at attention. "Sanna the Swamp Hag, your Grace. She commands the marsh Fae."

Though she wanted to recoil from the foul creature, Clíodhna gestured to the second prisoner. "Greetings to you, Sanna the Swamp Hag."

Beside her, Bodach let out a derisive bark of laughter. Clíodhna shot him a quick glare.

Instead of the polite greeting Wannaig offered, Sanna let out a new ululation and spat in Clíodhna's direction. Several guards snapped to attention and pulled their swords out, but Clíodhna waved them down. "Her disdain for me is understandable,. Do not react without my orders."

Sanna's eyes grew wide as she sat on the floor, her cry dying a horrible death. She shot an unreadable look toward her fellow prisoner.

Clíodhna stood. "I called you both here to answer for your crimes against Queen Áine. I judge you both guilty of rebellion, but I would allow you to say something on your behalf."

Sanna hissed, while Wannaig bowed his head once with solemn dignity.

Bodach opened his mouth, but Clíodhna spoke first. "Very well. As leaders of this rebellion, I hereby sentence you to banishment from Faerie. You are to dwell in the mortal world for seven of their cycle of seasons. Upon your return, I shall require a renewal of your vow of loyalty."

Her Consort yanked on her arm. "My Queen! Your punishment is much too lenient! They'll only foment rebellion again with their followers, many of whom reside in the mortal realm! Execution is the only answer here."

Clíodhna turned to him and in a clear voice, said, "Bodach, you will be silent unless I request your counsel."

Bodach's mouth gaped open. He still held her hand and this time, he tried to withdraw it, but she kept it tight. He settled back into his throne in a petulant sulk.

Wannaig's voice remained calm. "Your judgment is fair, my Queen. I give you my vow now, should you wish to accept it."

Sanna wasn't as accommodating. She raised one shaggy eyebrow. "Where must we go in the mortal world? Can we choose our home?"

"You may choose the area in which you wish to dwell. I have no preference or command. However, your behavior will be monitored. If you are acting against my interests, I will discover this perfidy."

With a wave of her hand, Sanna dismissed that concern. "I've done my protest. Now I want to be by myself for a while." She turned to glare at her captors. "Take me to a passage now."

The guards glanced at Clíodhna for approval, and she gave it with a nod. "Seven cycles of the season. I will send an emissary to inform you when you can return."

Once they'd left the hall, Bodach snatched his hand from hers. "You are a fool!"

Clíodhna lifted her chin and kept her voice even. "You will address me as your Queen or your Grace, as you prefer, Consort. Now, leave. I have other matters to attend to."

Bodach growled and for a moment, Clíodhna thought he would attack her. He took a step toward her and five guards stepped forward, each one stamping the butt of their spear on the floor in a precisely timed beat. The bark-skinned Fae glanced at them and growled again, stomping off in a huff.

Grimnaugh whispered, "That went better than I'd expected, your Grace."

She waved his comment away. "They only wanted their concerns addressed, and those died with the prior Queen. As the new Queen, they have no quarrel with me."

Grimnaugh frowned, scratching behind his ear. "It didn't hurt that you've befriended many of their people. In a way, they fought for you."

Clíodhna swiveled to face him, anger hard in the grim line of her lips. "Never say that again, Grimnaugh, not even in jest."

His eyes grew wide. "Yes, my Queen."

Chapter Seventeen

Bodach had disappeared after her judgment on the rebels, and Clíodhna relished the respite. She was eating a meal at court when Grimnaugh appeared in the arched door to the hall.

He came with dragging feet and a forlorn expression. His clothing was nothing but scorched scraps of fabric. Clíodhna didn't need to ask about his success. The answer was clear in every line of his body.

Court cleared as the courtiers all took their rest, so she led him to her antechamber to give his report.

The chamber, while much smaller than the throne room, was large enough to hold twenty people. Rose vines covered the walls on a delicate lattice.

Clíodhna sat on the couch and gestured for him to sit in a chair. "Am I to conclude that Queen Aoibheall has no wish to take part in my alliance?"

He closed his weary eyes. "You could come to that conclusion. I arrived at her court and met first with her Seneschal, then her Consort, and finally approached her at court. She gave no hint of her thoughts in her expression during my entire presentation. When I finished, she let the silence build until it grew almost painful."

Clíodhna considered such a technique a powerful tool and stored that away for future reference.

"When she spoke, she used a single word. 'No.' Then she lifted her hands and brought them down, as if throwing something. As soon as her arms rose, I ran. I'd heard of her preferred rejection in the past and had no intention of becoming a victim."

A servant brought in a platter of fruit. She refrained from speaking until he had left. She picked up a sweet, purple fruit and bit into it, after offering Grimnaugh the same. He took one but simply held it.

After she wiped the juice from her cheek, she asked, "Her preferred rejection?"

He shivered. "She blasted me with a ball of fire! I only missed getting roasted by running back and forth rather than in a straight line. I barely escaped but my clothing got singed." He held up a battered tunic with unmistakable burn marks down one side.

Clíodhna stood, anger prickling her skin. The sky darkened, despite its lack of clouds. "She attacked you? My official emissary?"

Grimnaugh's gaze flicked to the sky in panic. "My Queen! Please, don't react so. This is a mild rebuke for your request. Queen Aoibheall is well known for her temper. This isn't worth reacting to."

She crossed her arms and fixed him with a gimlet glare. "Not worth reacting to."

"Indeed, my Queen. In fact, I suggest we try the next Queen's realm. Grian might be more interested."

Clíodhna sat back on the couch and took another bite of her fruit. "Wasn't she my predecessor's sister? I'd think that would pre-dispose her against me."

Grimnaugh managed a mischievous grin. "The two were not on friendly terms."

"Hmm. Very well, Grian's realm shall be your next destination. Tell me what you know of her."

"Grian was Áine's sister. She's the pale, dim, winter sun to Áine's full, bright, summer sun. While the realm is always somewhat light here, and you have Cerul who can summon a facsimile of the sun itself, she rules the short days of the colder seasons in the mortal world. Her realm is darker, gloomier, and many of her creatures boast darker hearts."

Clíodhna let out a snort. "Queen Grian sounds like a delightful friend."

His bark of laughter made her heart warm as Grimnaugh put his fruit back and took another, peeled the thicker skin away, and chewed the flesh before speaking. "You might jest, but she may have use of you."

Clíodhna didn't care for the sound of that. "What use?"

"She has, in the past, expressed a love of the ocean."

"And what is that to me?"

His face broke into a grin. "You hold power over the sea."

Clíodhna blinked and sat up straight. "I do? Was someone supposed to inform me of this?"

Grimnaugh rolled his eyes, taking another bite of his fruit. "Where do you think you call your storms from?"

"Adhna said I had air magic. He taught me earth magic, but I had the natural call for air."

"You command water magic. The storms come from the sea, not from the air. The wind, yes, that comes from the air. A strong queen can call upon multiple sources of power, but from what I've seen, you're an ocean Queen."

Clíodhna blinked a few times, looking into the middle distance. "I grew up near the ocean, far to the southwest corner of the island. We lived on the beach, and I loved swimming with the dolphins."

"Yes, exactly that. You will again, I'm sure. *There* is where your true powers lie."

"What would Grian want of my power over the ocean, then?"

He gave a crafty grin and ate another section of his fruit. "That is what I mean to find out on my mission."

Clíodhna pressed her lips together. "Did you hear anything of Adhna during your visits?"

Grimnaugh fiddled with his fingers. "I still can't find out where Áine sent him on that last mission, nor have I heard of him since. He must be somewhere in the mortal world. Maybe he's looking after your children?"

That idea warmed Clíodhna's heart. "Perhaps so. I hope he is well. I hope they are well."

Much to Clíodhna's surprise, Queen Grian did agree to be part of a very loose alliance, but none of the others. Grimnaugh felt certain she only did so out of animosity for her sister. No matter that Clíodhna hadn't intended to usurp Áine, only that it happened, via Bodach's machinations.

Grian didn't want a visit from Clíodhna, though, according to Grimnaugh. She would agree to pledge safety for Clíodhna and her family, in exchange for the same, but had no wish to meet.

When she met with Grimnaugh in her antechamber, long after the court cleared, Clíodhna scowled at this detail.

"I suspect," Grimnaugh said, "she doesn't care for traveling much. Rumor has it she's never left her realm, even for battle."

"How does she lead her troops if she's not there?"

"She either sends her war leader, her Consort, or arranges the battles to be near her."

Clíodhna couldn't stifle a snort. "Arranges her battles? This isn't a game on a strategy board. These are the lives of our subjects!"

"The Queens hold a great deal of power, and if she wishes to use it for her own convenience, well, other Queens have used their power with less wisdom."

"And yet she wants my ocean power for something? Did she speak to you of that?"

"Yes, but in private. This would be a personal favor, you understand, not one between Queens. Are you willing to hear her request?"

A servant came in with mead. Clíodhna waited until they were alone again before nodding. "Tell me what she wants."

Grimnaugh poured mead into two goblets and handed her one. "She wants you to heal the ocean."

Clíodhna gaped at Grimnaugh. "She *what?*"

"Not the whole ocean! Just a part."

She sat back and took a sip. "Explain."

"There's a place in the mortal world where the ocean has been damaged by men, a place along the west coast. They throw their waste into the water and the sea life is suffering. Some creatures from her realm live there, Fae of the sea, and they've been complaining."

Clíodhna rose and began pacing. "But I can only go to the mortal world once again. I'm stuck here as Queen."

Grimnaugh made a sound in the back of his throat that might have meant agreement. "She's aware of your *géis*, and said the need is not urgent. When you *do* return, she asks that you spend some time healing that part of the sea."

If she had the power to do so, she would have done such healing anyhow, if she had the skill. Clíodhna wished she could find Adhna. He would be able to teach her how to heal the ocean. In the meantime, she needed to send an answer.

"You said humans lived nearby this damaged spot. Would they object to my work?"

He shrugged. "They dwell on an island not far away. I believe you can do your work from the mainland, without their direct knowledge."

"Very well. Tell her I agree to this boon. In return, I ask… I don't know. What should I ask as a personal favor, Grimnaugh? I can't waste this opportunity, but I'm not sure what might be within her power to grant."

He bit his lip, and a roguish grin spread across his mouth. "The most insidious, open-ended boon a Queen can ask for—a future favor."

"What if she refuses?"

The Fae shrugged. "She won't refuse. She wants the ocean to heal. It matters little to her when, as Fae live so long. The counter-favor might be similarly long-termed."

Clíodhna considered her initial reason for forming alliances with the Queens, to garner leverage against Bodach's power base. His defiance of her judgment on the rebels proved that he'd expected to have more power over her. He would certainly move against her soon, so she must prepare.

To that end, she called several courtiers for a meeting after court. Not all the courtiers; only those most sympathetic to her, rather than Bodach.

Clíodhna asked Grimnaugh and Cerul to gauge each courtier's loyalties and approach them privately. When they'd gathered, she bit her lip, counting the numbers. Only slightly more than half of the greater Fae had come. She searched for the young white-skinned Fae she'd met on her arrival at the court, but couldn't see him. Bodach must have nobbled the youngster already, more's the pity. He seemed sweet.

Still, she must move forward with her plan. Clíodhna had the servants seal the hall, stood on her dais, and cleared her throat. "I've assembled you to ask for your loyalty."

The courtiers murmured, confusion clear on their faces. One stepped up, a blocky, brown Fae from the outer marshes, near to the border of Grian's realm. "I don't understand, my Queen. You took our vows at your coronation."

"Obligatory vows to the new Queen, yes. I'm now requesting your true loyalty to my person. Asking, not demanding. If you prefer not to pledge yourselves to me, you may decline, and I will not punish you. I need to be able to count upon your heartfelt support."

She felt like a Chief begging his warriors to fight for him, but she must have actual, verbal, magical vows from them before they were dragged into a pitched battle with Bodach. He was probably out garnering similar support. To ignore such herself would be folly.

Cerul stepped forward, her head held high. She knelt before Clíodhna, bowing her head with perfect dignity. "I vow myself to you, my Queen. Until my blood runs cold and my body turns to dust. Until I walk with the Gods in *Tír na nÓg*. Until the memory of my power has faded."

A second Fae, one of the beautiful sea Fae, came forward next, and vowed themselves with similar words. One by one, each of the assembled gave their loyalty.

With each vow, her power grew. A tangible force surged into her, coursing through her veins and making her skin glow. When each had made their promise, she stood tall on her dais, shining with their love and regard. "The day may soon come where I shall call upon my host to march beside me. I now vow to you that I will do my best to be a fair Queen, and to protect you to the best of my abilities. I thank you for your trust in me."

They left in small groups, though a few stayed behind to ask her questions. She answered them each and, for the thousandth time, wished

Adhna stood by her side. He had so much more experience at this palace intrigue. Grimnaugh helped immensely, but he didn't have the initiative and influence she needed by her side.

Clíodhna wondered how long it would take one of her new inner court to betray her to Bodach.

Once they'd all left, she turned to Grimnaugh. "I need one more favor from you."

He grinned wide. "Just the one, my Queen?"

Clíodhna returned the grin, but then frowned. "I need you to find Adhna. His presence at my side is necessary. I don't care what you need to do or who you need to bribe. Find him."

Grimnaugh gave a single, sharp nod, and hurried away.

While she waited, Clíodhna held court, her heart skipping a beat each time a new Fae arrived. Each time, she hoped it was Adhna and Grimnaugh returning, but each time, she was disappointed.

The current court had lasted a horribly long time, but she didn't feel it was fair to cut off the waiting Fae just because she was weary. That had been the previous queen's habit, and she didn't want to repeat Áine's mistakes.

Clíodhna gestured for the current petitioner to continue their request. The lesser Fae listed every single slight their neighbor had committed over the last eon, in excruciating detail.

By this time, after a very long court session, she'd drunk three goblets of mead, and her attention drifted from his diatribe.

Her body didn't react the same to alcohol now that she'd gained that power from her inner court, but she still grew muzzy with too much.

Her mind drifted, remembering when she'd first met Adhna. He'd been so kind to her, teaching her so much. Then she remembered how well his hands understood her body, and her flesh craved his. She wanted him back with a sudden intensity.

Grimnaugh shuffled in at that moment, as if summoned by her musings. He came to her side, leaned over, and whispered, "I discovered news of Adhna."

She removed her hand from her breast. It must have drifted there in her mind-fog. The petitioner still droned on with his litany of complaints in a mind-numbing monotone.

Clíodhna sat straight and cut the petitioner off with a curt gesture. He halted mid-word. "I've developed a headache. Court is dismissed."

The petitioners shuffled off and soon they stood alone in the great hall, except for servants and a few straggling courtiers. She didn't want these privy to Grimnaugh's mission, so she walked to her antechamber, beckoning for him to follow.

Once she'd offered Grimnaugh refreshment and shooed the servants out, she folded her hands in her lap. "What did you find?"

He bowed his head. "Nothing good, your Grace."

Clíodhna's skin pebbled and her heart skipped a beat. "How so?"

He stared at his shoes. "I found no trace of him at any of the other courts, though a few didn't deign to answer."

She held her hand up. "I don't care which steps failed. Tell me what you found."

Grimnaugh cleared his throat again. "Bodach has him."

Clíodhna closed her eyes to keep from crying out in rage and frustration. "Bodach! May his rotten hide be eaten by a thousand beetles."

"Yes, your Grace. He may have had Adhna since he left on his mission, but I couldn't discover more details. Suffice to say, Bodach will use this to his advantage."

Jumping to her feet, she paced the antechamber. "Son of a diseased donkey! There's no telling what that creature has done to him."

Grimnaugh glanced up and his gaze flicked to the platter of fruits. She gestured for him to help himself. He picked up a tart, yellow fruit and bit deep, the juice dribbling down his chin. After he wiped it with his sleeve, he said, "Adhna is strong. He's been in similar situations in the past, with a Queen rather than a Consort. Still, Bodach's mind is twisted, and he delights in pain."

Clíodhna halted and narrowed her gaze at her assistant. "So I've noticed. We need to save him, Grimnaugh."

A doubtful expression crossed his face. "That won't be easy. Bodach is well-versed with imprisoning powerful beings."

"I've freed Adhna from one of his traps in the past." She continued pacing. "There's no doubt of your information?"

"None, your Grace. If I had any doubt, I would have told you."

Clíodhna imagined her hands around Bodach's neck, squeezing the life out of his treacherous soul. She wanted to see him beg and scream for his life, and she wanted to deny him that boon.

Unclenching her fists, she turned back to Grimnaugh. "We need a plan. It's a lucky thing we now have the pledged loyalty of most of my higher Fae and Queen Grian."

Grimnaugh gave a wry smile. "Not luck, my Queen. Sound planning on your part."

She waved the comment away. "Whichever, such loyalty will prove most useful. Adhna is well-liked by most of the high court. Every session, someone is asking about his return. I can use that to spur action."

He squinted up at her. "What are you thinking?"

Clíodhna set her mouth in a hard line. "I'm thinking Bodach will not give him up without a battle. He has a purpose in holding my lover, and he's biding his time for when he needs it. I don't mean to give him that advantage."

Grimnaugh finished his fruit and tossed the pit onto the platter. "Go on."

She rubbed her arms and raised her eyebrows. "Do you have any idea where he's holding Adhna?"

"A stronghold on the border, near Grian's realm. I've only been there once, long ago, and hope never to repeat the experience. A nasty place."

Clíodhna pursed her lips. That didn't sound promising. "And are you certain Adhna's there? Nasty how?"

"Yes, he's there. My agent in Bodach's guards assured me that he's seen Adhna in the bowels of the fortress. Bodach has infected the surrounding land with death. Nothing lives, not even in the soil."

A muscle in her jaw twitched. "He created a place in the mortal realm like that. A pit where he held Adhna. He must have done it again, but in Faerie."

Grimnaugh let out a long breath and clasped his hands. "The fortress is well-defended, your Grace. He has a great deal of followers and resources."

Clíodhna placed her hands on her hips. She thought back to the wars between the gods and what their tactical details might tell her. Many of the tales described great clashes between the *Fir Bolg* and the *Tuatha Dé Dannan*, and while these might be legends, they might hold clues to help her construct a battle plan.

"Do any of my inner court have battle experience?"

Grimnaugh pursed his frog-lips in consideration. "Your greatest asset would have been Sanna, who you just exiled to the mortal realm."

"Who I only exiled because Bodach insisted."

"Exactly. Other than Sanna, I judge Gabha to be a superior strategist."

Clíodhna scoured her memory of her loyal Fae, and one popped into mind. "Gabha? Is he the bronze smith I met when I first arrived at court? The stout Fae with black skin?"

"That's correct, your Grace."

"Excellent. Send him to me. We must make certain we can win before we make our move. Can you describe his defenses? How many troops does he have? What are their strengths and weaknesses?"

"I can find out, your Grace."

"Do that, and bring me whatever information you gather. Other than being a dead place, I want details of the terrain, the approaches, and their defensibility. What weapons he might command, both magical and mundane. We'll ask Gabha what else might be useful for our initiative."

As Grimnaugh left to fetch Gabha, Clíodhna stewed about what else she might have to do. She must call in her favor from Grian for this, as Bodach's dead lands marched along Grian's border. Grian might even be glad of the opportunity to rid them both of his power.

Gabha, his dark skin glistening in the low light, bowed as he entered. "How may I help you, my Queen?"

Clíodhna stood astride her horse, feeling silly in the frilly decorations over the battle armor. Her courtiers had draped both her and the horse with bronze armor so heavily, they could barely move, but Gabha insisted she be well-protected on the battlefield.

While she'd ridden horses all her life, it had taken much practice to learn how to stay astride with all the armor.

This Faerie mount spoke in her mind and had been trained as a battle steed. That made all the difference.

Cerul had used her talent to summon true wind and weather in Faerie, and even conjured a thunderstorm on the horizon. Clíodhna's first power had been over the weather, and she was glad to have that to draw upon.

While she had a bronze sword, Grimnaugh had assured her she wouldn't need to wield it. She held it only in case of a direct attack, but her host shouldn't allow Bodach's warriors to get so close. Still, Gabha had given her basic drills in the weapon.

Her host. That term sounded so odd, but she had no other description for the thousands of Faerie troops who marched along beside her.

Fae tall and small, human-like and not, tramped forward toward Bodach's dead land. Grian had assured her that her troops would join them along her own border, but asked her not to cross until the battle began.

When Clíodhna had quizzed Grimnaugh on why, his eyes had grown wide. "Do you not know? 'Tis the middle of the summer season, when the days in the mortal realm stretch the longest and the darkness grows short."

"Midsummer?" she glared at her assistant. "How does midsummer affect a battle in Faerie?"

"The veil between worlds affects any wielding of power, your Grace. Bodach's magic can slip into the mortal realm, as can yours. Those mortals might even perceive us, and join in the fighting."

She bit her lip. She didn't want to endanger any humans. But Bodach had discovered her purpose, so she had little choice.

Grimnaugh had reported that Bodach was gathering his own troops. If she waited too long, her enemy would grow too strong, and any incursion would become impossible. She must strike now if she had any hope of rescuing her mentor and lover. And holding onto her power in Faerie. And her life.

As they approached Bodach's fortress, the character of the land changed. The almost-butterflies no longer flew beside them. Tall grasses wilted and clung to the ground. Ponds grew into marshes and bogs. Trees grew gnarled and twisted and became dead hulks of lifeless wood.

Stones melted into horrific shapes, as if creatures had been frozen into a rictus of intense pain, lined the pathway into Bodach's demesne. Each one reached out to grab at those passing by, forever frozen in time. The buzz of insects silenced into the bubbling of noxious gases from the swamps. Those foul gases filled the air with intense miasma, making her choke and cover her mouth with her sleeve.

The tramp of thousands of feet, hooves, and claws drew toward the fortress, each face set in grim determination. Too many of those assembled had suffered at Bodach's hands.

Adhna was indeed well-loved and his imprisonment was enough reason for most of them to march at her command, even if they hadn't vowed loyalty. This assuaged her conscience that many of them might fall.

His fortress loomed in the distance, a black crag over a bare plain. Jets of smoke emerged from holes in the dirt, smelling of rotten eggs. Cerul, riding beside her, wrinkled her nose and Clíodhna flashed her a half-smile. The beautiful, elegant Fae would be out of sorts in this horrid landscape. But she needed Cerul's power over the light and darkness of Faerie to support her own weather magic.

Bodach's troops surrounded his fortress like a dark, bristling ocean. They undulated in the half-light, growling and screeching, much like Sanna the marsh Fae had. He must have garnered many of the marsh

Fae and the wild Fae, now that she'd banished their leaders to the mortal world. He must have been preparing for this a long time. Perhaps he'd even encouraged the other Fae to revolt in the first place, which set into motion both Queen Áine's death and her own rise to power.

But she still didn't understand *why* he wanted to place Clíodhna into power. Grimnaugh had assured her a Consort couldn't rule on his own without a Queen. He must have expected her to fall into line, a puppet to his desires, something to play with like a toy. When she'd been firm in her own opinions, he must have decided she wouldn't do, so he kidnapped Adhna to force her to comply.

But Adhna had been missing even before the prior Queen died, or so Grimnaugh believed. Bodach had been playing a long game. Regardless, he'd pay now.

Her troops formed a rough semi-circle around Bodach's forces. Grian's army stood on the other side, enclosing the area in an inescapable trap.

Had Bodach known of Grian's agreement? She hoped that detail had escaped his intelligence. With the other Queen's troops, they held the numeric advantage, but such things might count for naught if he'd had time to prepare for a siege.

Gabha had tried, over the course of their preparations, to outline the myriad of disasters that might befall them. They had no way of knowing how Bodach would fight back, react, or what weapons he had.

She stood in her saddle, surveying her War Chiefs, with Gabha in the lead. In her most strident, confident voice, she said, "Eat, drink, and ensure your arms are in working order. If they do not attack first, let us make ourselves ready for the day ahead."

Gabha and the other leaders nodded and passed the command down to the troops. Clíodhna dismounted and massaged her buttocks. As much as she'd practiced, it had been a while since she'd ridden for so long, and her muscles ached. Cerul also dismounted and offered her bread and cheese. She raised her eyebrows, knowing how difficult it was to find such food in Faerie.

Her friend chuckled. "I tricked a mortal into an ongoing exchange for bread, cheese, and honey. She only asked that I ensure her cow gave fresh milk through the winter. A more than fair bargain."

"Honey as well?"

Cerul stared at the ground. "I'm afraid I already ate the honey, my Queen. I'll save the next batch for you."

She clapped her hand on Cerul's shoulder. "Keep your honey, Cerul. You've more than earned the treat."

After they ate, Clíodhna gave Grimnaugh a nod. He saluted her and drew out a triple-curved ram's horn from the sling over his back. He held it to his lips and blew hard.

The sound shot bright and clear across the plain. Her host raised their weapons with a resounding cheer.

Though she couldn't see the details from the low hill she stood upon with her honor guard, Clíodhna watched the troops moving, like waves on the ocean shifting back and forth in a wicked tide. The ebb and flow of those who'd pledged their lives to her poured toward the enemy.

Archers let fly a volley of arrows, but most were deflected by the shield line. Then, the front lines marched forward, their spear tips pointed toward the enemy. Bodach's troops responded with a growl. They shook their own spears in defiance.

When the two lines met, the clash of the weapons grated in her ears. She wanted to clap her hands to keep the sound of her own Fae dying out. But Clíodhna owed it to them to hear their cries, to acknowledge their sacrifice for her and for Adhna.

The battle line wiggled and bent, first toward the fortress, and then back to her. A contingent of mounted Fae pierced into the marsh Fae, but the bog-oak people flanked from the left and repelled the attack.

Though the mounted Fae hacked at bog-oak limbs with abandon, the tree folk stomped stolidly forward, trampling their enemies until a clever Fae set a torch to one's branches. With their smoldering limbs, they retreated to regroup while the mounted knights advanced again.

An ululating cry from the right caught Clíodhna's attention, and a single marsh Fae ran for her, a bone sword held over his head.

She froze, unsure what to do, but then fumbled for the bronze sword at her side. Grimnaugh shouted and jumped in front of her, his only weapon the triple-curved horn. Cerul leapt forward and sliced down on the marsh Fae with her elegant bronze blade. The attacker fell and sizzled into a puddle of black ichor.

With a curl of her lip, Cerul wiped her blade until it shone, once again pristine. "I suggest you remain mounted, your Grace. That creature should never have gotten so close. You are safer there, and while you will be a more visible target, a lone attacker will have a more difficult path to you."

Still staring at the oozing puddle, Clíodhna shivered. Then she grabbed the saddle and pulled herself up, patting the sword once again in its sheath at her hip.

As the enemy pushed her troops back, Clíodhna glanced at the clouds Cerul had created. Now was her chance to contribute to the battle.

She drew upon the font of power within the air of Faerie, much diminished in this dead place. Clouds swirled and darkened into a thunderhead, and she pushed it toward his fortress, lightning crackling within it.

The light dimmed as the thunderclouds blocked out the ambient glow of the hills. Roiling clouds flashed and crashed as lightning struck the tallest spire of the tower.

As the spire crumbled into bits, Clíodhna grinned in intense satisfaction. The falling stone crushed several of Bodach's troops, but her own armies hadn't yet advanced to that point, so she felt no guilt as she prepared another volley of lightning.

Clíodhna lifted her arms as power crackled through her skin and bones and dropped them to bring the lightning again.

A bellow of rage drifted across the cacophony of battle. This made her grin even more widely. She prepared a third strike.

Something shimmered to her left, between her troops and Grian's. A glowing fog grew along the edge of her army, curling around the dead bits of land like a man caressing his lover's curves. Human-like Fae formed inside the shining mist, but they looked confused and terrified.

"Grimnaugh! Who are those new soldiers there? Are they our troops, or Grian's? Or is this some trick of Bodach's?"

He peered down into the mist. "I'm not sure, your Grace. I'll find out from Gabha." The frog-like Fae ran after the War Chief.

She couldn't make out many details, but one was wielding a scythe. Others didn't carry any weapons. Their clothing looked more like what human farmers would wear, rather than lesser Fae.

When Gabha rode to her side, she knew what he'd say. "Those aren't our troops, my Queen. Nor are they of Grian's or Bodach's forces."

Clíodhna's stomach roiled. "They're humans, aren't they?"

"Yes, my Queen, from what I can tell."

"Why are they here? They'll be killed in this battle."

The newcomers formed a circle against the strange creatures around them. Their fear was obvious in their posture and tentative swipes with the few weapons they had.

Grimnaugh pulled at his ear. "This must have something to do with the midsummer veil growing thin. The sheer amount of power concentrated here must have ripped a doorway into the mortal world. These might just be hapless peasants caught in the vortex."

Clíodhna swallowed as she stared at them. "Sweet Danú, they must be terrified. Send a contingent of mounted Fae to protect them, Gabha. If they wish to fight, give them weapons. If they wish to flee, bring them to safety. Back to the mortal world, if you can."

He bent at the waist. "Of course, my Queen."

As Gabha sent his mounted troops, Bodach's troops inched toward the small knot of humans. The mists still surrounded them, though it began thinning here and there. Men, women, even children stood terrified in that circle.

More people now emerged from the mists, but these newcomers strode forward with more purpose and confidence. They wore brown robes, and when Clíodhna squinted, she recognized Abbot Pátraic. "Son of a diseased donkey. What does he think he can do?"

Grimnaugh had gone off to help the humans, so no one was there to answer her question. Pátraic raised his crossed pieces of wood and his lips moved. He must be chanting his God's words, trying to fend off the evil of the Fae army.

Despite his danger, she chuckled at his conceit. As if their Christian God had power in Faerie.

When Grimnaugh and his contingent reached the first humans, an argument ensued. Some humans flocked to the frog-like Fae, pawing at him like beggars, while others grabbed weapons the Fae offered. Both Grian's and Clíodhna's troops formed a wedge to protect the interlopers.

Pátraic strode through both lines to confront Bodach's troops. He held his cross up high and continued chanting, his monks following him with their heads held high.

A few glanced at the Fae armies surrounding them with apprehension, but they still followed their Abbot. Clíodhna had to admit he showed little fear or hesitancy. At least he believed in his ideals, no matter how much he twisted them to his own purposes.

One group of humans with weapons had joined her forces, while a smaller group joined Grian's forces. More huddled in fear, cowering from the din of the surrounding battle, mostly women and children.

Not all the women huddled afraid. Several grabbed the offered bronze swords and joined in with battle cries worthy of the Morrígan.

The nearest of Bodach's army were a group of swamp Fae and reptilian creatures not unlike Grimnaugh. One jumped high and landed amidst the frightened humans, making them scatter with screams.

A young girl, suddenly alone, screeched in terror as the creature grabbed her hair and lifted her high. She swung like a toy as his mouth came closer to her face.

A monk with a fringe of dark curls around his bald head whirled and smacked the Fae on the back of the head with a wooden cudgel. The Fae dropped his prey and faced this new threat, his mouth slavering.

The monk glanced at the girl, who ran into the arms of a waiting man. Once she fled, the monk smashed what passed for the Fae's nose.

Clíodhna lost sight of the two combatants as more mist swirled to obscure her view. Grimnaugh and two other Fae were working some magic, which she felt more than saw. They formed a glowing arch between them, a rip between the worlds, sturdier than the accidental one the humans slipped through.

One by one, they led the frightened humans back to their own realm. Some of those fighting dropped their swords to join them. Others noticed the door but kept fighting.

She gestured for her War Chief, speaking with two of his sub-chiefs. "Gabha!"

He hurried to her side after dismissing them. "Yes, my Queen?"

"How goes the battle? I need updates."

"We're doing well enough. Bodach has held firm, but three of our units have penetrated his stronghold. One reports that he's inside and almost to the prison."

Her eyes widened. "Truly? I couldn't tell from here. You have excellent intelligence."

Gabha bowed low. "It's what I do, my Queen. Have you discovered the source of the unexpected civilians below?"

The stragglers disappeared through the glowing arch, but the monks still fought, with Pátraic at their head. She wished the odious priest would leave with the rest of his people. "They're from a village in the mortal world."

"Do you know them?"

"I do." The curly-haired monk, the one who'd saved the little girl, glanced up at her, and her heart skipped. *Odhrán!*

Even at this distance, she recognized her one-time lover. She gasped and clasped her hands. "Gabha, I need to get down there. Now!"

"What? Your Grace, that is most unsafe! I urge you to reconsider."

Clíodhna spun to glare at him. "Are you questioning my orders, War Chief?"

He took a few steps back. "No, no, of course not, my Queen! As you command." Mounting his horse, he gathered a small guard, and they climbed down the hill. Toward Odhrán.

With each step, she came closer to him. Around her, the clash of blades faded into a buzz of white noise, of no more concern to her than bees.

When she came within shouting distance of the monks, a few glanced back at this new threat. Odhrán let his gaze linger before he turned back to chant with his Abbot.

She must make sure she didn't imagine him. "Odhrán!"

He turned again, and his blue eyes and dimple answered her heart.

With a final glance toward his Abbot, he abandoned the fighting monks and ran to her. She dismounted and opened her arms for her lover.

It had been so long since she'd held him in his arms. Just that one, sweet night during the thunderstorm, the one time he'd been completely hers. Now, he was here with her, smelling of fear and sweat and home.

After a fierce embrace, he held her shoulders. "Clíodhna? Is it you? Everyone's sure you died long ago!"

Then she spied the sprinkle of silver in his hair and beard, silver streaks that had never been there in the young man she'd known. How long had she been gone from the mortal world?

Odhrán stared into her eyes. "You haven't changed at all, Clíodhna. How is that even possible? Where have you been all these winters?"

Winters. How many winters? How had her children changed? She opened her mouth to speak, but nothing came out. Instead, she pulled him into another hug.

After a moment's hesitation, he clung to her, digging his fingers into her back. She gasped again, unable to breathe.

Grimnaugh ran up to her. "My Queen, most of the humans are back in their world, but the chanting ones refuse to go! A few others won't listen and seem to be enjoying the fight, but those chanters are unarmed, save a few with clubs." He glanced at Odhrán. "They wield them well, to be sure, but they are no match for Bodach's forces."

Odhrán glanced down at the frog-like Fae. "Are you of the Fae? Why do you call her the Queen?"

Grimnaugh glanced back and forth between Clíodhna and Odhrán. "Because she is! What do you think, foolish mortal? That I just go up to any old person and make them my Queen?"

After stifling a giggle, Clíodhna put her hand on Odhrán's shoulder. "It's a long story. I promise I'll tell you when I can. Right now, we have a battle to win. Will you convince the other humans to return home? We don't want them injured."

Odhrán shot a glance toward Pátraic, still chanting at the top of his lungs. A twisted, black Fae twice his size swung at him, but he used his gilded crozier to block the blow, twisting it around and jabbing it at his attacker's face. The Fae backed up several steps, letting another soldier take his place.

"I can try, but Pátraic's convinced we've been invaded by demons from Hell."

Clíodhna let out a snort. "I can see his point. The troops he's fighting possess more than their fair share of evil. That's what your Hell is, right? A home for evil?"

He flashed a harried grin. "I miss our conversations, Clíodhna. Yes, close enough. How can I find you again when this is over? I've moved back to your village."

She glanced at Grimnaugh and then back to Odhrán. "Let's survive this and I'll try to find you. I still have a tower to destroy."

The last humans, even those who'd been joyfully fighting beside her troops, disappeared through Grimnaugh's glowing archway between worlds. It snapped shut and her skin itched. Very few of Bodach's fighters remained on the battlefield. Grian's and her own Fae troops flooded the plain.

She searched the milling Fae soldiers for Gabha, when Bodach emerged from the crowd, striding toward her. Two of his sub-chiefs carried something between them, something slung in a low litter and wrapped in dark cloth. Clíodhna caught her breath and her heart raced. Had they been too late? Had Bodach killed Adhna before they'd the chance to rescue him?

If so, he would pay the price. Her rage bubbled up within her, and she bunched her fists. Her shoulders tensed and she gathered her storm clouds again, ready to expiate her wrath on every single member of Bodach's troops, if need be.

Then, the form in the litter moaned.

Her rage forgotten, Clíodhna ran to the litter and knelt. She lifted the blanket from one end with gentle fingers.

The face she found might have been Adhna's, once. Now, battered, bruised, cut, and stained with filth, it bore little resemblance to her beloved teacher and lover.

Her rage flooded back but she clenched her jaw, refusing to let her emotions carry her away. Adhna was alive and she had him safe now. That's what mattered.

Bodach and his troops faded back into the crowd. With dispatch, she had Adhna taken to her palace, leaving Gabha to finish the battle and mop up the victories.

Chapter Eighteen

Fae healed quickly, but it still took a long time for Adhna's wounds to heal. His bruises eventually faded to yellow and his cuts closed. Even his broken bones mended, eventually. But his spirit was dimmer.

She placed him at her side as Consort, despite his protests. "I do not wish this place empty, and you are far better a Consort than Bodach would ever be. Besides, you are much more beloved by the court than he."

Her lover gave her a careful bow. "My Queen, as much as I appreciate the thought, Bodach is still strong. Even with his defeat, he's given up little raw power. He will contest this appointment."

Clíodhna straightened her shoulders with a confidence she didn't have. "We shall see what happens then."

When Bodach did show his face again in Clíodhna's court, he stormed into the great hall, actual fire smoldering on his bark-skin in places.

She waved a hand before her nose. "Bodach, please douse yourself. Your flesh stinks when it burns."

He scowled first at her and then at Adhna sitting on the Consort's throne. "Adhna, you may have usurped my place in appearance, but you know I still hold the power of the Consort. That position is more than who the Queen favors with her foolish notions and ill-considered lust."

Gabha, who'd quietly come up behind the bark-skinned Fae, placed a condescending hand on Bodach's shoulder. Bodach shrugged it off without even glancing at him.

Clíodhna lifted her chin. "That may be true, but for now, Adhna stands by my side. You are not welcome in my court, Bodach. Go back to your fortress. And have a care if you try to betray me again. Next time, I shall not be so gracious."

Her posturing was mostly bluff, but she hoped Bodach didn't know that. While Her predecessor had held unquestionable power, Clíodhna grasped at strings, hoping to hold her net in place before it unraveled. Strength and confidence were the only weapons she had left to wield.

Bodach glowered at each of them, but when he returned his gaze to her, he gave a sly half-smile. "Have a care yourself, *my Queen*." These last two words he hissed with exaggerated care. "The people you hold dear do not all live under your protection."

Before she reacted to his obvious threat, he vanished. She bolted to her feet. "How can he do that in my very court? I thought none could perform such magic in my seat of power?"

She turned to Adhna in question, but he just gave an apologetic shrug. "Bodach still has great power, my Queen. I warned you of this. A defeat in battle didn't diminish it, not by a considerable degree. He just sent you a very strong warning and a very real challenge."

She sat back on her throne, the chill in her blood making her shudder. Etromma, Donn, Aileran, Rumann, and now Odhrán. They were all vulnerable. Sure, she had Grian's assurance and whatever protection she might offer but their powers were severely limited in the mortal realm.

Clíodhna drew in a deep breath. "I must go back, Adhna. I must protect them."

His eyes turned sad. "You can only go back once, remember?"

Clíodhna shut her eyes and bit her lip. "I remember. Many winters have passed, and I need to see my children again. I must do what I can."

"I have some advice, if you'll heed it."

She raised her eyebrows, inviting his suggestion.

He cleared his throat. "When you return, live alone for a time before you seek your family out. Living in Fae is… habit forming. The mortal world can be a shock."

Shaking her head, Clíodhna clenched her fists. "I need to protect those I love, Adhna."

He held out his hands, palms down. "I can protect them for a while longer. Go find a place to be alone. Work the favor Grian asked of you, to clean that bit of the sea. Otherwise, you may make mistakes you cannot fix."

Despite her worries, she recognized the wisdom in his words. "Very well. Thank you."

Grimnaugh cleared his throat. "What about your throne, my Queen?"

Clíodhna glanced around at the handful of remaining courtiers. Her petitions had grown fewer after the battle. Many of the complaints had been because of his loyal followers. "I will appoint a Regent while I'm gone."

She glanced at Gabha, and then at Cerul, who stepped up next to the War Chief. "Will you two be willing to work as co-Regents in my absence?"

As one, they nodded. Cerul gave her a slight smile of encouragement.

"You should be able to send messages to me if needed, but I trust you both to have the common sense and strength to withstand pressure from the likes of Bodach."

With a glance to the other Fae, Gabha asked, "May we keep your assistant, Grimnaugh? Much of the court etiquette is a mystery, but he understands each detail."

Clíodhna placed a hand on the frog-like Fae's shoulder. "Will you help my co-Regents, my friend?"

Grimnaugh let out a grunt of agreement. "Only if you promise me one thing, my Queen."

"If it's within my power to grant, it's yours."

"When you return, may I leave the court?"

She felt like he'd punched her in the gut. "Are you so unhappy in your position? Have I mistreated you?"

He held up his hands, and his eyes grew wide. "No, no, my Queen! You've been kind to me. But I need rest. These events have worn me out, and I must be away from the court for a while."

"It seems we both need a rest. Very well. I so grant your leave. And you, Adhna? Will you ask for leave as well?"

He nodded. "I tire more easily than before my ordeal, my love. But I will come to you in the mortal realm soon. You are still in need of teaching." His eyes twinkled at the last, and she returned his grin.

The mortal world seemed both unchanged and utterly different. After so long in Faerie, the mortal realm was muted and mundane, filled with mud and bugs and itchy skin.

As per Adhna's suggestion, Clíodhna built a simple shelter near the beach, not too far from the shore where she grew up. The roundhouse gave shelter from the summer storms, and she spent some time reliving her youth. Her time in Faerie and the seashore invigorated her spirit, despite her mortal body growing older with aches and pains.

While Clíodhna had always delighted in solitude, she still longed for male company. But she wasn't ready to share her peace with anyone else.

She spent her days swimming in the salty sea. A few of the larger residents, dolphins, came to find who was swimming in their realm. Their chittering inquiries were incomprehensible to her, but they'd play with her in the waves.

The dolphins offered no judgment, no intrigue, and no danger. They demanded nothing from her but laughter, a wage more readily gifted each day.

Years of worry and stress slipped away as she swam with the dolphins and remembered her youth.

Before he left her, Adhna had shown her how to heal the ocean, as per Queen Grian's request. Then, she'd told him to return to Faerie.

He furrowed his brow. "I should be there to protect you, my Queen."

She'd waved away his concern. "I haven't aged at all. It will be difficult enough to convince them I'm their mother without a stranger with me."

He gave a reluctant nod. "Very well. I'll wait for you in the cave near the standing stones. Come there when you're ready to return."

An island sat just off the shore, covered with Christian monks. Human waste from such a large community of men poisoned the water below, harming the sea life.

As Clíodhna healed her own soul, she healed the ocean, too. She couldn't destroy the waste, but she could disperse it into the wider ocean, diminishing its poisonous effects. Thus, she completed Grian's favor, though she would have done this task anyhow.

One day, a storm angled across the horizon toward the shore. Churning water brought shoals of fish, and her dolphins friends feasted on these.

After that, she'd conjure storm cells whenever her dolphin friends came near, giving them a proper feast during their visit.

After all, proper Gaelic hospitality demanded such efforts, did it not?

After a few such meals, one dolphin pushed his soft-skinned snout under her hand. She patted him, but he did it again. Intrigued, she cocked her head, wishing she could speak to him.

The dolphin moved until her hand touched his fin, and when she gripped it, he chittered. Taking this as approval, she grabbed it with both hands and, with tentative bravery, mounted the dolphin like a horse.

The dolphin chittered again and leapt up, dragging her along. He swam into the crashing waves, up and over, again and again.

At first, she held on for dear life. Then, when she realized he was just giving her a thrilling ride rather than trying to drown her, she laughed in delight.

From that day, they fell into a routine. She brought up a storm to churn up a meal, and the dolphins took her on rides across the waves. Sometimes, they brought her to islands dotting the coast. Other times, they took her out into the wide, empty ocean.

Every now and then, a massive whale swam beside them, or other dolphin pods. A few sharks might come close, but her dolphin friends poked their gills to make them go away.

There came a day when she didn't look forward to swimming with the dolphins as much as she had. Instead, she looked inland, wondering where her children were. The time had come to seek her family. With great reluctance, she said goodbye to her maritime friends, and began her trek home.

As Clíodhna tramped along the flooded path towards her village, she wished she had her Fae horse.

She chuckled at her idea. A horse? How grand had she become now? She'd never needed a horse to ride into the village in the past. Her time as Queen had spoiled her.

When she arrived and strode to the center square, she held her chin high, glancing at each villager's face. No one looked familiar.

One woman's face tugged at her memory, but she didn't recognize her when their eyes met.

Etromma should be at the blacksmith's home, as she'd married Tirechan. Was his father still alive, or had the boy taken over the forge?

Clíodhna followed her nose to the acrid smell of the blacksmith's fire. Black smoke billowed from the flames, rising into the sky like a beacon. The hammering of iron made her flinch. She must be sensitive to the substance now, like the other Fae.

After taking a deep breath against her fears and fighting the urge to flee, she walked to the roundhouse and peered through the doorway, standing open to catch the breeze on this warm summer day. The interior seemed dark and empty. She made her way around the back, where the blacksmith toiled at his work.

The *tink, tink, tink* of his hammer was almost a song, a chant she sang under her voice. *Find me now. I am here. Find me now.* Would Etromma have changed much? How many children did she have now?

A youngish man, his chest stripped bare and covered in soot and sweat, stood over the anvil. His hammer tapped a red-hot ingot, forming it into a long shape.

She cleared her throat to get his attention.

He glanced up and nodded once, speaking in a gruff tone. "I'm almost at a point I can stop. Bide a few moments and I'll be right with you."

The young man examined the metal, doused it in a barrel, and then hammered a few more bits. He dunked it again, billows of steam pouring out of the water. After peering at his work again, he put it aside, along with his hammer. Then he grabbed a cloth and mopped his face before pulling on a brown *léine.*

He held his hands out to her, palms up. "I welcome you to my hearth. What do you seek?"

She placed her hands over his in greeting. "I come seeking information of my kin. Her name is Etromma."

The blacksmith's face broke into a smile. "You seek my mother? I'm afraid she's far away, in the north. She moved near her brother."

Clíodhna swallowed her disappointment. "In the north?"

"Oh, yes. The church sent Donn there to work on the cathedral many seasons past, and Etromma went along to help care for him after Da died."

"Tirechan died?"

The young man nodded. "Aye, about two winters past. Trampled by a horse on a trade journey."

She placed a hand over her heart. "I'm so sorry. Oh, I forgot to introduce myself! I'm Clíodhna."

His eyes grew wide. "Clíodhna? That's Etromma's mother's name."

In a cautious tone, she said, "Yes, that's me."

He backed up a few steps, his hands out. "You couldn't be. You're too young. She died winters ago." His voice faded to a whisper. "Are you… are you a spirit?"

She threw her head back and laughed. "No, of course not! I never died. I went away for a while, that's all. And now I've returned. What's your name, lad?"

He visibly swallowed and his eyes darted toward the roundhouse and back to her, but he gathered enough courage to speak. "I'm called Pátraic."

The name punched her in the gut. "Like the abbot? Does he still live here?"

The lad gave a nod, still nervous. "He just came back, after winters traveling around the country. Uncle Donn asked Ma to name me for him. They call me *Pátraic Óg*, to tell us apart."

Had Adhna even told Etromma or Donn about Rumann? Maybe Aileran still lived nearby. Clíodhna pondered that before asking, "And Aileran? Does he still live near here?"

Pátraic Óg's shoulders drooped and he stared at the ground. "He died many winters ago. A fever took him in the night."

Clíodhna caught her breath and her knees turned weak. She stumbled toward the log bench and sat upon it.

While covering her face in her hands, she tried not to give in to the tears. Not here, not in front of her grandson.

Aileran, dead. Etromma and Donn, in some far away county. In the north? Should she travel there to find them?

She glanced up, her face streaked with unwanted tears. "What about my youngest son, Rumann?"

His face lit up. "Rumann? But of course we know of him! I didn't realize he's your son, though. He lives near the bend of the river. He has a wife and several young sons. Rumann's a fisherman. Would you like me to take you there?"

A tiny bubble of hope grew in her heart. Clíodhna didn't want to frighten it or burst it, so she clamped on the burgeoning joy until she met Rumann.

Pátraic Óg offered his hand and drew her to her feet. He closed the furnace door and banked the fire before they left.

The path seemed half-familiar, but the foliage looked different. How many winters had she spent in Faerie? A dozen? More, if Rumann had grown, with a family of his own. Twenty?

He'd wouldn't even remember her. Adhna had taken him to the mortal realm before he could crawl. What would she have to do to convince him she was his mother? What would she do if he refused to accept her?

As they approached the clearing, she realized they were coming to her own home. Rumann lived where she'd raised her family. The notion made her heart warm, and that small bubble of hope burst into something stronger, something magical and intense.

Two boys played outside. The younger one, perhaps about seven winters old, was the very image of Adhna, his dark hair tied back with a thong. Both glanced up as they approached.

Pátraic Óg shouted toward the roundhouse. "Rumann! Rumann, I brought you a visitor."

Clíodhna held her breath as a man emerged. His dark brown hair unkempt, but his belly well-fed, he glared at them both. He crossed his arms and asked, in a querulous voice, "Well? Who is it?"

Clíodhna stepped forward, her hands out in greeting. "Rumann, you may not recognize me, but we've met before. Sure, you would have been much too young to remember me, but I'm—" Her breath caught for a moment. "I'm your mother."

Rumann continued to glare at her, but the boys, who'd been watching this drama unfold, both gasped. The youngest one ran inside, emerging with another boy and a thin woman with reddish hair.

The woman looked Clíodhna up and down with a sour expression and clutched Rumann's arm, making her relationship with him clear. "Who's this, then?"

The woman's face seemed familiar. Clíodhna gave her a warm smile. "I'm Rumann's mother, but he hasn't seen me since before he could crawl. Are these your children, then?"

Three boys stood behind them, ranging from the youngest brown-haired boy to a well-grown youth of perhaps twenty winters. They stared at her with varying degrees of curiosity and judgment.

That youngest boy, the one who looked most like Adhna, peeked out from behind his mother's skirt, his eyes wide.

The woman narrowed her eyes. "His mother, eh? First, you're barely older than he is. How can you be his mother? And if you are, where in God's good name have you been all these winters? He's not seen hide nor hair of you since he was a babe, as you say. Why should we believe you?"

Clíodhna glanced at the roundhouse. "I lived here, before Rumann came. My eldest, Etromma, married the blacksmith's boy, Tirechan. Then came Donn, and sweet baby Aileran. Aileran would have been barely older than Rumann then."

Rumann let out a short bark of laughter. "He was four winters older than me, woman. You should get your facts straight before you try to muscle your way into this family."

Then she remembered the time she'd spent in Faerie, and realized her mistake. "Well, four winters is a small difference, compared to the gap between Donn and Aileran. Let's see, when Etromma had fifteen winters, Donn had thirteen. That's when Aileran came. I bore you five winters later, a twenty-winter span in total."

Doubt crept across Rumann's angry expression. He glanced at his eldest and turned back to her, his eyebrows raised. "You're too young."

Clíodhna flashed him a wide smile and shrugged. "I married young and have been living by the sea for many seasons. The ocean air does wonders for the skin."

He glanced sidelong at his wife. "What do you think, Mugain?"

Chapter Nineteen

With some reluctance, Clíodhna's family accepted her into their home. She promised to help care for the children and help with the housework, an offer which Mugain gladly accepted.

Clíodhna finally remembered where she'd seen Mugain; Donn had been sweet on her, so many winters ago. Since Donn had pursued life with the Christians rather than take a wife, she'd married Rumann. She was twelve winters older than her youngest son, but they seemed content.

It took longer for the children to grow comfortable around her. The eldest, Éanna, with broad shoulders and dirty blond hair, gave her only sullen looks and sidelong glances.

The middle child, Niall, was biddable enough, though he grew quiet when she came near. He had his mother's red locks and was perhaps two or three winters older than the youngest, Fingin.

This lad was the shy one, with dark wavy hair so similar to Adhna's. He was eight winters old, thin and pale. He fished with his father but showed little joy in the work.

Clíodhna, used to be in charge of her own household and then being a Queen in Faerie, chafed at being the good-mother, a tolerated presence, barely heeded nor honored.

That first morning, she rose before dawn, as she had during her mortal life. After so much time in Faerie, she was eager to greet the dawn and bask in the warmth and beauty of the sunrise. In the darkness, Clíodhna climbed her favorite hill and sat cross-legged on the same stone she'd first met Adhna at.

After drawing in a deep breath, with tendrils of earth power, she felt a familiar thrill as energy flowed through her body. In and out she breathed, drawing in the power and releasing it, centering her soul to her spot on this mortal land.

As the first rays of sun burst through the low layers of clouds on the horizon, the sky was bathed in deep peach and violet. When the light chased twilight into the dark recesses of shadow, more power bathed her soul.

Clíodhna tipped her face back to relish in the light, closing her eyes. The bees buzzed around her, and a sparrow alighted on her arm as the golden dawn broke across the hilltops.

"You haven't forgotten how."

With a knowing grin, she opened her eyes and turned to Adhna. "It's not something the body forgets."

Her lover sat behind her, wrapping his legs around her and hugging her back to his chest. She rocked back against him, secure in his embrace.

"How did your meeting with your family go? I presume, since you stayed the night, that they accepted your return."

"For the most part. They have some doubts, but they'll come around."

Adhna squeezed her once. "Would you like me to stay?"

"I think I will be well enough for now. The youngest child, Fingin, seems to be a kind lad. I'd like to get to know him better before I return."

"Very well. I'll help Cerul and Gabha in their co-Regency and return when I can."

He faded into nothing and her back turned cold in the dawn chill. Clíodhna hugged herself, trying to convince herself that she'd made the right decision, sending him away. Especially with Odhrán possibly in the village.

At the thought of Odhrán, a smile crept over her face and her blood warmed, counteracting the morning chill. But she couldn't go find him just yet. After having spent far too much time away from her family, she meant to get to know them now.

Clíodhna wiped her hands off on her *léine* and ran down the hill, eager to see her family again. She'd prepare them breakfast and start the day right.

But when she returned to the roundhouse, it was empty. After cursing at herself for missing them, she realized they must have gone into the village.

Were they also followers of the Christ? Would they be at the monk's morning service? Etromma and Donn had both attached their lives to this new religion. If she wished for her family to accept her, she might have to do the same, at least in name.

Besides, she might see Odhrán.

Clíodhna strode down the path toward the village. When she got to the abbey, she stared at the empty chapel building in confusion. Then singing came from another building, and she remembered the monks had been crafting a new place for their services.

Walking through the garden, full and lush with the summer's growth, she found the grand new hall. Rounded arches soared high into the sky with worked stone, a truly elegant sight, for the mortal world. It paled in comparison to anything in Faerie, though.

Voices chanted in a measured rhythm, but she didn't understand the words. They must be singing in that Roman language. The doorway stood open and welcoming, but she paused, her heart racing.

What if Odhrán was there and didn't want to see her? What if that abbot banished her again? What if no one recognized her?

She tamped down on her doubts, got control of her panicked heart, and strode forward with far more confidence than she possessed.

Clíodhna had expected the interior to be dark and crowded, like the chapel. Instead, tall open windows in the arches let in the morning light, illuminating the church and making the dust motes glitter.

The space filled with song, an almost physical force which embraced her. A few heads turned when she came in, but most concentrated on the music.

At the far end of the room, Abbot Pátraic stood next to a long table draped in white. The table held a golden cross and several other items. Clíodhna took her place in the back row, searching for her family or anyone else she might recognize.

When the song ended, the deadening silence grew oppressive. Then the abbot spoke into the emptiness, breaking the spell.

He lectured in the other language, intoning his words with a practiced rhythm. Clíodhna glanced at more faces. None of the surrounding people looked familiar.

Had she been gone so long? Twenty winters didn't change people so much. She ought to be able to recognize the younger selves within their older bodies. Yet so many people were crowded within the walls, twice the population of the village she'd known.

A flash of pale blonde hair streaked with white caught her eye and, stripping away the winters in her imagination, she recognized Ita. She must speak to her old friend afterwards.

Pátraic stepped back as another monk came forward. He spoke in their own language and told a story about three strangers who had come to a village in search of help. No one would help them, each one turning the strangers away from their doors. Then, one man welcomed the strangers into their home, offering to feed them and wash their feet.

Once their hosts made the strangers comfortable, the visitors revealed themselves as angels, and commended their host for offering hospitality.

When he finished his story, the monk clasped his hands together. "So always welcome strangers into your home, for you may welcome angels, unbeknownst to you."

Since this custom fit in with the Gaelic tradition of welcoming guests, Clíodhna approved. While caring for others in hopes of a potential reward didn't have the same honor as caring for others because it was the right thing to do, some people required more incentive.

Perhaps she'd come home at a propitious time, just after this reminder to welcome strangers. It seemed odd to be a stranger in her own home. But this wasn't her home, not any longer.

After the service, she sought her own family first. Clíodhna tried to find Mugain's red hair, but found Rumann's scowling face, instead. She pushed through the crowd to stand next to her son.

A hand on her shoulder made her turn. Odhrán's ice-blue eyes stared at her with wide wonder. "Clíodhna? Can it be you? Merciful Mother!" He touched his forehead, chest, then each shoulder.

She took in a shuddering breath. He'd aged since she saw him last, even at the battle. His beard had fetching gray streaks and his hair had disappeared. No curly fringe around the edges, but a flawless shiny dome from ear to ear. She gave him a grin and dared to touch the smooth skin.

He gave her a rueful grin, showing his dimple. "Ah, yes, my hair. A vanity of my youth. I held on to my rapidly retreating locks for many

316

seasons, only shaving the tonsure required of the church, but that time has passed. They call me Maol Odhrán now, after my bald head." He rubbed the back of his skull.

"Clíodhna? Clíodhna, is that you? How can it be?" She turned at Ita's voice, wavering with incredulity.

Odhrán gripped her shoulder. "I must go. Come visit me in the gardens, later."

With a hasty nod to the monk, she turned and clasped Ita into a hug. Her friend's bones seemed thin and brittle. Clíodhna pulled back, studying the changes in her face. "Ah, how I've missed you, my friend."

Ita narrowed her gaze. "The real Clíodhna wouldn't have said such a thing."

Chuckling, Clíodhna shrugged. "We all change with the seasons, Ita. How's your family? Have you been faring well? And has this village doubled in size or is there some festival I'm not aware of?"

Ita glanced over her shoulder at the knot of people congregating around the abbot, but most of the village had gone home. "It's difficult to adjust to so many, that's true enough. We've been getting more and more as the abbey grew. We need to speak, but not here."

Clíodhna's stomach knotted at her clipped tone. Her friend led her away from the church, and they sat on the wall of the well in the town square.

Ita pursed her lips and stared at the church. "At first, craftsmen working on the buildings came, then tanners and weavers to provide them with clothing. Chandlers, coopers, all manner of tradesmen followed. They brought their families and cleared more of the forest for their farms."

"They've cleared the forest?" Clíodhna glanced around as if she'd missed this huge change, but the woods nearby still stood.

Her friend waved her hand. "Not here. The other side of the village, along the river. The river water has been fouled with waste from the tannery. They were kind enough to build downstream, but it still stinks."

"I've been away so long. So many changes, it's hard to understand them all. I'm staying with my son, Rumann, but—"

Ita's eyes grew wide. "What? Rumann's your son? I had no idea! Donn told Mugain and Rumann to move in there when he left. I think he still had guilt over breaking off their engagement. But when did you have Rumann? You'd disappeared for winters already."

Confusion spinning in her mind, Clíodhna closed her eyes. "I'll tell you all I can."

Ita pressed her lips together. "I don't understand why you couldn't come back for a visit. The coast isn't *that* far away. Not even your children knew how to find you. I raised Aileran as best I… but…" Her words choked off with a sob.

While clasping her hands tight, Clíodhna said, "I heard he died of a fever, but I didn't find out until yesterday. What happened?"

With a mighty sniff, Ita shut her eyes. "He was only seven winters old. He was becoming a real help around the farm, and my daughter took him everywhere with her. One day, his stomach was bothering him, and I put him into bed. His skin seemed cooler in the night but then, when I woke… he was gone. His body was cold already."

The other woman glanced up, anger in her eyes. "That's when I tried to find you. You said not to, but I had runners out searching for any word of you. I found nothing. Nothing! Not one sign of you across the countryside. It's as if you vanished in a puff of smoke."

Clíodhna ground her teeth together. She should have known Ita wouldn't accept the story without digging in, but she had to craft her tale. Ita had always been a gossip. The lie had only been a slight bend of the truth.

True, Clíodhna had spent her time away from everyone she'd known in a distant place, just in Faerie rather than the mortal realm on the ocean.

"I needed to be by myself, after Oisinne… I just couldn't face anyone. Not for a long time. Then, once my mind had healed, I'd gotten used to being alone. I didn't want to be around others, especially anyone who'd known my husband."

Ita shook her head. "He was a handful, true enough. He never did recover his wits."

Blinking, Clíodhna leapt to her feet. "Recovered? What do you mean, recovered? He died! I saw lightning strike him, and his corpse burnt and smoking!"

After letting out a snort. "That one. No, he didn't die. 'Twould have been far kinder if he had. Instead, he lingered on in agony, passed from one household to the other. No one had room to care for him. His skin had been so scorched, and his bones so broken, he was like an infant. A querulous, mad infant, capable of great violence. Etromma tried to care for him, but even she couldn't stand it."

Clíodhna didn't want to ask, but she must. "What happened to him?"

Ita gave a shrug. "No one else would take him. Since we couldn't find you on God's green earth, he crawled around with a begging bowl. Finally, the monks took him in. They cared for him for a few moons before they sent him to another of their houses, one which specialized in healing. We haven't seen hide nor hair of the poor creature since."

Poor creature. Her husband, burnt to a crisp by her own magic. She'd left him for dead but had instead abandoned him to the whims of fate. Clíodhna had expected guilt at having left her children, but this fresh attack of shame left her breathless.

A chill swept over her and her skin pebbled. She rubbed her arms, but it didn't help. Oisinne might still be alive. A shell, a husk of his former self. His mind had already fled, but she'd destroyed his body. What had been left of the man she'd married so many seasons ago? Should she search for him?

Ita broke into her guilty reverie. "Word came from the monks that he finally died last winter. They'd had a bitter season, and his body didn't have the defenses against the cold. 'Tis a mercy, to be sure. Poor man."

And the monks had taken him in, despite his ruined state. Maybe the Christians had some good notions, despite their indoctrination and hate. Or not all of them harbored such intense hatred as Abbot Pátraic had shown her.

Clíodhna placed a gentle hand on her friend's arm. "Thank you, Ita. I am glad someone took care of him, and that he didn't die alone."

Then, true to her nature, Ita related the news of others in town. Of the chandler's grandson marrying the baker's daughter, of the tanner's wife and her affair with a monk.

Clíodhna bit her lip at that, thinking of her night with Odhrán, but that news must have faded with time. Her mind drifted to Odhrán as Ita spoke, and she wondered when she should seek him in the gardens.

Ita slapped her hands on her knees. "Well, the horses won't muck out their own stalls. I must get home. My eldest does his best, but the house still needs a woman's hand to run things. Will I see you at tomorrow morning's service?"

Clíodhna agreed with reluctance. She didn't mind attending but didn't want to risk encountering Pátraic. Still, if she participated in their rituals, he'd have little to complain about.

As Ita left, Clíodhna returned to the abbey grounds. Searching through the gardens, she found only an older monk, basking in the late morning sun. Odhrán must have other duties, so she'd need to seek him out later.

She ambled home, noting differences as she walked. The old oak which had stood at that bend was only a blackened stump jutting out of the ground. The pines along the left side had grown considerably taller and almost blocked out the sun. Was it already midday? She'd forgotten how much Ita talked, and she'd lost track of the day.

Something rustled in the brush. She'd expected a squirrel or groundhog, but a young *sidhe* peeked shyly from around her pine tree. She waved and ducked back into hiding.

With a grin, Clíodhna walked on with a lighter step. Despite the increase in people and the disturbing story of so much forest cut down, some Fae still lived on the land. That heartened her purpose.

She'd try to teach her grandchildren something of the Fae. Clíodhna felt she must counteract the condemnation of the Good Folk spouted by the likes of Pátraic.

With this in mind, as soon as he finished his chores, she pulled Fingin away. She drew him down to the river, where he seemed at home and comfortable. She'd teach him to honor the Fae, to see them in their hiding places. Maybe she might even teach him to speak with them.

Her grandson held her hand with tentative strength. He'd never be a powerful man, as his frame remained slight. Clíodhna had seen him flinching whenever Rumann yelled, and she suspected her son beat the boy.

Where had he learned such violence? Certainly not from her. And Oisinne hadn't been part of his life. Had Rumann been bullied as a boy, without her to protect him? She wanted to protect Fingin, as beatings could damage such a frail child. She'd try to counteract such cruelty with some kindness.

"Now, young man, what can you tell me about the creatures who live in the water?"

She didn't get to meet Odhrán in the garden, after all. The church had sent him to another church location, some island off the west coast, the day after she returned from Faerie.

He'd sent her a message of apology with another monk. Despite the kind message, she felt somehow cheated of a reunion with her ex-lover.

In the meantime, her body seemed to be catching up with the seasons she'd spent in Faerie. Her skin grew thinner and she developed wrinkles. A streak of white formed in her black hair. When she rose in the pre-dawn darkness, her bones complained at the chill.

And her son was a cruel man. He beat his wife and his children on a regular basis. Keeping in mind her status as a guest, she tried to keep her opinions to herself, but it wasn't easy.

At one point, Rumann's temper was so strong, it gave Clíodhna nightmares of Oisinne's cruelty. Had her time in Fae made her less able to endure the hardships of the mortal world?

Rather than scream at her own son and risk his wrath, she escaped for the summer.

Clíodhna traveled back to the ocean, to the place she first returned after Faerie. Her crude shelter had fallen, but she built a new one. Away from all the people, alone except for the beasts of the land, air, sea, she relished her own company.

Clíodhna swam in the ocean every day. Her white streak grew wider as she played with the dolphins and dove into the waves, reliving her youth. It helped to rejuvenate her mind and her spirit, if not her body.

She gathered a pod of six dolphins who became her friends, bringing her seaweed and shellfish and taking her out into the water. Clíodhna felt like a dolphin herself, she spent so much time in the salt sea.

She also practiced her magic, drawing from the massive power of the ocean before her. Adhna had taught her to draw a bare tendril from the earth, so she practiced with pulling a small rivulet from the ocean. In time, her mastery over each element grew as did her confidence.

To amuse the dolphins, she created shapes from the water, dancing along the surface. She formed fish shapes to leap along the edge of the shore as the dolphins chittered their amusement and delight.

When the days grew shorter and the nights grew longer, Clíodhna returned to Rumann's home.

And when the time for Odhrán's return came closer, she counted the days until she could meet her friend again.

She'd been relieved at the delay, as she could get to know her family more, to settle back into her place in the village. And to determine if Abbot Pátraic still detested the sight of her.

Clíodhna still considered him a vile dogmatist, but he acted as if she didn't exist, other than a polite nod when they passed each other. A few times, she thought she detected a glint of that fervent extremism, but the spark faded quickly. He never spoke a word to her.

Content with this arrangement, she kept out of his way. Without a mad husband to care for, or children to raise, she found this much easier than before. She had a freedom she'd never experienced. No true responsibilities, no heavy goals or projects. She only had Fingin's education in honoring the Fae.

She'd spoken to a few of the villagers about the wild folk. Most ignored her or shook their heads at her odd notions. A few had built a relationship with their own Fae, the ones who lived inside a well or along the edge of the woods. Most didn't have the bravery for such disobedience of their church, though.

Fingin, despite being a rather simple lad, was full of joy when he first spoke to the Fae. They danced on the water for him and touched his nose with their fingers, making him giggle like a joyful babe.

She enjoyed many a lazy afternoon with her grandson, showing him the ways of the Fae, of nature, and of his own abilities. His father had no interest in the lad, spending his attention on his eldest boy and his own mug of ale.

Clíodhna tried to speak to Rumann, guilt coloring her words. "I didn't want to leave you, Rumann. But where I went, it was too dangerous, especially for an infant. I needed to make sure you were safe."

He cast her a withering glance, his jaw clenched tight. He took a swig of his ale and slammed it on the wooden table. "I don't care why you abandoned me. Stop trying to excuse it."

"At least let me explain—"

He cut her off with a wave of his hand. Since that hand still held the mug, a splash of ale swirled out and spilled on the floor. "I grew up without your help, and I'll manage my family the same way."

Her temper flared at his words. "The way you're managing young Fingin? You barely look at the poor lad. He needs affection, Rumann."

He growled and stood, looming over her with menace. "Look, woman. You're my mother, so I won't turn you out, but you aren't to meddle, understand? You leave my family to me and go about your business."

Clíodhna seethed with the need to answer with sarcasm and rage, wanting to slap the insolent fool into some sense. But he outweighed her by a lot and stood several heads taller. If she angered him too much, he'd beat her, as well.

Someday, when she left again, she'd give him a piece of her mind. Maybe even sooner.

Clíodhna sat on a bench in the garden, waiting for Odhrán to arrive. She fidgeted with the edge of her sleeve, far more nervous than she ought to be. He said he'd be there at dusk, but she wasn't certain how he figured dusk. Different people marked it in different ways. When the sun dipped below the hills? When the sky went totally dark?

She fiddled with the end of her braid, which she'd arranged to hide the streak of white hair and chuckled at her own silly vanities.

A shuffle behind her made her turn, but it was a different monk strolling by. She didn't know his name but they exchanged cordial nods and he disappeared amongst the ornamental flowers.

How much would Odhrán have changed in all this time? Would he still be interested in her friendship? She'd asked this question a thousand times since he'd left. When she'd gotten word of his return, her heart raced so fast she needed to sit.

She'd turned into a giddy girl, ready to walk out with her suitor for the first time. While she loved Adhna with all her heart, and Odhrán had been living his life in the mortal world for a score of winters without her, her heart knew what it wanted.

Clíodhna wiped at her face, mopping the sweat away and waited.

This time, her old friend walked toward her. Odhrán's bald head shone in the afternoon sun. Her face flushed as he came near and held her hands out. He squeezed hers tight but didn't embrace her.

Somewhat discomfited by this, she settled on the bench. He sat beside her and turned to face her. "I'm gratified you waited. The abbot held me up, and I apologize for being late."

Her giddiness cooled with his formal words. Clíodhna took a deep breath. "I've looked forward to speaking with you, Odhrán. It's been much too long."

He gave her a half-smile. "It's been at least four winters since that magical battle, and over fifteen before that when you left us."

"Four winters? It was a short time for us in Faerie."

His eyes grew wide, twinkling with eager anticipation. "Faerie, yes, you must tell me all about that! If I hadn't seen it with my own eyes, I would never have believed such a thing. Abbot Pátraic was quite incensed with everyone involved."

"Oh? Did he blame them? He shouldn't have."

Odhrán frowned, looking toward the church building. "He did. In fact, he cursed those who took up arms to help in the battle."

She narrowed her eyes. "What sort of curse?"

"Something vile about turning into a vicious hound when they lose their temper. I tried to persuade him to remove it, that such a curse would bring evil to himself, but he refused to listen. He *did* relent enough to make them protectors. At least they have a noble purpose now. He calls them the *faoladh*."

Odhrán cast his eyes to his feet. "He often refuses to listen. I consider it a failing on my part that I couldn't get him to recant. He responded by sending me away, his favorite answer to insolence."

Clíodhna gave a chuckle. "Is that why he sends you away so often, then?"

While shrugging one shoulder, he said, "That must be why. Either that, or he can't stand my face." He turned to her and traced his finger along her braid, just at the bit of white peeking through. "Why do you hide this? Such a lovely, distinctive feature. You should display this badge of wisdom with pride."

On an impulse, Clíodhna cupped her hands on his cheeks. "I've dreamed of your face, Odhrán. Over all that time, I still treasure you."

Their eyes locked for just one heart-breaking moment before he pulled back, blinking several times. "I dreamt of you often, Clíodhna. And I cherish the time we spent together. But we can only ever be friends now. We can never have more."

After he dropped her hands, she clasped them in her lap, staring at them to keep from bursting into tears. It had been so long since they'd been together. He must have found another love during the long seasons traveling.

Besides, what she loved most about him had been their conversations, not his physical love, though that had been lovely. Once she got her emotions under control, she glanced up again.

Odhrán was staring at his own hands, lost in thought. She placed her hand on his shoulder, making him look up, his eyes begging for understanding. She granted him a sad smile. "We'll always be friends. I'm content as long as we keep that friendship. It's the part of us I cherished the most."

His tentative smile deepened into genuine pleasure. "I worried so much about this talk. I even delayed returning out of worry you'd detest me."

She clasped his hand again and squeezed. They needed no more words.

Chapter Twenty

Dappled sunlight speckled the rocks as they peered into the swirling water. A strand of Clíodhna's hair fell into her face, a strand from the white streak. She tucked it behind her ear with exasperation. "Fingin, do pay attention. Now, see how this dark stuff edges the water sprite's fins? Something poisonous is in the water."

The boy peered at the sprite's damaged fin and glanced up at his grandmother. "But what made that happen?"

Wrinkling her nose, Clíodhna glanced upriver. "Judging from the stink of urine, that tanner's to blame. He dumps waste into the water, with no heed to how it hurts the wildlife or Fae. I've a mind to speak to him about it."

Fingin bowed his head. "I don't like the tanner. He's loud. His voice hurts my head."

With a chuckle, Clíodhna patted the boy on his shoulder. "He's loud, true enough. But I can be louder if I put my mind to it. Would you like to come along? Or do you prefer to go home?"

He stuck out his chin. "I want to come with you. If I go home, Da will give me work to do."

They walked along the shore to the tanner's roundhouse, the huge workshop in the back perched on a low cliff over the river. Even as they watched, someone tossed a bucket of sludge out the window and into the water below. The stink of urine, lime, and salt drifted from the noxious waste, making them both sneeze.

With Fingin in tow, Clíodhna marched up to the workshop door and peered in. She could make out very little in the dim interior, but something moved along the far wall. She knocked on the door frame to get their attention.

A man's voice boomed out. "What? Who is it?"

"Clíodhna, from the village. I'd like to speak to you about that poison you just dumped in the river."

"Poison? What are you talking about? It's just dirty water. I've been doing it for seasons. All the tanners do. That's why we set up downriver from the village."

She crossed her arms and lifted her chin. "While that's appreciated, it's hurting the wildlife and the Fae. You need to find another method of disposal."

The big man emerged from the shadows. Clíodhna backed up a few steps. He stood a good arms-length taller than she, with broad shoulders and muscled arms. He scowled down at them both. "The wildlife and the Fae, is it? Oh, isn't that a precious thing? You're nothing but a mere woman and a half-grown child. Begone, the both of you."

Fingin shrunk away, but Clíodhna planted her feet and glared up at the big man. "I will not begone, as you so command. I'll stay until you promise a solution."

He curled his lip and flexed his upper arm muscles, an obvious attempt at intimidation. She clenched her jaw as the wind whipped her hair. The sky darkened with storm clouds racing across the sun. Since the day had been mild, the tanner glanced up in surprise. A peal of thunder echoed across the hills.

His stance didn't seem so intimidating now, nor his manner so threatening. The tanner took a step back, glancing around him. "What's happening? What are you doing?"

After placing a hand over her heart, Clíodhna asked, "Me? How could I be doing anything? I'm a mere woman and this but a half-grown child. Surely, you aren't frightened of us?"

Thunder boomed, louder this time, and the first few drops fell on the dry ground.

"What's wrong, big man? It's just a thunderstorm. I thought you liked loud noises? Or is that only when you're making them?"

His eyes fixed on Clíodhna's face and for a moment, she thought he'd lunge at her. She shoved her instinct to flee down and forced herself to smile in the face of danger. After all, she'd faced Bodach and his entire army. She could stare down one mortal tanner.

Fingin whimpered beside her, clutching her leg. When she spared a glance for her grandson, he was staring at the sky with frightened eyes.

With a sigh, she let the thunderstorm fade away. "Take this as a warning. The Fae are under my protection. Damage them at your own peril."

Taking Fingin's hand, she walked away with slow dignity. Let him stew over that for a while. *A mere woman, indeed.* A pity she couldn't reveal her own status as Faerie Queen to this abhorrent fool.

When they returned home, Rumann and Mugain were nowhere to be seen. The older boys worked in the yard, and she bid Fingin to join them. She needed a break from the lad.

While she loved teaching him, patience had never been her greatest virtue, and he didn't learn quickly. Oh, his heart was huge and his kindness knew no limits, but to retain knowledge took a great deal of work and practice.

Clíodhna sat in her alcove, considering what she should do that evening. Odhrán had asked her to join him in the abbey garden. She often met him there and talked deep into the night. He ought to be sleeping, but he stole time for her. But he couldn't meet her until dusk.

Clíodhna had to admit, she was getting bored. She grew weary of her work in the mortal realm, where she had no real power. She ached to return to Faerie, as if the very land called her back. That draw simmered as a slow-burning need, an itch that called for constant scratching. A hum only heard within her heart.

She glanced at her shelves and took out the white fabric package, the brooch Adhna had gifted her. After unwrapping it, she traced the intricate gold and silver traced animal shapes on the brooch.

Adhna had told her that she needed to pass the brooch on. She couldn't choose Rumann. Donn and Etromma lived far away. Rumann's eldest sons subsisted in dim cruelty, like their father. She'd seen it in their bullying of Fingin.

Maybe Patraic Óg? She shook her head. It wasn't the lad's fault, but Clíodhna shuddered whenever she heard that name. There was magic in names, after all. How could she gift the Fae brooch to someone who shared a name with her persecutor?

Fingin was her only choice, but he was only eight winters old. Would he be old enough to handle such power? Would he be able to command power like hers, the ability to call up storms at will? No, Adhna had said each magical talent would be different.

Clíodhna glanced up as someone darkened the doorway. As if the thought of him had conjured the Fae, Adhna gave her a smile. She rose to greet her lover in a warm embrace. "Adhna, how did you know I was thinking of you?"

He glanced down at the brooch in her hand. "Do you need to ask? I'm connected with the magic in that brooch. Of course, I came when you held it with such intense concentration."

Ruefully, she clutched the piece of jewelry. Imbued with Adhna's own magic, why wouldn't it act as a summoning tool? "I was just thinking I should choose someone to gift it to."

He cupped her cheeks in his hand and gave her a gentle kiss to the lips. "You're wise to choose someone now. In fact, the brooch wasn't the only thing that called me back to you. Faerie needs you to return."

Panic flooded her imagination. "Why? What's Bodach done? Is Cerul in trouble? Gabha? What about Grimnaugh?"

He let out a laugh. "Calm down, Clíodhna. Nothing so dire. Yes, Bodach has been stirring up trouble. With the throne empty, he's been riling up the lesser Fae and nobbling the higher court. He's glommed onto that poor lad, Ammatán, intent on turning him into an agent of madness."

"Oh, that poor, sweet child."

"Cerul has tried to counteract his efforts, but her power is limited. He's still the strongest of the court, and with you gone, the strongest in Faerie. The longer you're gone, the more the other Fae believe his lies. We need you back before he gathers too many powerful allies."

She chewed on her lower lip. "That means I must gift the brooch to Fingin before I leave. And that I can never come back."

Adhna gave her a sad smile. "That's true, my dearest love. I'll help you with that transfer, and then I must bring you home."

Adhna left to wait for them at the standing stones while Clíodhna braided her hair and wound it around her head.

Then, she sought out Fingin, who was mucking out the stables. "Fingin! Stop that now. I have something for you."

The boy ran to her and tossed the pitchfork against the wall. After recalling her own pain when Adhna had gifted her the brooch, she hoped it wouldn't hurt the lad too badly. She didn't dare tell him what they'd be doing but had to trust in the boy's sense of adventure. He had a natural curiosity to go with his sympathy for the Fae.

Clíodhna led him up the path, past the looming guardian stones, and into the stone circle. The boys eyes grew wide, but he stayed silent. Adhna stood in the woods with his staff, hidden by the summer leaves, but she caught his gaze.

He nodded once and she took in a deep breath. Kneeling by Fingin, she said, "I have a gift for you, child. You must keep it safe and secret from everyone, do you understand?"

He gave a frightened nod.

The twelve stones reached for the sky in the growing dusk. Clíodhna drew in the wind as they approached, making the clouds swirl in the overhead darkness.

She took Fingin's hand, sensing the boy's rising terror, and held tight. She wished she could give him some confidence, some bravery, but he'd have to learn that on his own. The only thing she could give him tonight was the legacy of the brooch.

Thunder boomed and the temperature plummeted. Wind tugged at their clothing as Clíodhna patted her tightly braided hair.

Inside the circle, she told Fingin, "Stand here, boy. You must stay here, no matter what happens. Do you understand? I have some work to do before the ceremony."

"Ceremony?"

"Shush now! All will be clear in time."

While pulling the wind around her, she marched the perimeter of the stones. Adhna had taught her the words in the language of their ancestors, words of power that unlocked the energy of the stones. Sparks of power flowed through her body and out of her fingers as she encircled the stones once, twice, three times. While mist embraced them, sparks shone out as bright as the full moon.

On the third circuit, she commanded the sparks to dance. With her hands, she guided them into complex patterns which described the ancient powers.

Swirling in groups of three, intertwining lines, and animals like those etched on the brooch. Symbols carved upon the ancestor stones, pictures from seasons so long past that even ancient memories had turned to legend and to myth.

Clíodhna's hair stood on end as she completed the dance and commanded the sparks to coalesce into a single strike of lightning. She directed it to the center of the circle, just past where Fingin huddled in abject fear.

The poor boy, frightened out of his wits, scrambled away from the strike. To his credit, he didn't leave the circle. Instead, he crawled to the largest stone, the north-facing sentinel, and cried tears which washed away in the rain.

Clíodhna strode to where the lightning had struck, the acrid odor of charred earth burning her nose. She raised her arms, still singing in that ancient language. She called down the gods in the words Adhna had taught her over several patient seasons.

Mysterious Manannán and Aebh, rulers of the mists!
Shield us with your cloak.

334

Brilliant Grian and Elatha of the sun and the moon!
Transport us with your silver craft.
Powerful Tuireann of the thunder bolts!
Guard us with your fury.
Honored Cailleach, the ruler of ice and snow!
Keep us in your arms.

Her hair had escaped from her braid, whipping in the wind like sea eels. She called the light down to her, commanding the energy into ancient power shapes.

As she bid the energy to depart, to go back to its home in the sky, she felt a thousand winters younger. Clíodhna hadn't felt old before, but now she stood ready to take over the world.

Fingin's eyes grew wide with horror.

"Now, child, are you ready for your legacy?"

He didn't answer, but she reached into her bag and drew the brooch out. She held it out in its white fabric wrapping and unfolded each edge with ceremonial dignity. Green gemstones shone bright in the dark mists.

Despite his terror, Fingin reached out to touch the brooch. Clíodhna wanted to snatch it away, to spare the child the inevitable pain, but fate demanded her compliance.

When he grasped it, he screeched and collapsed, his scream cutting through her soul. Thunder boomed and lightning ripped across the sky. She sat cross-legged and placed his head in her lap, stroking his hair and rocking him.

When lightning struck beside her, Fingin whimpered and burrowed into her arms. She needed to get him out of the storm.

Too weak from her conjuring to banish the weather, Clíodhna shoved the brooch in her pouch and lifted her grandson. With Adhna's help, they carried him down to the roundhouse.

As they descended the fairy hill, through the stones and the mist, her energy trickled back. Not much, but enough to keep her from collapsing.

They tucked him into his bed. He snuggled into his covers and didn't seem to have taken too much harm from the transfer of the brooch's power. Still, she'd be anxious until he woke.

Her hair fell into her eyes again, and she pushed it behind her ear with impatience. Then she stared at the lock that used to be white. It had turned black again.

Angry voices came from outside. Her mind racing, Clíodhna stumbled to the door to peer out into the stormy darkness. The rain had stopped, but the wind still whipped, and the stink of wet, burning wood was everywhere.

Several men carried spitting torches, muttering amongst themselves. In the forefront stood Abbot Pátraic.

Behind Pátraic, the tanner glowered with hatred in his eyes. Clíodhna cursed her own hasty actions at his workshop. Now she must reap the reward for her temper.

Clíodhna grabbed Fingin's pitchfork and strode outside, planting her feet wide. Holding a weapon, any weapon, gave her confidence. "Why have you come to my home, Abbot Pátraic?"

He raised his decorated crozier high. He'd dressed in his ceremonial white robes with a sparkling gold and purple scarf draped across the back of his neck. It hung straight in front of him, showing off detailed embroidery. The same entwined animal shapes from the brooch danced on his scarf.

"I come to accuse you of being in league with the devil, of working with the evil forces he spews forth from fiery hell. I come to burn a wanton."

He pounded his crozier on the bare ground three times. The men behind him raised their torches and shouted in avaricious glee at his ringing proclamation.

She gave him a scowl. "You're mad, Abbot Pátraic. I don't even know your devil."

The tanner stepped forward, pointing a stained finger at her with malice. "She does! She threatened me with his wrath!"

Clíodhna rolled her eyes. "I did no such thing. I told you to stop dumping your disgusting mess into the river. You'd burn me for telling you not to foul our water supply?"

He growled at her and stepped back, as another man to stepped forward. "She told my wife to make friends with the Good Folk living in our hearth."

Pátraic nodded as if this qualified as credible evidence for Clíodhna's evil ways. Had these people ever been her friends? She saw no women, and only a few monks she didn't recognize. Odhrán wasn't among them. For once, she wished Rumann was here. Even *he* wouldn't allow an angry mob to burn his own mother.

Adhna whispered in her ear. "They won't listen to reason. They're too filled with prejudice and hate for the Fae. Our only chance is to flee to the stones. We don't have the strength to fight so many."

She glanced up the path toward the stones. Perhaps they could lose them in the Fae mists. Clíodhna gave him a single nod.

As if they'd rehearsed it, they ran on either side of the mob. Clíodhna, wishing she was at full power, pelted down the glittering path, begging Danú to guide her steps and keep her from stumbling.

Behind her, angry shouts erupted. They yelled orders but were slow to organize. Perhaps they didn't want to chase down a mere woman, as the tanner had called her. Just maybe, a few remembered the last time they'd tried to kill her.

If they came too close, she'd give them another memory. By Danú, she'd give them an experience that would sear their soul and keep them from ever getting a good night's rest again.

As Adhna ran at her side, Clíodhna's anger grew as she climbed the hill, running through the darkness along the glittering path. She passed the black sentinel stones while shouts faded behind them. They'd almost reached the sanctuary of the circle when their hunters emerged from the forest.

One snatched at her sleeve, ripping a great tear in it. She jerked away, but another grabbed Adhna, pinning his arms in a hug. This one held tight, and he brought his torch to the Fae's hair.

She screeched and thrust her pitchfork at Adhna's captor. He backed off, but not before Adhna's shoulder was scorched.

The mob fanned out around their prey, encircling both with feral glee in their eyes. She glanced toward the stone circle, black in the dim mist. The flickering torchlight reminded Clíodhna of her powers.

She threw her head back in a mighty laugh and got the satisfaction of Pátraic's expression of grim satisfaction slipping a notch.

Adhna elbowed her and slipped her something. She took the bronze leaf-shaped knife. Ancient power oozed from it, and a slow smile spread across her face.

While raising the knife in one hand and the pitchfork in the other, Queen Clíodhna, Queen of the Faeries, called down the storm.

At least, she tried to call the storm. Her magic had been drained earlier, and only a faint breeze answered her call, swirling the mist.

Frustrated, she screamed into the night. Their attackers, after a moment's hesitation, threw off their caution and came closer. Step by step, they drew their circle tighter. Pátraic chanted in his harsh language as the men called out insults and names.

"Fae-lover! You sleep with the devil every night!"

"Go away, back to hell!"

"Wanton of the night!"

She growled and brandished her weapons, making one or two step back, but most of them wouldn't be intimidated by a woman, no matter how well armed. Sweat dripped into her eyes and her mouth and she spat out the salty liquid.

The circle of hunters kept growing tighter, and eventually, they were in the stone circle, surrounded by angry men.

Clíodhna risked a quick glance at Adhna, but he looked just as exhausted as her. They should never have transferred the brooch to Fingin today.

She tried a second time to draw down the weather to her command. This time, it listened to her, but the power was reluctant and sluggish. She needed time to pull it to a full fury.

With a flash of inspiration, she moved to pulling power from the earth rather than the sky. This was easier, and soon, a strand of earth power funneled into the sky like a fountain. Clíodhna shouted in sheer jubilation as it rushed through her and into the roiling storm clouds.

Wind cut through the stone circle, making the torches gutter. Each man stared upward as thunder boomed around them. A few stepped back, but their fellows pulled them back into the circle.

Adhna chanted under his breath behind her. She recognized the words, similar to those Grimnaugh had used to rip a hole between the mortal realm and Faerie. She needed to give him time to complete his spell.

The storm still fought her command, so she sent the next wave of power out to the local Fae, hoping they'd heed her call.

Wind whistled by the stones and icy needles of rain stung their faces as the men stepped closer again, now inside the stone circle themselves.

A few wild Fae popped up along the tree line, skulking just out of reach. Not the elegant river Fae or ethereal creatures of the wind. Instead, she spied the grotesquely shaped earth and rock Fae, gnarled and dark as a mossy stone.

One large Fae flashed Clíodhna a wicked grin and then gave the tanner's cloak a firm tug. The tanner whirled around, his torch hitting the face of the man crowded behind him. That man shoved the tanner. "What are you playing at, man? Stop messing around."

A rock Fae yanked another man's ankle, making him stumble into his neighbors. Then a third Fae blew out a torch.

As the Fae bedeviled the attackers, Clíodhna had time to raise her power again. This time, she funneled it into three lightning strikes between her and the mob. This drove them back further, despite their determination.

Pátraic shouted from relative safety beyond the stones, his crozier held high. "Don't let her sorcery drive you back, fools! She commands demons to distract you! Kill the demons and then you can then kill her!"

The men turned on the wild Fae, their torches looming even in the driving rain. The tanner shoved his torch into one Fae's face, making the creature screech in anguish. Another man did the same, and soon, the living Fae fled the stone circle, but seven lay in scorched piles of death.

Adhna cut through the veil and a doorway rimmed in fire appeared. He grabbed her hand. "Now! We must go now!"

"Some Fae are still alive! We must save them."

"No, they came to your call, as they must. You're their Queen. They sacrificed themselves with willing hearts. We must leave!"

With one more glance of pity for the crumpled bodies and a stare of hatred toward Pátraic and his brutes, Clíodhna stepped through the rip in the veil.

Chapter Twenty-One

Clíodhna had expected to come to a place she recognized. Perhaps near her palace, or Adhna's cozy roundhouse. Instead, they arrived in the middle of a horrible blight.

Black, noxious goo covered what might have once been healthy trees. Though the hills rolled in a pleasant undulation, bracken and weeds jutted from the ground with skeletal claws. A miasma of rotted vegetation and the stink of a corrupt soul drifted across them.

Clíodhna clutched at Adhna's arm. "Why did you bring us here?"

He shook his head. "I had no choice in my destination. Faerie doesn't stay in a fixed place in relation to the mortal world."

She tried to find some identifying characteristic in the landscape. "Where are we?"

Her mentor cast his gaze to the horizon and pointed. "There. That's the palace spire."

Clíodhna squinted, and made out a hair-thin line against the dim light, as if someone had scratched a smooth rock with their fingernail.

After heaving a deep sigh, she put her hands on her hips. "I suppose we have to travel on foot, don't we?"

With a half-smile, Adhna shook his head. "Indeed, we don't. I knew we'd have to travel." He whistled several sweet tunes, an anodyne to the surrounding corruption. The tune manifested into white sparks and ambled away. "Now we wait."

In just a few heartbeats, hoof beats pounded across the blight, bright and cheerful. Two large white horses, perfectly matched, came close with their heads held high. Each bowed to her and she clapped her hands in delight. "Adhna! I've missed your cleverness." She gave him a lingering kiss that promised more.

Clíodhna mounted her steed while Adhna got on his, and they journeyed back to her palace.

Despite all her time in the mortal realm, she looked forward to sitting on her throne again, watching the courtiers' dance, and hearing Cerul sing. She did not look forward to seeing Bodach again, though. "Is Bodach the reason for this disgusting mess?"

Adhna wrinkled his nose. "After the big battle, his power spilled into other areas. Not all of Faerie has succumbed to his filth, but parts have. Even if you destroyed him now, some bits of the land would still call him lord."

"If I destroyed him now. But I can't, can I?" She made it more of a statement than a question.

Adhna pursed his lips. "You can limit his power, but only by being there to hold the reins. He's too powerful to destroy or imprison, and much too powerful to banish. He'd be even more dangerous in the human realm. Bodach finds a great delight in madness, and seeing what he can do to stir up such things in humans."

Adhna glanced at her and then down to the trail so fast, she knew he had more information. "What, Adhna? What has he stirred up already?"

He closed his eyes. "I believe part of your husband's madness came from Bodach's interference. And Pátraic's hatred of you smells of Bodach, too. The Christian didn't turn to madness, but Bodach took his incredible prejudice and twisted it into zealotry. He may mellow without constant goading, but I can't tell how much is native bigotry and how much is Bodach's pressure."

So much of her heartbreak over the last seasons stemmed from either her husband's madness or Pátraic's hatred. Clíodhna clenched her fists until the strap of the reins bit into her palms. "Very well. He will reap the reward for what he's sown."

Adhna flashed her a glare. "You cannot punish him directly. You've already shown yourself a match for him, but you can't defeat him. He'll use that to his advantage in any pitched battle. You should pretend to be under his influence and bide. In time, you can remove him from power."

She snorted, making her horse toss his head and whinny. "And how long will that take? I'm not a patient woman, Adhna."

He laughed, the merry sound a wonderful counterpart to the poisonous environment. "No, one could never accuse you of having too much patience, my love. But you are no longer a woman. You are a Faerie Queen. You have eons to make your move, and when you do, it will be legendary."

The pride in her mentor's voice made her grin. "I'll at least make him pay for it a little now. That will satisfy me... for a while."

When they arrived at the palace grounds, courtiers flocked to follow her into the palace. Adhna spoke to a few as they entered.

She didn't dismount, even in the grand hall. Bodach's corruption hadn't affected this part of Faerie, not yet, for which she drew solace. Instead, she rode the white horse into court.

Several courtiers moved aside with startled exclamations and some eager smiles. Also, a few angry glares, which she made careful note of.

Bodach was lounging on the throne—*her* throne—sideways, while Cerul fed him sections of fruit. As Clíodhna's horse approached, he scrambled up from the throne and shooed the other Fae away, tossing the remaining fruit into the corner.

After stepping down the dais, Bodach held out his arms. "My Queen! I did not expect you back so soon."

Standing tall in her saddle, her voice boomed through the space. "You mean, you didn't expect me back at all. How dare you? How dare you usurp my place and corrupt my land? You will pay for this, Bodach, and despite your predilection for pain and madness, you will *not* enjoy your punishment."

His sycophantic smile slipped a notch, and she nodded to the guards Adhna had fetched. "Take him."

Nine guards approached the bark-skinned Fae. Bodach turned on the guards, claws out as he snarled, "You won't dare lay hands on me!"

Her voice turned ice-cold as she gestured for a second wave of guards. Twenty-seven Fae now surrounded him. "They will. And you will not fight them, for any injury you do to my own guards, you will pay for, three-fold."

Something in her voice must have hit home, for Bodach's eyes widened and he sheathed his claws. The guards took him away, with ungentle hands.

Once he'd been removed from the throne room, she sought Grimnaugh's frog-like face. He emerged from the corner he'd been cowering in. She grinned and took him into her arms. "I've missed you, my friend."

When she stood, she curled her lip at the state of mess on her throne. "Let's have this cleaned before I sit, shall we? I don't want a trace of Bodach left. I know I must let him return someday, but not yet. Please, not yet."

The magnetic poles have shifted. Powers ignite in their veins. But are their emerging Unhidden talents strong enough to defend them from annihilation?

Anna Taylor is barely holding her anxiety at bay. With scales growing on her body and shocking magic now at her command, the teacher flees after being outed by a student and attacked by an angry mob.

Can Anna, Max, and the squad stem a tsunami of chaos and death? Start reading *Taming of the Few* to defend a powerful destiny today!

www.GreenDragonArtist.com/Books

Thank You!

Thank you so much for enjoying Age of Druids. If you've enjoyed the story, please consider leaving a review so other readers can discover Clíodhna's adventures!

If you would like to get updates, sneak previews, sales, and a FREE short story and a FAMILY TREE, please sign up for my newsletter.

www.GreenDragonArtist.com

Other Books by This Author

**See all the books available
through Green Dragon Publishing at
*www.GreenDragonArtist.com/Books***

Historical Note

Dear Readers,

As you embark on the evocative journey through the pages of "Age of Druids," I am excited to provide you with a glimpse into the historical inspirations that shape the tapestry of this gripping narrative.

Set against the backdrop of Ireland in the year 470CE, I've thrown the conflict between old, pagan ways and the new, Christian ways into high gear. One character, Abbot Patricius, is especially fervent about this change. As you might guess, I based this character on St. Patrick, though I ascribed a lot of cruelty to my version that may not have been true of the historical man.

Details about the early monastery, such as their services, the love feast, and their gardens, were as close as I could determine from my research to monasteries of the time.

When I was worldbuilding my version of Faerie, I researched the Queens associated with each area of Ireland. There are many different versions of these legends, but I tried to stick with the older sources. While Irish Fairies in the sources don't have 'courts' as is described in Scottish legends, I created one in my world, but that wasn't based on any lore.

As for the battle, this is very loosely tied to a local legend, that of St. Patrick, werewolves, and the town of Ossory. Some of this is based on Norse tales and the writings of Gerald of Wales who, it must be said, isn't the most reliable of sources. In these tales, an entire village opposed St. Patrick, and as punishment, he cursed the people of that town to periodically change into wolves but retain their human intelligence.

"Age of Druids" explores the intricate dance between old and new, tradition and transformation. As Clíodhna faces the shadows of persecution and the allure of the unknown, the story unfolds as a testament to the resilience of a pagan woman in a world in turmoil.

About the Author

Christy Nicholas writes under several pen names, including Rowan Dillon, CN Jackson, and Emeline Rhys. She's an author, artist, and accountant. After she failed to become an airline pilot, she quit her ceaseless pursuit of careers that began with the letter 'A' and decided to concentrate on her writing. Since she has Project Completion Compulsion, she is one of the few authors with no unfinished novels.

Christy has her hands in many crafts, including digital art, beaded jewelry, writing, and photography. In real life, she's a CPA, but having grown up with art all around her (her mother, grandmother, and great-grandmother are/were all artists), it sort of infected her, as it were. She wants to expose the incredible beauty in this world, hidden beneath the everyday grime of familiarity and habit, and share it with others. She uses characters out of time and places infused with magic and myth, writing magical realism stories in both historical fantasy and time travel flavors.

Social Media Links:
Blog: www.GreenDragonArtist.net
Website: www.GreenDragonArtist.com
Facebook: www.facebook.com/greendragonauthor
Instagram: www.instagram.com/greendragonartist9
TikTok: www.tiktok.com/@greendragonauthor